# MEN OF WRATH

### CREATED BY
## AARON & GARNEY

image

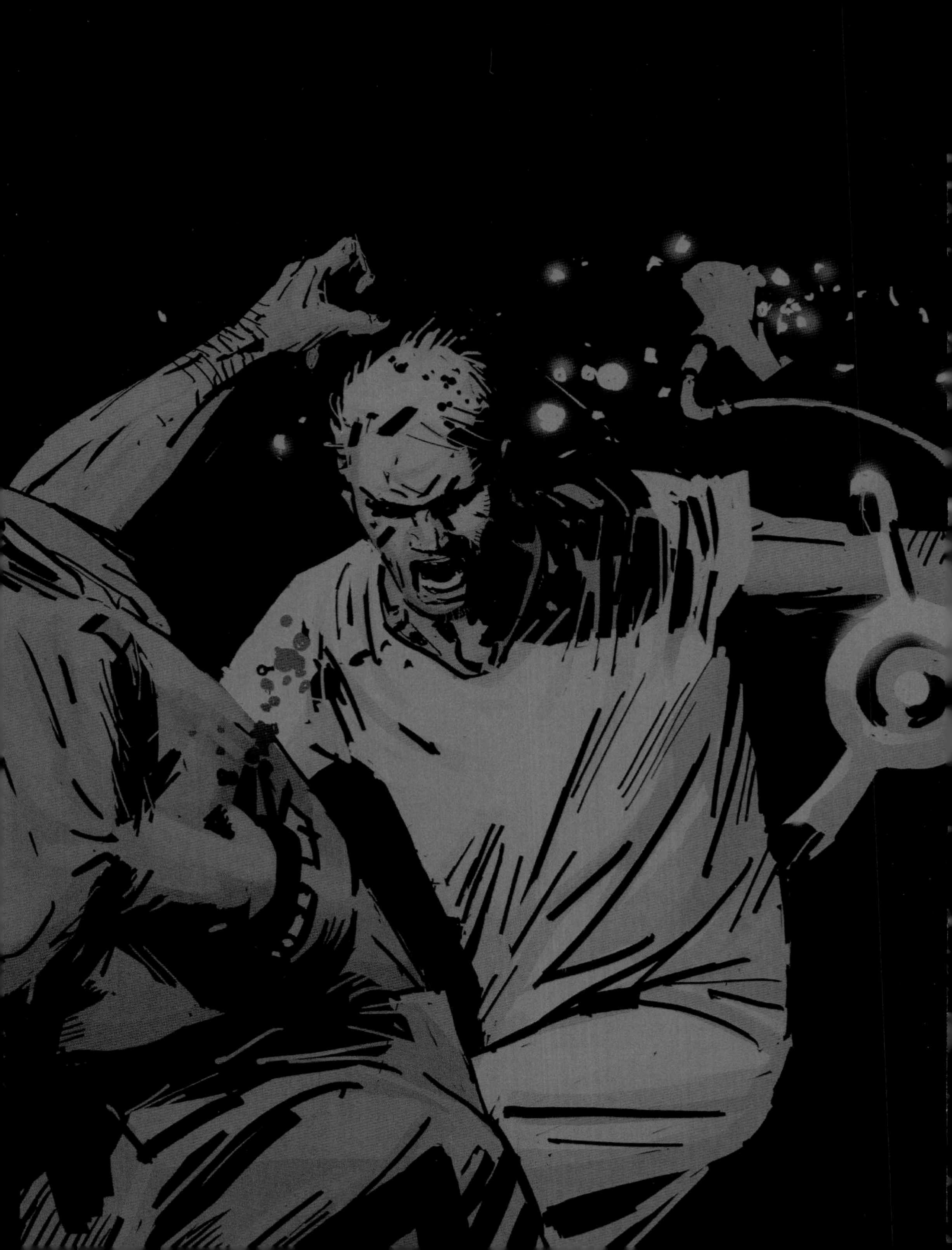

# MEN OF WRATH

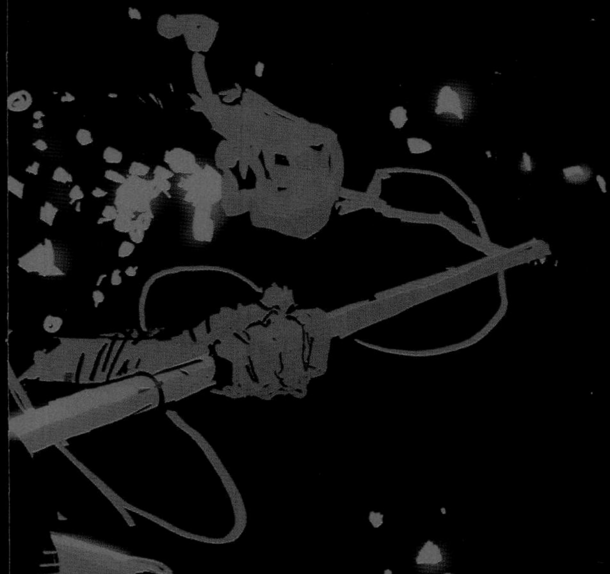

## JASON AARON
WRITER

## RON GARNEY
ARTIST

## MATT MILLA
COLORS

## JARED K. FLETCHER
LETTERS

## SEBASTIAN GIRNER
EDITOR

image

IMAGE COMICS, INC.

ROBERT KIRKMAN: CHIEF OPERATING OFFICER

ERIK LARSEN: CHIEF FINANCIAL OFFICER

TODD MCFARLANE: PRESIDENT

MARC SILVESTRI: CHIEF EXECUTIVE OFFICER

JIM VALENTINO: VICE PRESIDENT

ERIC STEPHENSON: PUBLISHER / CHIEF CREATIVE OFFICER

COREY HART: DIRECTOR OF SALES

JEFF BOISON: DIRECTOR OF PUBLISHING PLANNING & BOOK TRADE SALES

CHRIS ROSS: DIRECTOR OF DIGITAL SALES

JEFF STANG: DIRECTOR OF SPECIALTY SALES

KAT SALAZAR: DIRECTOR OF PR & MARKETING

DREW GILL: ART DIRECTOR

HEATHER DOORNINK: PRODUCTION DIRECTOR

NICOLE LAPALME: CONTROLLER

IMAGECOMICS.COM


JARED K. FLETCHER - LOGO + BOOK DESIGN

METIME AROUND 1900, MY GREAT-GREAT-GRANDFATHER, IRA AARON, STABBED A MAN
ATH IN AN ARGUMENT OVER SOME SHEEP.

S YOUNG SON, SAMMIE, WAS THERE AND WITNESSED THE KILLING. IT WAS HIS KNIFE THAT W
ED IN THE STABBING.

ARS LATER, IN 1924, SAMMIE AARON, MY GREAT-GRANDFATHER, WOULD MEET HIS OW
RANGE DEMISE.

'D DIE OF RABIES, AFTER BEING BITTEN BY A RABID DOG.
OM THIS DARK LITTLE BIT OF MY OWN FAMILY HISTORY WAS BORN **MEN OF WRATH.**

A AND RUBEN RATH ARE THE CULMINATION OF A LONG, BLOODY CYCLE OF SOUTHERN VIOLENC
E THAT'S BEEN PASSED DOWN FROM FATHER TO SON OVER THE COURSE OF A CENTURY. A
HAT STARTED WITH SOME SHEEP, WILL ONLY END WHEN EVERYONE DIES.

IS MAY BE THE DARKEST, MEANEST THING I'VE EVER WRITTEN. AND IF YOU'VE READ SOME
WORK ON **WOLVERINE** OR **SCALPED** OR **SOUTHERN BASTARDS**, YOU KNOW I'M NO STRANGER
INGS DARK AND MEAN. BUT THERE'S SOMETHING PERSONAL ABOUT ALL THIS AS WELL.

HATEVER WAS PASSED DOWN TO ME FROM IRA AARON, DOWN THROUGH HIS DOOMED S
MMIE, DOWN THROUGH GENERATIONS OF ALABAMA FARMERS AND COAL MINERS AND REBE
D PREACHERS AND THE OCCASIONAL MURDERER, I'M NOW PASSING ON TO YOU.

ANKS FOR READING **MEN OF WRATH**. THANKS FOR JOINING THE FAMILY.
UPPOSE I SHOULD INTRODUCE YOU TO YOUR NEW RELATIVES.

IS ISN'T THE FIRST TIME THAT RON GARNEY AND I HAVE KILLED A BUNCH OF PEOPLE TOGETH
T EVEN CLOSE. OUR FIRST COLLABORATION CAME BACK IN 2008, IN THE PAGES OF **WOLVERI**
R A STORY CALLED "GET MYSTIQUE." AFTER THAT, THERE WAS **WOLVERINE WEAPON X** A
**TIMATE CAPTAIN AMERICA** AND MOST RECENTLY, **THOR GOD OF THUNDER**.

ROUGHOUT MUCH OF THAT, WE TALKED ABOUT THE IDEA OF DOING SOMETHING LIKE TH
METHING THAT WAS OURS. SOMETHING THAT WAS REAL. SOMETHING THAT WAS MEA
METHING THAT RON COULD CUT LOOSE ON IN A WAY HE NEVER HAD BEFORE.

N'S A GUY WHO'S DONE IT ALL AT THIS POINT, IN TERMS OF MAINSTREAM SUPERHERO COMI
'S HAD LEGENDARY RUNS FOR BOTH MARVEL AND DC. HE'S DRAWN THE MOST POPUL
HARACTERS IN THE WORLD. HE'S BODYSLAMMED PEOPLE IN BARS. BUT HE'S NEVER DC
METHING LIKE THIS. THIS IS RON'S FIRST CREATOR-OWNED SERIES. HIS FIRST TRUE CRI
ORY. HIS FIRST CHANCE TO SHOW YOU JUST HOW DARK AND MEAN HE CAN BE.

INING RON AND I ON OUR MURDEROUS QUEST ARE A MOTLEY CREW OF CRACK CRAFTSMEN A
LTY ROGUES, INCLUDING COLORIST EXTRAORDINAIRE MATT MILLA, LETTERING GURU JAF
ETCHER AND EDITOR/PART-TIME GERMAN NINJA SEBASTIAN GIRNER.

HAT'S QUITE THE LINE-UP. THE MEN OF **MEN OF WRATH**. FEAR AND RESPECT THEM ALL.

HO KNOWS, WE MIGHT JUST GET THIS BAND BACK TOGETHER SOMEDAY AND DO THIS ALL AGA
HERE ARE DEFINITELY SOME MORE STORIES I'D LIKE TO TELL WITH THESE MEN OF WRATH.

ORE STORIES ABOUT SHEEP AND DOGS AND HORSES. OH, THOSE POOR POOR HORSES. MO
ORIES ABOUT FATHERS AND SONS. ABOUT DEBTS NO HONEST MAN COULD PAY. ABOUT DEE
AWED MEN WHO FIND IT EASIER TO KILL THAN TO LIVE. ABOUT WHAT IT MEANS TO BE A RA

NTIL THEN, I GUESS I'LL SEE YA AT THE FAMILY REUNIONS. BRING LOTS OF BEER. AND

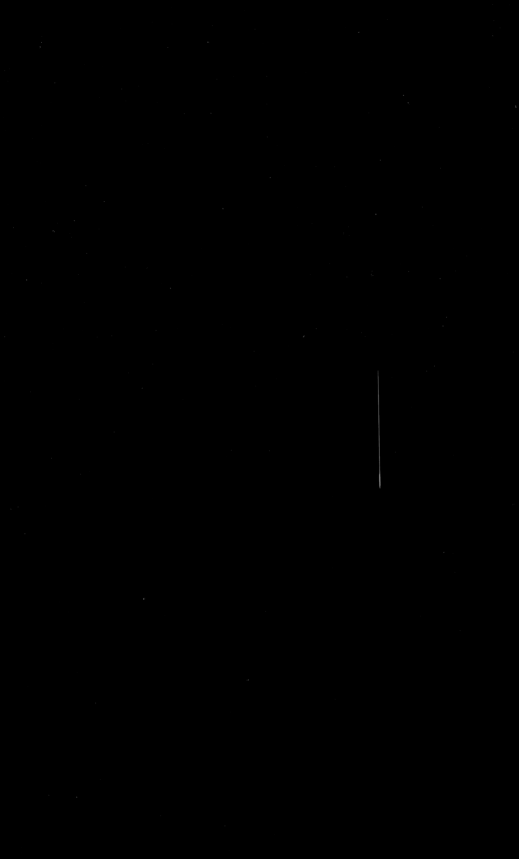

# CHAPTER ONE

## AMONG THE SHEEP

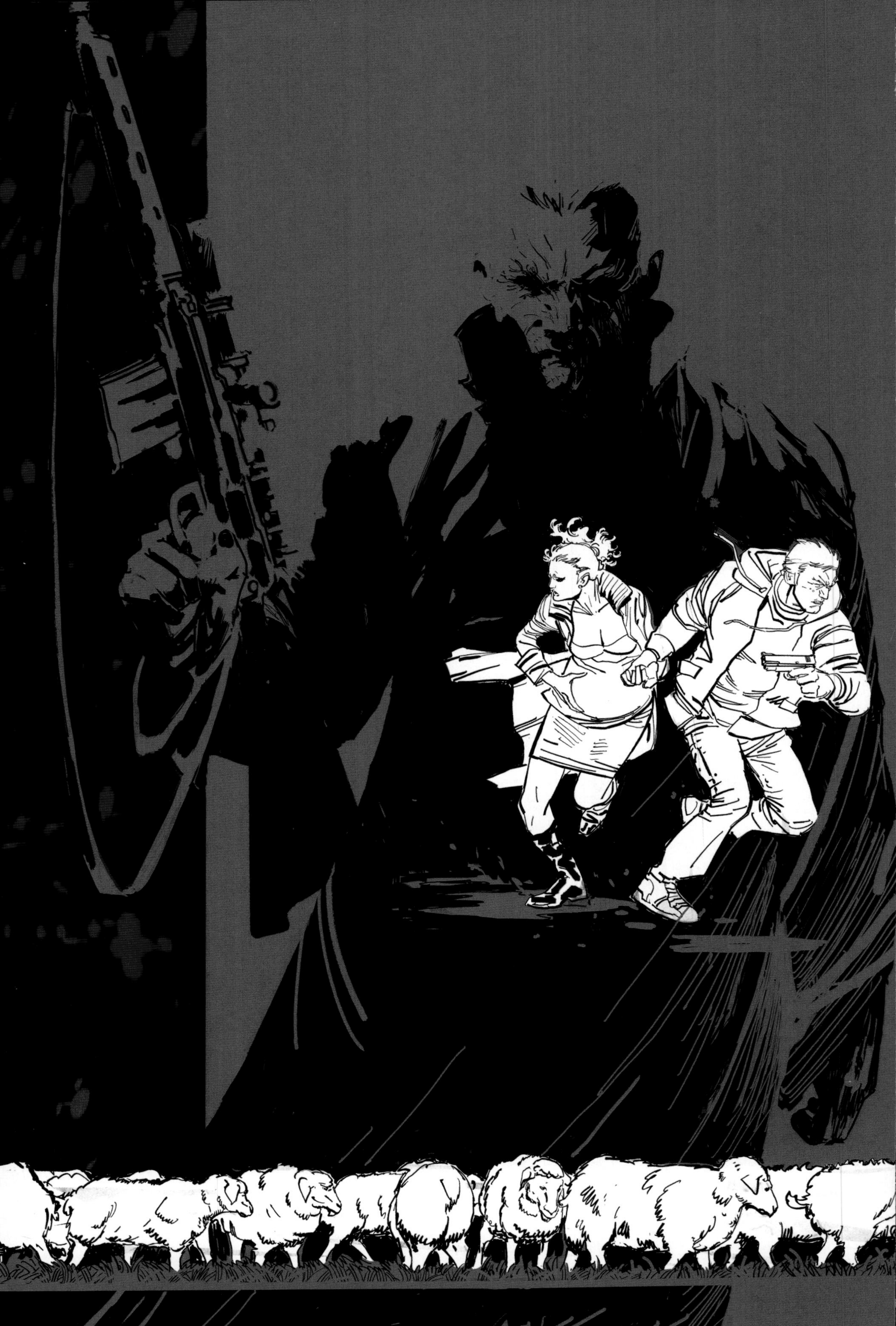

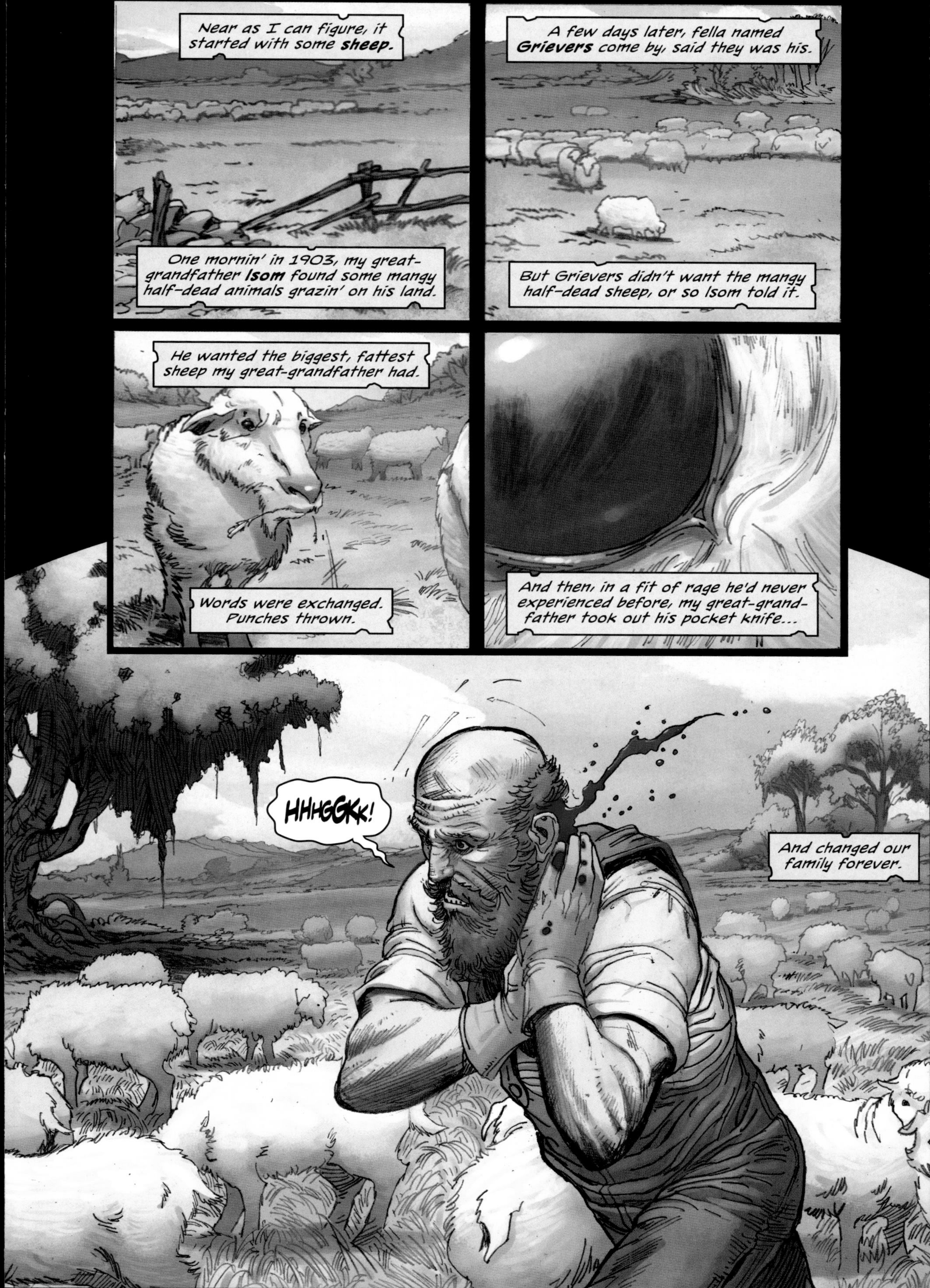

Near as I can figure, it started with some **sheep.**
One mornin' in 1903, my great-grandfather **Isom** found some mangy half-dead animals grazin' on his land.
A few days later, fella named **Grievers** come by, said they was his.
But Grievers didn't want the mangy half-dead sheep, or so Isom told it.
He wanted the biggest, fattest sheep my great-grandfather had.
Words were exchanged. Punches thrown.
And then, in a fit of rage he'd never experienced before, my great-grandfather took out his pocket knife...
HHHGGKK!
And changed our family forever.

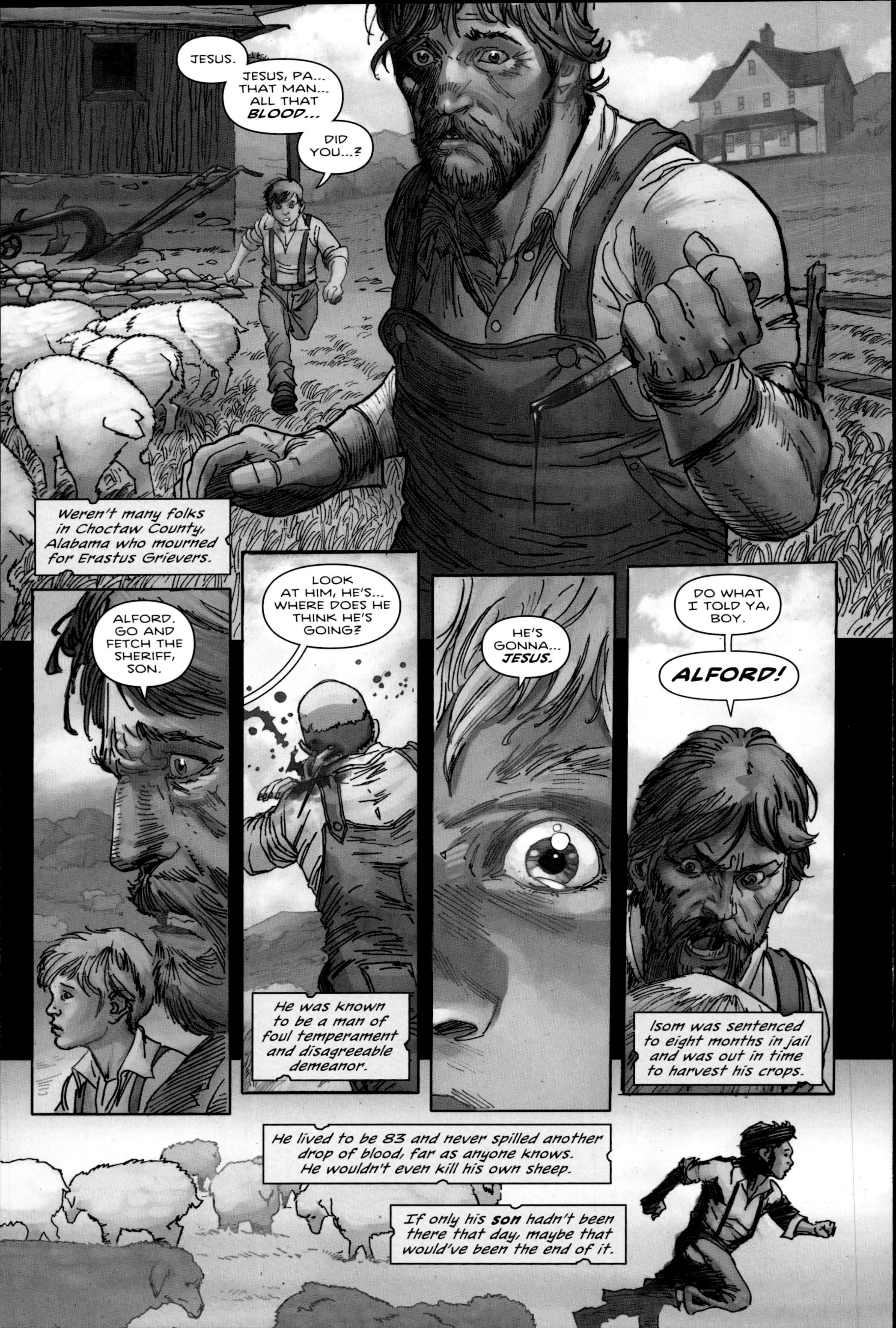
JESUS.
JESUS, PA... THAT MAN... ALL THAT BLOOD...
DID YOU...?
Weren't many folks in Choctaw County, Alabama who mourned for Erastus Grievers.
ALFORD. GO AND FETCH THE SHERIFF, SON.
LOOK AT HIM, HE'S... WHERE DOES HE THINK HE'S GOING?
He was known to be a man of foul temperament and disagreeable demeanor.
HE'S GONNA... JESUS.
DO WHAT I TOLD YA, BOY.
ALFORD!
Isom was sentenced to eight months in jail and was out in time to harvest his crops.
He lived to be 83 and never spilled another drop of blood, far as anyone knows. He wouldn't even kill his own sheep.
If only his son hadn't been there that day, maybe that would've been the end of it.

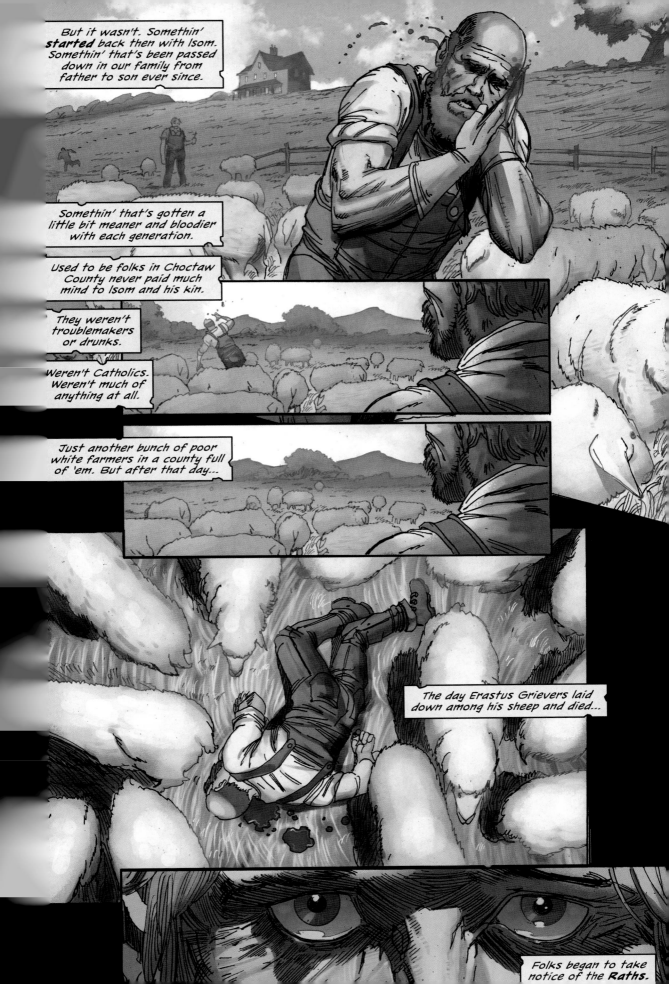

But it wasn't. Somethin' **started** back then with Isom. Somethin' that's been passed down in our family from father to son ever since.

Somethin' that's gotten a little bit meaner and bloodier with each generation.

Used to be folks in Choctaw County never paid much mind to Isom and his kin.

They weren't troublemakers or drunks.

Weren't Catholics. Weren't much of anything at all.

Just another bunch of poor white farmers in a county full of 'em. But after that day...

The day Erastus Grievers laid down among his sheep and died...

Folks began to take notice of the **Raths.**

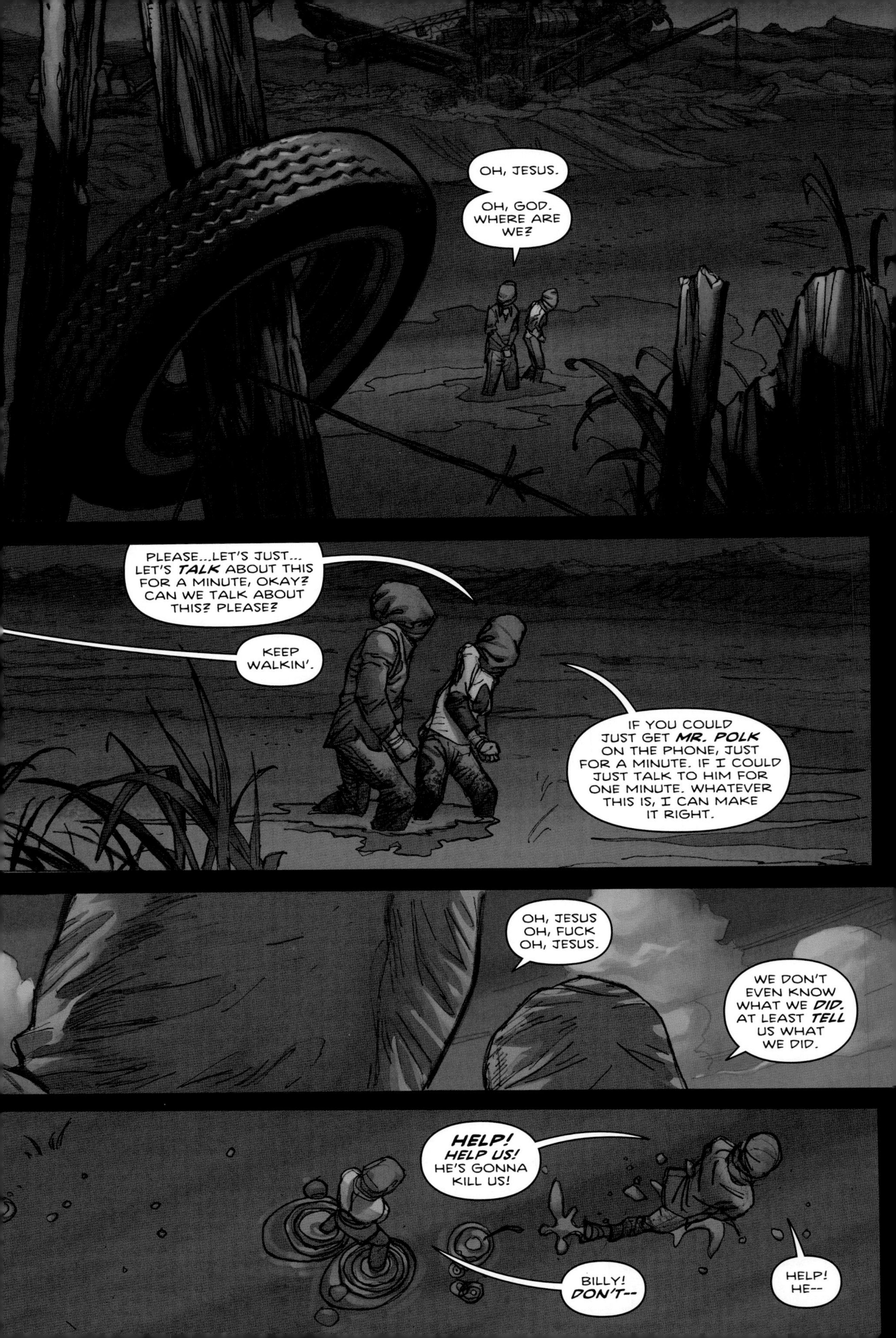
OH, JESUS.
OH, GOD. WHERE ARE WE?
PLEASE...LET'S JUST... LET'S TALK ABOUT THIS FOR A MINUTE, OKAY? CAN WE TALK ABOUT THIS? PLEASE?
KEEP WALKIN'.
IF YOU COULD JUST GET MR. POLK ON THE PHONE, JUST FOR A MINUTE. IF I COULD JUST TALK TO HIM FOR ONE MINUTE. WHATEVER THIS IS, I CAN MAKE IT RIGHT.
OH, JESUS OH, FUCK OH, JESUS.
WE DON'T EVEN KNOW WHAT WE DID. AT LEAST TELL US WHAT WE DID.
HELP! HELP US! HE'S GONNA KILL US!
BILLY! DON'T--
HELP! HE--

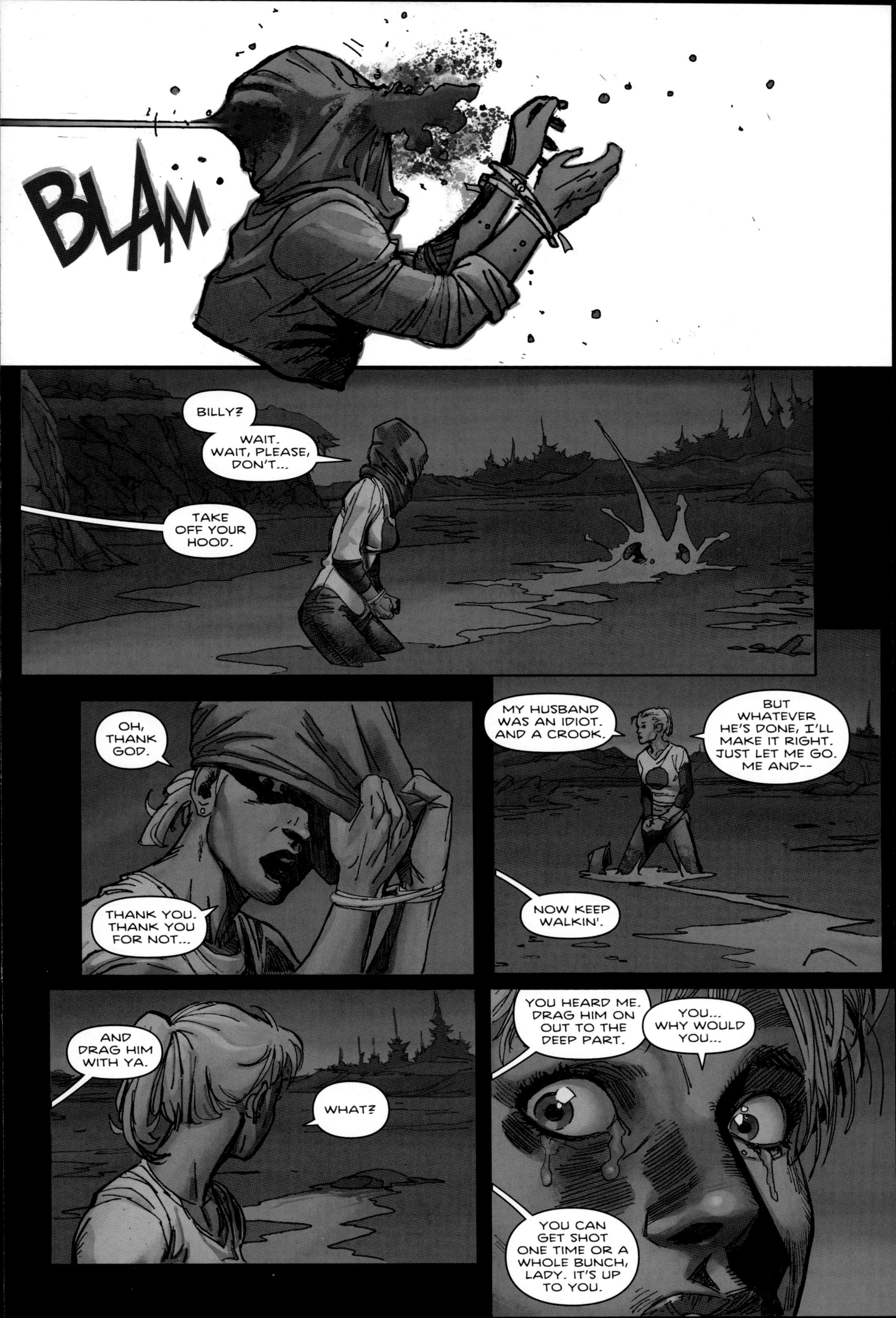
BLAM
BILLY?
WAIT. WAIT, PLEASE, DON'T...
TAKE OFF YOUR HOOD.
OH, THANK GOD.
THANK YOU. THANK YOU FOR NOT...
MY HUSBAND WAS AN IDIOT. AND A CROOK.
BUT WHATEVER HE'S DONE, I'LL MAKE IT RIGHT. JUST LET ME GO. ME AND--
NOW KEEP WALKIN'.
AND DRAG HIM WITH YA.
WHAT?
YOU HEARD ME. DRAG HIM ON OUT TO THE DEEP PART.
YOU... WHY WOULD YOU...
YOU CAN GET SHOT ONE TIME OR A WHOLE BUNCH, LADY. IT'S UP TO YOU.

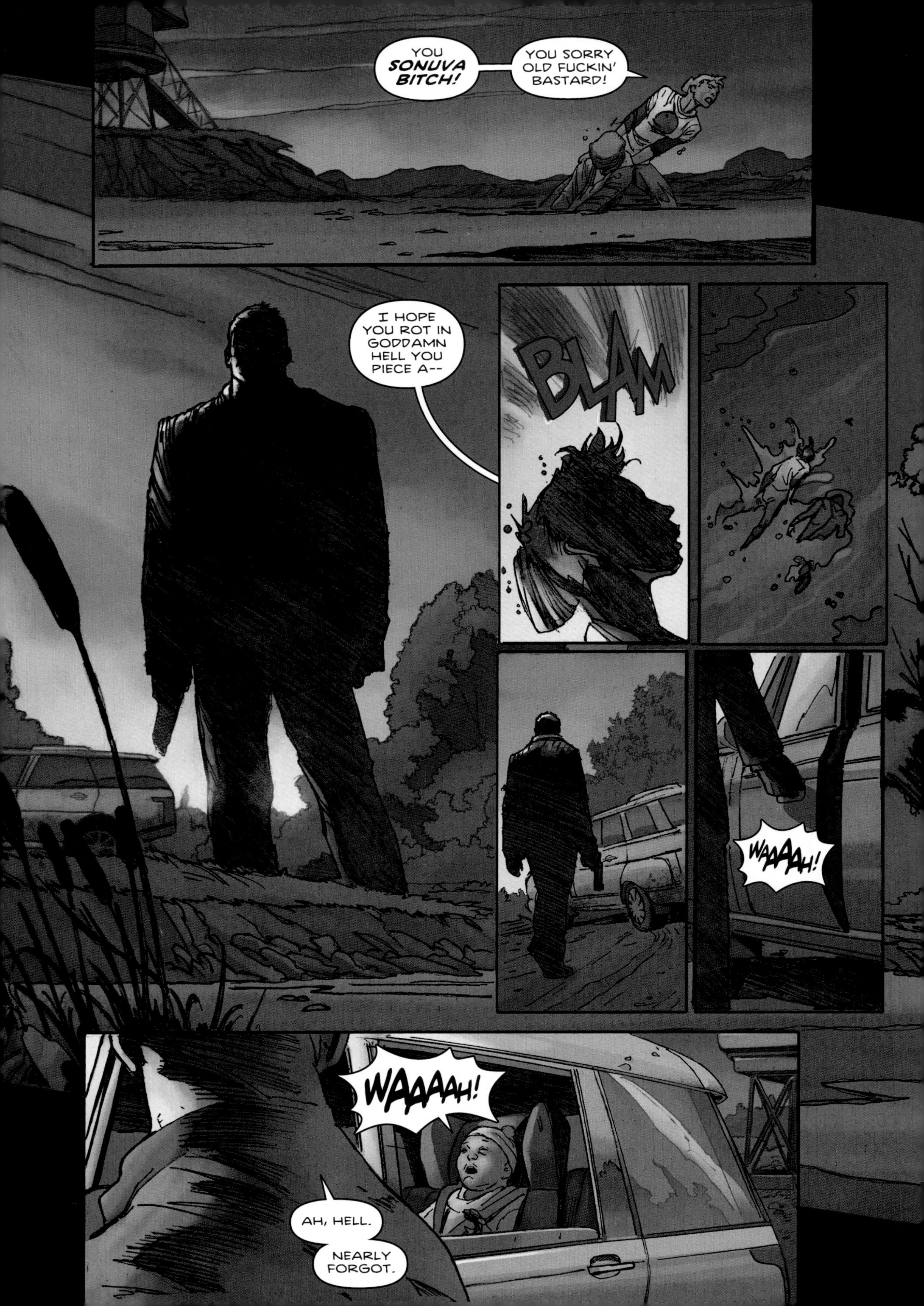
YOU *SONUVA BITCH!*
YOU SORRY OLD FUCKIN' BASTARD!
I HOPE YOU ROT IN GODDAMN HELL YOU PIECE A--
BLAM
WAAAAH!
WAAAAH!
AH, HELL.
NEARLY FORGOT.

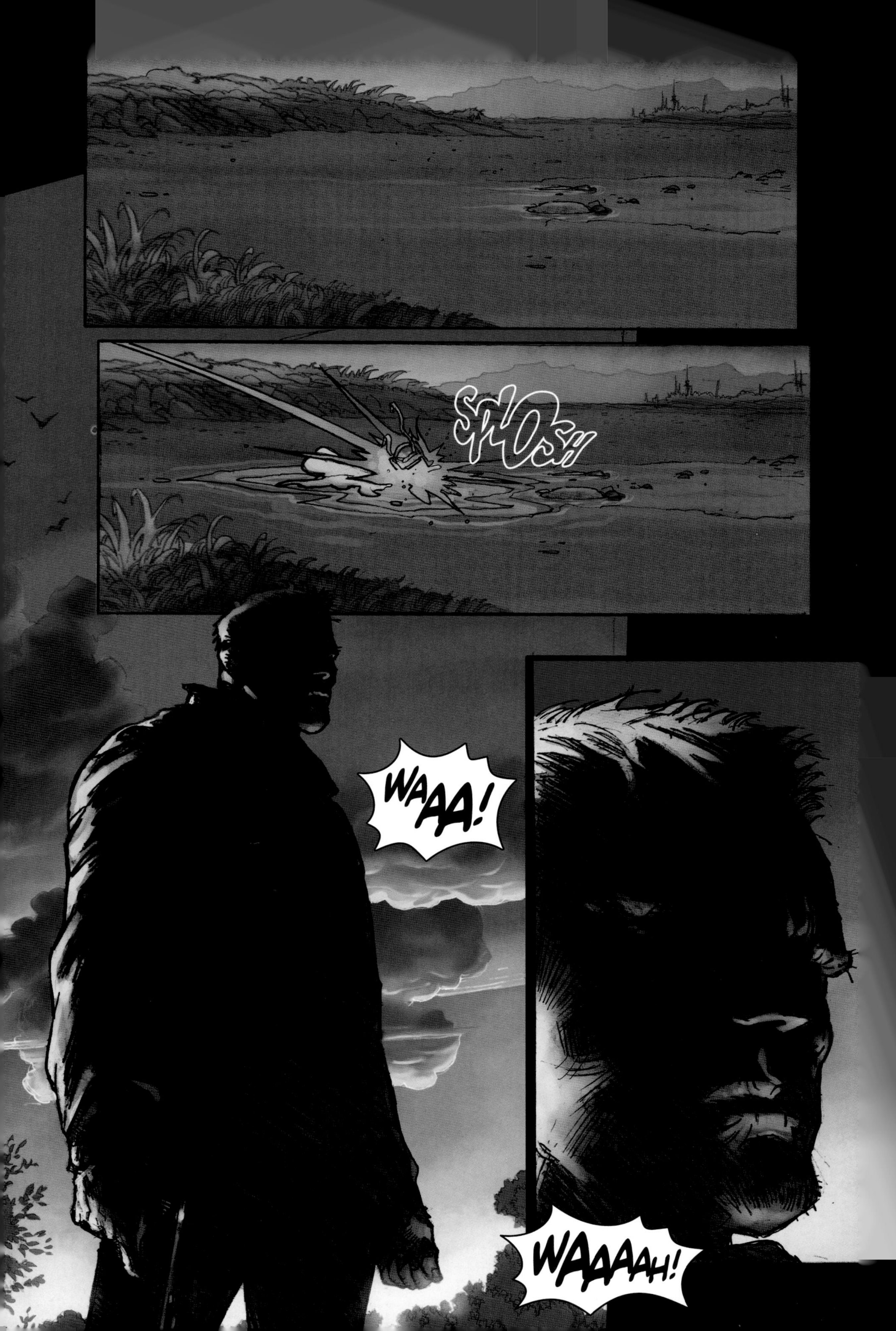
SPLOOSH
WAAA!
WAAAAH!

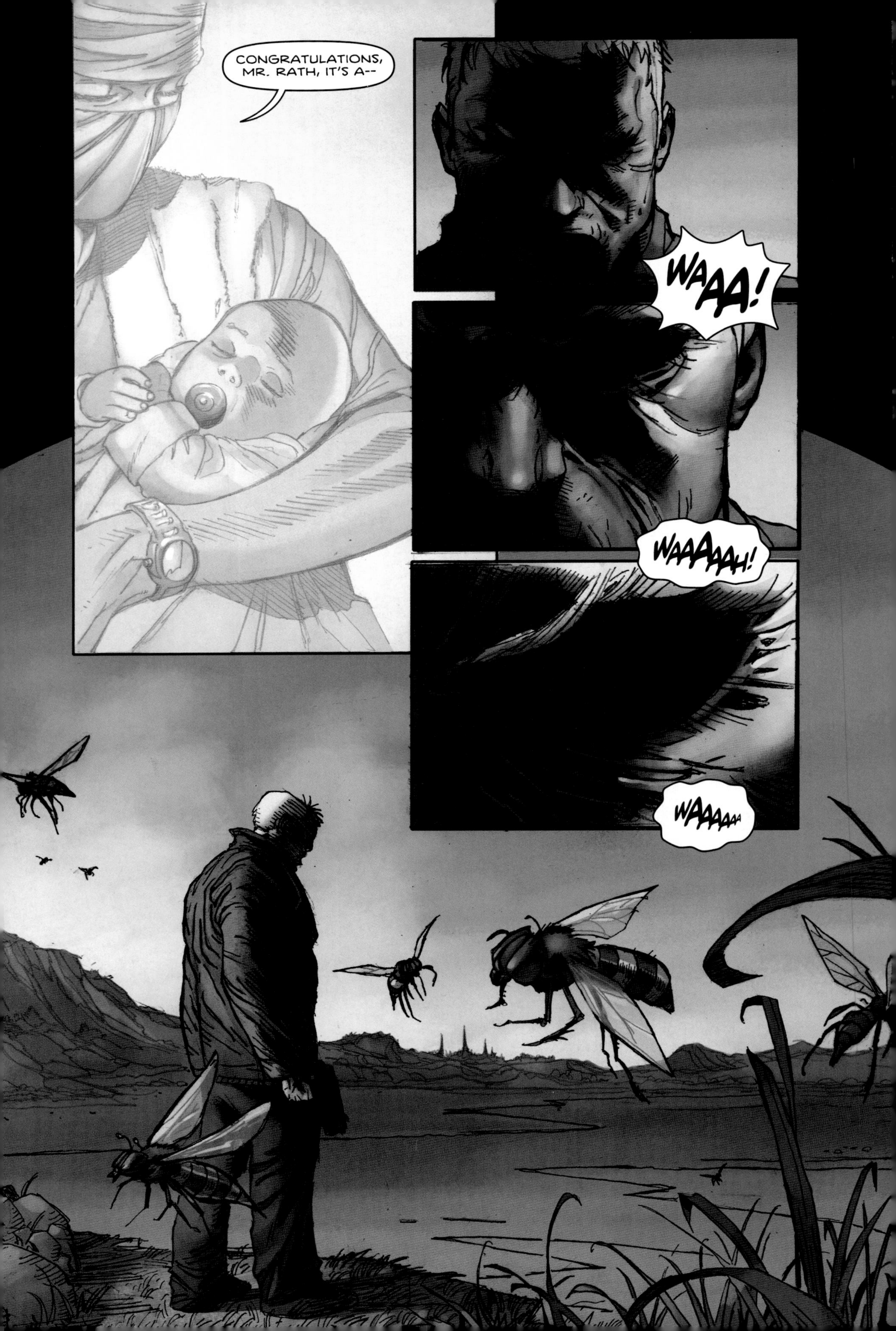
CONGRATULATIONS, MR. RATH, IT'S A--
WAAA!
WAAAAAH!
WAAAAAA

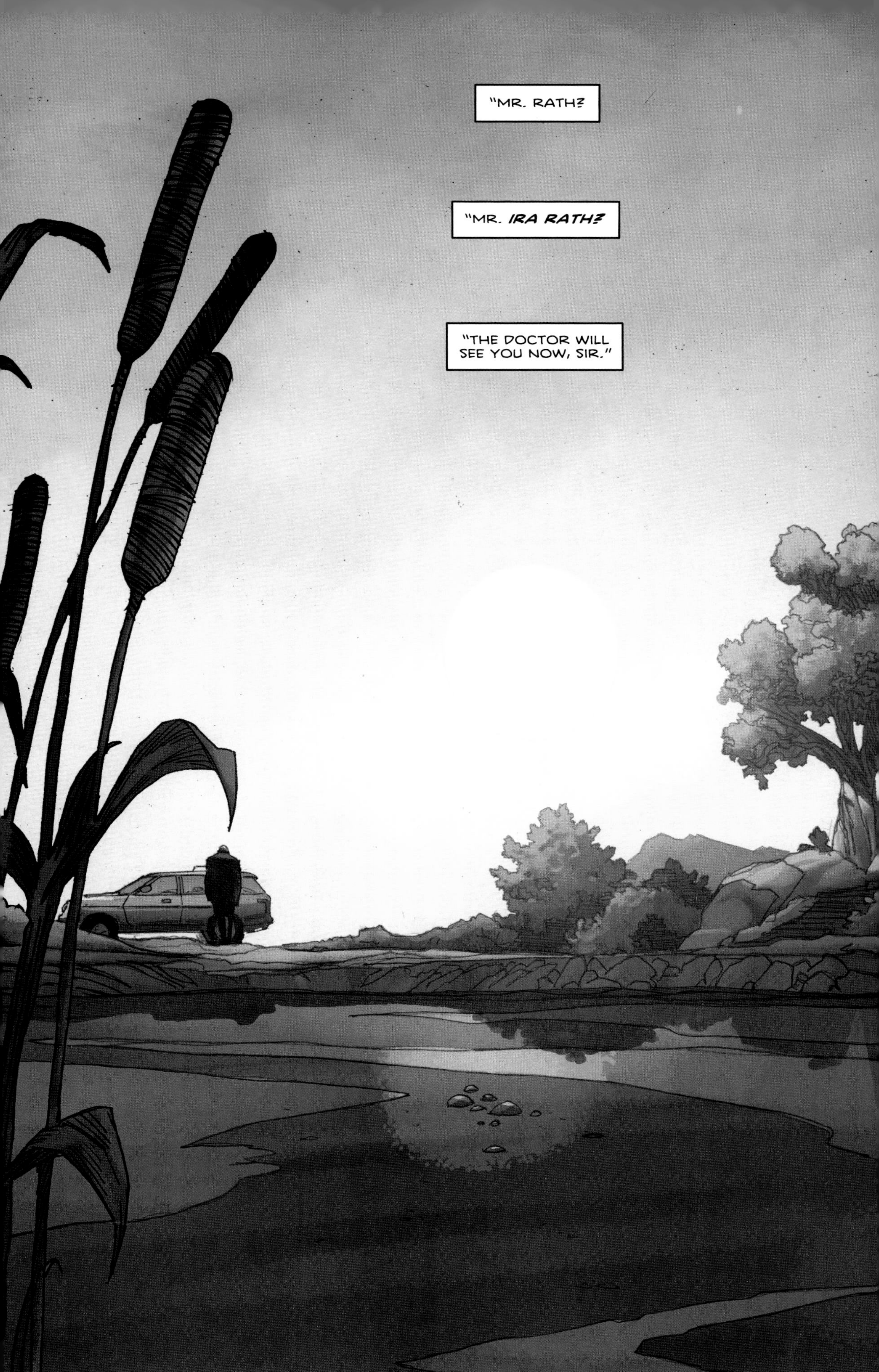
"MR. RATH?
"MR. IRA RATH?
"THE DOCTOR WILL SEE YOU NOW, SIR."

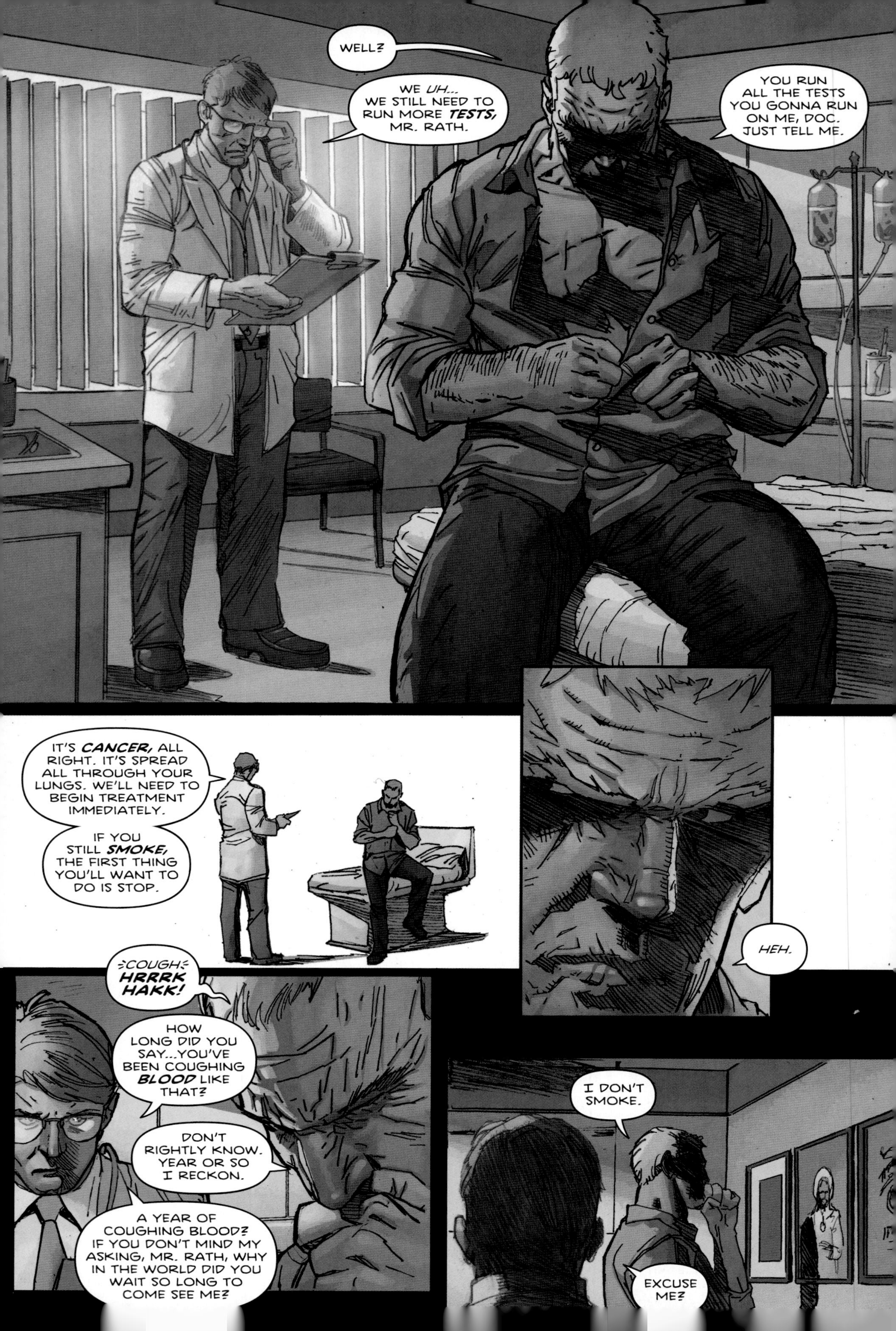
WELL?
WE UH... WE STILL NEED TO RUN MORE TESTS, MR. RATH.
YOU RUN ALL THE TESTS YOU GONNA RUN ON ME, DOC. JUST TELL ME.
IT'S CANCER, ALL RIGHT. IT'S SPREAD ALL THROUGH YOUR LUNGS. WE'LL NEED TO BEGIN TREATMENT IMMEDIATELY.
IF YOU STILL SMOKE, THE FIRST THING YOU'LL WANT TO DO IS STOP.
HEH.
COUGH
HRRRK HAKK!
HOW LONG DID YOU SAY...YOU'VE BEEN COUGHING BLOOD LIKE THAT?
DON'T RIGHTLY KNOW. YEAR OR SO I RECKON.
A YEAR OF COUGHING BLOOD? IF YOU DON'T MIND MY ASKING, MR. RATH, WHY IN THE WORLD DID YOU WAIT SO LONG TO COME SEE ME?
I DON'T SMOKE.
EXCUSE ME?

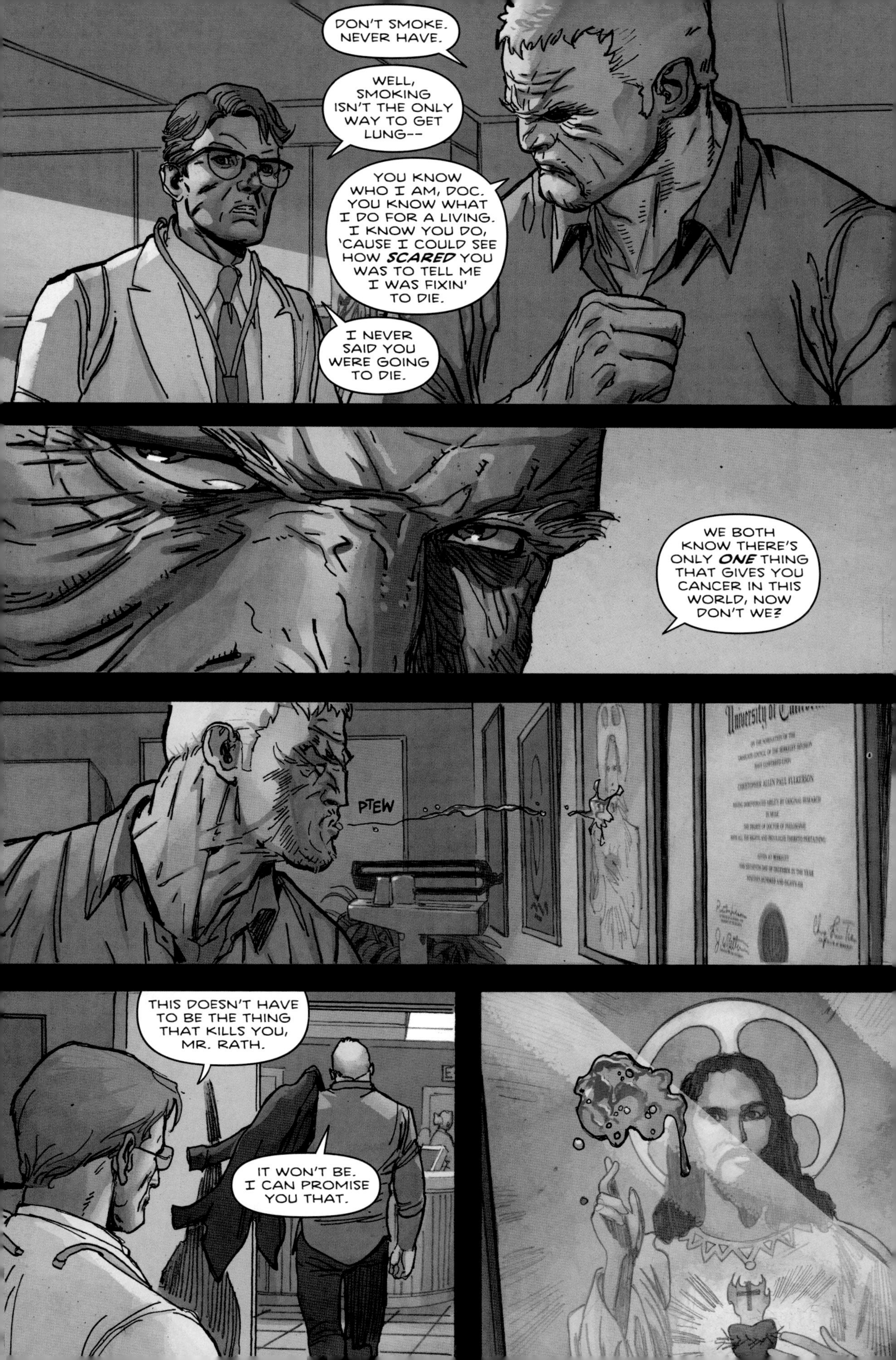
DON'T SMOKE. NEVER HAVE.
WELL, SMOKING ISN'T THE ONLY WAY TO GET LUNG--
YOU KNOW WHO I AM, DOC. YOU KNOW WHAT I DO FOR A LIVING. I KNOW YOU DO, 'CAUSE I COULD SEE HOW *SCARED* YOU WAS TO TELL ME I WAS FIXIN' TO DIE.
I NEVER SAID YOU WERE GOING TO DIE.
WE BOTH KNOW THERE'S ONLY *ONE* THING THAT GIVES YOU CANCER IN THIS WORLD, NOW DON'T WE?
PTEW
THIS DOESN'T HAVE TO BE THE THING THAT KILLS YOU, MR. RATH.
IT WON'T BE. I CAN PROMISE YOU THAT.

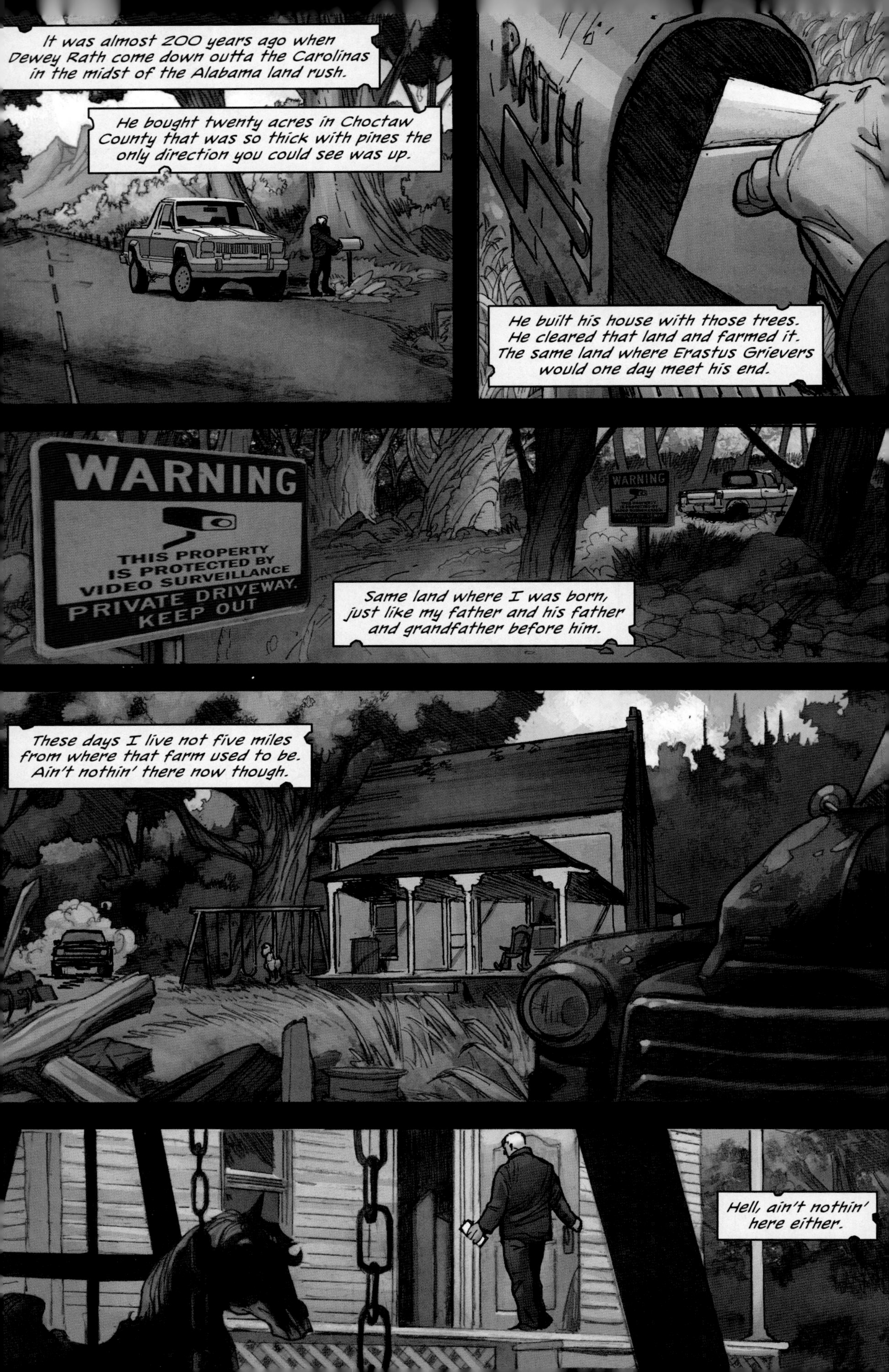
It was almost 200 years ago when Dewey Rath come down outta the Carolinas in the midst of the Alabama land rush.
He bought twenty acres in Choctaw County that was so thick with pines the only direction you could see was up.
RATH
He built his house with those trees. He cleared that land and farmed it. The same land where Erastus Grievers would one day meet his end.
WARNING
THIS PROPERTY IS PROTECTED BY VIDEO SURVEILLANCE
PRIVATE DRIVEWAY. KEEP OUT
WARNING
Same land where I was born, just like my father and his father and grandfather before him.
These days I live not five miles from where that farm used to be. Ain't nothin' there now though.
Hell, ain't nothin' here either.

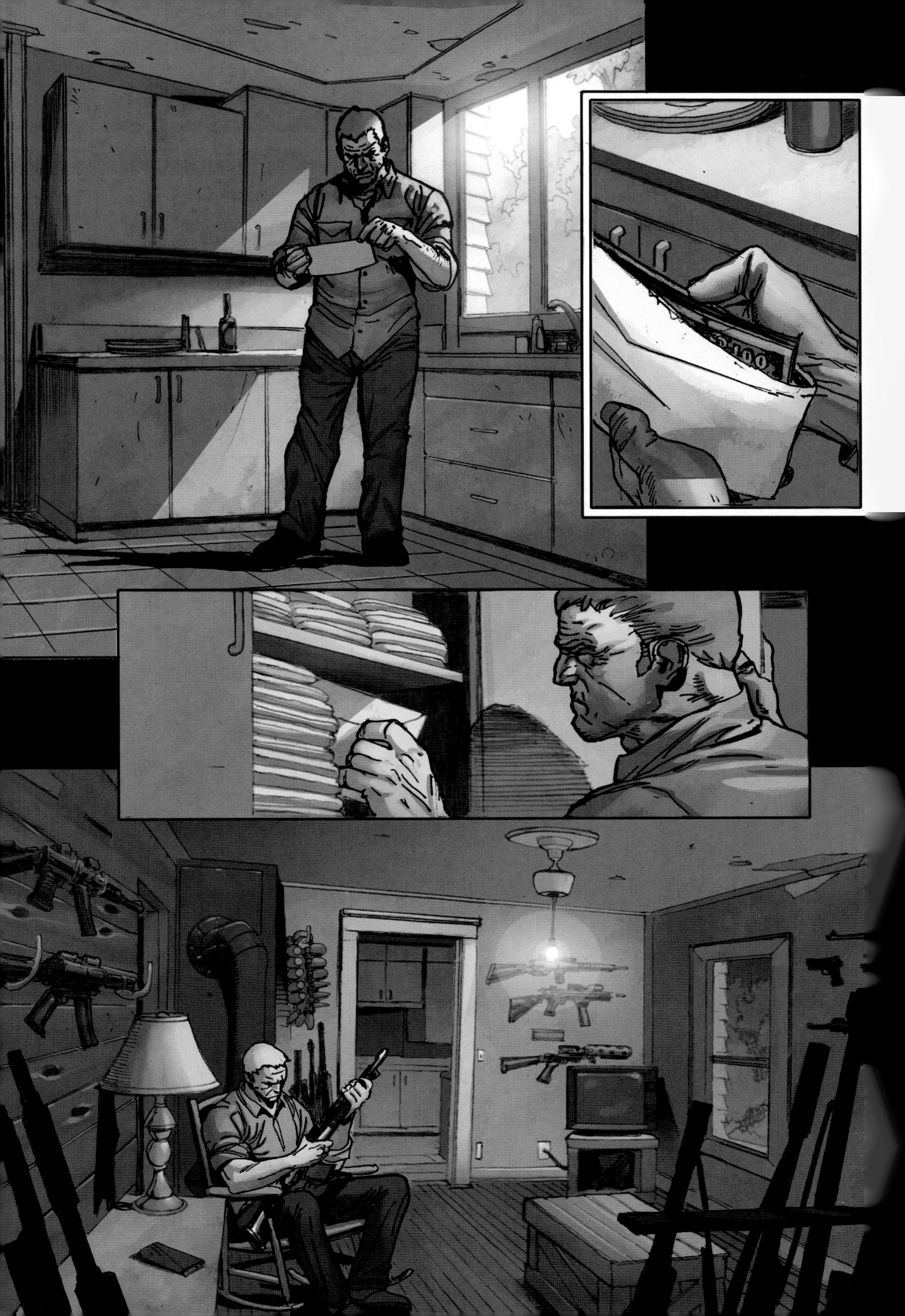

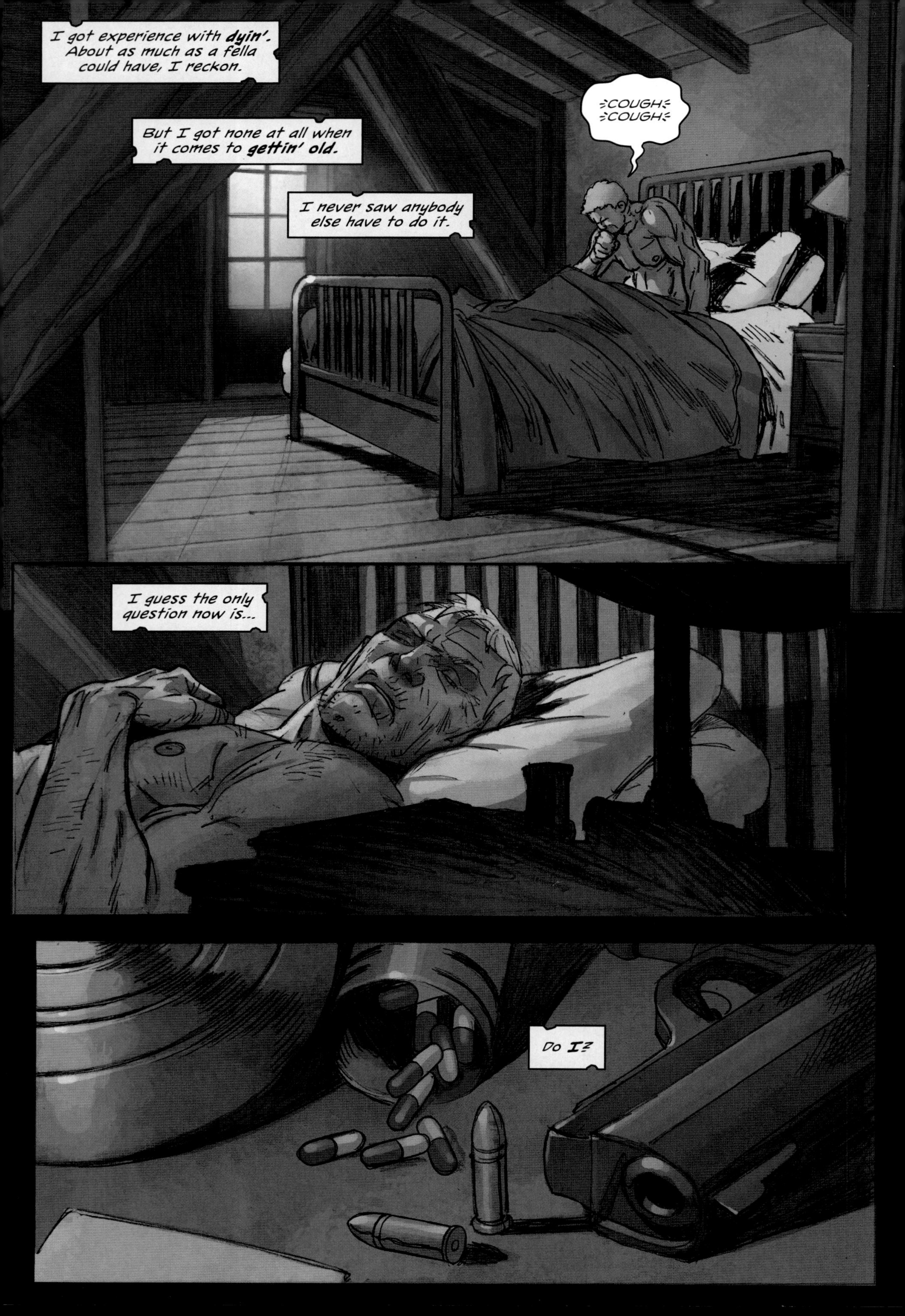
I got experience with dyin'. About as much as a fella could have, I reckon.
But I got none at all when it comes to gettin' old.
I never saw anybody else have to do it.
COUGH COUGH
I guess the only question now is...
Do I?

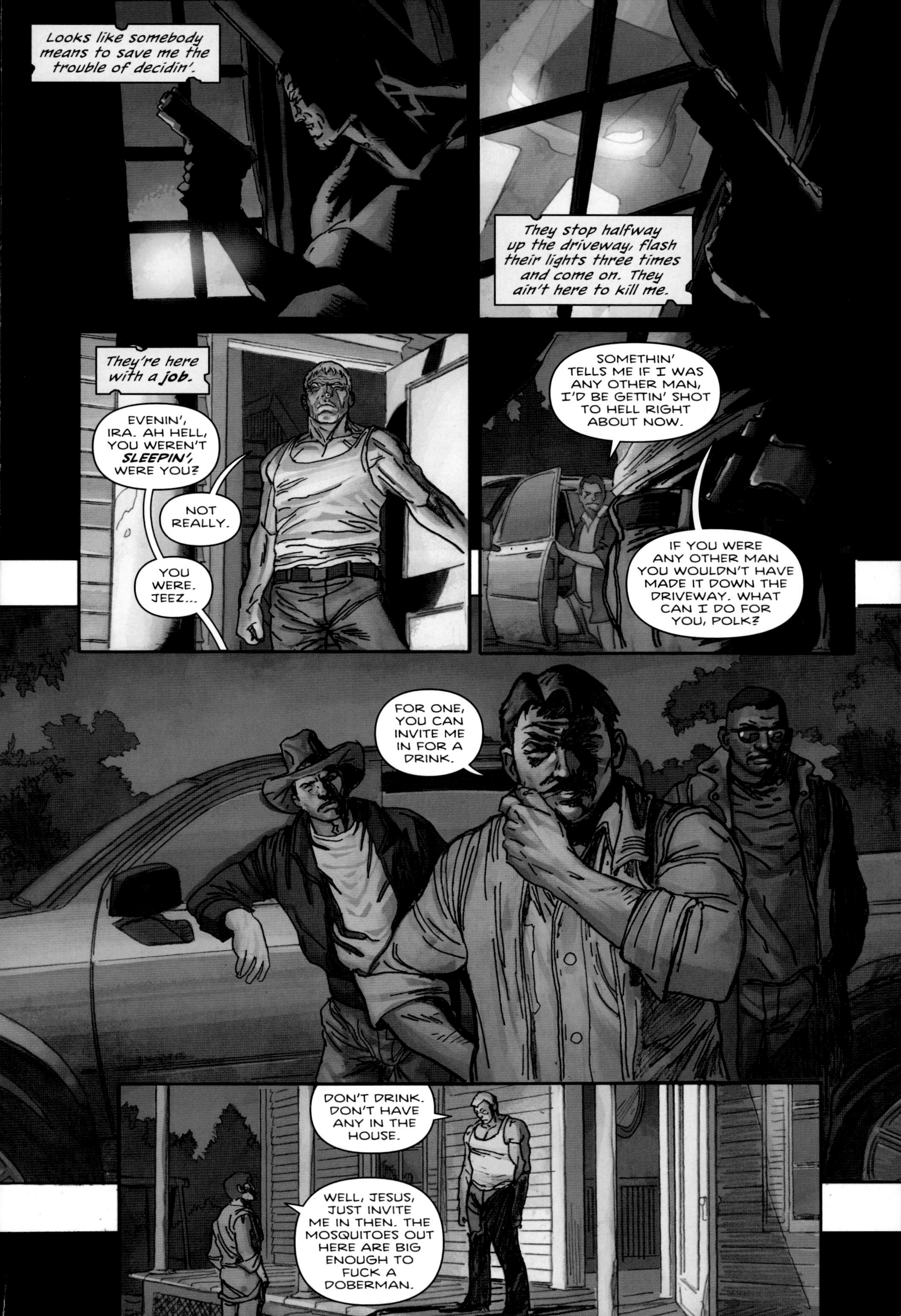
Looks like somebody means to save me the trouble of decidin'.
They stop halfway up the driveway, flash their lights three times and come on. They ain't here to kill me.
They're here with a job.
EVENIN', IRA. AH HELL, YOU WEREN'T SLEEPIN', WERE YOU?
NOT REALLY.
YOU WERE. JEEZ...
SOMETHIN' TELLS ME IF I WAS ANY OTHER MAN, I'D BE GETTIN' SHOT TO HELL RIGHT ABOUT NOW.
IF YOU WERE ANY OTHER MAN YOU WOULDN'T HAVE MADE IT DOWN THE DRIVEWAY. WHAT CAN I DO FOR YOU, POLK?
FOR ONE, YOU CAN INVITE ME IN FOR A DRINK.
DON'T DRINK. DON'T HAVE ANY IN THE HOUSE.
WELL, JESUS, JUST INVITE ME IN THEN. THE MOSQUITOES OUT HERE ARE BIG ENOUGH TO FUCK A DOBERMAN.

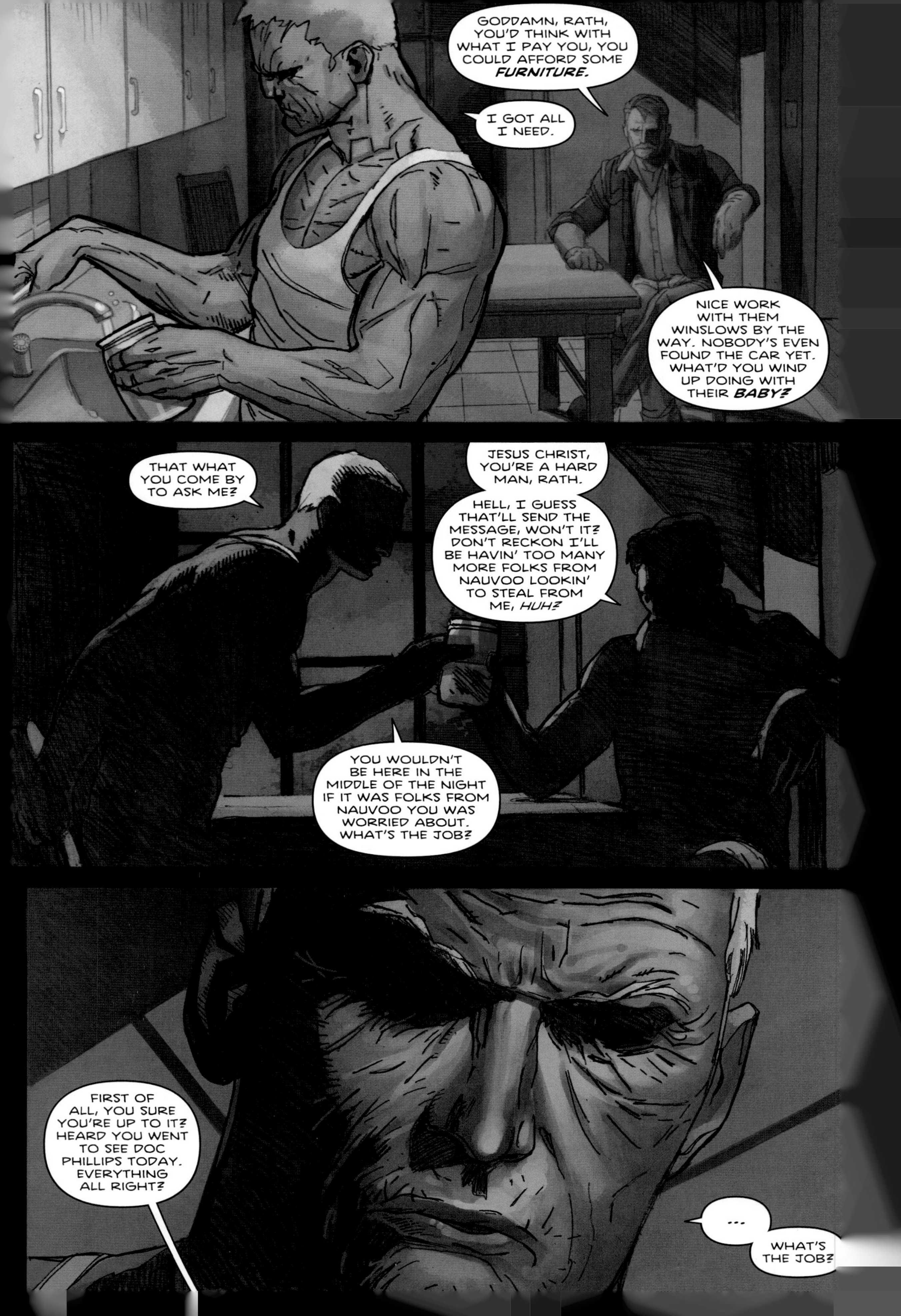
GODDAMN, RATH, YOU'D THINK WITH WHAT I PAY YOU, YOU COULD AFFORD SOME FURNITURE.
I GOT ALL I NEED.
NICE WORK WITH THEM WINSLOWS BY THE WAY. NOBODY'S EVEN FOUND THE CAR YET. WHAT'D YOU WIND UP DOING WITH THEIR BABY?
THAT WHAT YOU COME BY TO ASK ME?
JESUS CHRIST, YOU'RE A HARD MAN, RATH.
HELL, I GUESS THAT'LL SEND THE MESSAGE, WON'T IT? DON'T RECKON I'LL BE HAVIN' TOO MANY MORE FOLKS FROM NAUVOO LOOKIN' TO STEAL FROM ME, HUH?
YOU WOULDN'T BE HERE IN THE MIDDLE OF THE NIGHT IF IT WAS FOLKS FROM NAUVOO YOU WAS WORRIED ABOUT. WHAT'S THE JOB?
FIRST OF ALL, YOU SURE YOU'RE UP TO IT? HEARD YOU WENT TO SEE DOC PHILLIPS TODAY. EVERYTHING ALL RIGHT?
...
WHAT'S THE JOB?

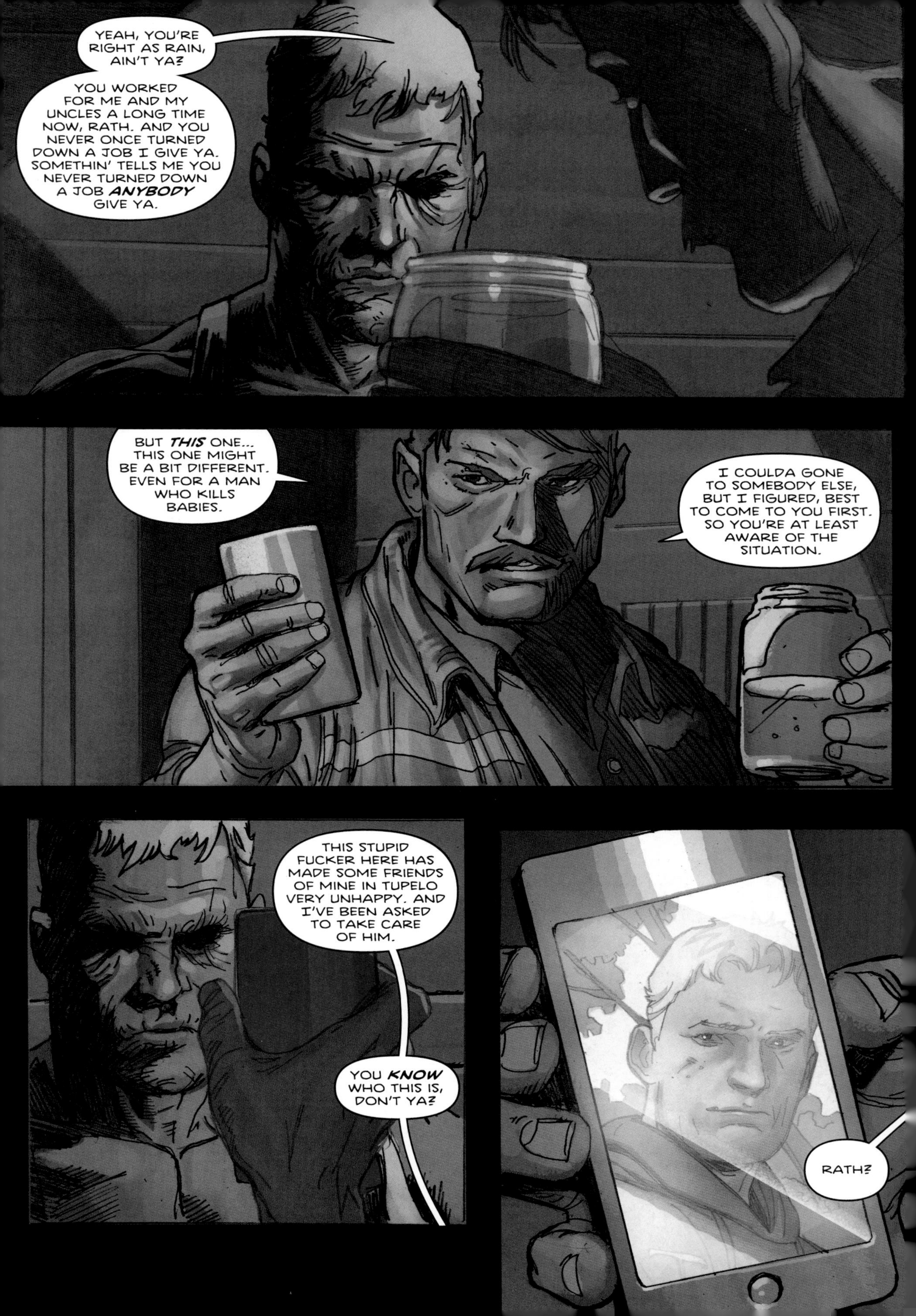
YEAH, YOU'RE RIGHT AS RAIN, AIN'T YA?
YOU WORKED FOR ME AND MY UNCLES A LONG TIME NOW, RATH. AND YOU NEVER ONCE TURNED DOWN A JOB I GIVE YA. SOMETHIN' TELLS ME YOU NEVER TURNED DOWN A JOB ANYBODY GIVE YA.
BUT THIS ONE... THIS ONE MIGHT BE A BIT DIFFERENT. EVEN FOR A MAN WHO KILLS BABIES.
I COULDA GONE TO SOMEBODY ELSE, BUT I FIGURED, BEST TO COME TO YOU FIRST. SO YOU'RE AT LEAST AWARE OF THE SITUATION.
THIS STUPID FUCKER HERE HAS MADE SOME FRIENDS OF MINE IN TUPELO VERY UNHAPPY. AND I'VE BEEN ASKED TO TAKE CARE OF HIM.
YOU KNOW WHO THIS IS, DON'T YA?
RATH?

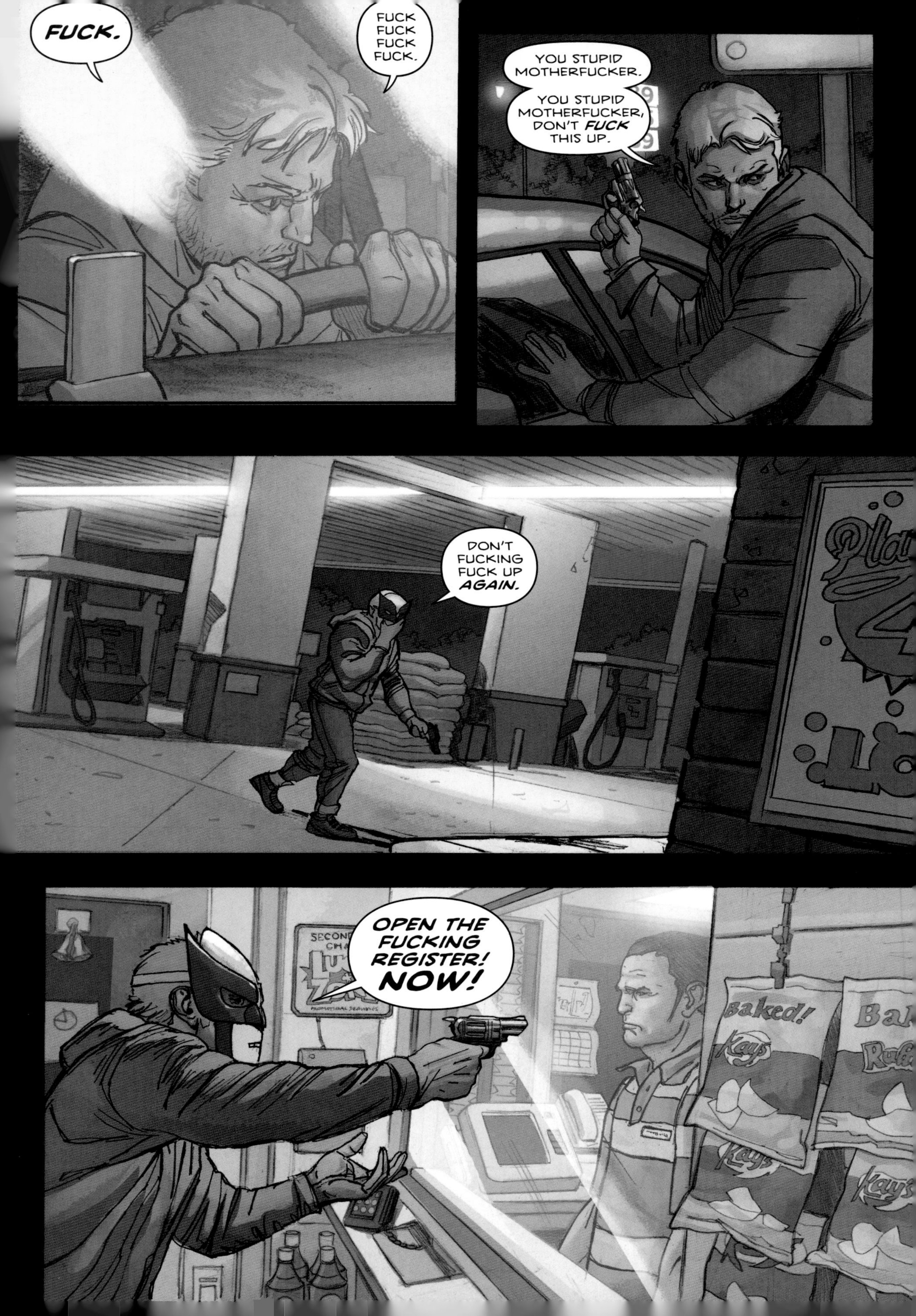

FUCK.
FUCK FUCK FUCK FUCK.
YOU STUPID MOTHERFUCKER.
YOU STUPID MOTHERFUCKER, DON'T FUCK THIS UP.
DON'T FUCKING FUCK UP AGAIN.
OPEN THE FUCKING REGISTER! NOW!
Baked!
Kay's

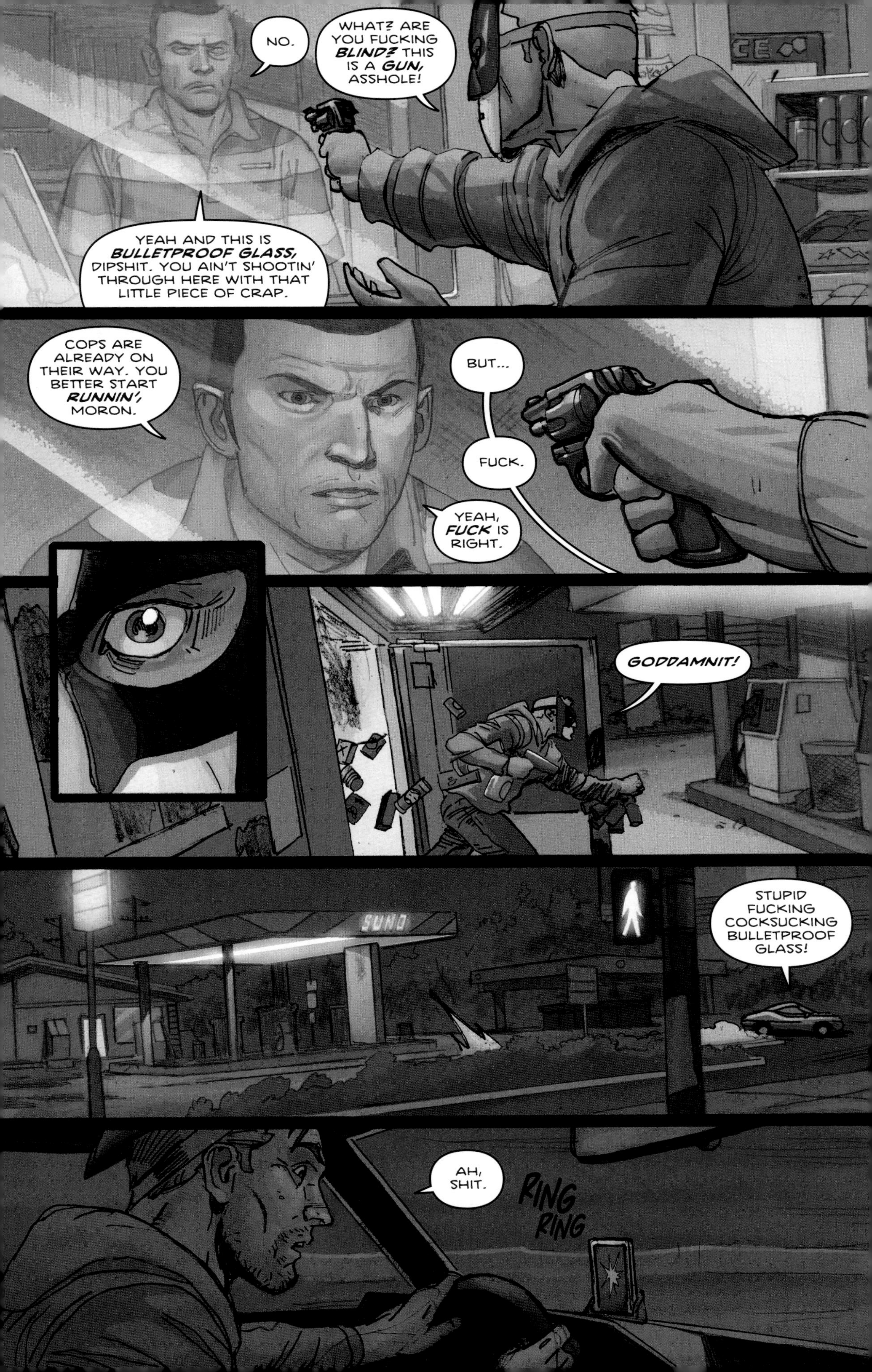
NO.
WHAT? ARE YOU FUCKING BLIND? THIS IS A GUN, ASSHOLE!
YEAH AND THIS IS BULLETPROOF GLASS, DIPSHIT. YOU AIN'T SHOOTIN' THROUGH HERE WITH THAT LITTLE PIECE OF CRAP.
COPS ARE ALREADY ON THEIR WAY. YOU BETTER START RUNNIN', MORON.
BUT...
FUCK.
YEAH, FUCK IS RIGHT.
GODDAMNIT!
SUNO
STUPID FUCKING COCKSUCKING BULLETPROOF GLASS!
AH, SHIT.
RING
RING

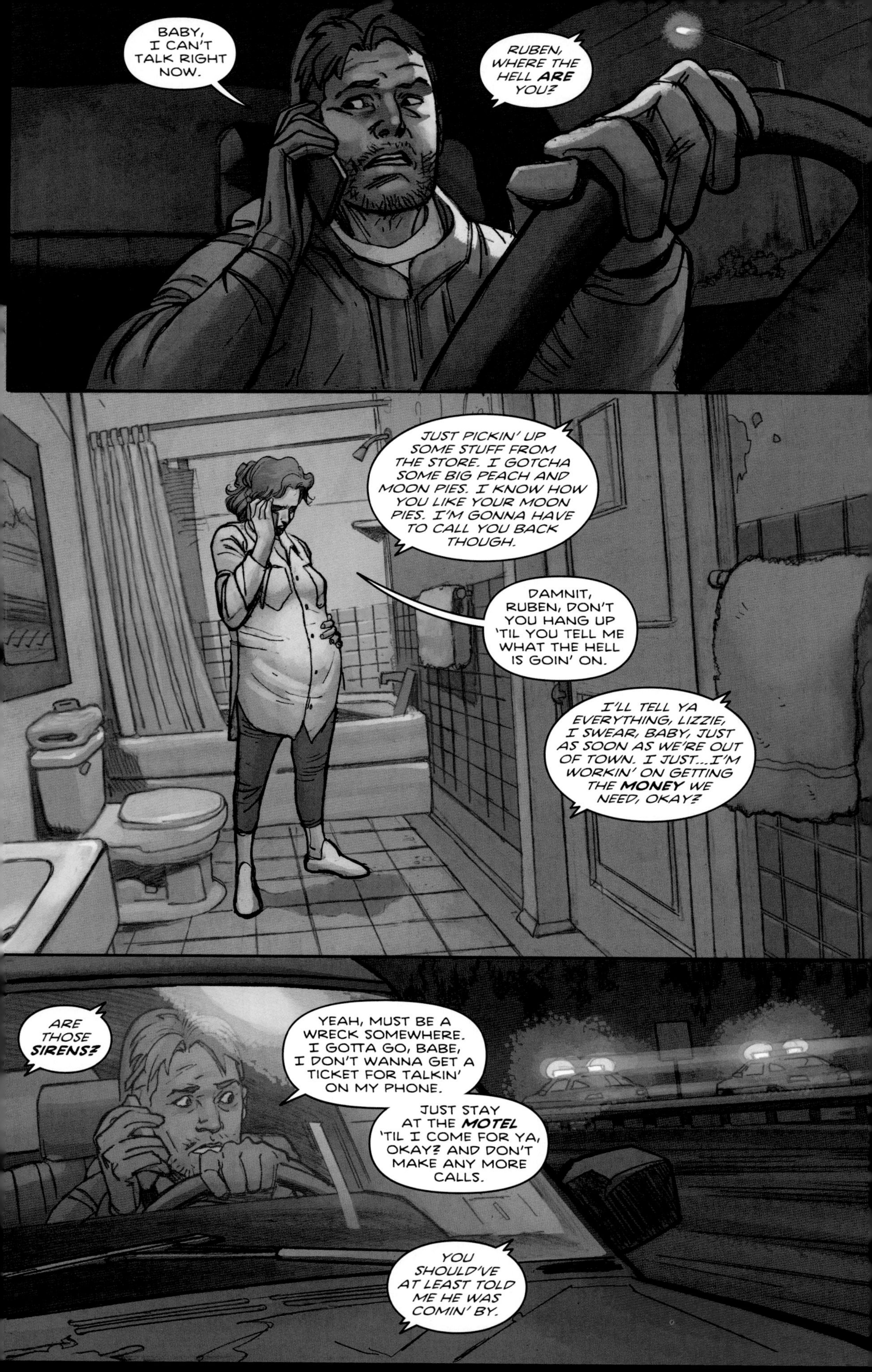
BABY, I CAN'T TALK RIGHT NOW.
RUBEN, WHERE THE HELL ARE YOU?
JUST PICKIN' UP SOME STUFF FROM THE STORE. I GOTCHA SOME BIG PEACH AND MOON PIES. I KNOW HOW YOU LIKE YOUR MOON PIES. I'M GONNA HAVE TO CALL YOU BACK THOUGH.
DAMNIT, RUBEN, DON'T YOU HANG UP 'TIL YOU TELL ME WHAT THE HELL IS GOIN' ON.
I'LL TELL YA EVERYTHING, LIZZIE, I SWEAR, BABY, JUST AS SOON AS WE'RE OUT OF TOWN. I JUST...I'M WORKIN' ON GETTING THE MONEY WE NEED, OKAY?
ARE THOSE SIRENS?
YEAH, MUST BE A WRECK SOMEWHERE. I GOTTA GO, BABE, I DON'T WANNA GET A TICKET FOR TALKIN' ON MY PHONE.
JUST STAY AT THE MOTEL 'TIL I COME FOR YA, OKAY? AND DON'T MAKE ANY MORE CALLS.
YOU SHOULD'VE AT LEAST TOLD ME HE WAS COMIN' BY.

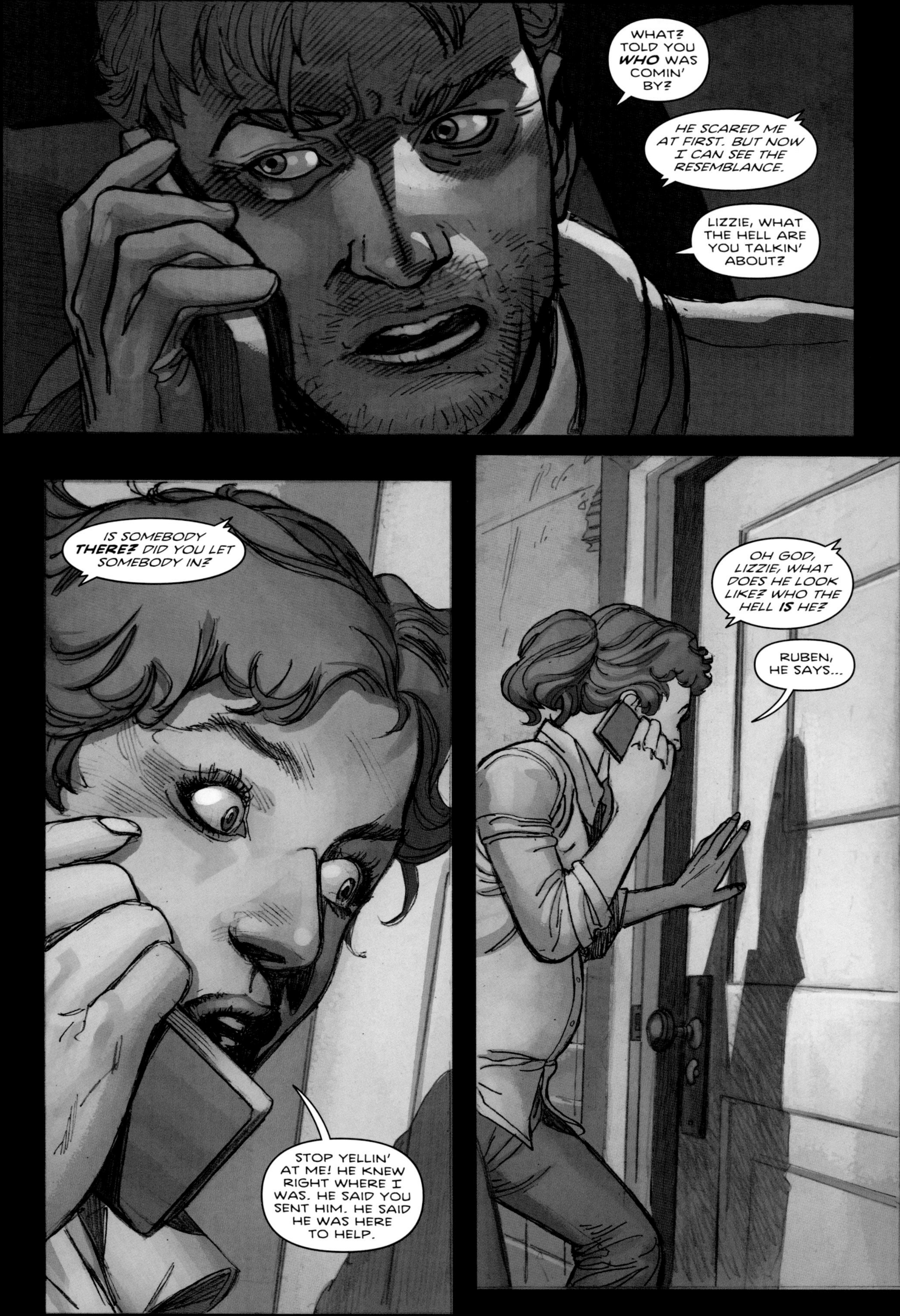

WHAT? TOLD YOU **WHO** WAS COMIN' BY?
*HE SCARED ME AT FIRST. BUT NOW I CAN SEE THE RESEMBLANCE.*
LIZZIE, WHAT THE HELL ARE YOU TALKIN' ABOUT?
*IS SOMEBODY* ***THERE?*** *DID YOU LET SOMEBODY IN?*
STOP YELLIN' AT ME! HE KNEW RIGHT WHERE I WAS. HE SAID YOU SENT HIM. HE SAID HE WAS HERE TO HELP.
*OH GOD, LIZZIE, WHAT DOES HE LOOK LIKE? WHO THE HELL* ***IS*** *HE?*
RUBEN, HE SAYS...

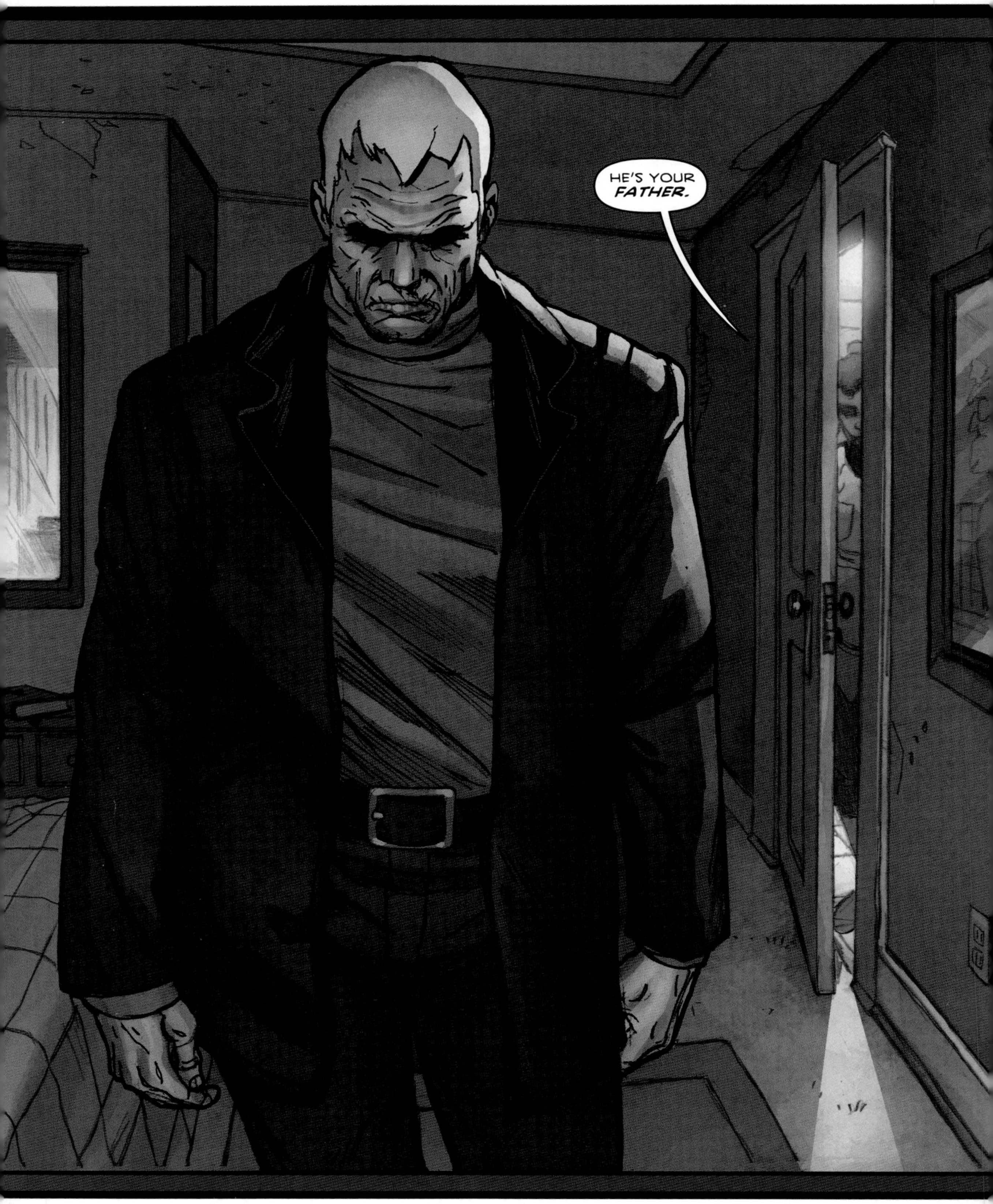
HE'S YOUR *FATHER.*

# CHAPTER TWO

## HEIR OF THE DOG

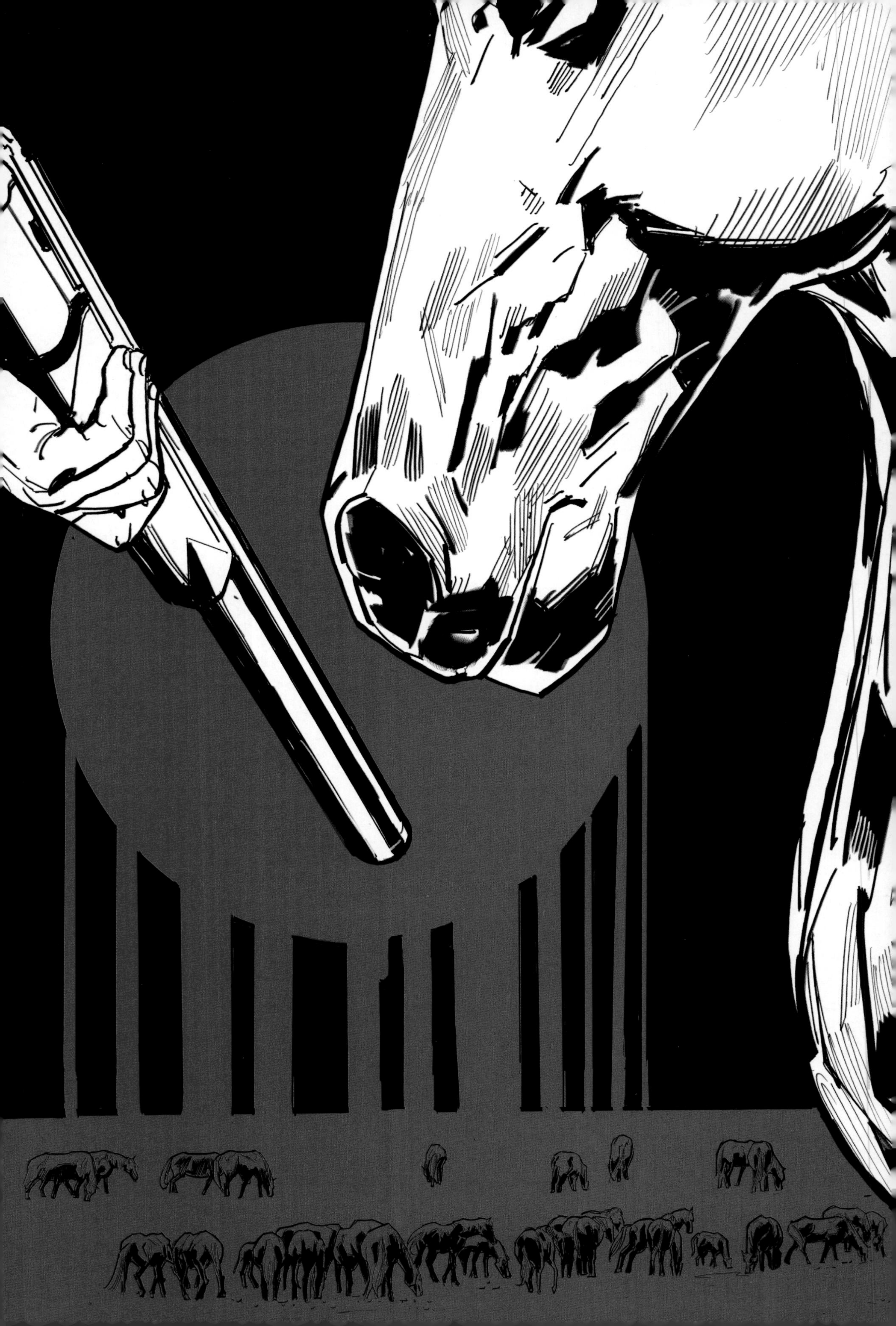

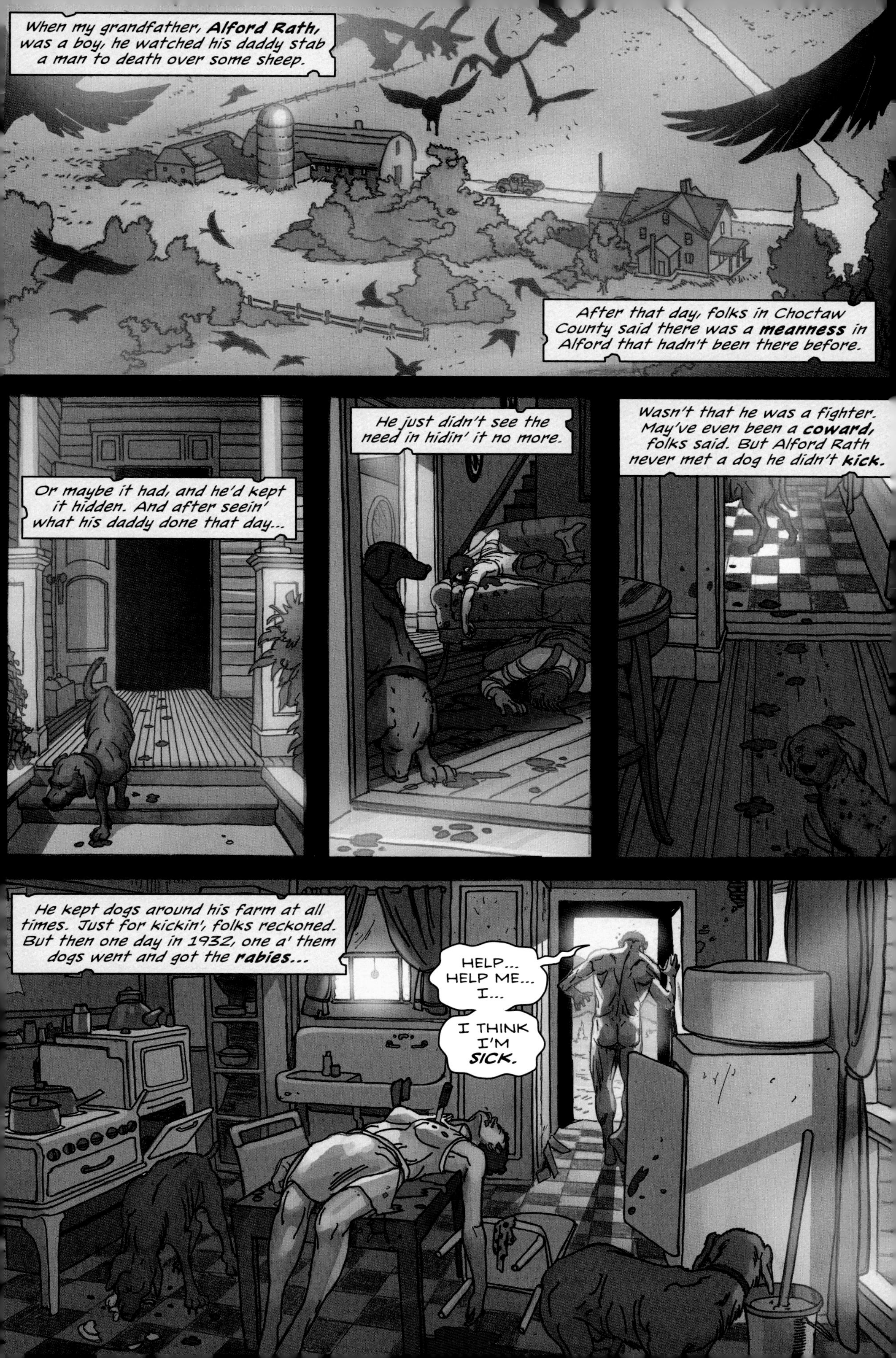
When my grandfather, **Alford Rath,** was a boy, he watched his daddy stab a man to death over some sheep.
After that day, folks in Choctaw County said there was a **meanness** in Alford that hadn't been there before.
Or maybe it had, and he'd kept it hidden. And after seein' what his daddy done that day...
He just didn't see the need in hidin' it no more.
Wasn't that he was a fighter. May've even been a **coward,** folks said. But Alford Rath never met a dog he didn't **kick.**
He kept dogs around his farm at all times. Just for kickin', folks reckoned. But then one day in 1932, one a' them dogs went and got the **rabies...**
HELP... HELP ME... I...
I THINK I'M **SICK.**

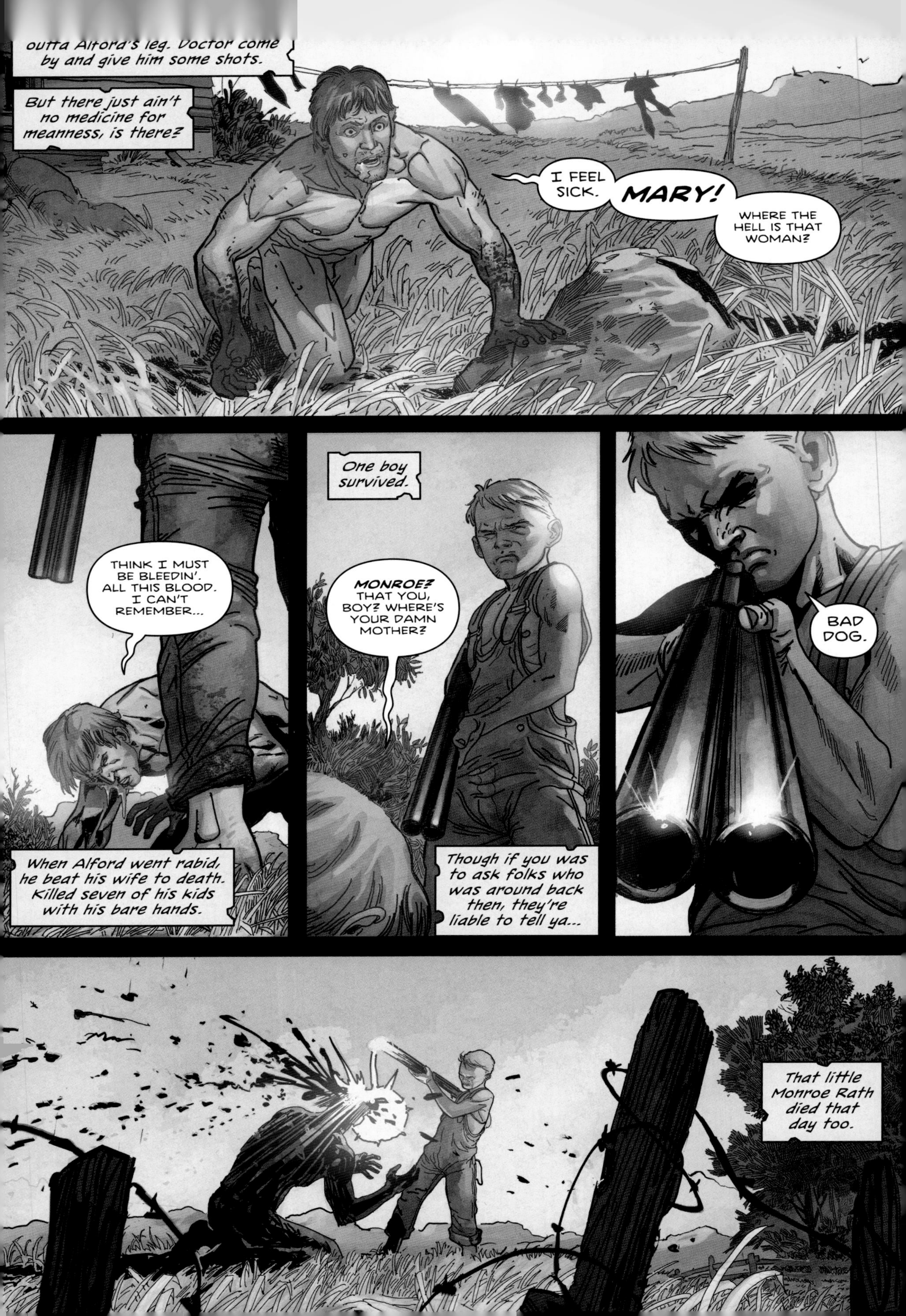

outta Alford's leg. Doctor come by and give him some shots.
But there just ain't no medicine for meanness, is there?
I FEEL SICK.
MARY!
WHERE THE HELL IS THAT WOMAN?
THINK I MUST BE BLEEDIN'. ALL THIS BLOOD. I CAN'T REMEMBER...
When Alford went rabid, he beat his wife to death. Killed seven of his kids with his bare hands.
One boy survived.
MONROE? THAT YOU, BOY? WHERE'S YOUR DAMN MOTHER?
Though if you was to ask folks who was around back then, they're liable to tell ya...
BAD DOG.
That little Monroe Rath died that day too.

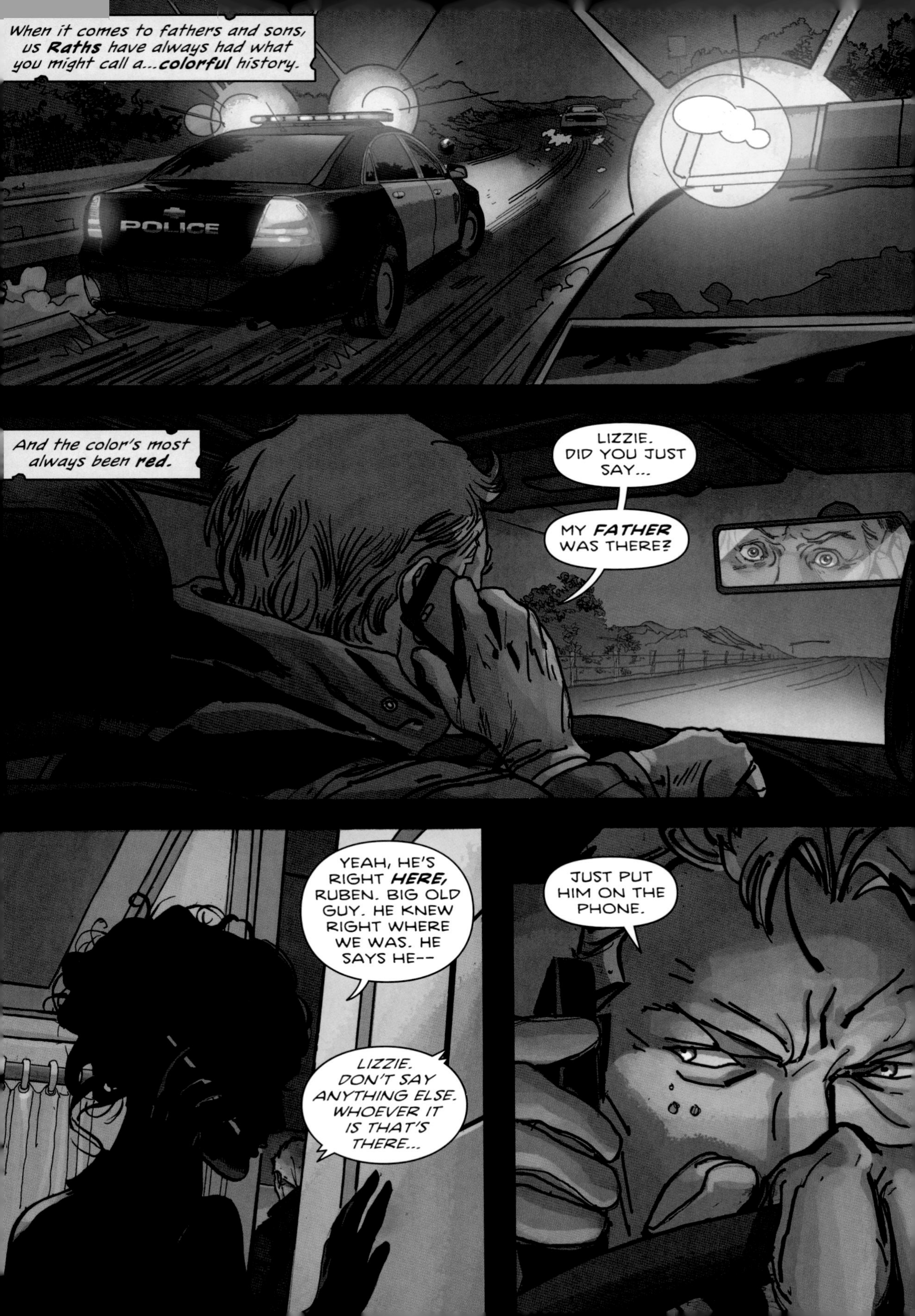
When it comes to fathers and sons, us Raths have always had what you might call a...colorful history.
POLICE
And the color's most always been red.
LIZZIE. DID YOU JUST SAY...
MY FATHER WAS THERE?
YEAH, HE'S RIGHT HERE, RUBEN. BIG OLD GUY. HE KNEW RIGHT WHERE WE WAS. HE SAYS HE--
LIZZIE. DON'T SAY ANYTHING ELSE. WHOEVER IT IS THAT'S THERE...
JUST PUT HIM ON THE PHONE.

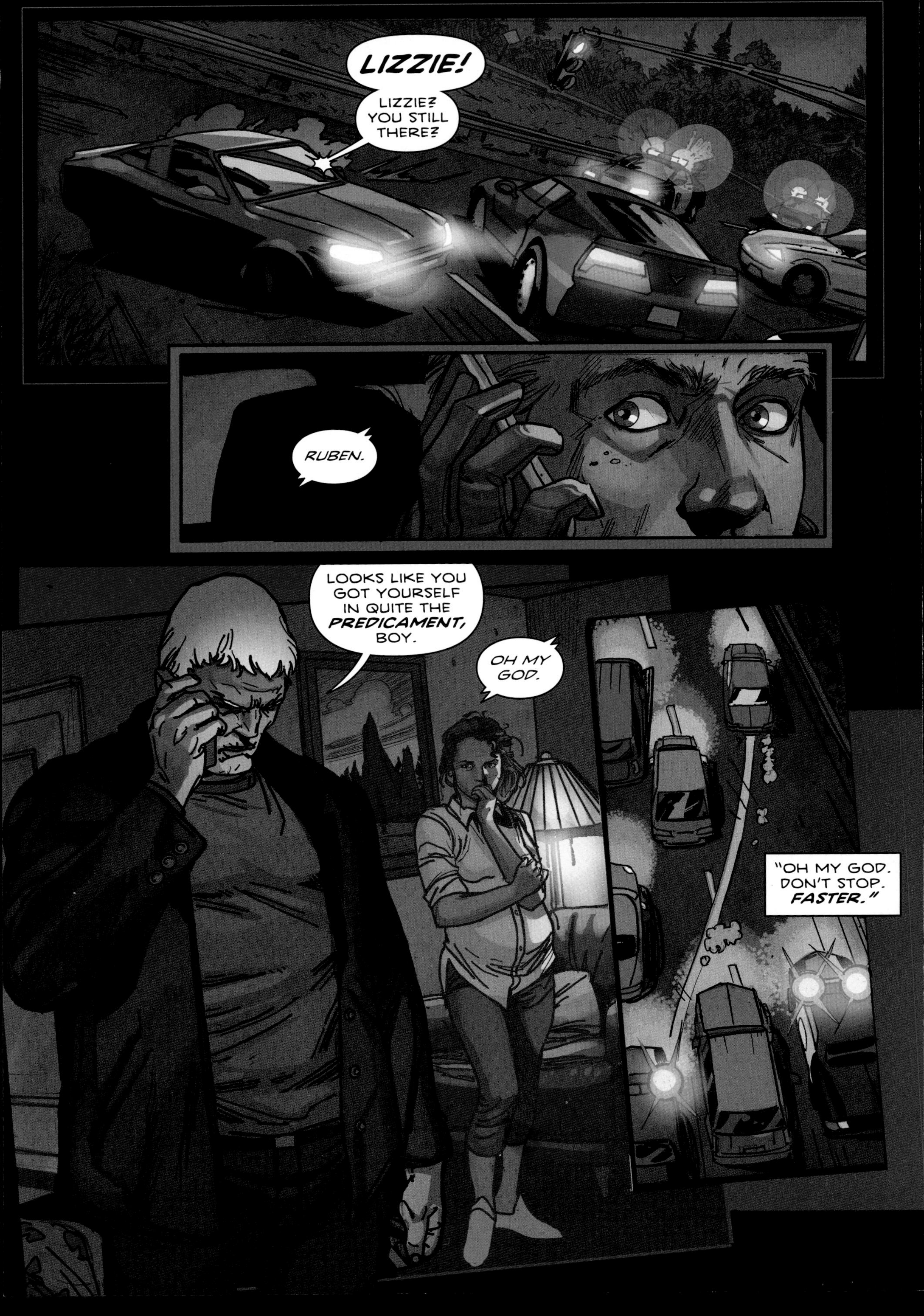
LIZZIE!
LIZZIE? YOU STILL THERE?
RUBEN.
LOOKS LIKE YOU GOT YOURSELF IN QUITE THE PREDICAMENT, BOY.
OH MY GOD.
"OH MY GOD. DON'T STOP. FASTER."

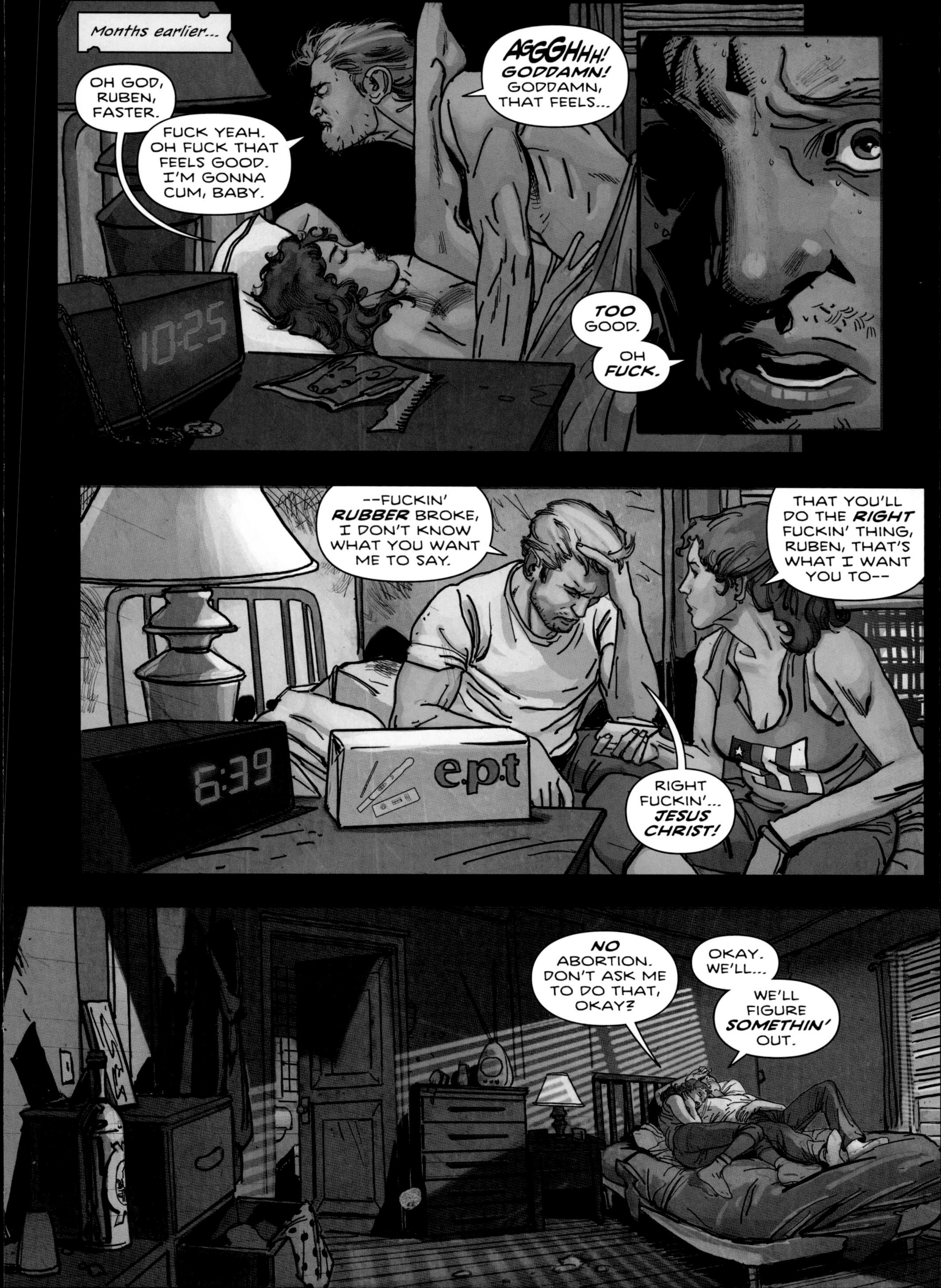
Months earlier...
OH GOD, RUBEN, FASTER.
FUCK YEAH. OH FUCK THAT FEELS GOOD. I'M GONNA CUM, BABY.
AGGGHHH! GODDAMN! GODDAMN, THAT FEELS...
TOO GOOD.
OH FUCK.
10:25
--FUCKIN' RUBBER BROKE, I DON'T KNOW WHAT YOU WANT ME TO SAY.
THAT YOU'LL DO THE RIGHT FUCKIN' THING, RUBEN, THAT'S WHAT I WANT YOU TO--
RIGHT FUCKIN'... JESUS CHRIST!
6:39
e.p.t
NO ABORTION. DON'T ASK ME TO DO THAT, OKAY?
OKAY. WE'LL...
WE'LL FIGURE SOMETHIN' OUT.

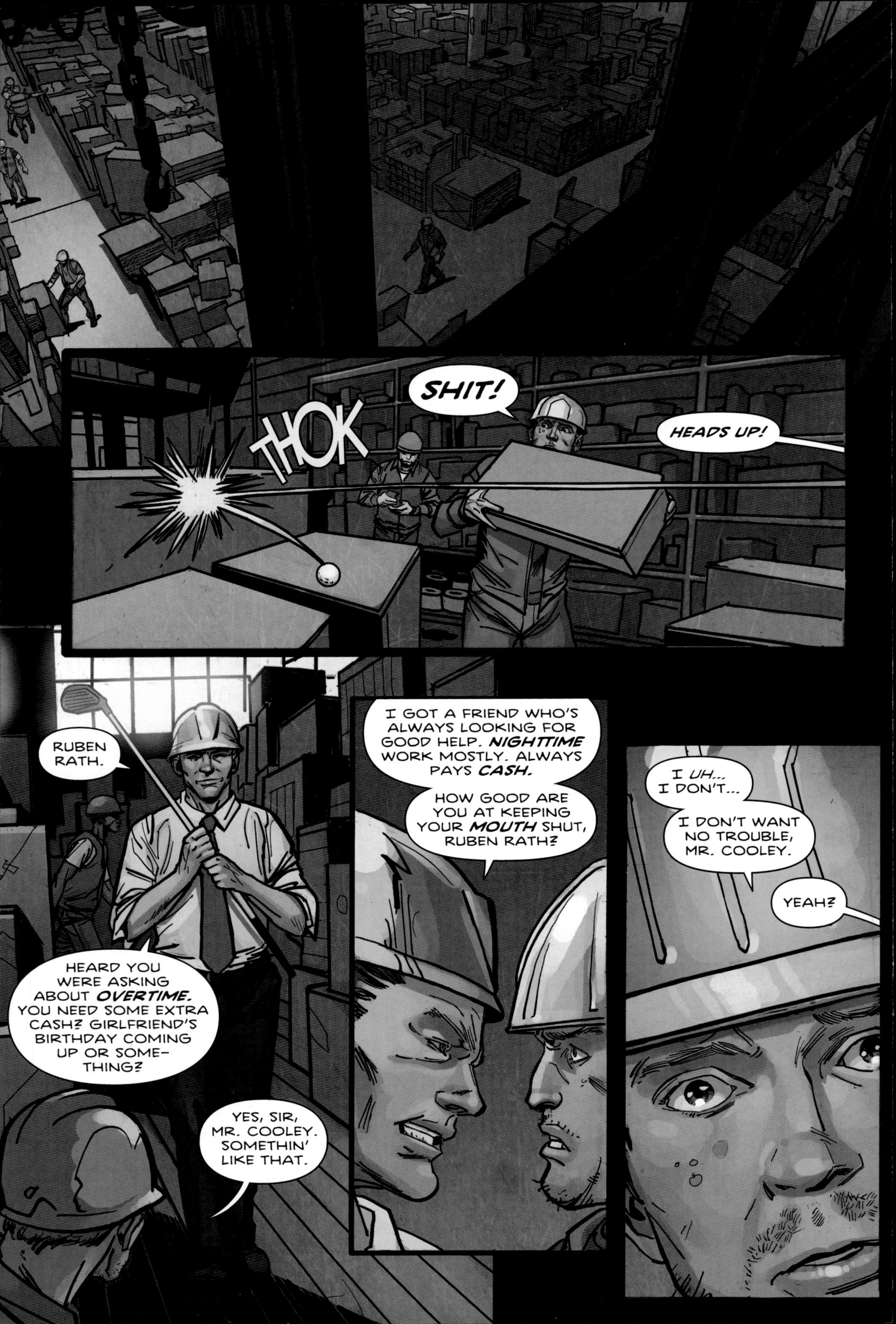
THOK
SHIT!
HEADS UP!
RUBEN RATH.
HEARD YOU WERE ASKING ABOUT OVERTIME. YOU NEED SOME EXTRA CASH? GIRLFRIEND'S BIRTHDAY COMING UP OR SOME-THING?
YES, SIR, MR. COOLEY. SOMETHIN' LIKE THAT.
I GOT A FRIEND WHO'S ALWAYS LOOKING FOR GOOD HELP. NIGHTTIME WORK MOSTLY. ALWAYS PAYS CASH.
HOW GOOD ARE YOU AT KEEPING YOUR MOUTH SHUT, RUBEN RATH?
I UH... I DON'T...
I DON'T WANT NO TROUBLE, MR. COOLEY.
YEAH?

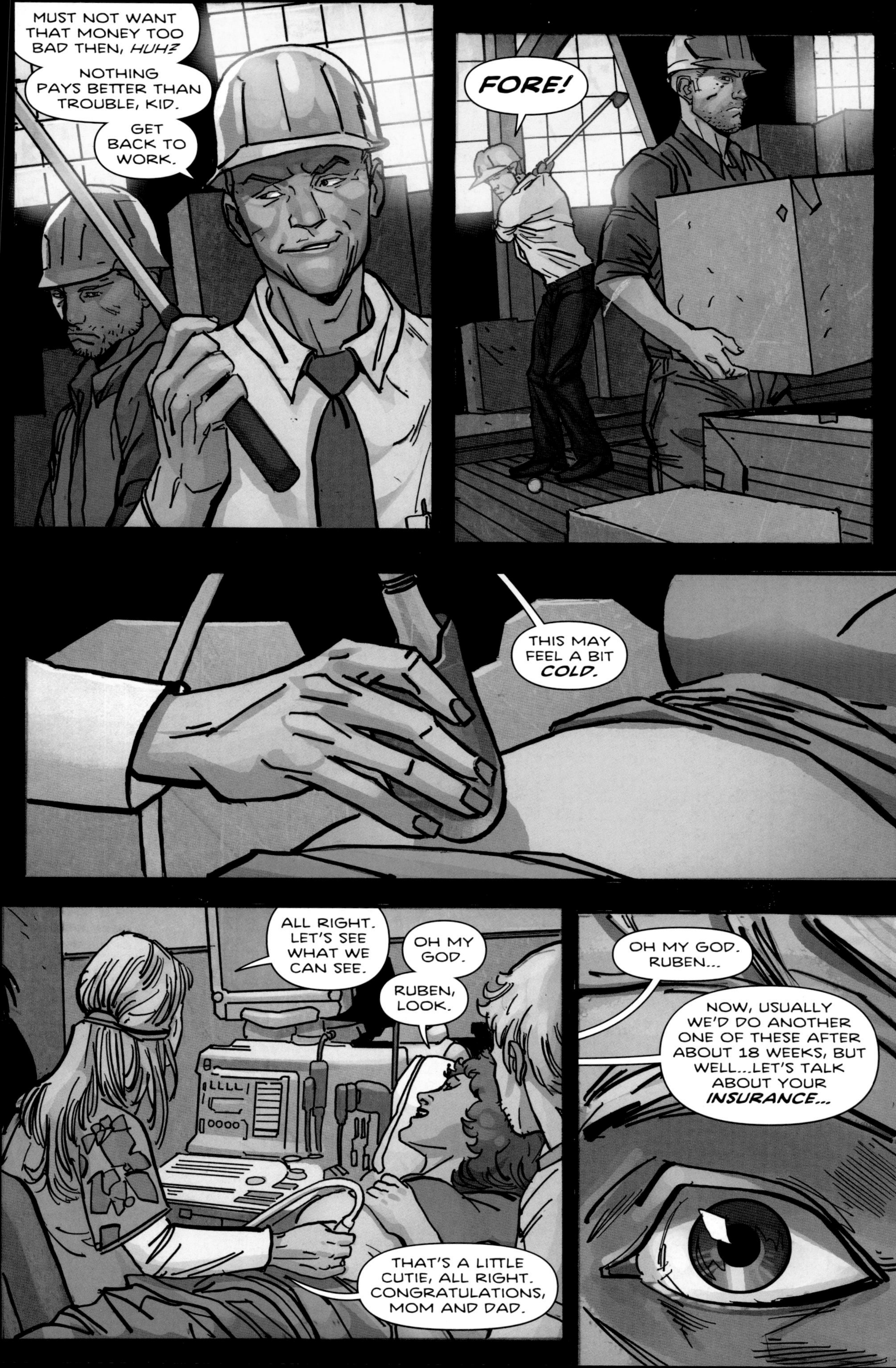
MUST NOT WANT THAT MONEY TOO BAD THEN, *HUH?*
NOTHING PAYS BETTER THAN TROUBLE, KID.
GET BACK TO WORK.
*FORE!*
THIS MAY FEEL A BIT *COLD.*
ALL RIGHT. LET'S SEE WHAT WE CAN SEE.
OH MY GOD.
RUBEN, LOOK.
THAT'S A LITTLE CUTIE, ALL RIGHT. CONGRATULATIONS, MOM AND DAD.
OH MY GOD. RUBEN...
NOW, USUALLY WE'D DO ANOTHER ONE OF THESE AFTER ABOUT 18 WEEKS, BUT WELL...LET'S TALK ABOUT YOUR *INSURANCE...*

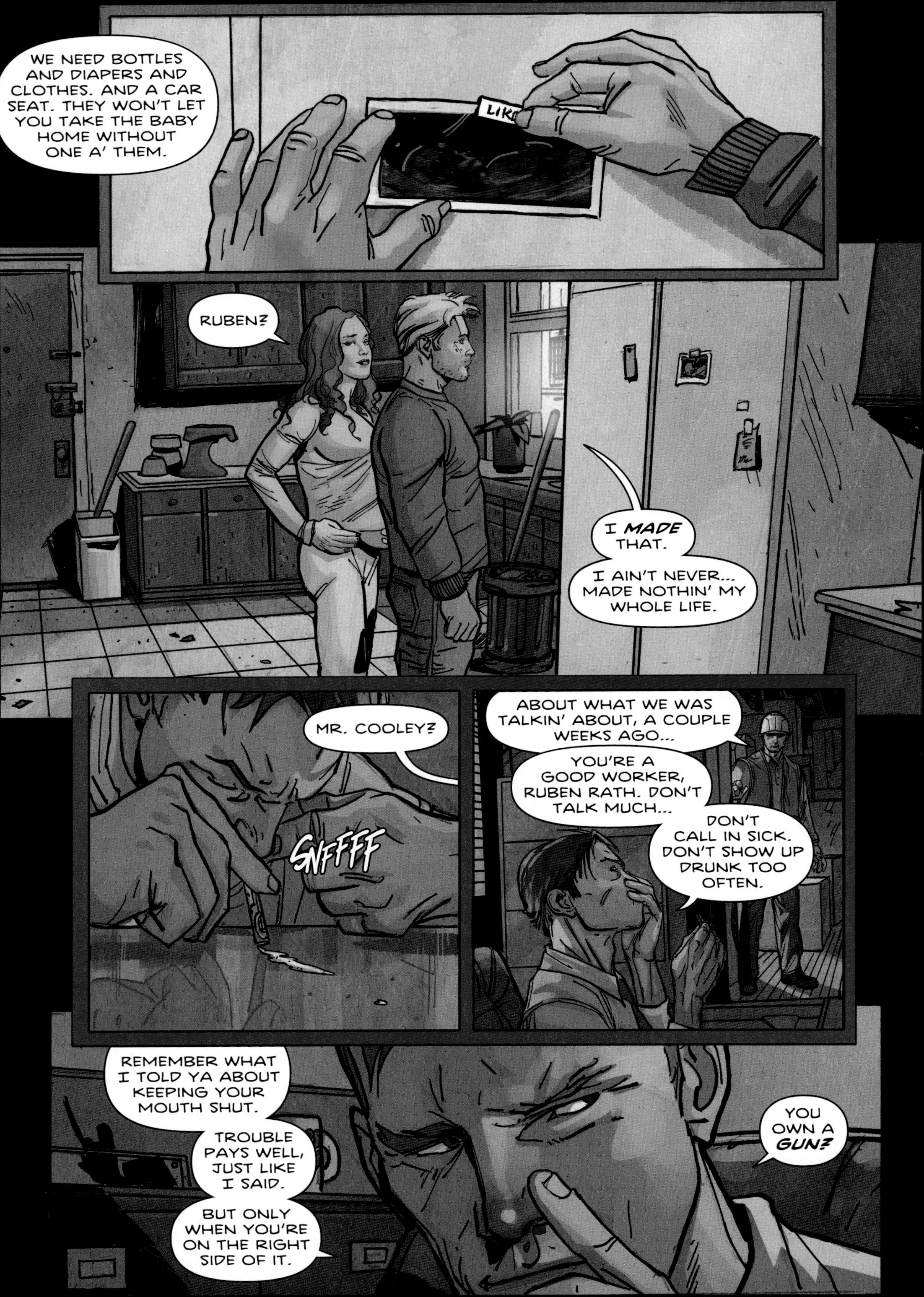
WE NEED BOTTLES AND DIAPERS AND CLOTHES. AND A CAR SEAT. THEY WON'T LET YOU TAKE THE BABY HOME WITHOUT ONE A' THEM.
RUBEN?
I *MADE* THAT.
I AIN'T NEVER... MADE NOTHIN' MY WHOLE LIFE.
MR. COOLEY?
SNFFFF
ABOUT WHAT WE WAS TALKIN' ABOUT, A COUPLE WEEKS AGO...
YOU'RE A GOOD WORKER, RUBEN RATH. DON'T TALK MUCH...
DON'T CALL IN SICK. DON'T SHOW UP DRUNK TOO OFTEN.
REMEMBER WHAT I TOLD YA ABOUT KEEPING YOUR MOUTH SHUT.
TROUBLE PAYS WELL, JUST LIKE I SAID.
BUT ONLY WHEN YOU'RE ON THE RIGHT SIDE OF IT.
YOU OWN A *GUN*?

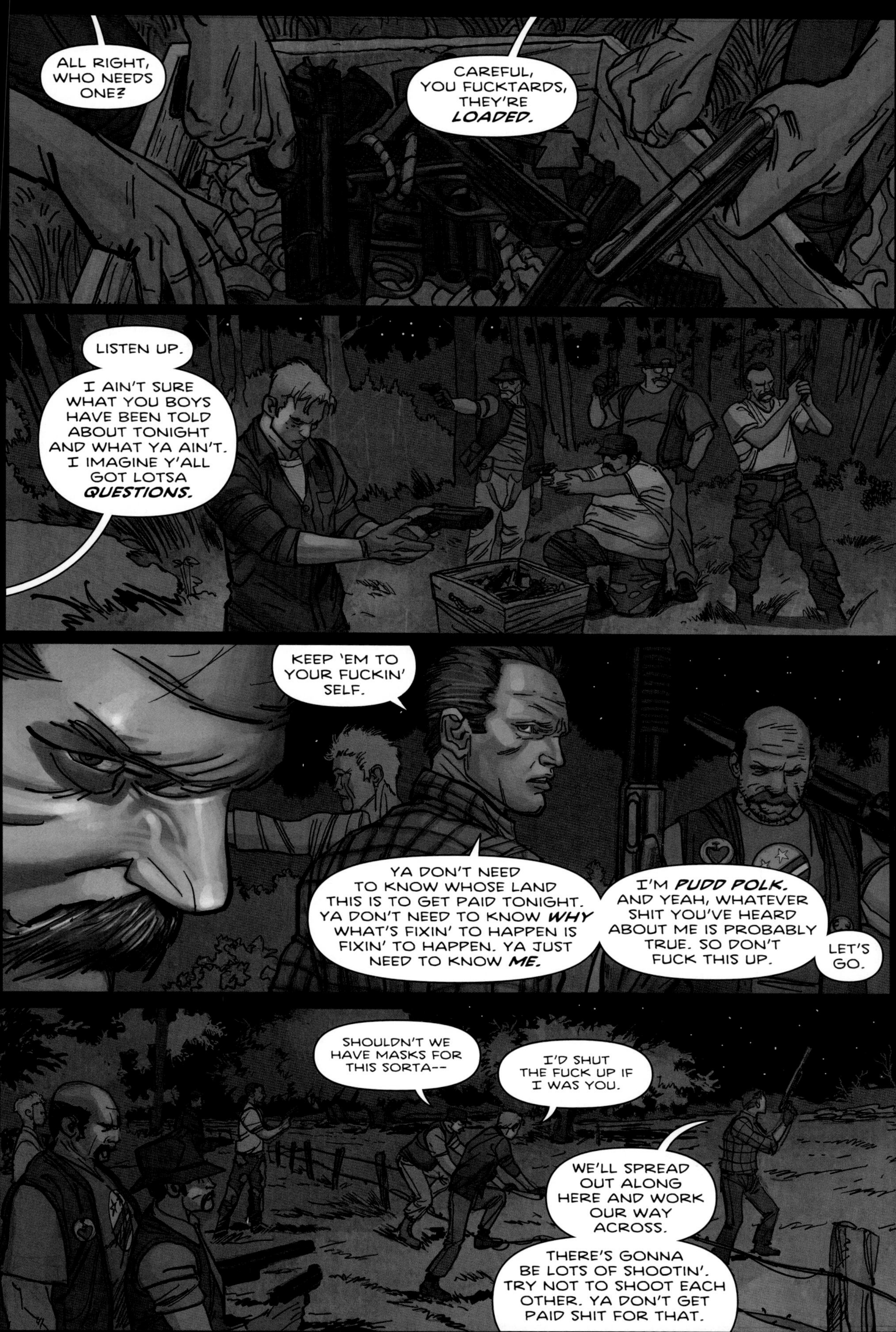
ALL RIGHT, WHO NEEDS ONE?
CAREFUL, YOU FUCKTARDS, THEY'RE *LOADED.*
LISTEN UP.
I AIN'T SURE WHAT YOU BOYS HAVE BEEN TOLD ABOUT TONIGHT AND WHAT YA AIN'T. I IMAGINE Y'ALL GOT LOTSA *QUESTIONS.*
KEEP 'EM TO YOUR FUCKIN' SELF.
YA DON'T NEED TO KNOW WHOSE LAND THIS IS TO GET PAID TONIGHT. YA DON'T NEED TO KNOW *WHY* WHAT'S FIXIN' TO HAPPEN IS FIXIN' TO HAPPEN. YA JUST NEED TO KNOW *ME.*
I'M *PUDD POLK.* AND YEAH, WHATEVER SHIT YOU'VE HEARD ABOUT ME IS PROBABLY TRUE. SO DON'T FUCK THIS UP.
LET'S GO.
SHOULDN'T WE HAVE MASKS FOR THIS SORTA--
I'D SHUT THE FUCK UP IF I WAS YOU.
WE'LL SPREAD OUT ALONG HERE AND WORK OUR WAY ACROSS.
THERE'S GONNA BE LOTS OF SHOOTIN'. TRY NOT TO SHOOT EACH OTHER. YA DON'T GET PAID SHIT FOR THAT.

YOU GET PAID...FOR SHOOTIN' *THEM.*

FIFTY DOLLARS CASH FOR EVERY HORSE YA KILL.

AND NO ARGUIN' OVER WHO KILLED WHAT. WE'LL CHECK THE FUCKIN' SLUGS IF WE GOT TO.

READY?

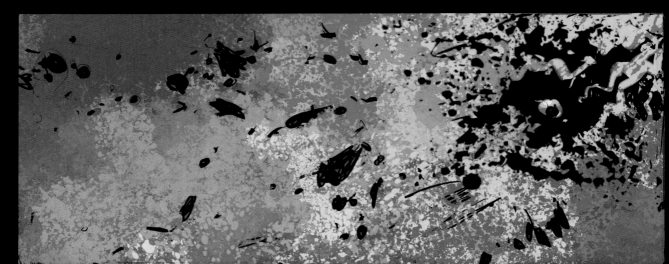

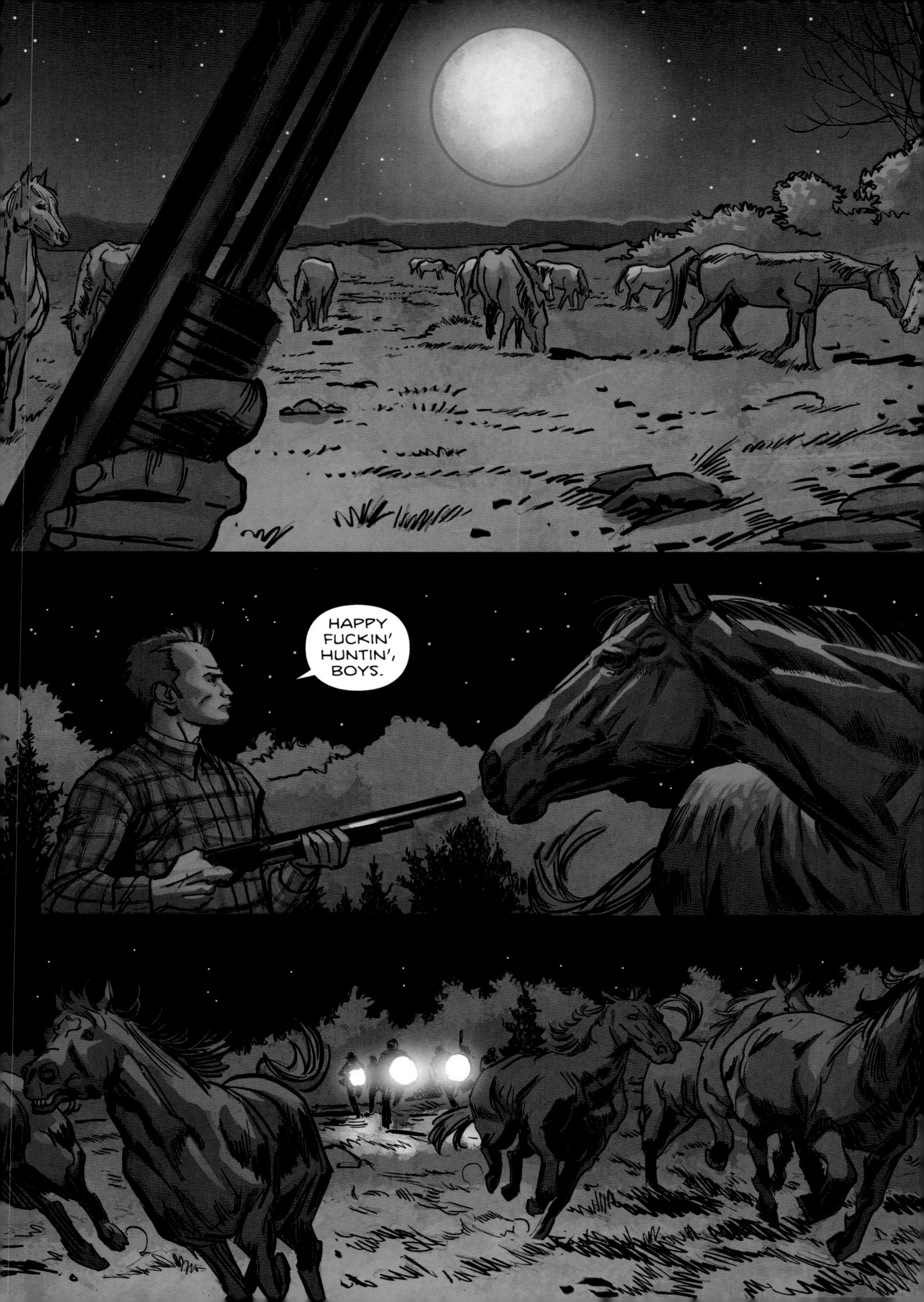
HAPPY FUCKIN' HUNTIN', BOYS.

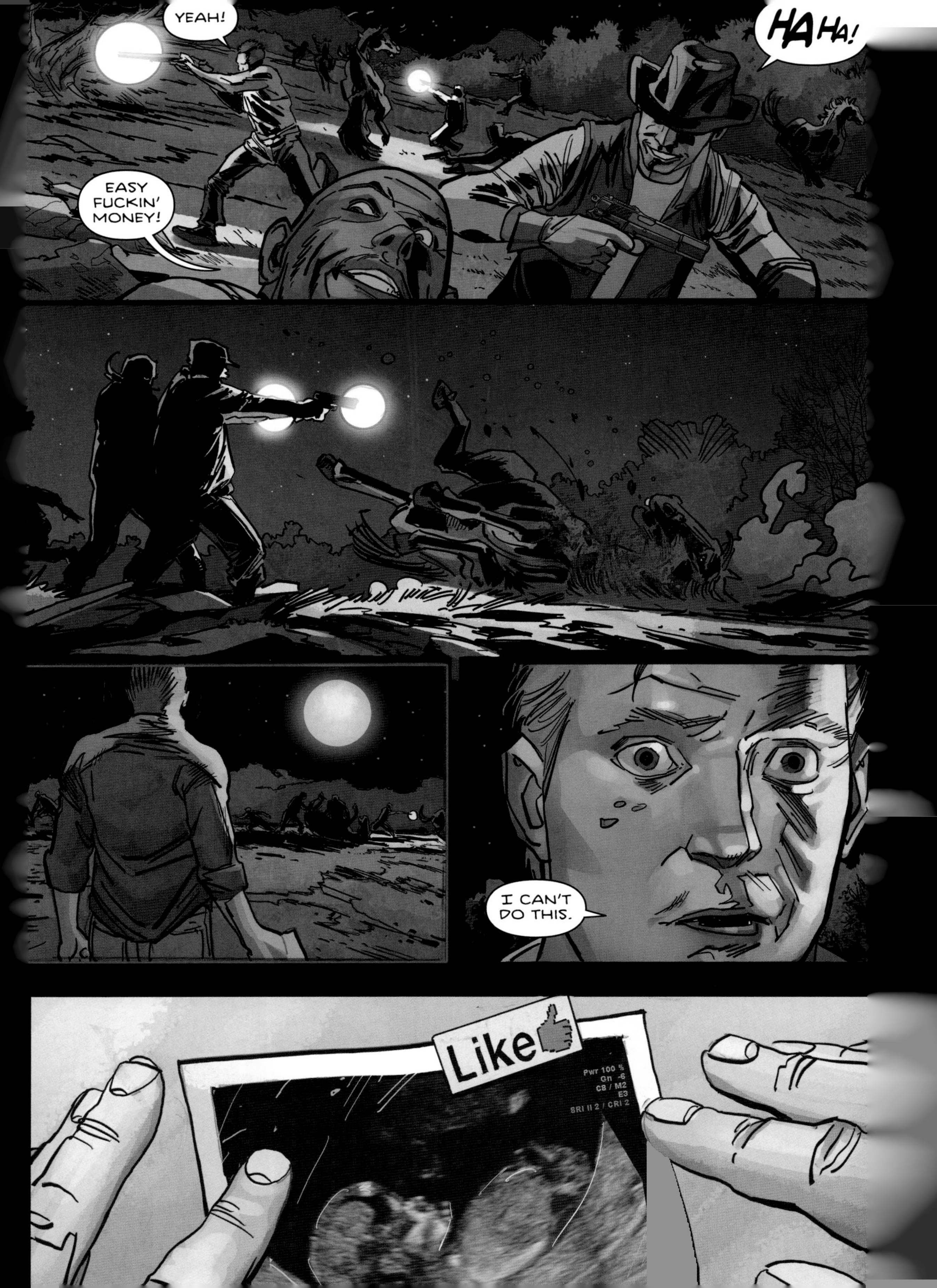
YEAH!
HA HA!
EASY FUCKIN' MONEY!
I CAN'T DO THIS.
Like
Pwr 100 %
Gn -6
C8 / M2
E3
SRI II 2 / CRI 2

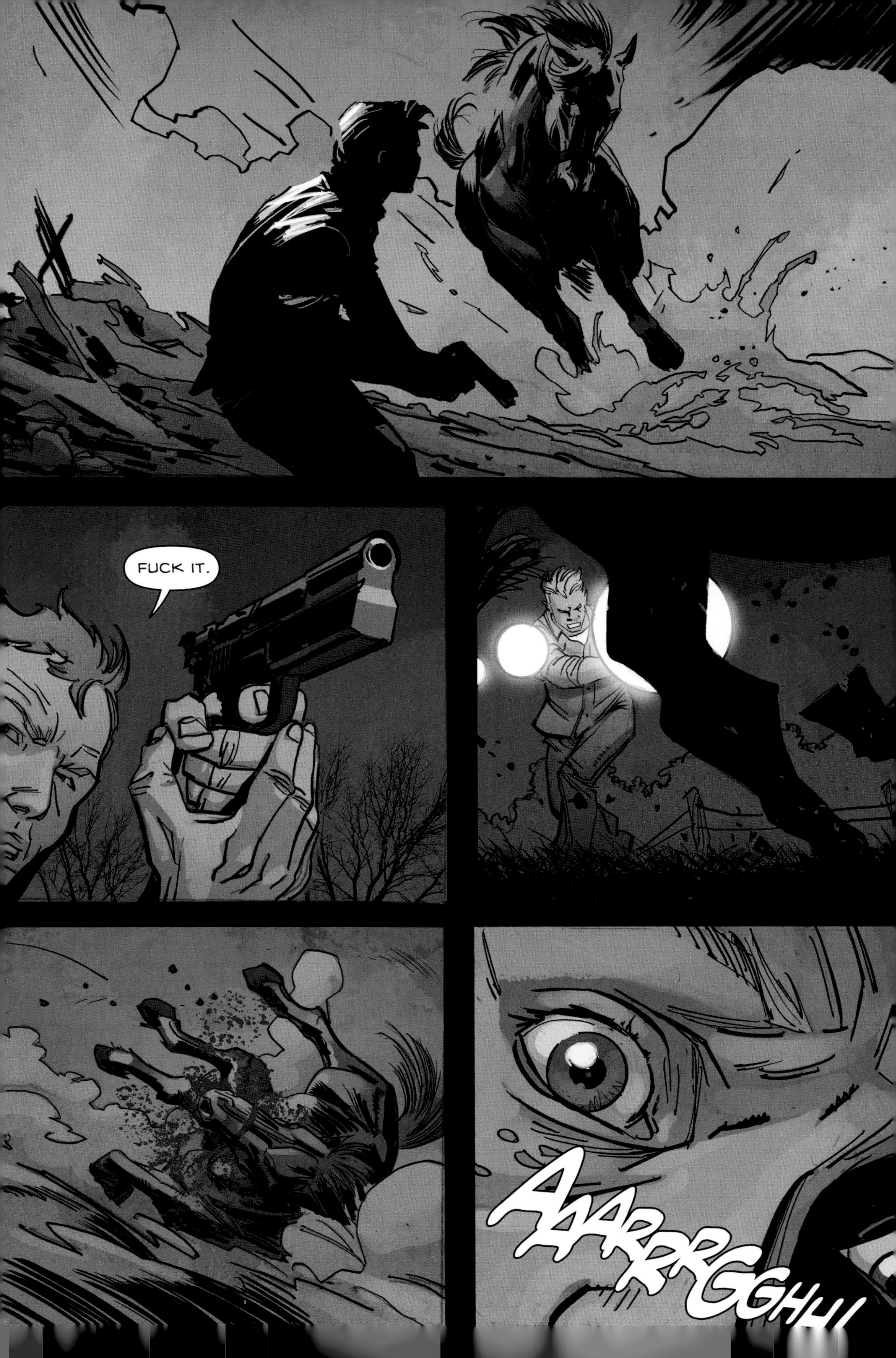
FUCK IT.
AAARRRGGHH!

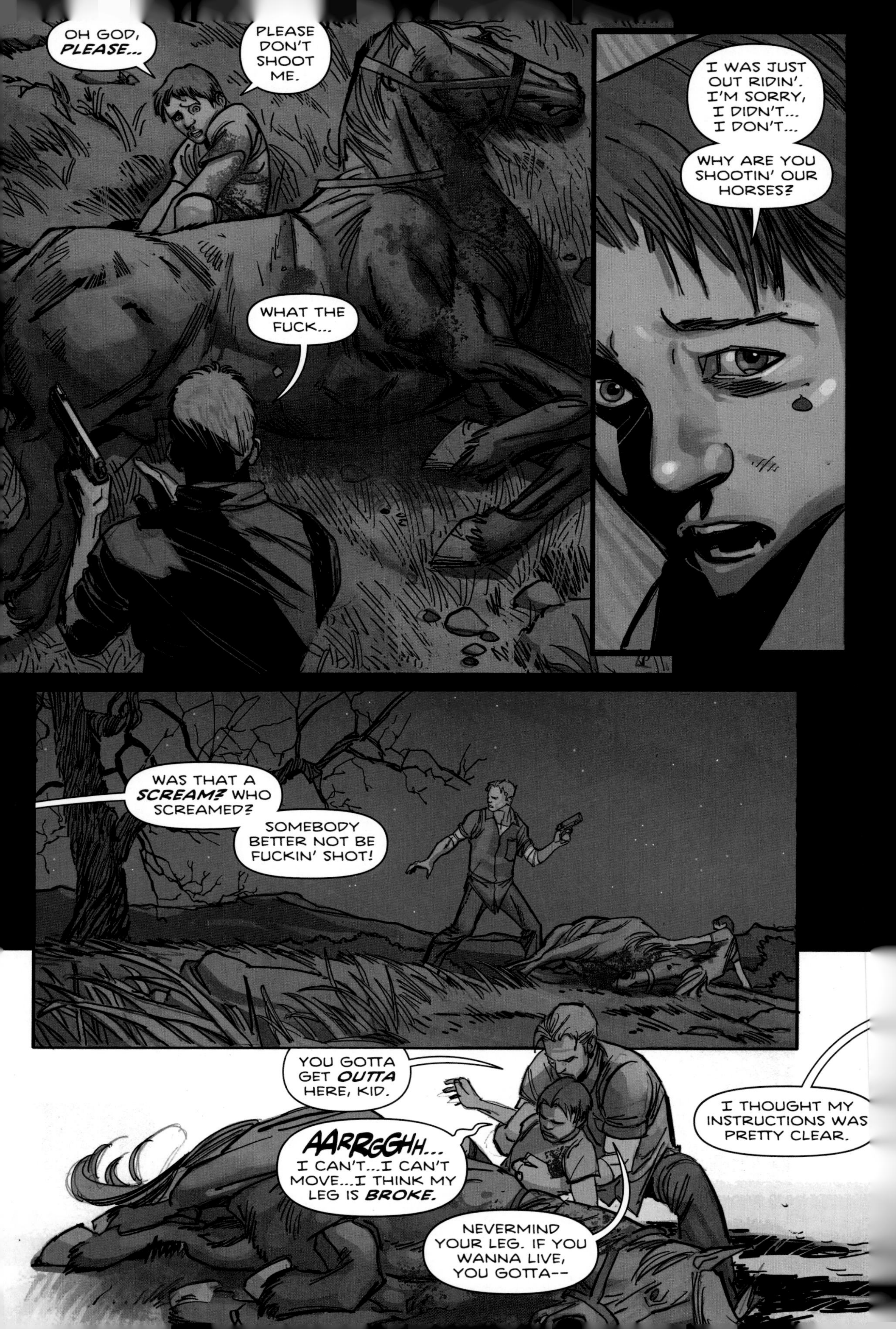
OH GOD, *PLEASE...*
PLEASE DON'T SHOOT ME.
WHAT THE FUCK...
I WAS JUST OUT RIDIN'. I'M SORRY, I DIDN'T... I DON'T...
WHY ARE YOU SHOOTIN' OUR HORSES?
WAS THAT A *SCREAM?* WHO SCREAMED?
SOMEBODY BETTER NOT BE FUCKIN' SHOT!
YOU GOTTA GET *OUTTA* HERE, KID.
AARRGGHH... I CAN'T...I CAN'T MOVE...I THINK MY LEG IS *BROKE.*
NEVERMIND YOUR LEG. IF YOU WANNA LIVE, YOU GOTTA--
I THOUGHT MY INSTRUCTIONS WAS PRETTY CLEAR.

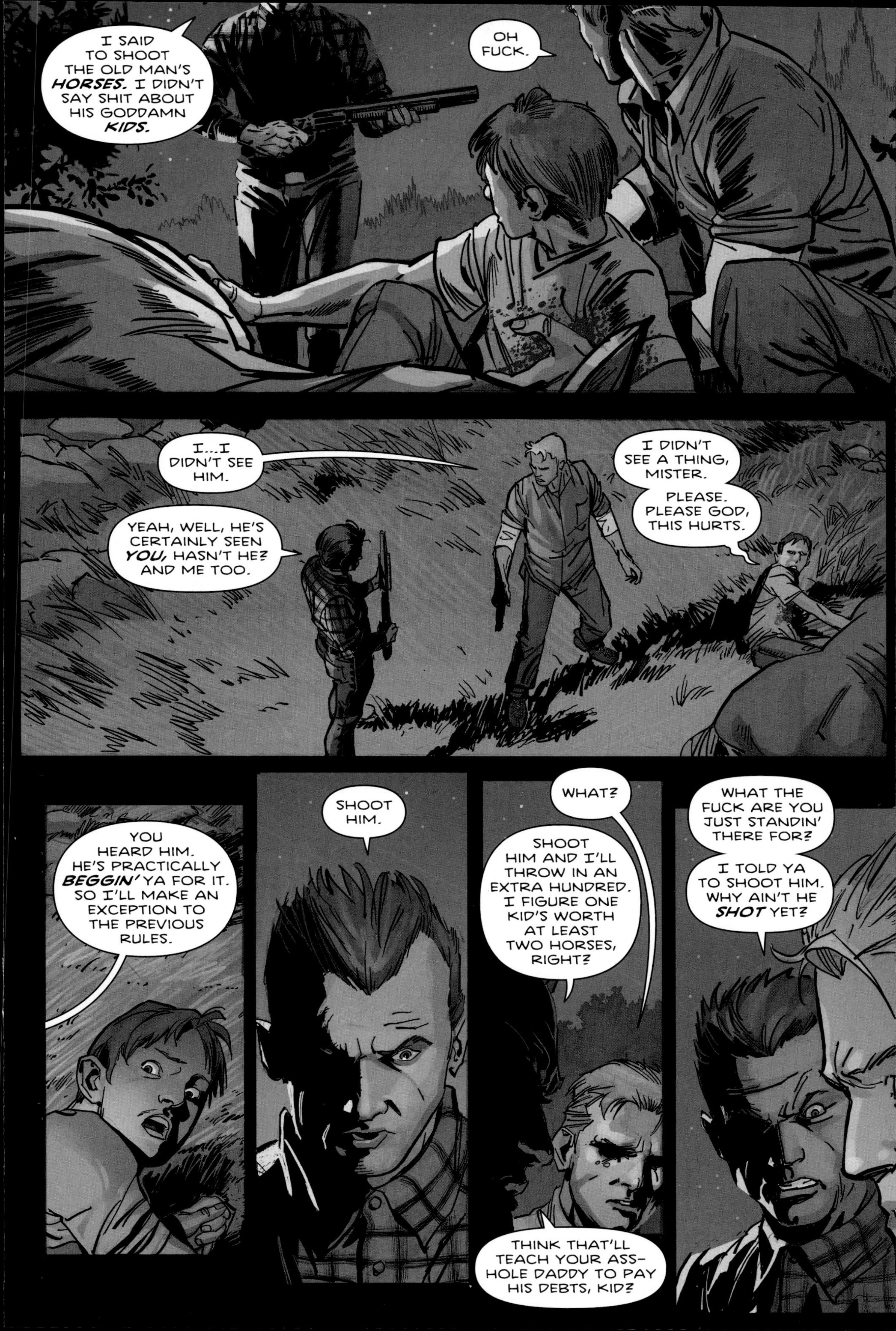
I SAID TO SHOOT THE OLD MAN'S HORSES. I DIDN'T SAY SHIT ABOUT HIS GODDAMN KIDS.
OH FUCK.
I...I DIDN'T SEE HIM.
YEAH, WELL, HE'S CERTAINLY SEEN YOU, HASN'T HE? AND ME TOO.
I DIDN'T SEE A THING, MISTER.
PLEASE. PLEASE GOD, THIS HURTS.
YOU HEARD HIM. HE'S PRACTICALLY BEGGIN' YA FOR IT. SO I'LL MAKE AN EXCEPTION TO THE PREVIOUS RULES.
SHOOT HIM.
WHAT?
SHOOT HIM AND I'LL THROW IN AN EXTRA HUNDRED. I FIGURE ONE KID'S WORTH AT LEAST TWO HORSES, RIGHT?
THINK THAT'LL TEACH YOUR ASS-HOLE DADDY TO PAY HIS DEBTS, KID?
WHAT THE FUCK ARE YOU JUST STANDIN' THERE FOR?
I TOLD YA TO SHOOT HIM. WHY AIN'T HE SHOT YET?

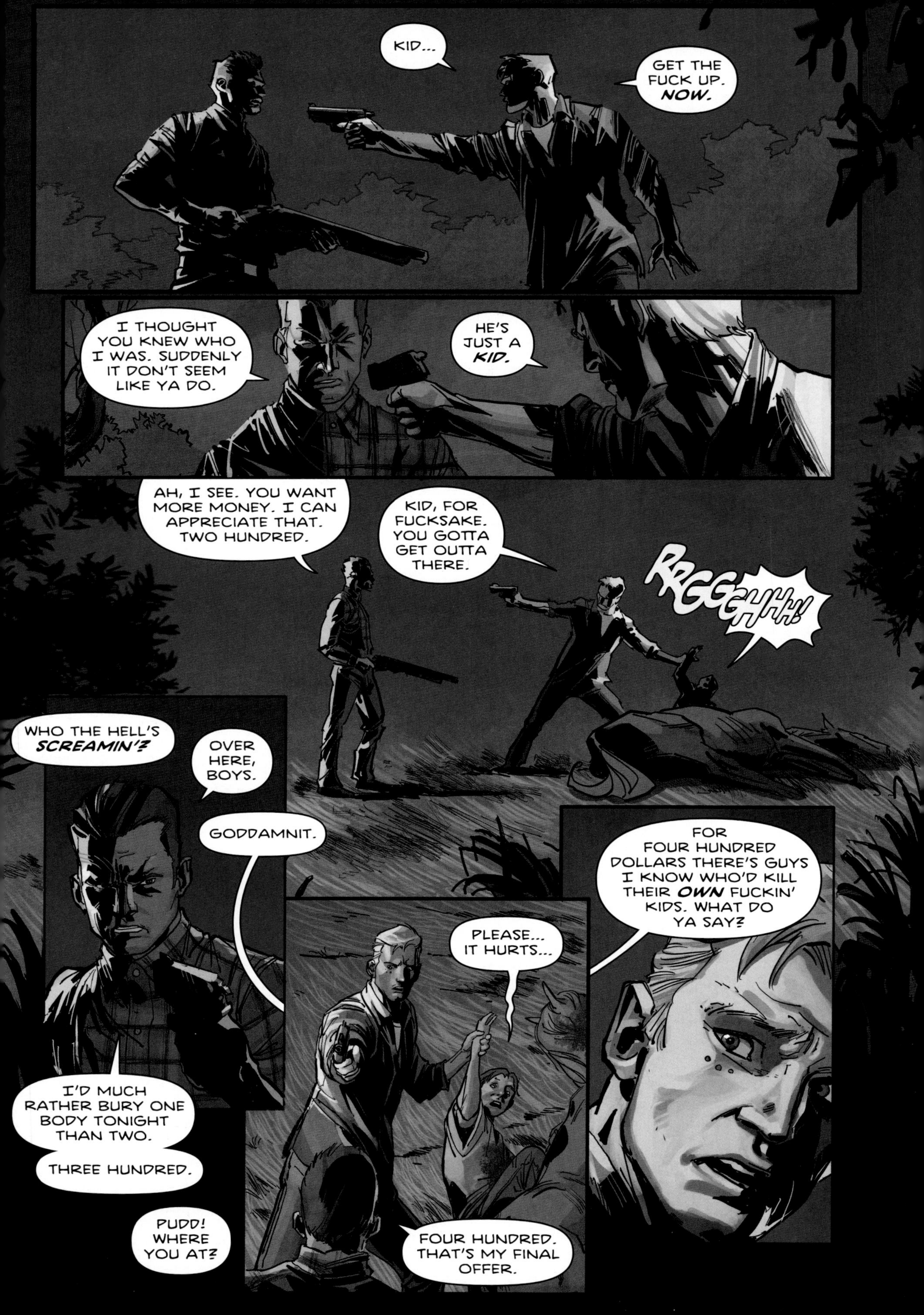
KID...
GET THE FUCK UP. NOW.
I THOUGHT YOU KNEW WHO I WAS. SUDDENLY IT DON'T SEEM LIKE YA DO.
HE'S JUST A KID.
AH, I SEE. YOU WANT MORE MONEY. I CAN APPRECIATE THAT. TWO HUNDRED.
KID, FOR FUCKSAKE. YOU GOTTA GET OUTTA THERE.
RRGGGHHH!
WHO THE HELL'S SCREAMIN'?
OVER HERE, BOYS.
GODDAMNIT.
I'D MUCH RATHER BURY ONE BODY TONIGHT THAN TWO.
THREE HUNDRED.
PUDD! WHERE YOU AT?
PLEASE... IT HURTS...
FOUR HUNDRED. THAT'S MY FINAL OFFER.
FOR FOUR HUNDRED DOLLARS THERE'S GUYS I KNOW WHO'D KILL THEIR OWN FUCKIN' KIDS. WHAT DO YA SAY?

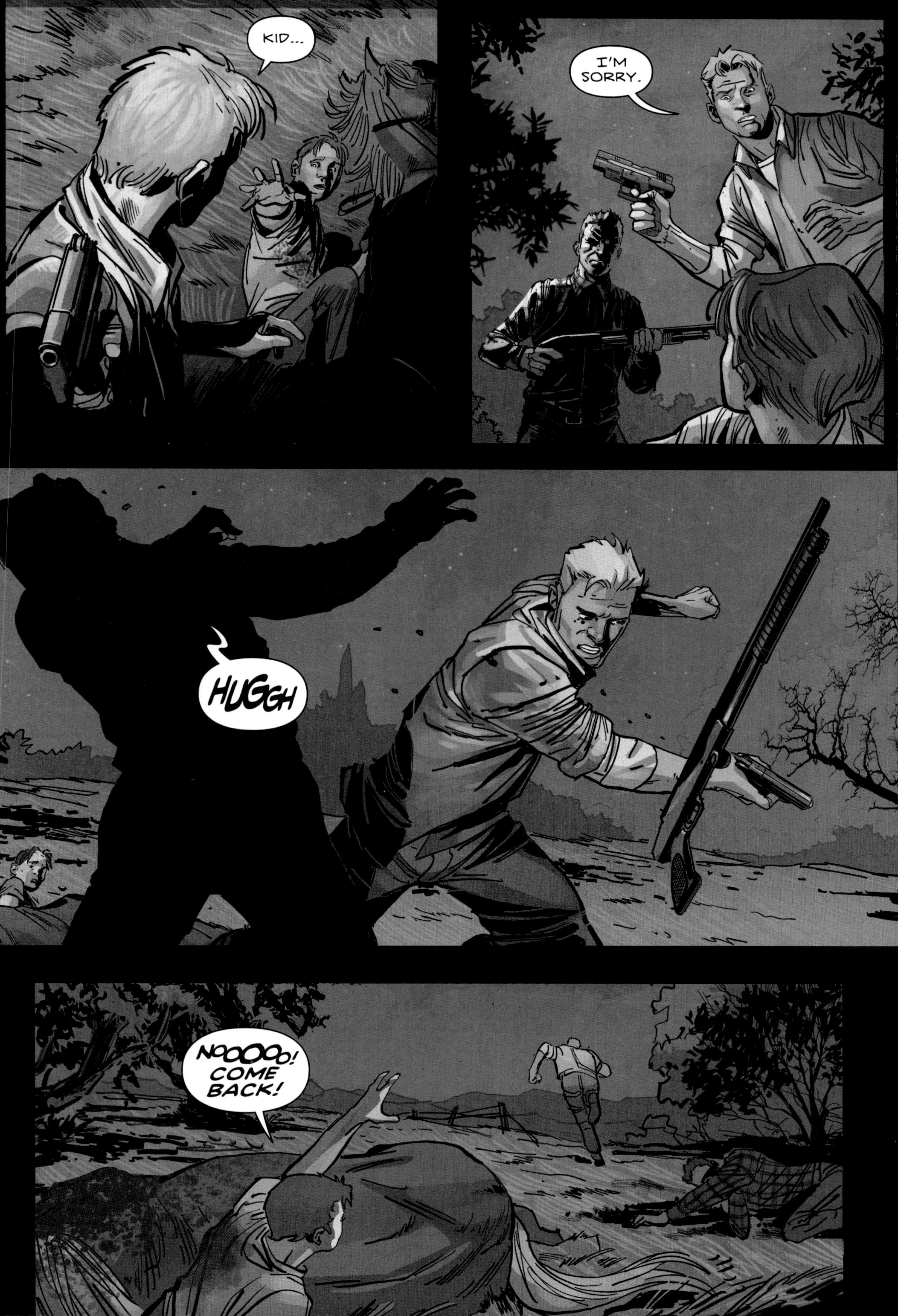
KID...
I'M SORRY.
HUGGH
NOOOOO! COME BACK!

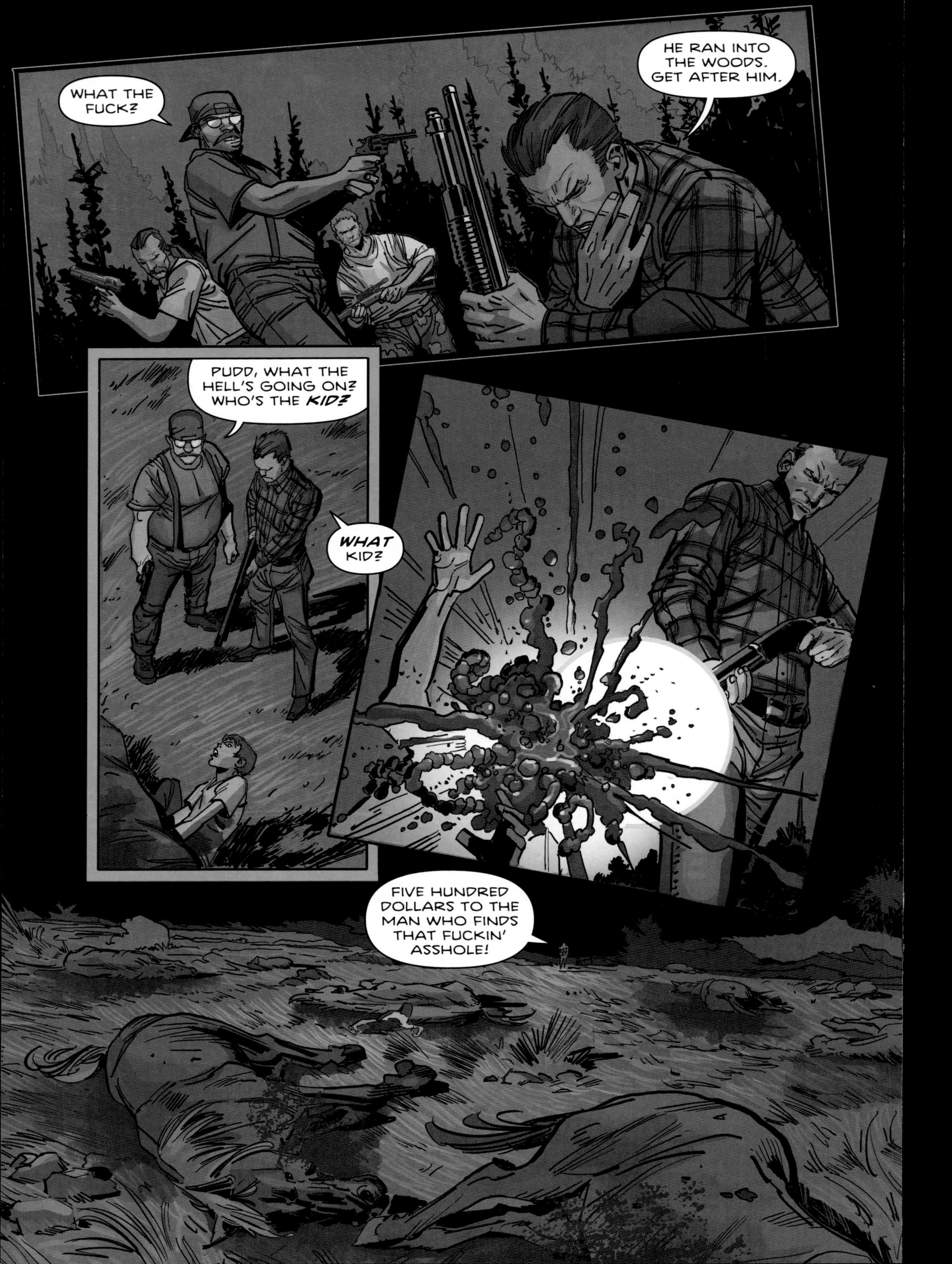
WHAT THE FUCK?
HE RAN INTO THE WOODS. GET AFTER HIM.
PUDD, WHAT THE HELL'S GOING ON? WHO'S THE KID?
WHAT KID?
FIVE HUNDRED DOLLARS TO THE MAN WHO FINDS THAT FUCKIN' ASSHOLE!

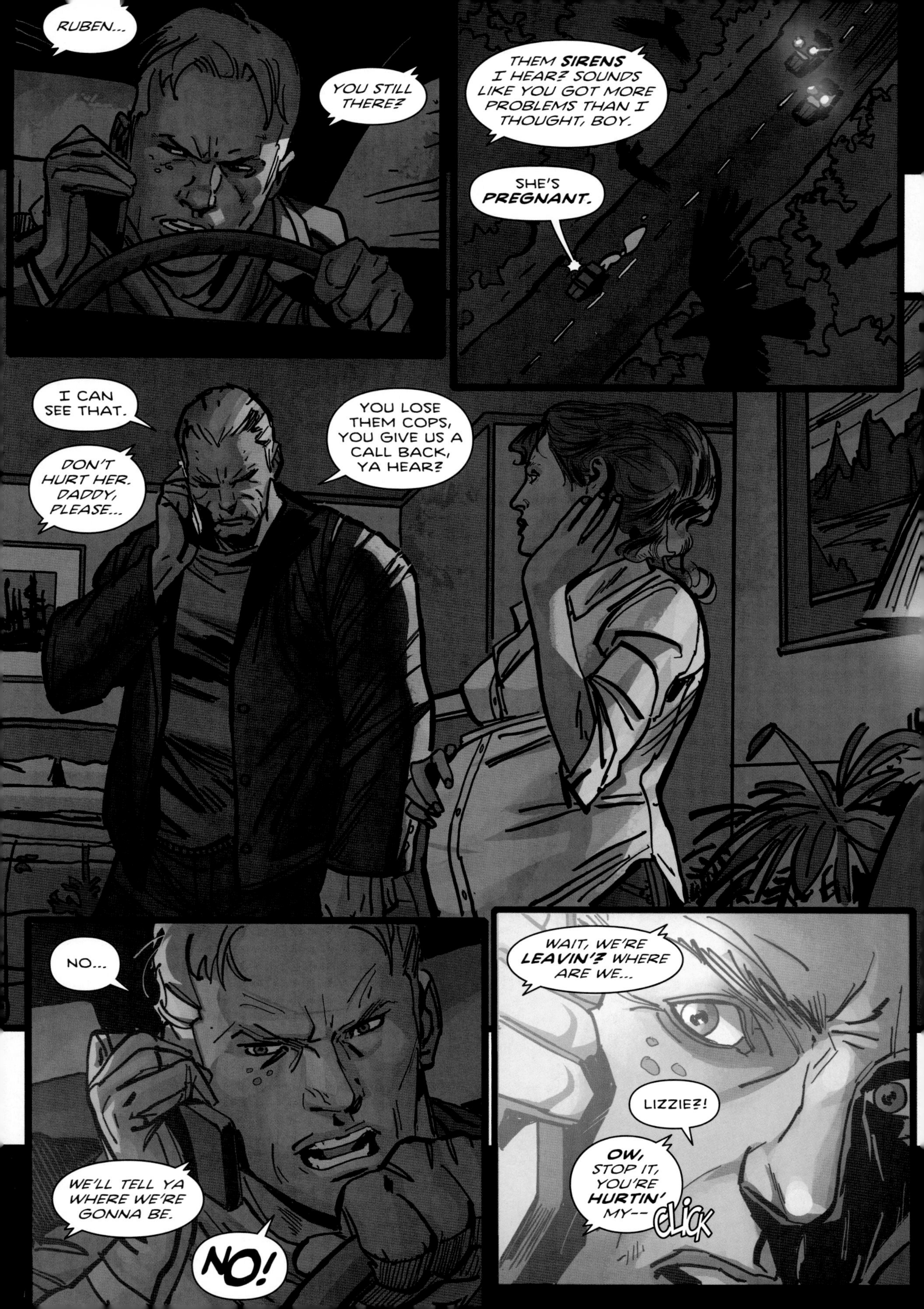
RUBEN...
YOU STILL THERE?
THEM **SIRENS** I HEAR? SOUNDS LIKE YOU GOT MORE PROBLEMS THAN I THOUGHT, BOY.
SHE'S ***PREGNANT.***
I CAN SEE THAT.
*DON'T HURT HER. DADDY, PLEASE...*
YOU LOSE THEM COPS, YOU GIVE US A CALL BACK, YA HEAR?
NO...
WE'LL TELL YA WHERE WE'RE GONNA BE.
NO!
WAIT, WE'RE ***LEAVIN'?*** WHERE ARE WE...
LIZZIE?!
**OW,** STOP IT, YOU'RE **HURTIN'** MY--
CLICK

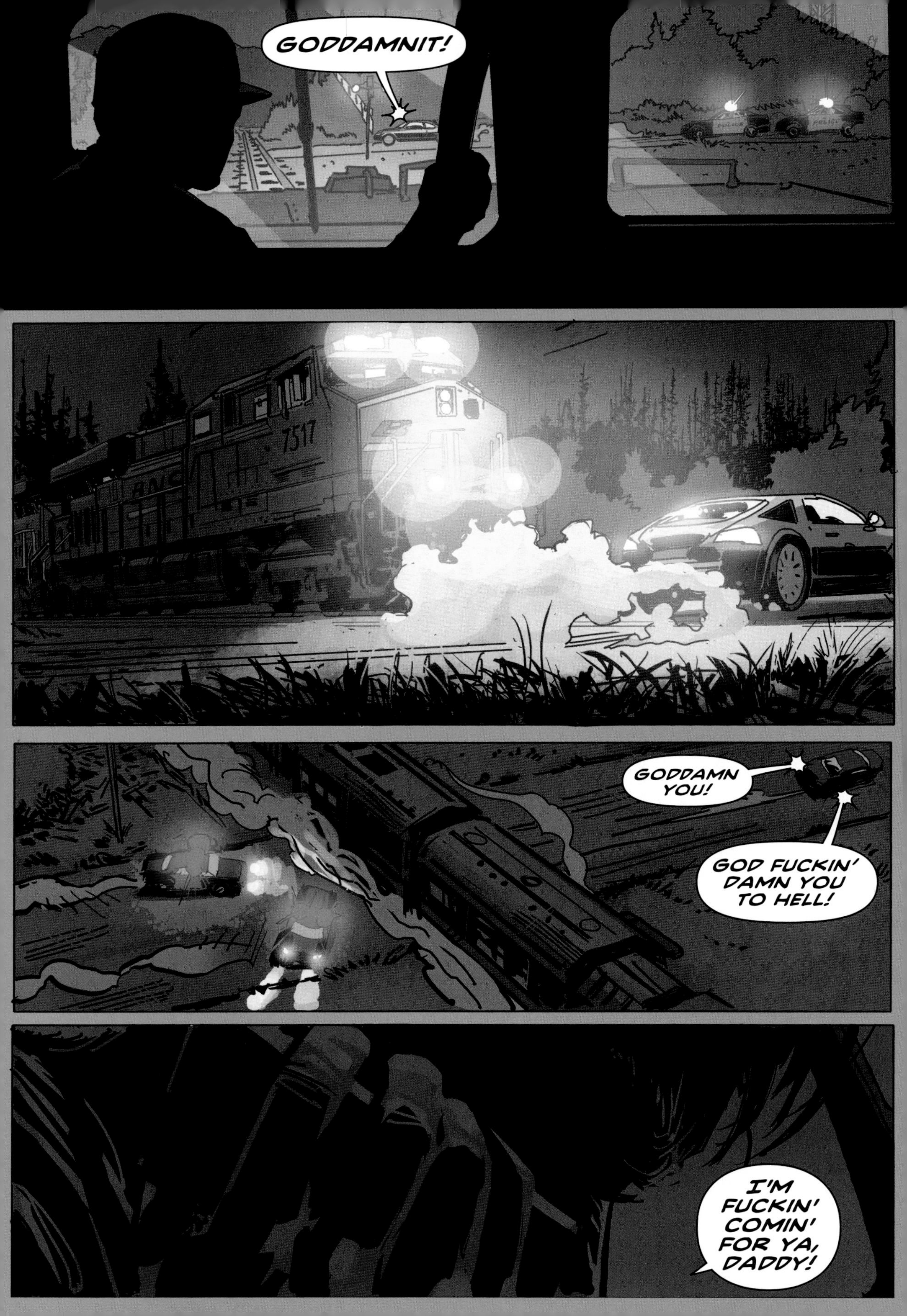
GODDAMNIT!
GODDAMN YOU!
GOD FUCKIN' DAMN YOU TO HELL!
I'M FUCKIN' COMIN' FOR YA, DADDY!

# CHAPTER THREE

## DECORATION DAY

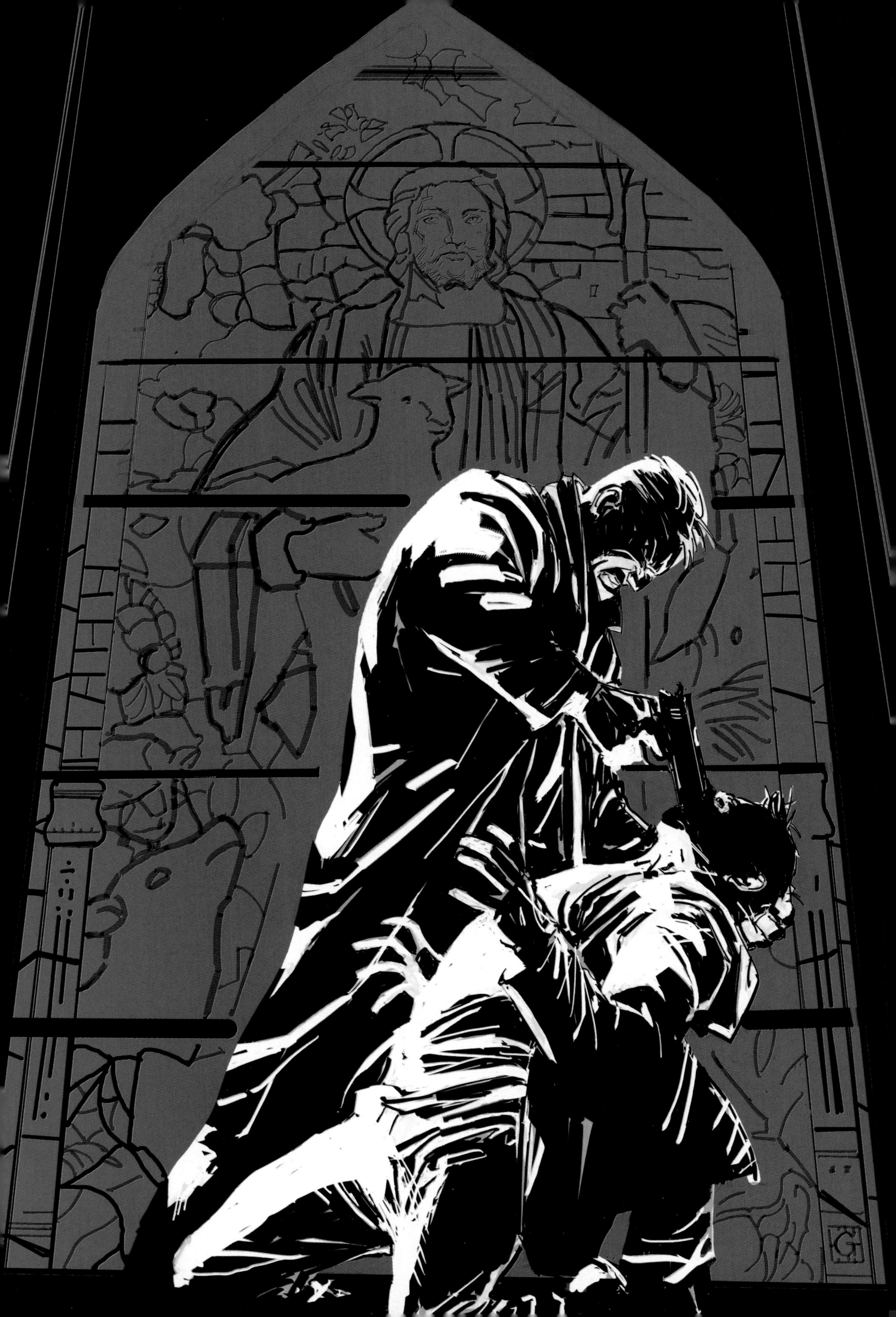

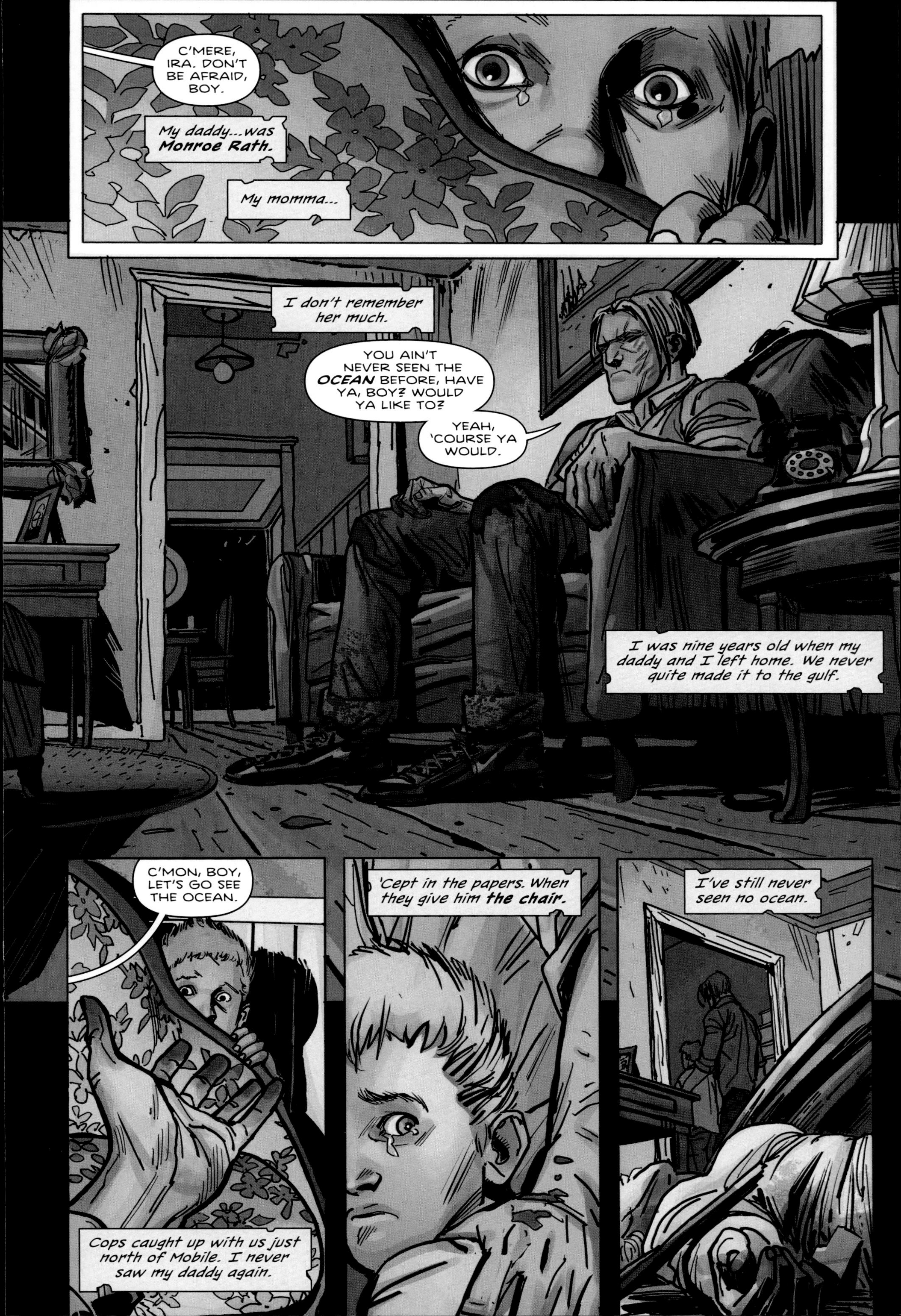
C'MERE, IRA. DON'T BE AFRAID, BOY.
My daddy...was Monroe Rath.
My momma...
I don't remember her much.
YOU AIN'T NEVER SEEN THE OCEAN BEFORE, HAVE YA, BOY? WOULD YA LIKE TO?
YEAH, 'COURSE YA WOULD.
I was nine years old when my daddy and I left home. We never quite made it to the gulf.
C'MON, BOY, LET'S GO SEE THE OCEAN.
Cops caught up with us just north of Mobile. I never saw my daddy again.
'Cept in the papers. When they give him the chair.
I've still never seen no ocean.

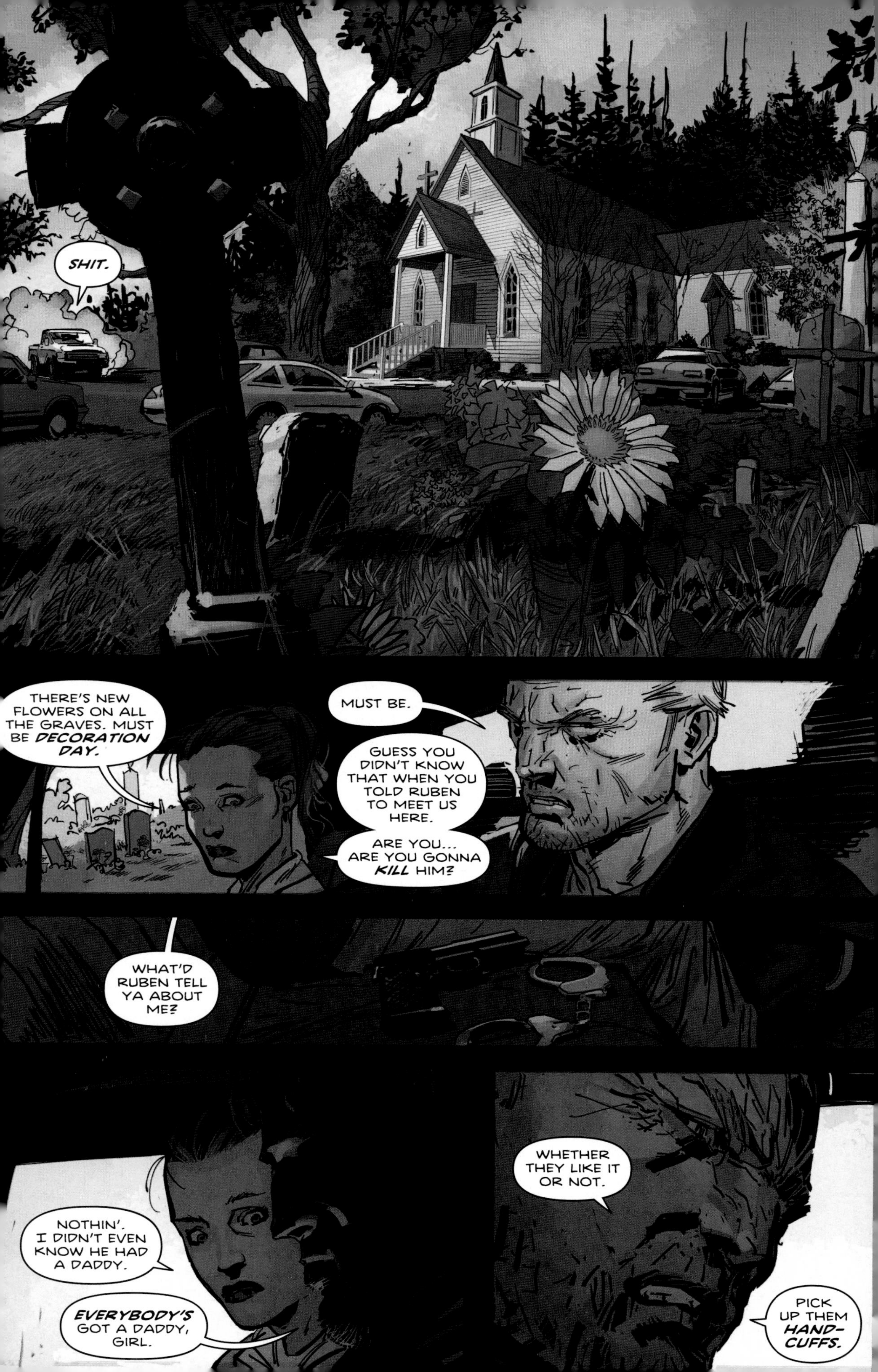
SHIT.
THERE'S NEW FLOWERS ON ALL THE GRAVES. MUST BE DECORATION DAY.
MUST BE.
GUESS YOU DIDN'T KNOW THAT WHEN YOU TOLD RUBEN TO MEET US HERE.
ARE YOU... ARE YOU GONNA KILL HIM?
WHAT'D RUBEN TELL YA ABOUT ME?
NOTHIN'. I DIDN'T EVEN KNOW HE HAD A DADDY.
EVERYBODY'S GOT A DADDY, GIRL.
WHETHER THEY LIKE IT OR NOT.
PICK UP THEM HAND-CUFFS.

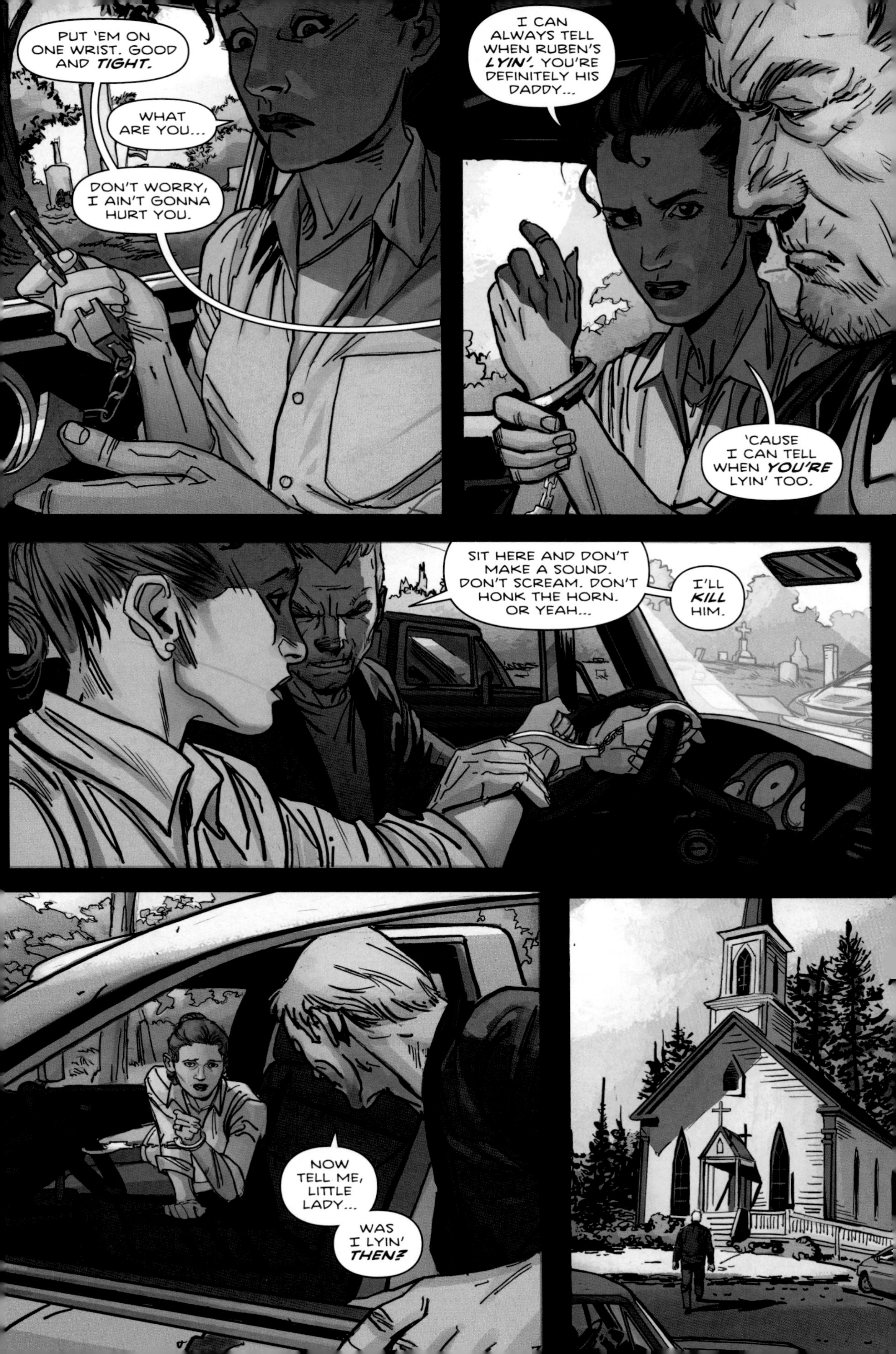
PUT 'EM ON ONE WRIST. GOOD AND TIGHT.
WHAT ARE YOU...
DON'T WORRY, I AIN'T GONNA HURT YOU.
I CAN ALWAYS TELL WHEN RUBEN'S LYIN'. YOU'RE DEFINITELY HIS DADDY...
'CAUSE I CAN TELL WHEN YOU'RE LYIN' TOO.
SIT HERE AND DON'T MAKE A SOUND. DON'T SCREAM. DON'T HONK THE HORN. OR YEAH...
I'LL KILL HIM.
NOW TELL ME, LITTLE LADY...
WAS I LYIN' THEN?

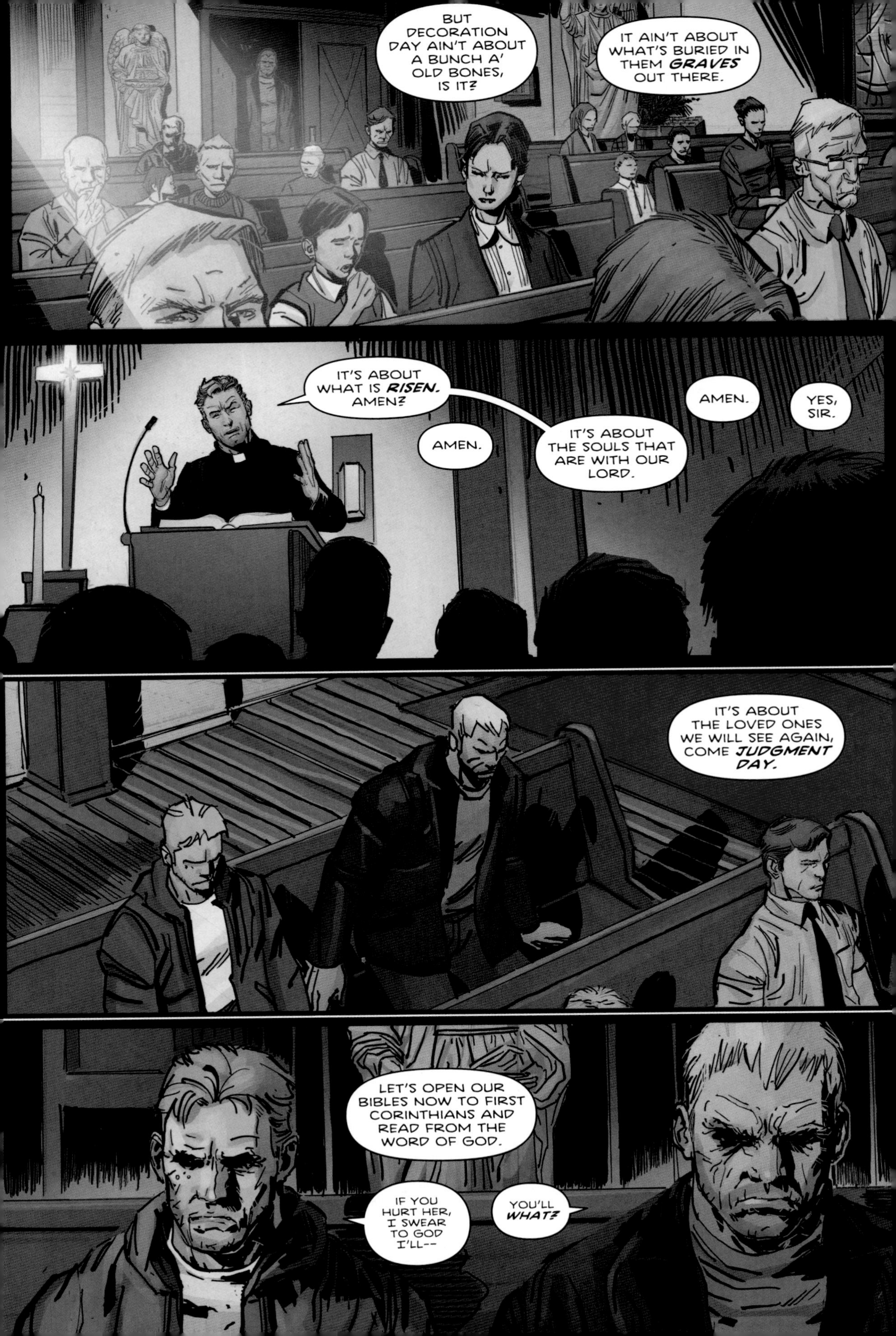
BUT DECORATION DAY AIN'T ABOUT A BUNCH A' OLD BONES, IS IT?
IT AIN'T ABOUT WHAT'S BURIED IN THEM GRAVES OUT THERE.
IT'S ABOUT WHAT IS RISEN. AMEN?
AMEN.
IT'S ABOUT THE SOULS THAT ARE WITH OUR LORD.
AMEN.
YES, SIR.
IT'S ABOUT THE LOVED ONES WE WILL SEE AGAIN, COME JUDGMENT DAY.
LET'S OPEN OUR BIBLES NOW TO FIRST CORINTHIANS AND READ FROM THE WORD OF GOD.
IF YOU HURT HER, I SWEAR TO GOD I'LL--
YOU'LL WHAT?

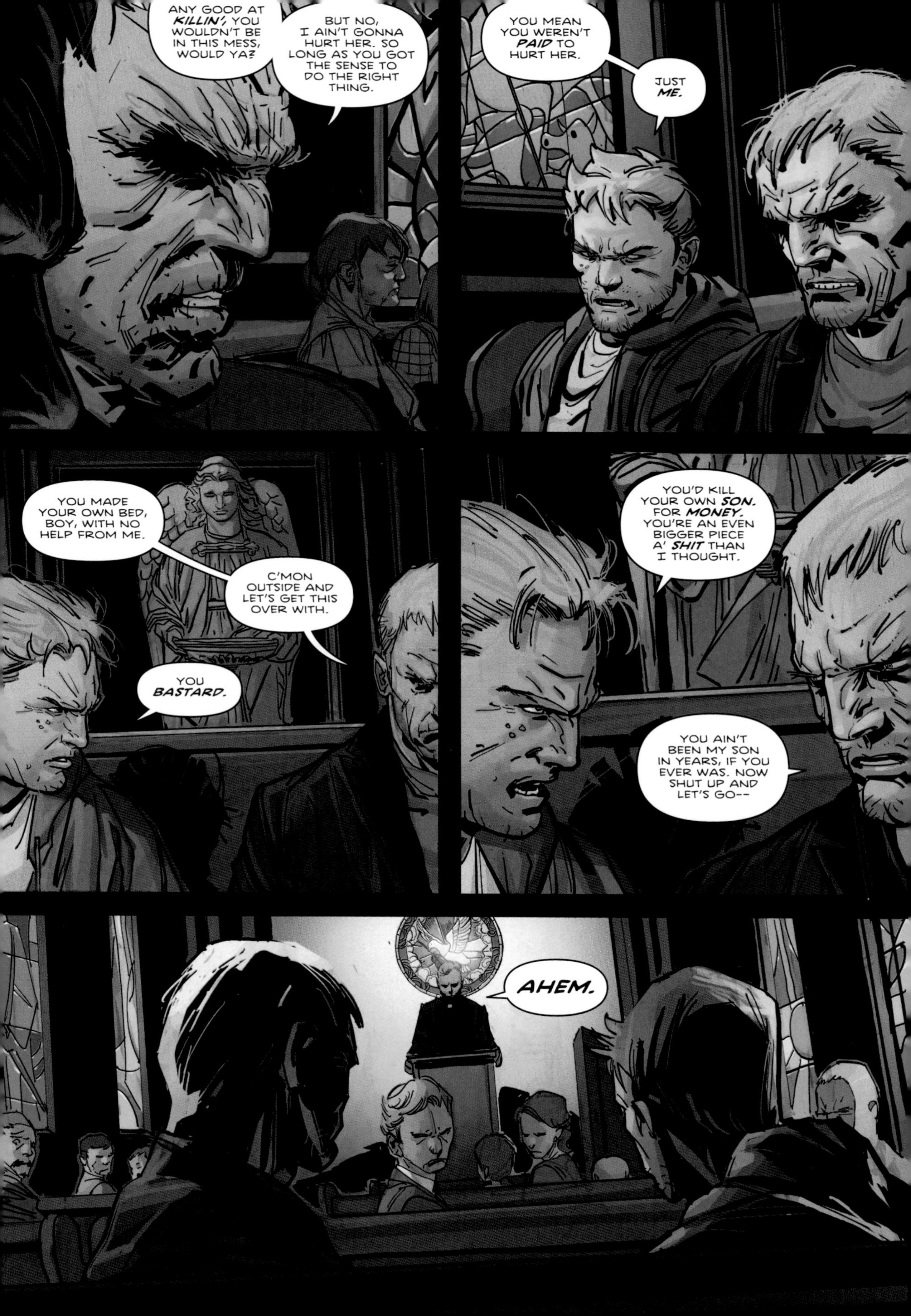
ANY GOOD AT KILLIN', YOU WOULDN'T BE IN THIS MESS, WOULD YA?
BUT NO, I AIN'T GONNA HURT HER. SO LONG AS YOU GOT THE SENSE TO DO THE RIGHT THING.
YOU MEAN YOU WEREN'T PAID TO HURT HER.
JUST ME.
YOU MADE YOUR OWN BED, BOY, WITH NO HELP FROM ME.
C'MON OUTSIDE AND LET'S GET THIS OVER WITH.
YOU BASTARD.
YOU'D KILL YOUR OWN SON. FOR MONEY. YOU'RE AN EVEN BIGGER PIECE A' SHIT THAN I THOUGHT.
YOU AIN'T BEEN MY SON IN YEARS, IF YOU EVER WAS. NOW SHUT UP AND LET'S GO--
AHEM.

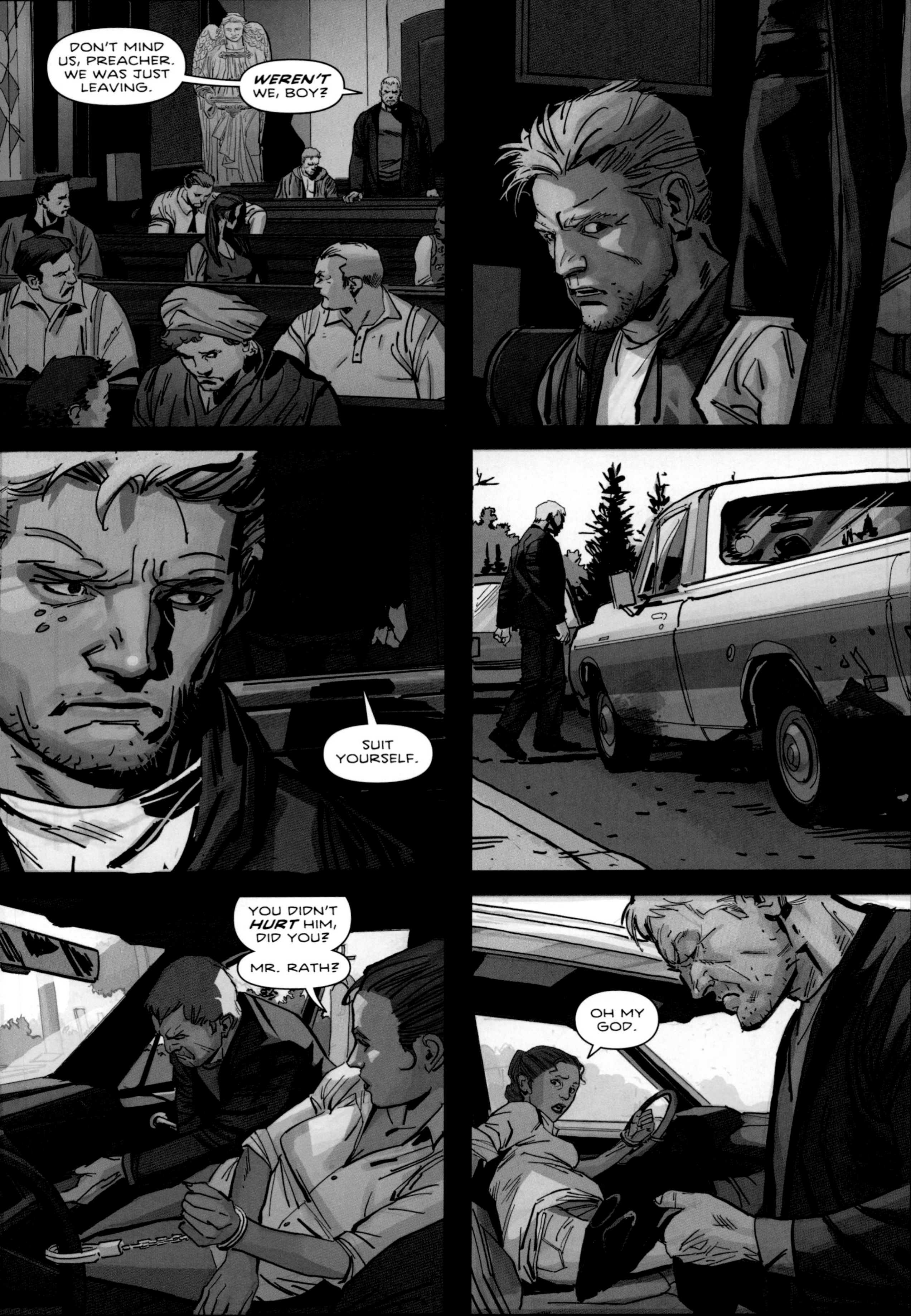
DON'T MIND US, PREACHER. WE WAS JUST LEAVING.
WEREN'T WE, BOY?
SUIT YOURSELF.
YOU DIDN'T HURT HIM, DID YOU?
MR. RATH?
OH MY GOD.

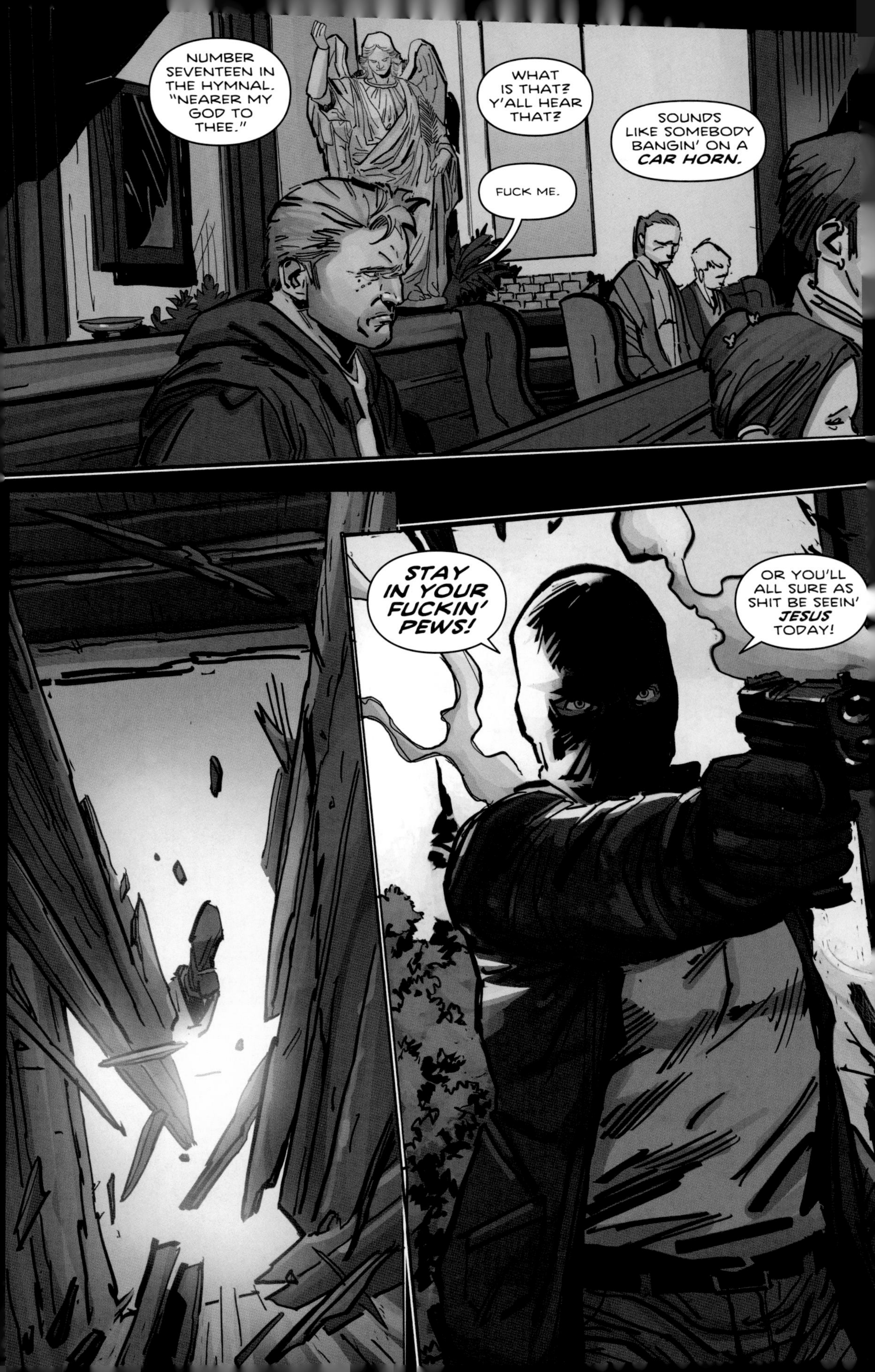
NUMBER SEVENTEEN IN THE HYMNAL. "NEARER MY GOD TO THEE."
WHAT IS THAT? Y'ALL HEAR THAT?
SOUNDS LIKE SOMEBODY BANGIN' ON A CAR HORN.
FUCK ME.
STAY IN YOUR FUCKIN' PEWS!
OR YOU'LL ALL SURE AS SHIT BE SEEIN' JESUS TODAY!

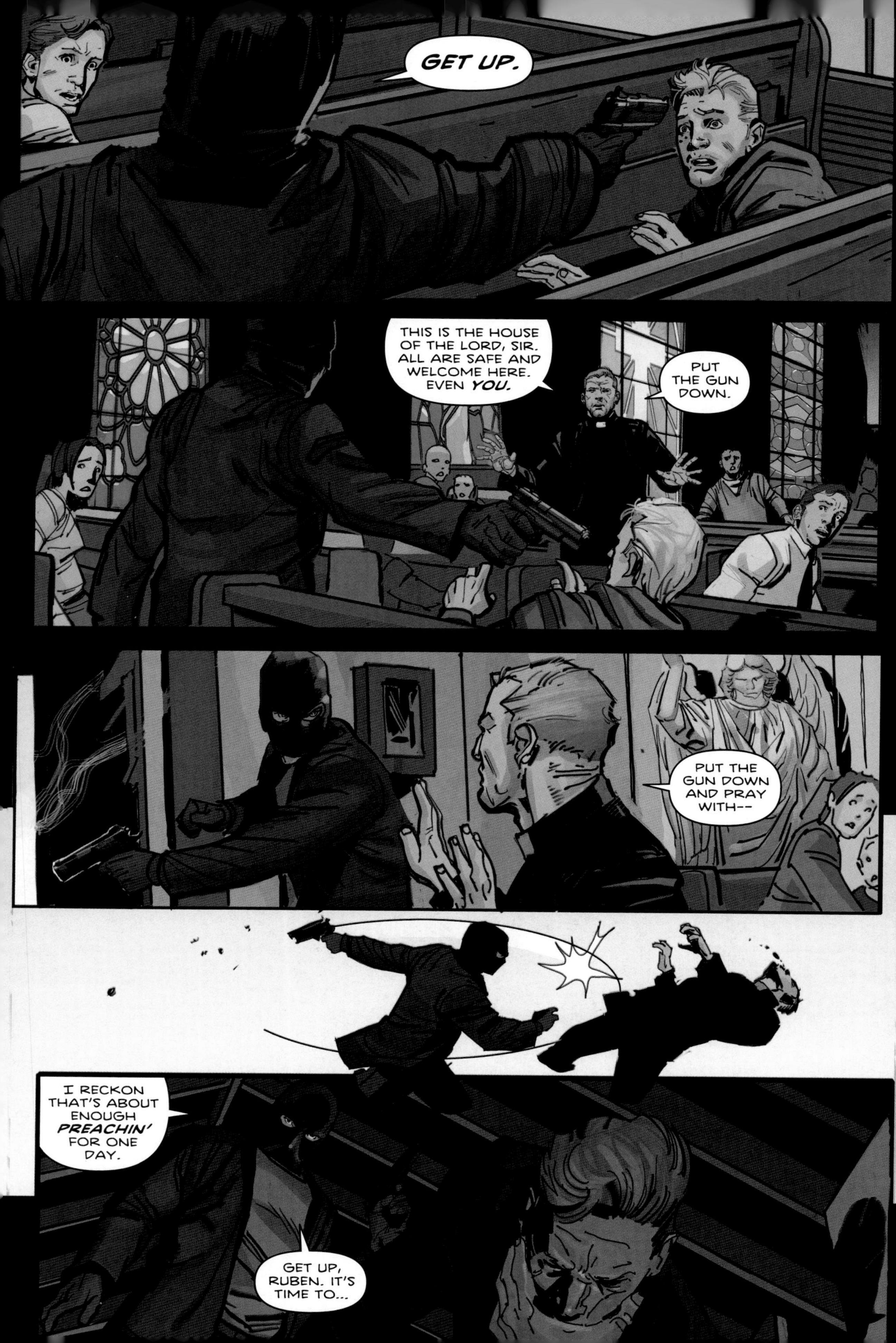

GET UP.
THIS IS THE HOUSE OF THE LORD, SIR. ALL ARE SAFE AND WELCOME HERE. EVEN YOU.
PUT THE GUN DOWN.
PUT THE GUN DOWN AND PRAY WITH--
I RECKON THAT'S ABOUT ENOUGH PREACHIN' FOR ONE DAY.
GET UP, RUBEN. IT'S TIME TO...

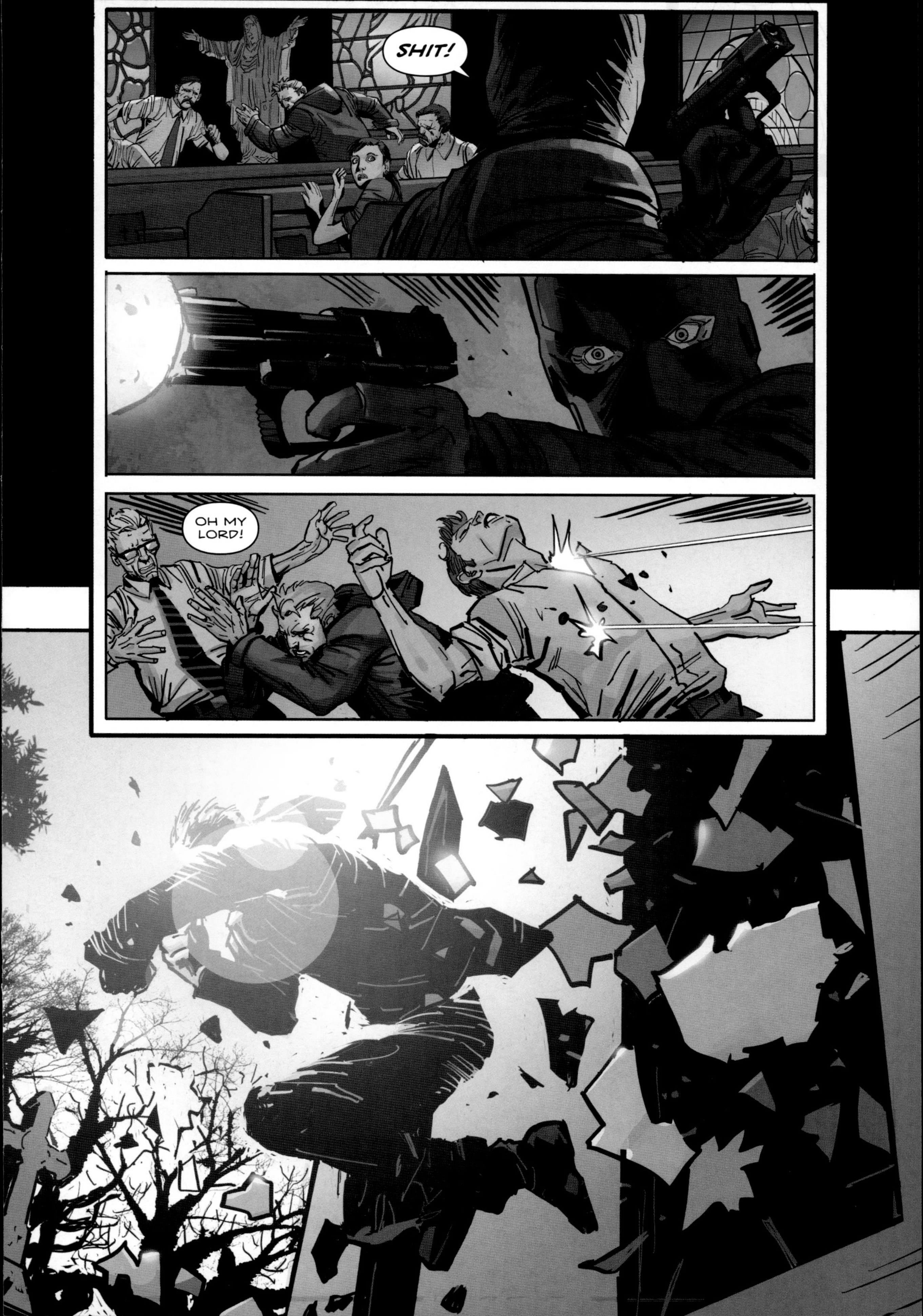
SHIT!
OH MY LORD!

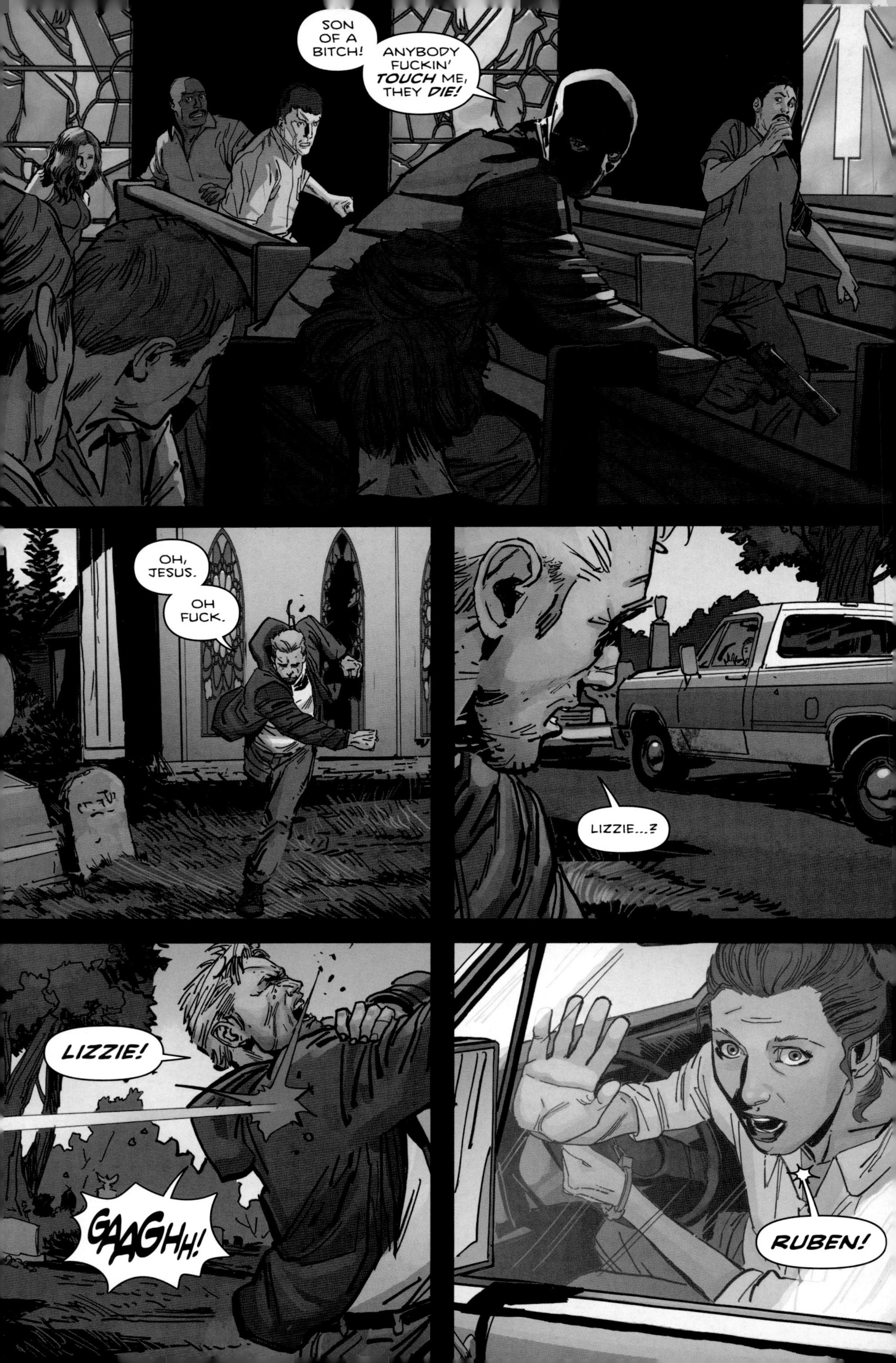
SON OF A BITCH!
ANYBODY FUCKIN' TOUCH ME, THEY DIE!
OH, JESUS.
OH FUCK.
LIZZIE...?
LIZZIE!
GAAGHH!
RUBEN!

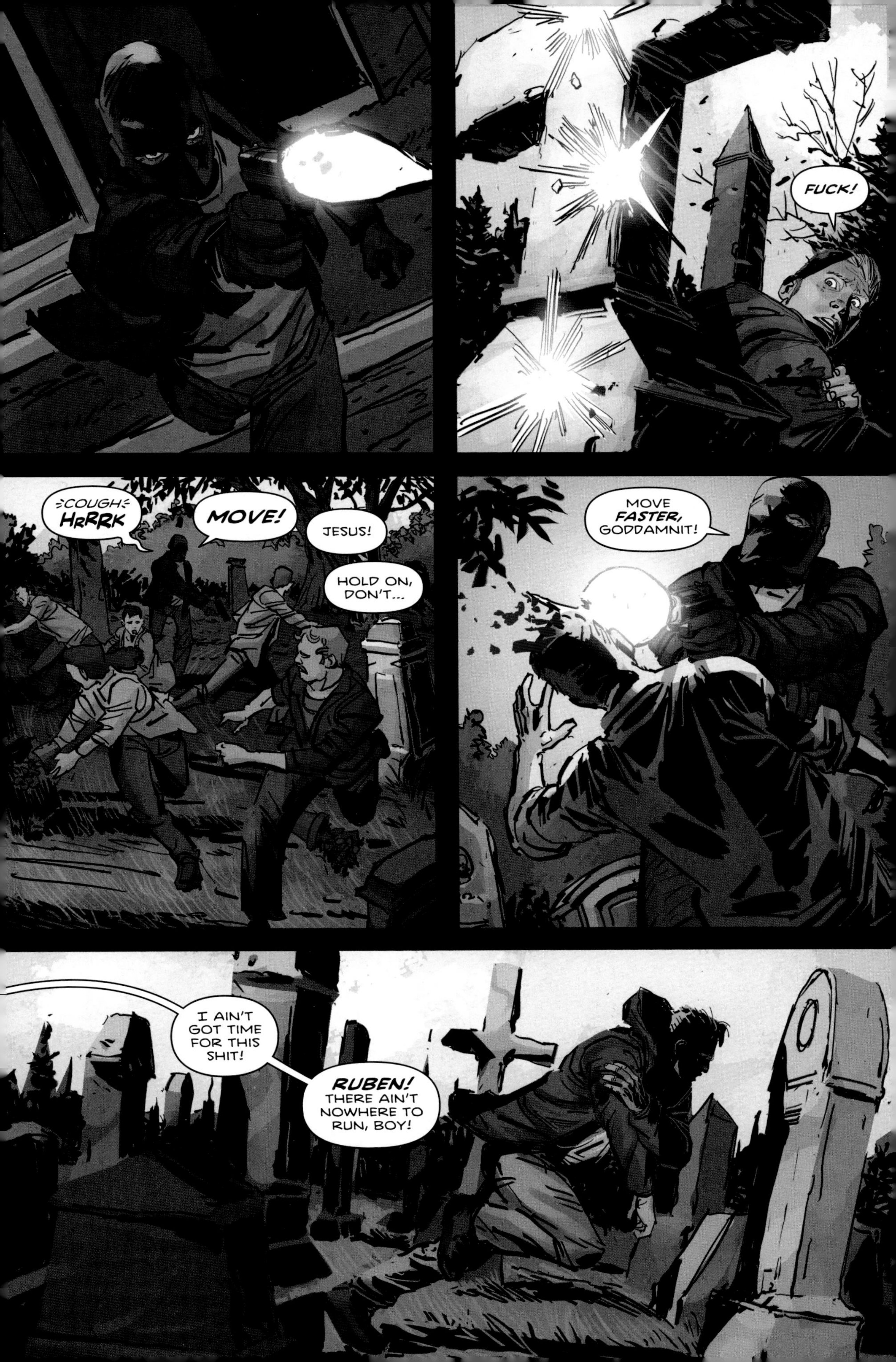
FUCK!
COUGH
HRRRK
MOVE!
JESUS!
HOLD ON, DON'T...
MOVE FASTER, GODDAMNIT!
I AIN'T GOT TIME FOR THIS SHIT!
RUBEN! THERE AIN'T NOWHERE TO RUN, BOY!

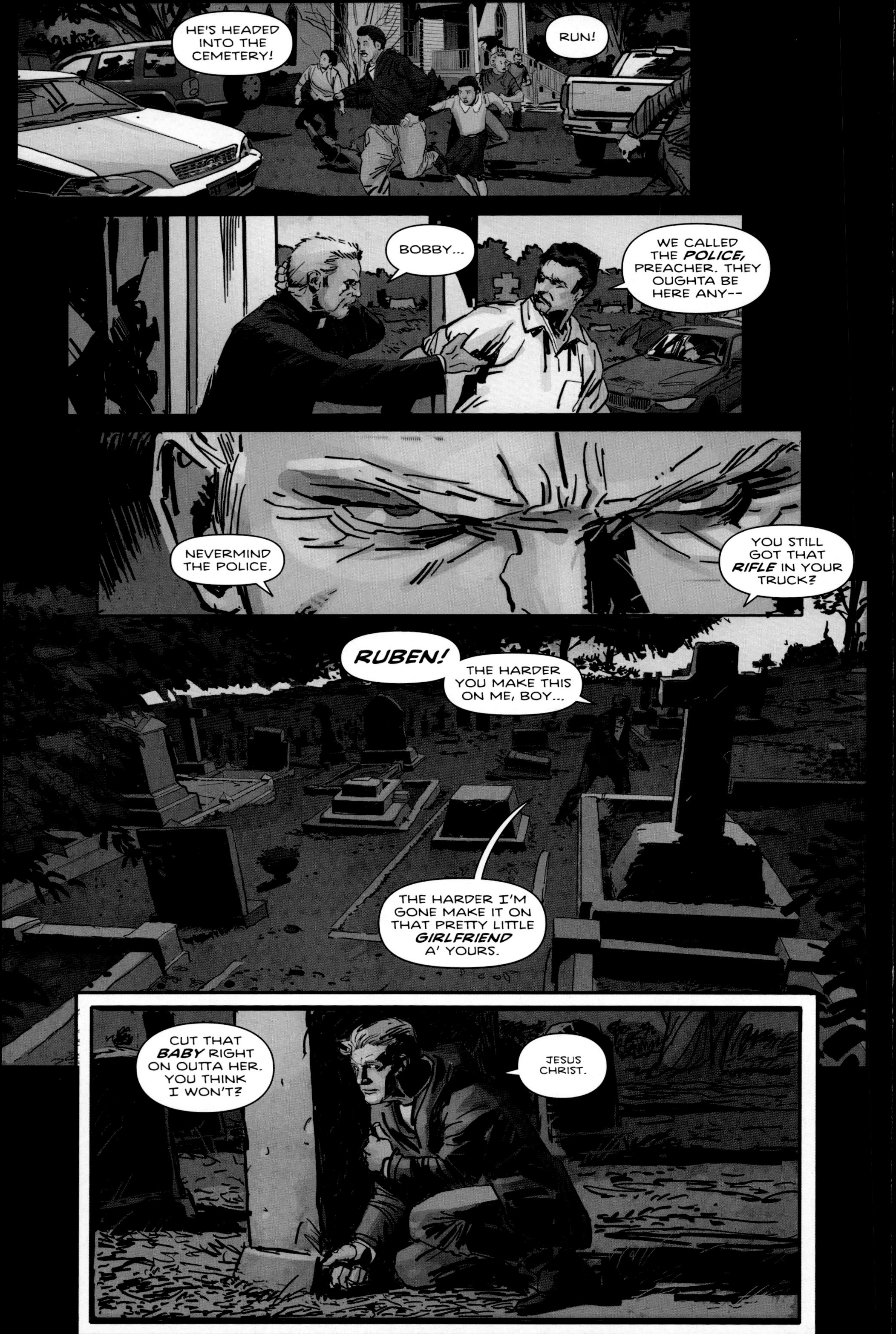
HE'S HEADED INTO THE CEMETERY!
RUN!
BOBBY...
WE CALLED THE POLICE, PREACHER. THEY OUGHTA BE HERE ANY--
NEVERMIND THE POLICE.
YOU STILL GOT THAT RIFLE IN YOUR TRUCK?
RUBEN!
THE HARDER YOU MAKE THIS ON ME, BOY...
THE HARDER I'M GONE MAKE IT ON THAT PRETTY LITTLE GIRLFRIEND A' YOURS.
CUT THAT BABY RIGHT ON OUTTA HER. YOU THINK I WON'T?
JESUS CHRIST.

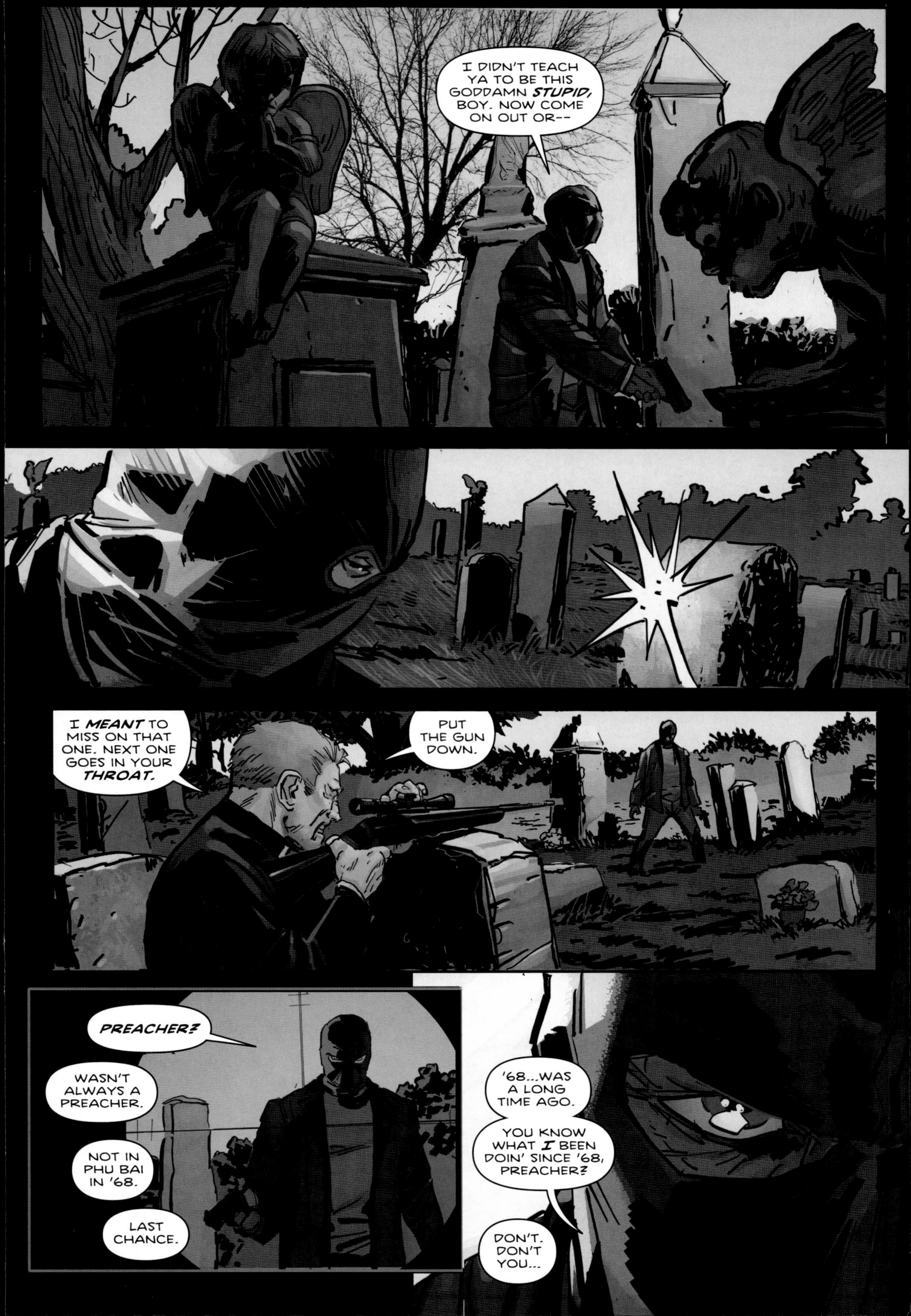
I DIDN'T TEACH YA TO BE THIS GODDAMN STUPID, BOY. NOW COME ON OUT OR--
I MEANT TO MISS ON THAT ONE. NEXT ONE GOES IN YOUR THROAT.
PUT THE GUN DOWN.
PREACHER?
WASN'T ALWAYS A PREACHER.
NOT IN PHU BAI IN '68.
LAST CHANCE.
'68...WAS A LONG TIME AGO.
YOU KNOW WHAT I BEEN DOIN' SINCE '68, PREACHER?
DON'T. DON'T YOU...

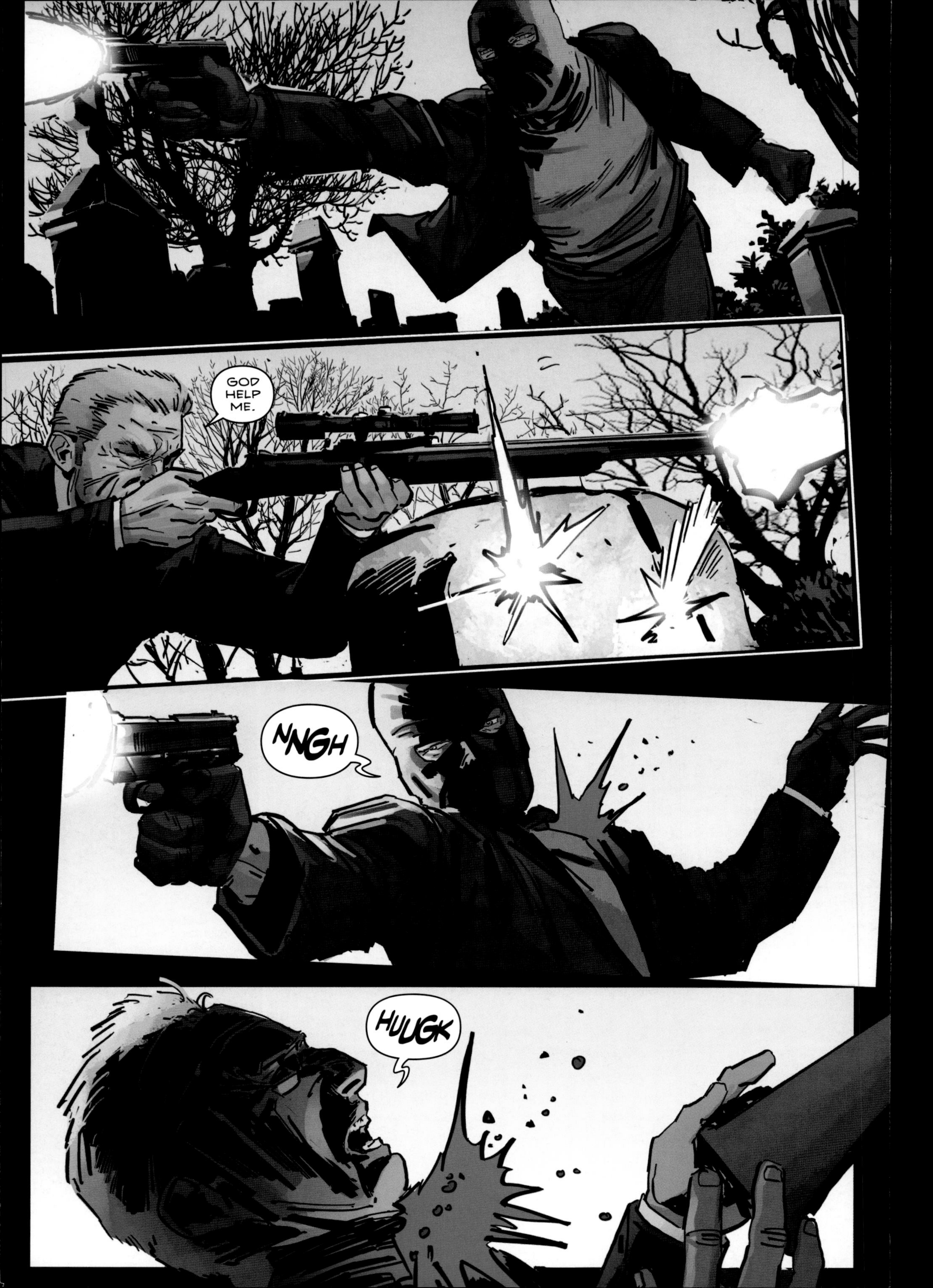
GOD HELP ME.
NNGH
HUUGK

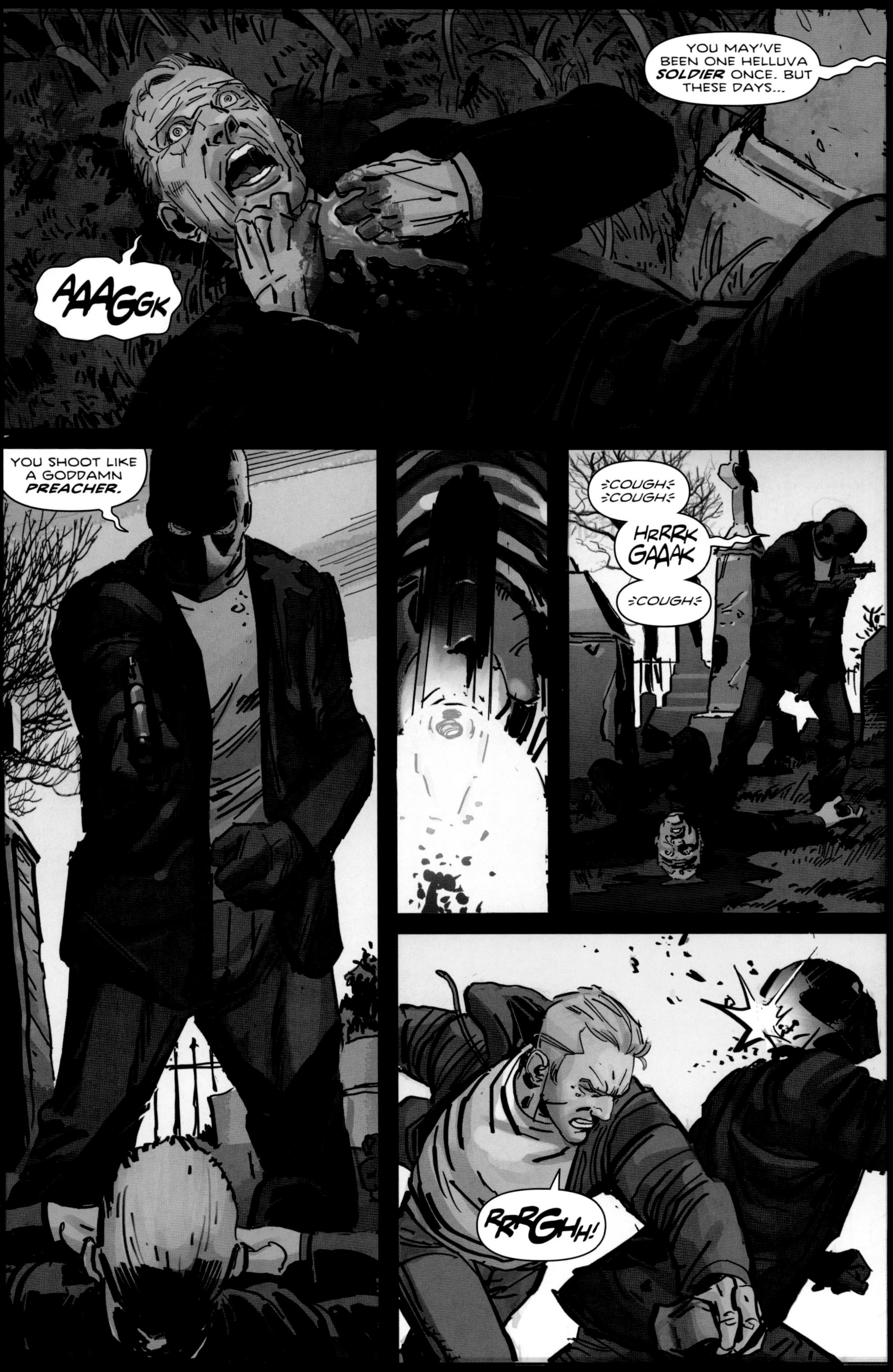

YOU MAY'VE BEEN ONE HELLUVA SOLDIER ONCE. BUT THESE DAYS...
AAAGGK
YOU SHOOT LIKE A GODDAMN PREACHER.
COUGH COUGH
HRRRK GAAAK
COUGH
RRRGHH!

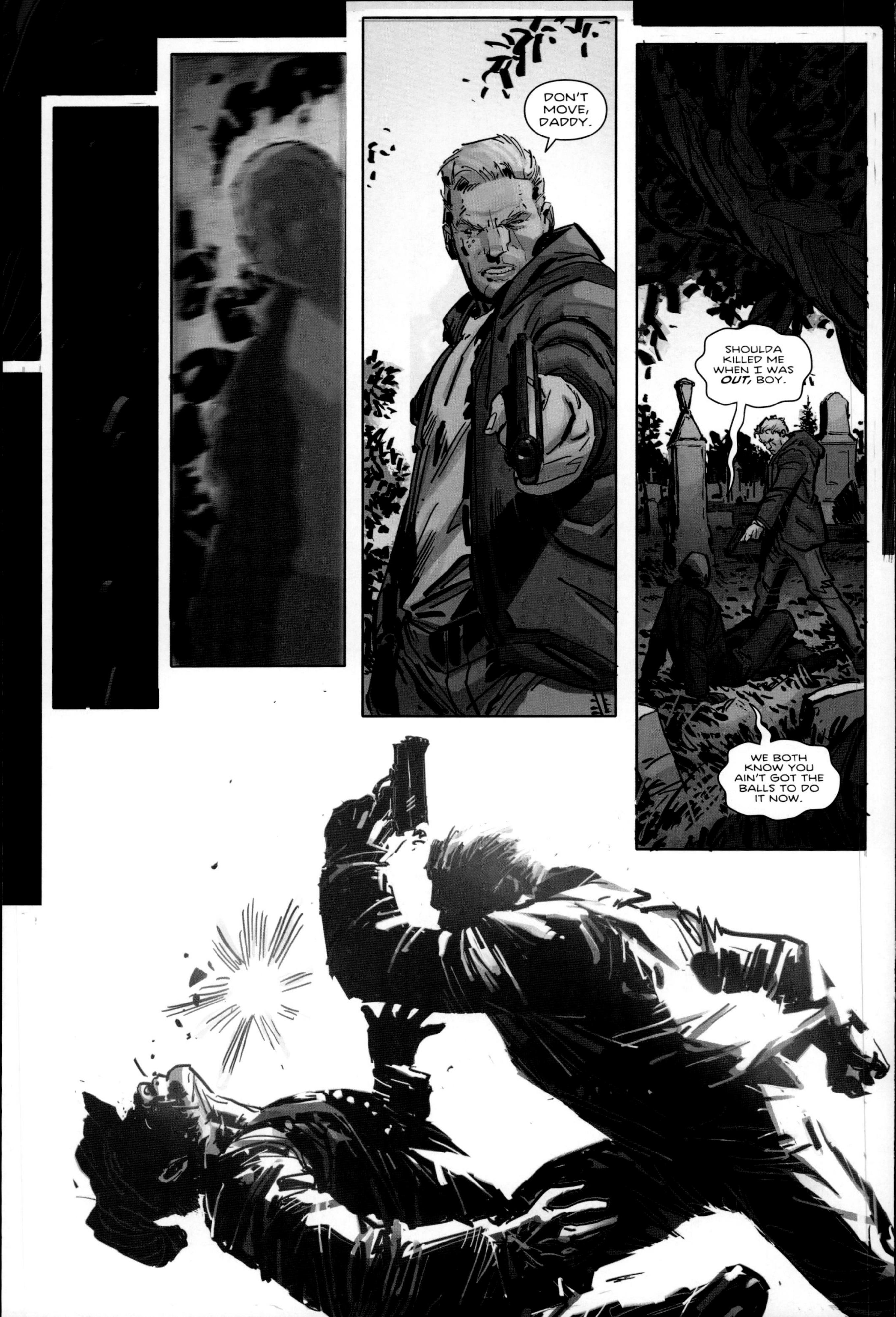
DON'T MOVE, DADDY.
SHOULDA KILLED ME WHEN I WAS OUT, BOY.
WE BOTH KNOW YOU AIN'T GOT THE BALLS TO DO IT NOW.

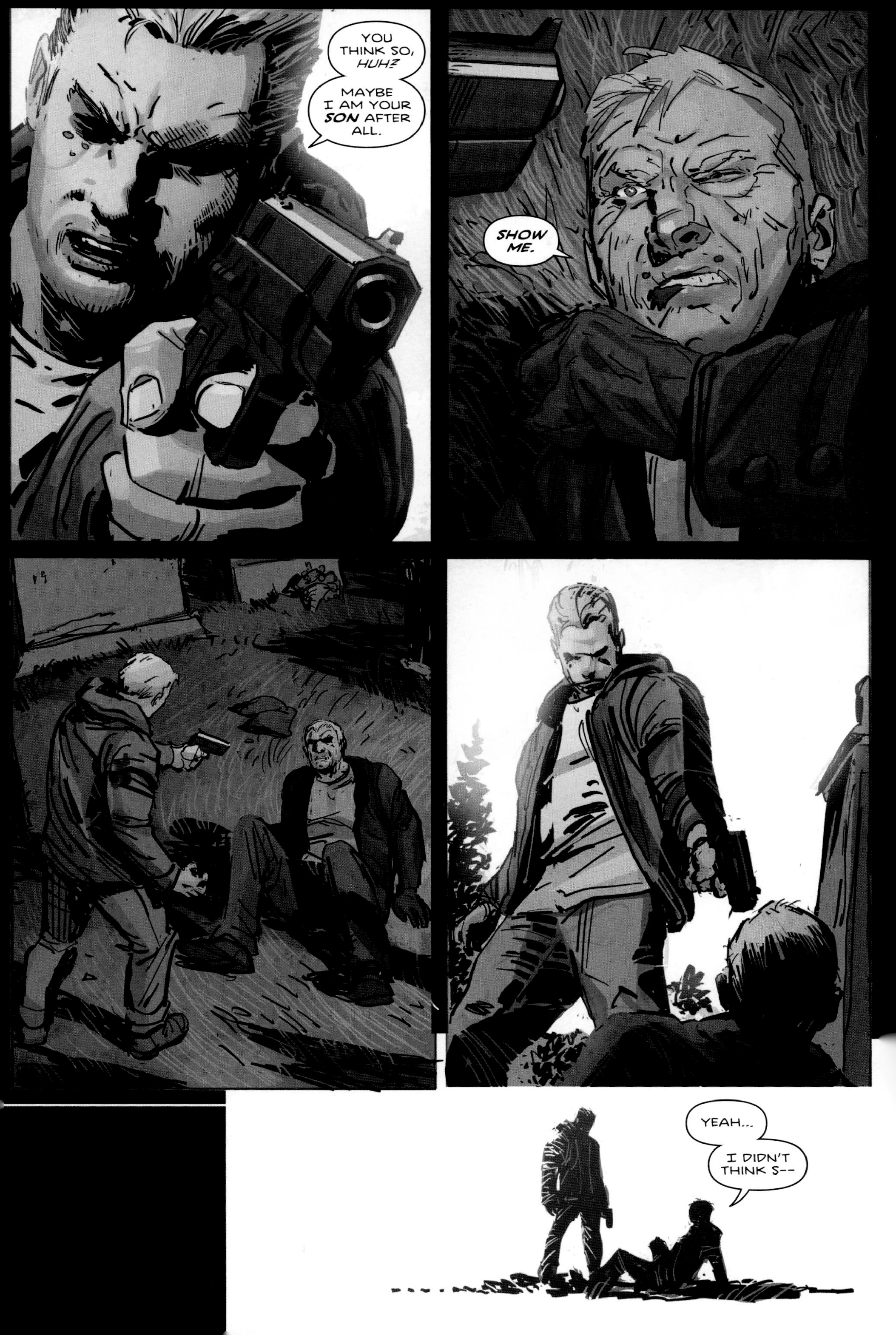
YOU THINK SO, *HUH?*
MAYBE I AM YOUR **SON** AFTER ALL.
*SHOW ME.*
YEAH...
I DIDN'T THINK S--

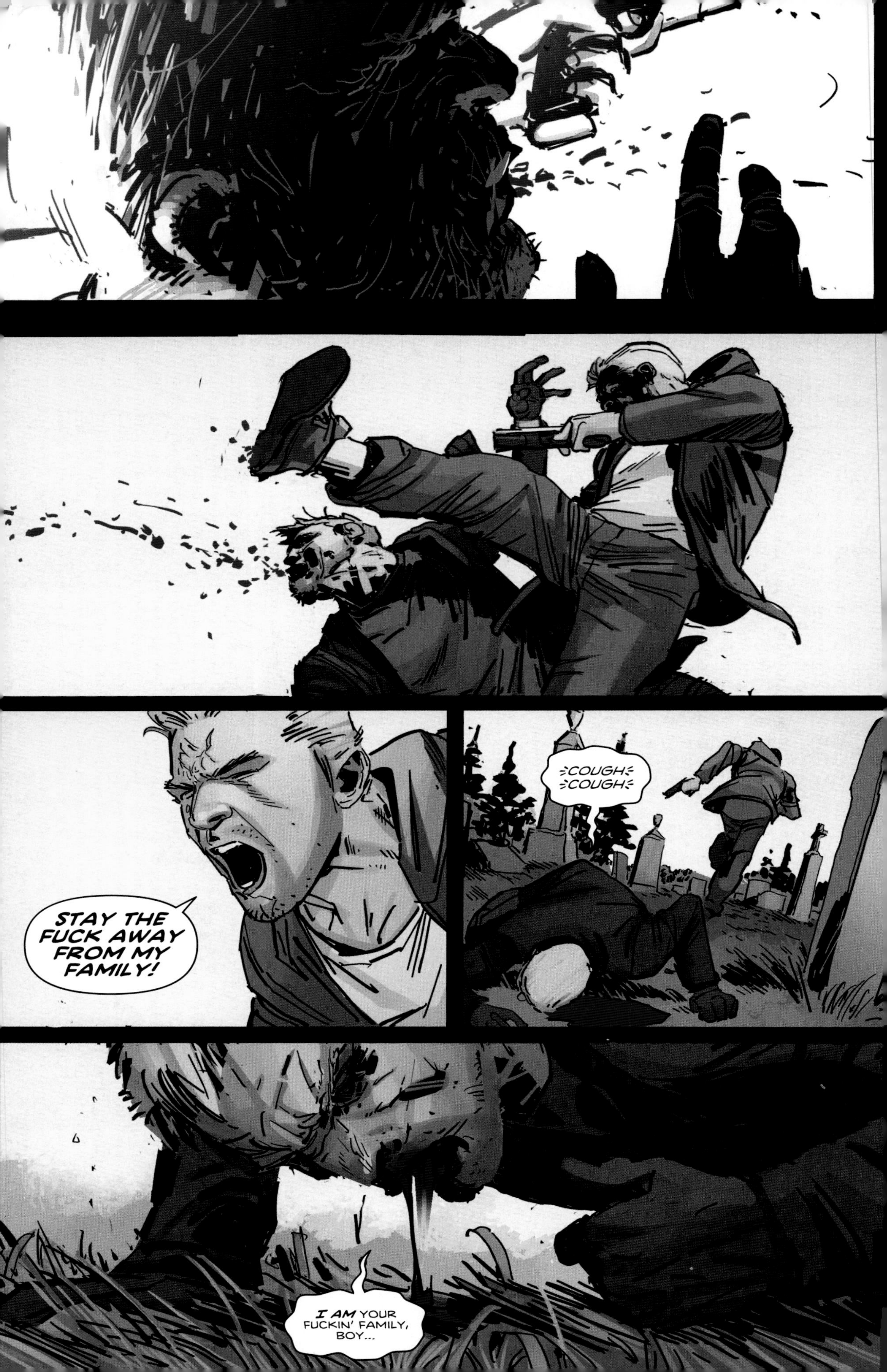
STAY THE FUCK AWAY FROM MY FAMILY!
COUGH COUGH
I AM YOUR FUCKIN' FAMILY, BOY...

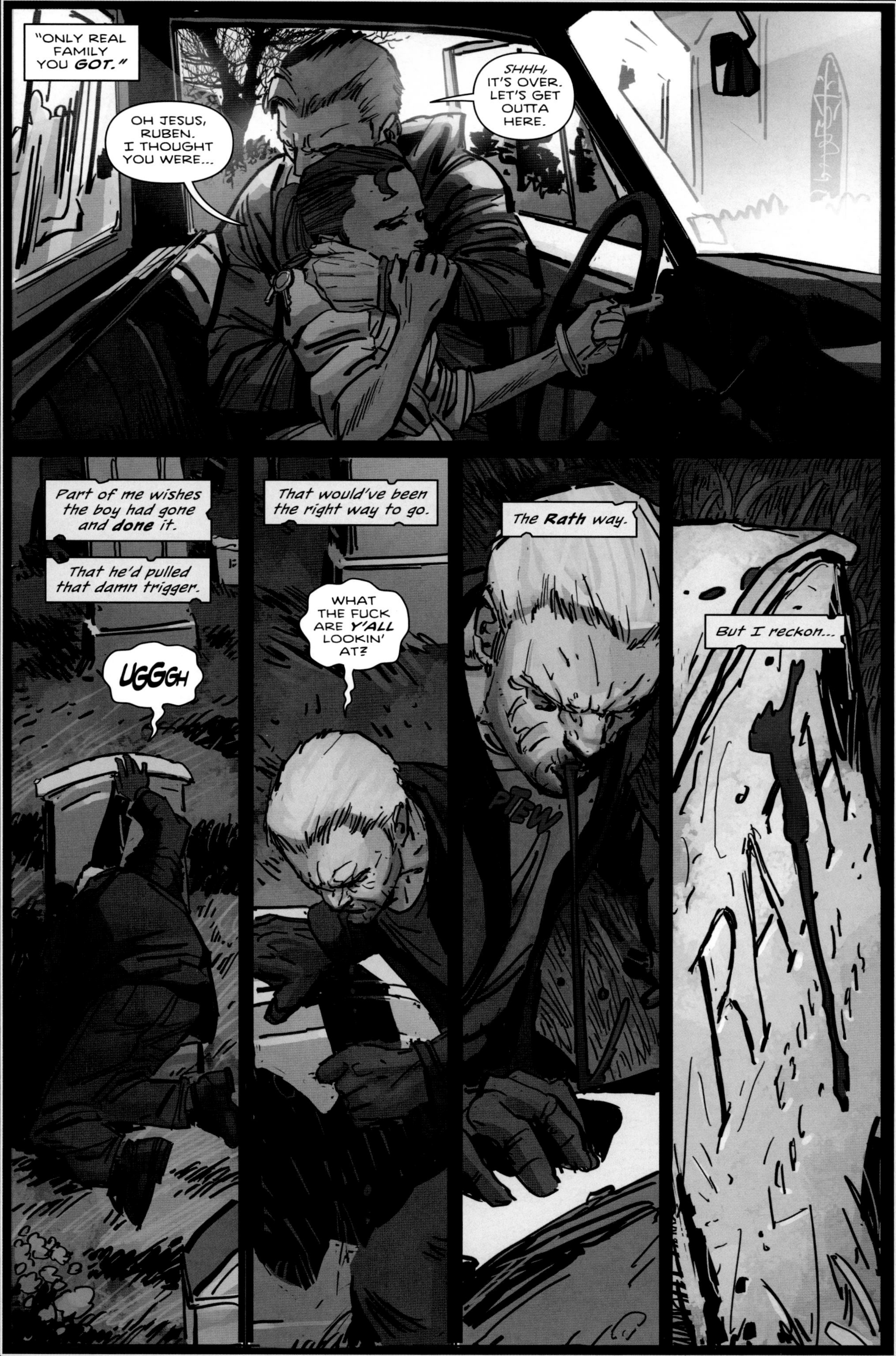
"ONLY REAL FAMILY YOU GOT."
OH JESUS, RUBEN. I THOUGHT YOU WERE...
SHHH, IT'S OVER. LET'S GET OUTTA HERE.
Part of me wishes the boy had gone and done it.
That he'd pulled that damn trigger.
UGGGH
That would've been the right way to go.
WHAT THE FUCK ARE Y'ALL LOOKIN' AT?
The Rath way.
PTEW
But I reckon...

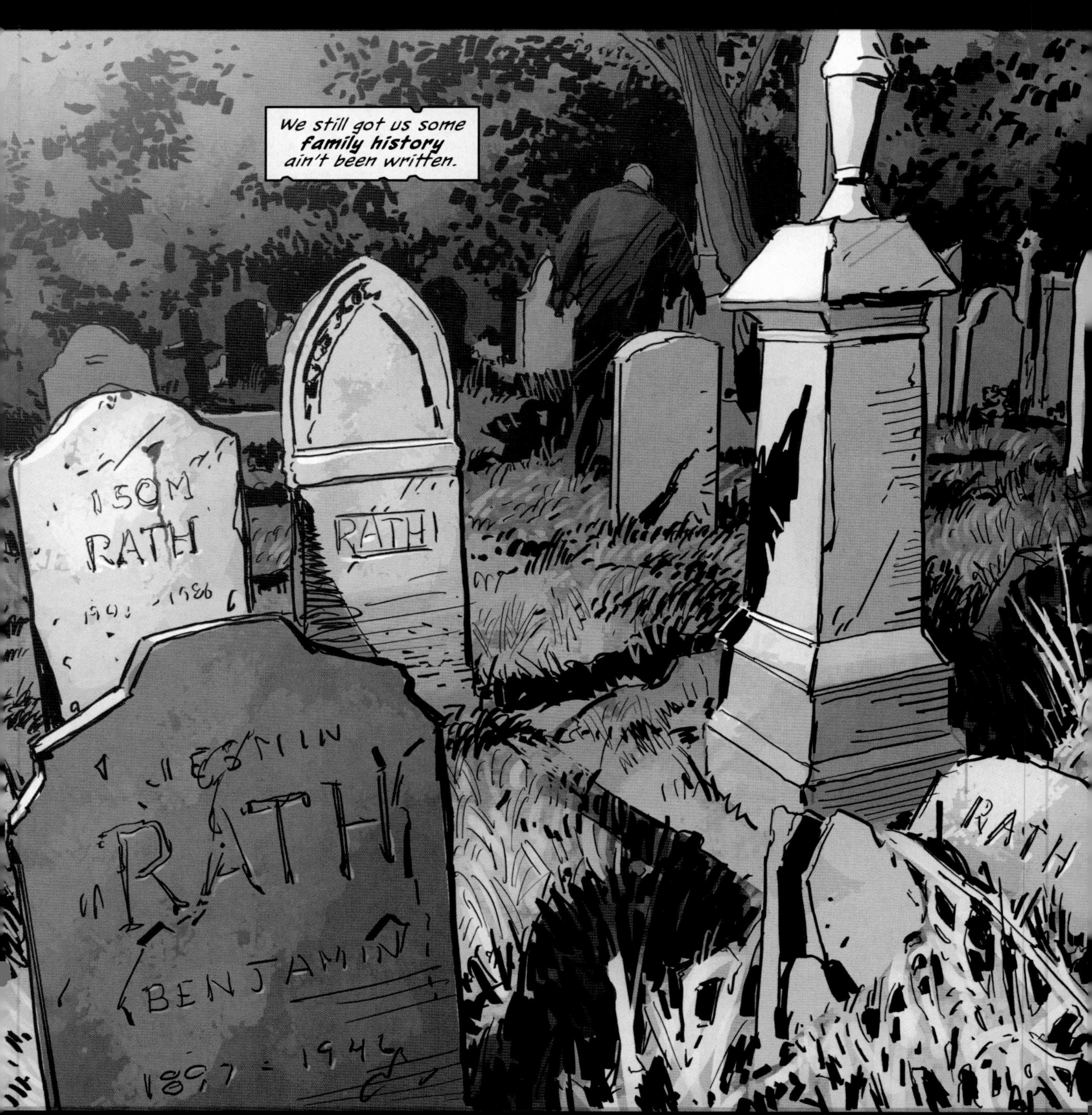
We still got us some ***family history*** ain't been written.
ISOM RATH
RATH
RATH BENJAMIN
RATH

# CHAPTER FOUR

## MY FATHER'S HOUSE

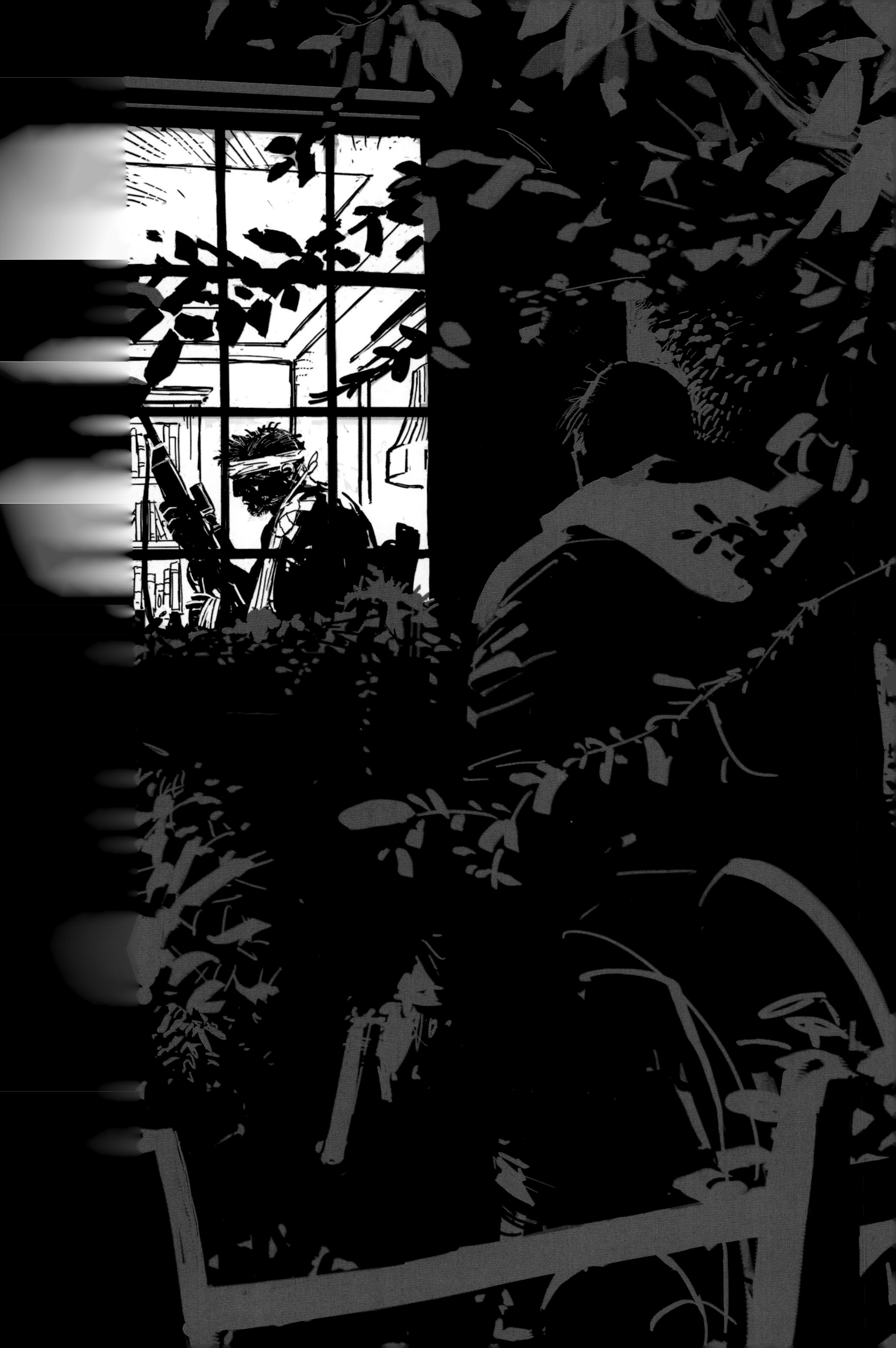

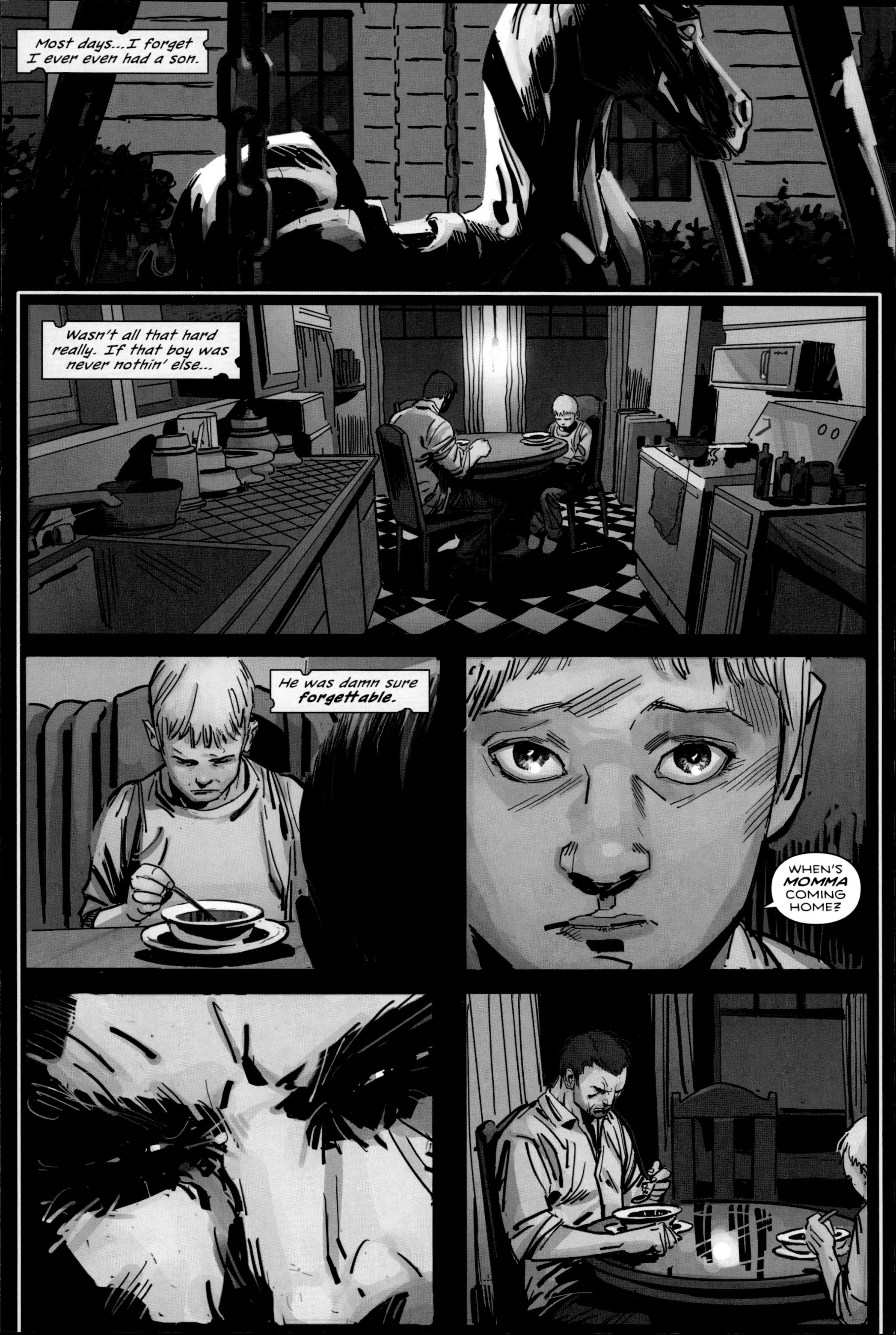
Most days...I forget I ever even had a son.
Wasn't all that hard really. If that boy was never nothin' else...
He was damn sure forgettable.
WHEN'S MOMMA COMING HOME?

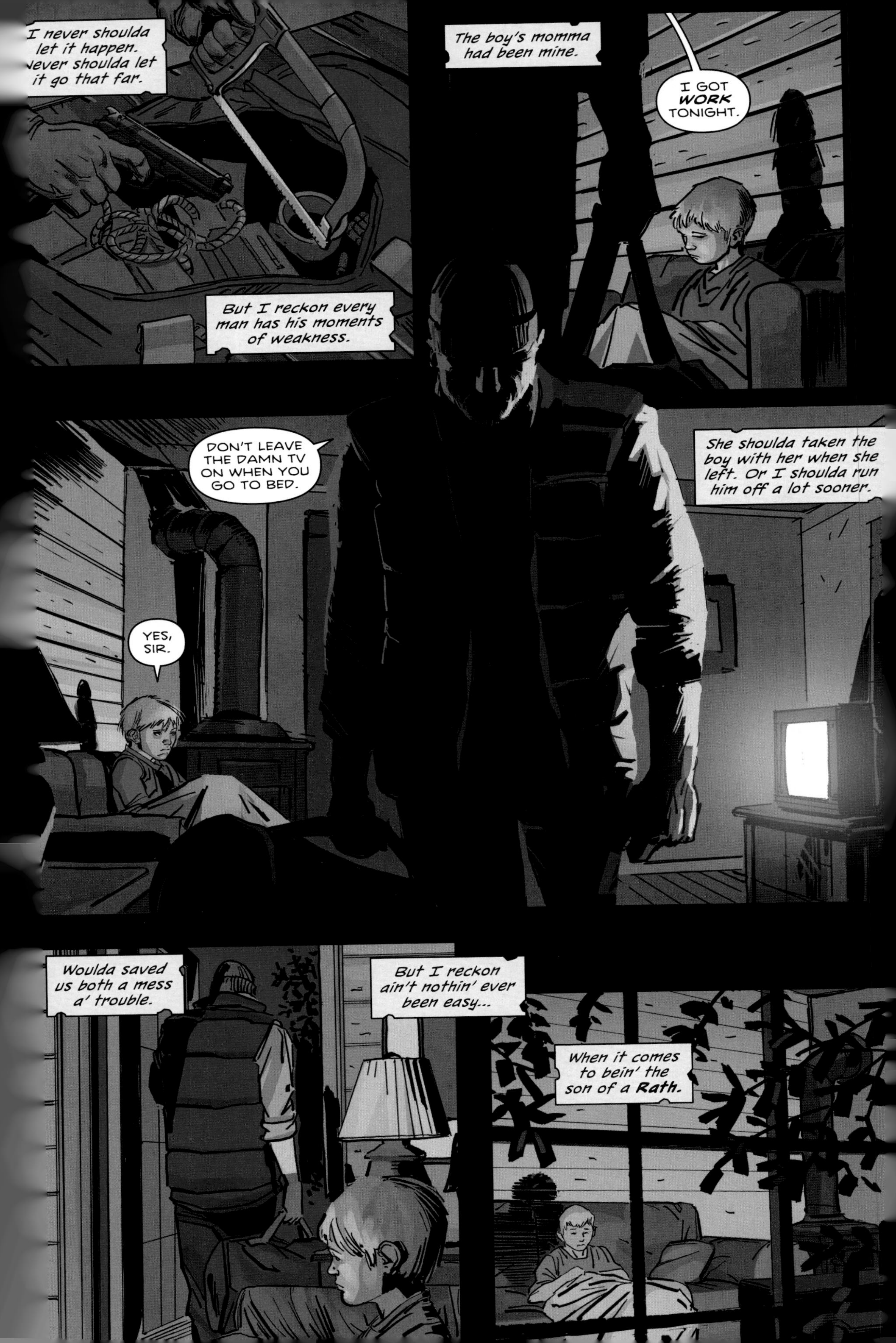
I never shoulda let it happen. Never shoulda let it go that far.
But I reckon every man has his moments of weakness.
The boy's momma had been mine.
I GOT WORK TONIGHT.
DON'T LEAVE THE DAMN TV ON WHEN YOU GO TO BED.
YES, SIR.
She shoulda taken the boy with her when she left. Or I shoulda run him off a lot sooner.
Woulda saved us both a mess a' trouble.
But I reckon ain't nothin' ever been easy...
When it comes to bein' the son of a Rath.

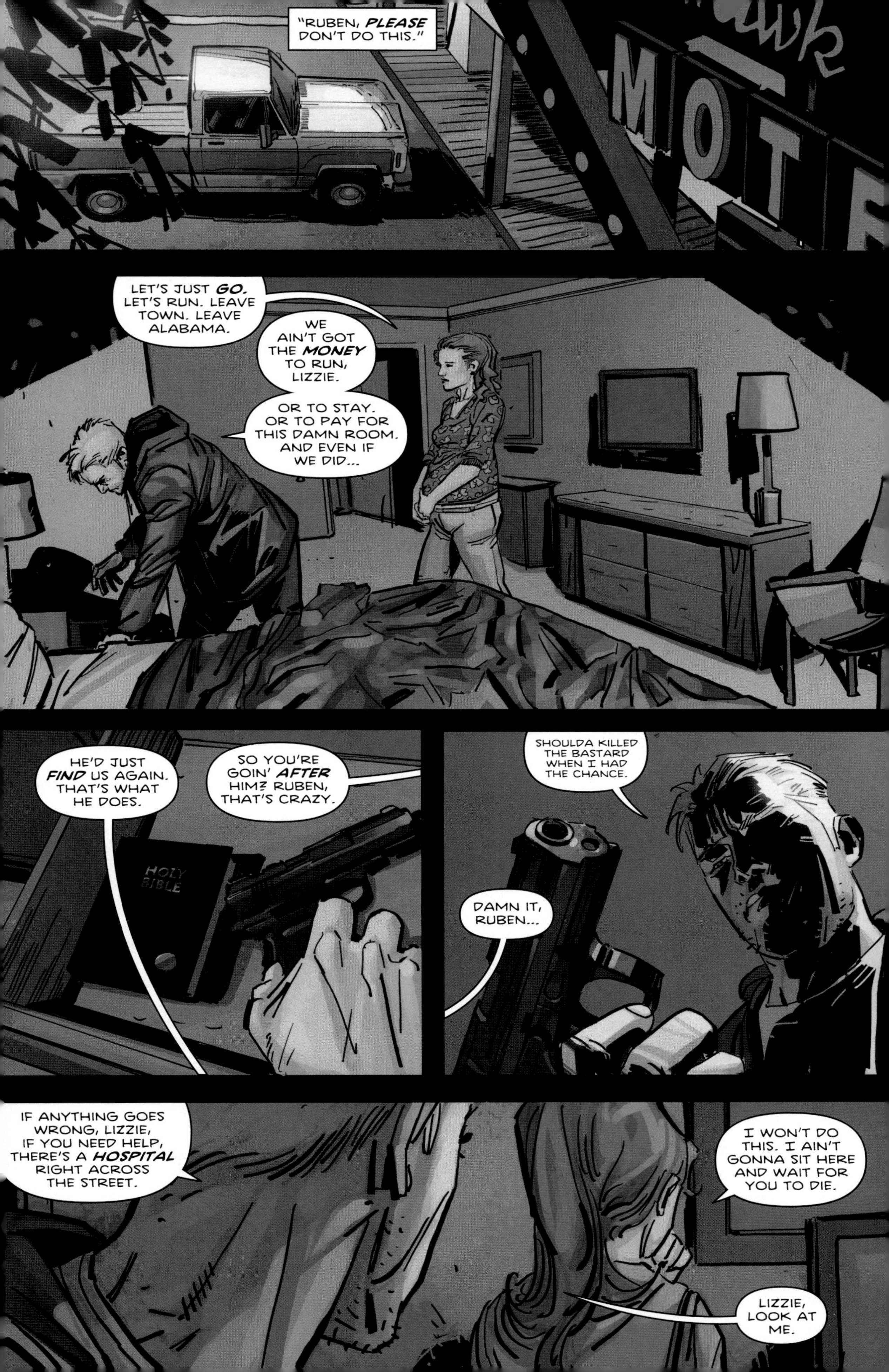
"RUBEN, PLEASE DON'T DO THIS."
MOTE
LET'S JUST GO. LET'S RUN. LEAVE TOWN. LEAVE ALABAMA.
WE AIN'T GOT THE MONEY TO RUN, LIZZIE.
OR TO STAY. OR TO PAY FOR THIS DAMN ROOM. AND EVEN IF WE DID...
HE'D JUST FIND US AGAIN. THAT'S WHAT HE DOES.
SO YOU'RE GOIN' AFTER HIM? RUBEN, THAT'S CRAZY.
HOLY BIBLE
SHOULDA KILLED THE BASTARD WHEN I HAD THE CHANCE.
DAMN IT, RUBEN...
IF ANYTHING GOES WRONG, LIZZIE, IF YOU NEED HELP, THERE'S A HOSPITAL RIGHT ACROSS THE STREET.
I WON'T DO THIS. I AIN'T GONNA SIT HERE AND WAIT FOR YOU TO DIE.
LIZZIE, LOOK AT ME.

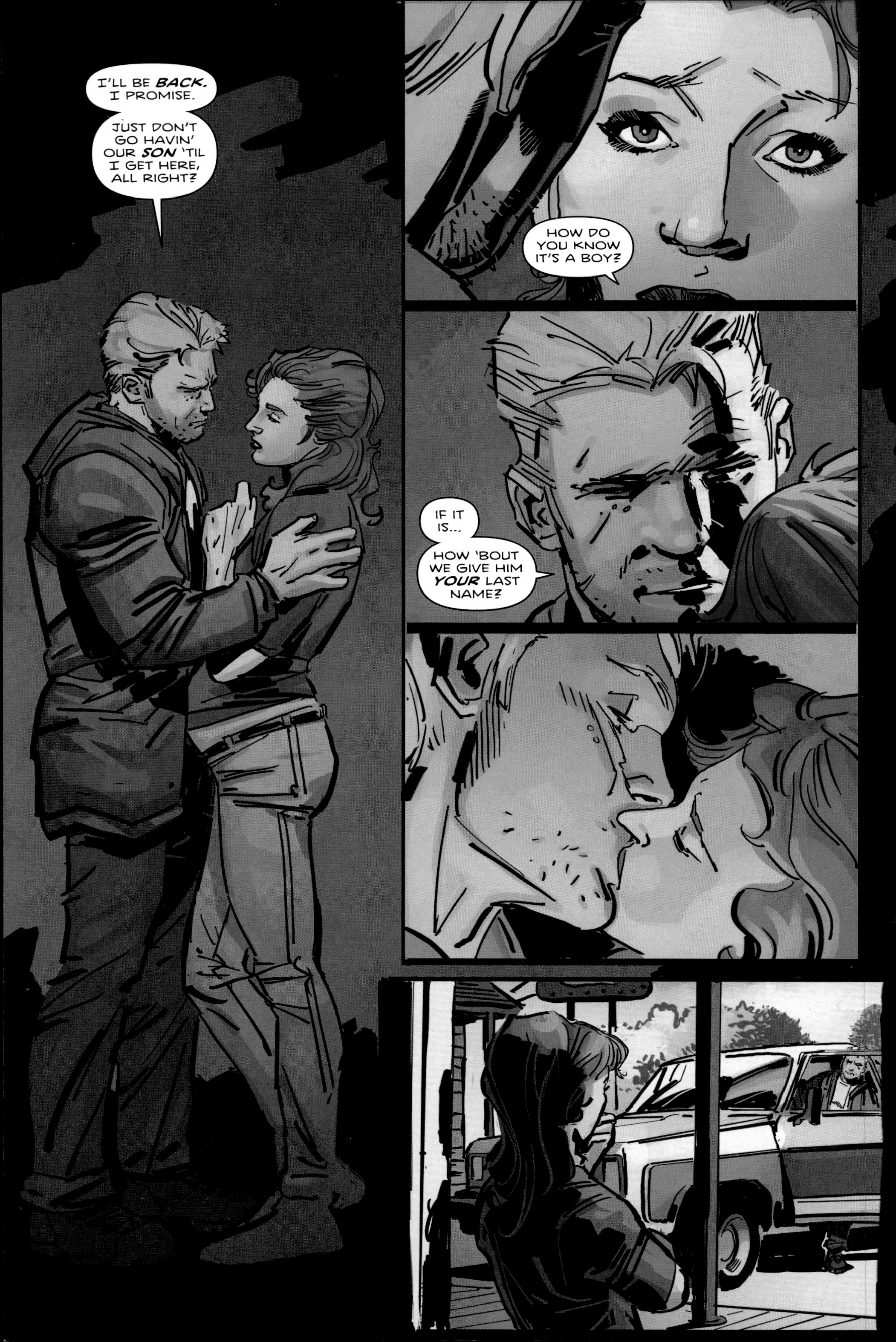
I'LL BE **BACK.** I PROMISE.
JUST DON'T GO HAVIN' OUR **SON** 'TIL I GET HERE, ALL RIGHT?
HOW DO YOU KNOW IT'S A BOY?
IF IT IS...
HOW 'BOUT WE GIVE HIM **YOUR** LAST NAME?

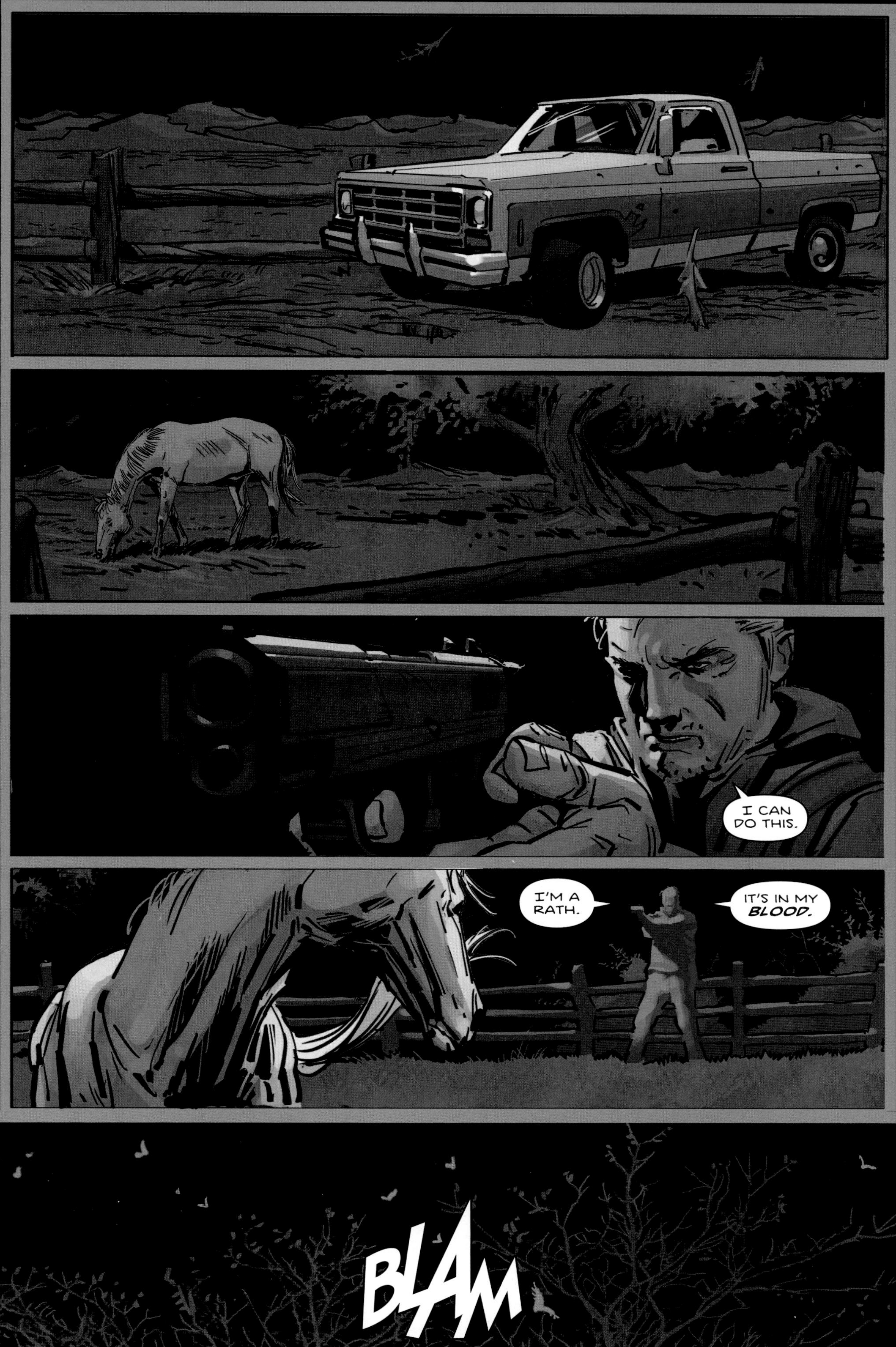
I CAN DO THIS.
I'M A RATH.
IT'S IN MY *BLOOD.*
BLAM

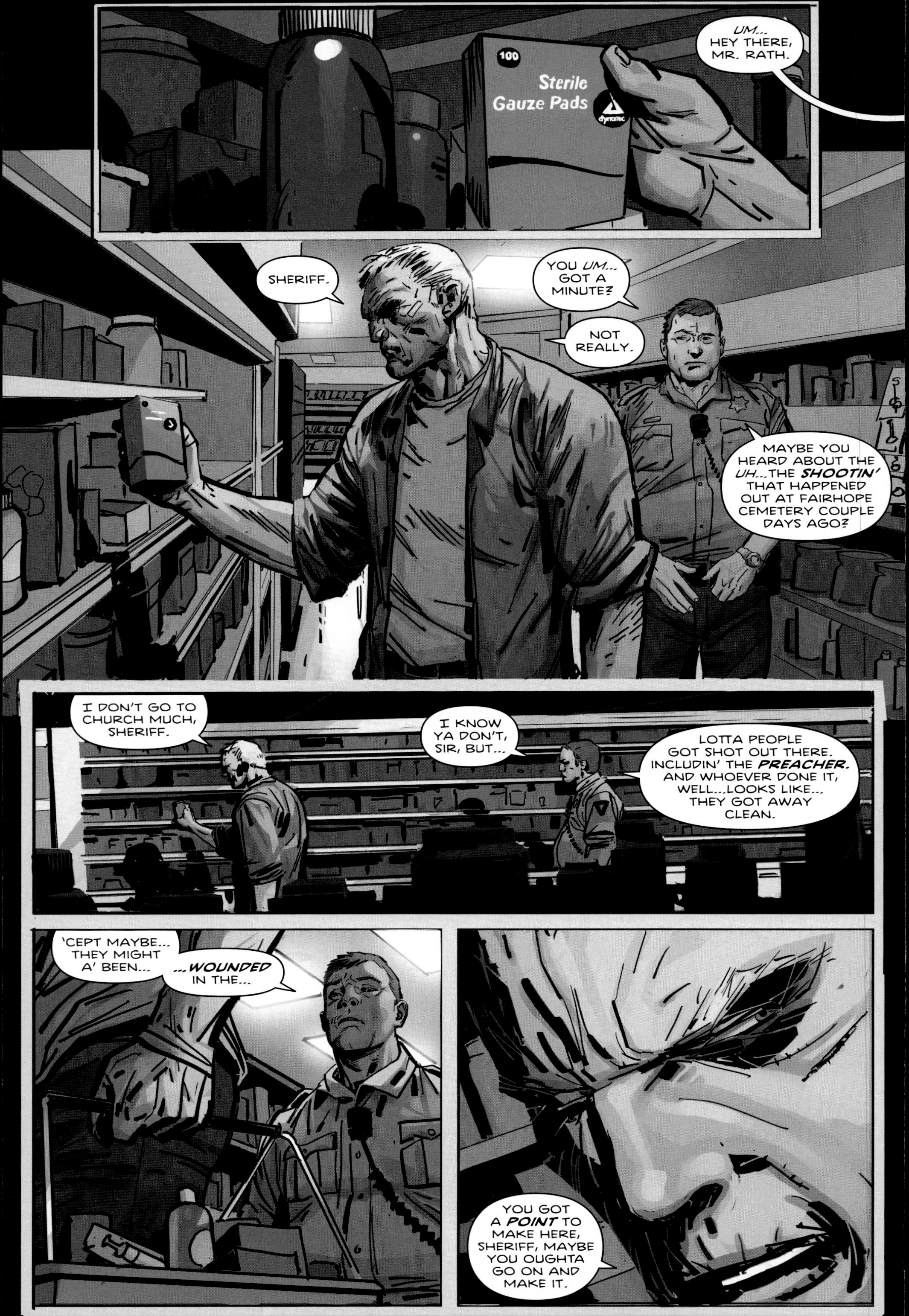
100
Sterile Gauze Pads
UM... HEY THERE, MR. RATH.
SHERIFF.
YOU UM... GOT A MINUTE?
NOT REALLY.
MAYBE YOU HEARD ABOUT THE UH... THE SHOOTIN' THAT HAPPENED OUT AT FAIRHOPE CEMETERY COUPLE DAYS AGO?
I DON'T GO TO CHURCH MUCH, SHERIFF.
I KNOW YA DON'T, SIR, BUT...
LOTTA PEOPLE GOT SHOT OUT THERE. INCLUDIN' THE PREACHER. AND WHOEVER DONE IT, WELL... LOOKS LIKE... THEY GOT AWAY CLEAN.
'CEPT MAYBE... THEY MIGHT A' BEEN...
...WOUNDED IN THE...
YOU GOT A POINT TO MAKE HERE, SHERIFF, MAYBE YOU OUGHTA GO ON AND MAKE IT.

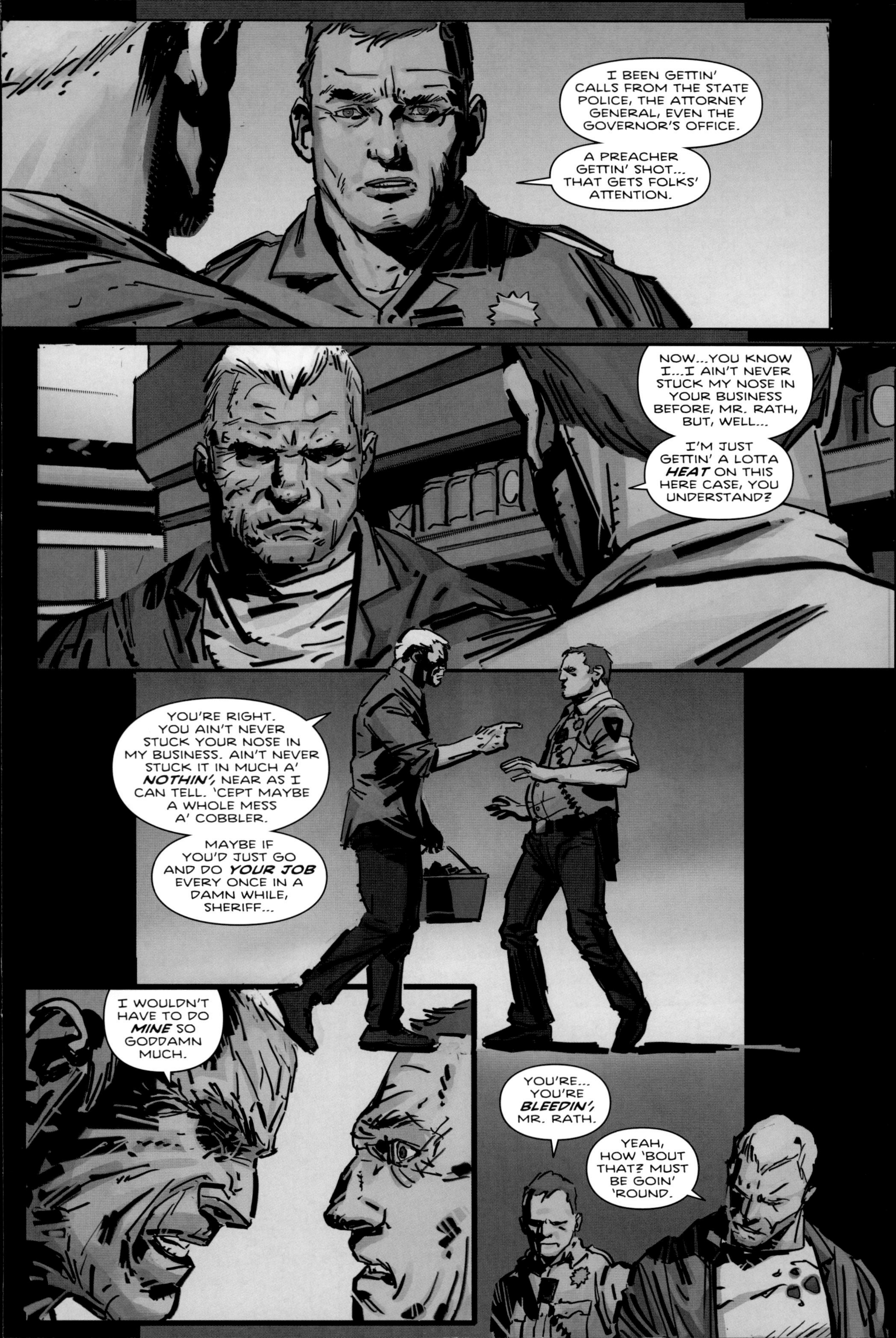
I BEEN GETTIN' CALLS FROM THE STATE POLICE, THE ATTORNEY GENERAL, EVEN THE GOVERNOR'S OFFICE.
A PREACHER GETTIN' SHOT... THAT GETS FOLKS' ATTENTION.
NOW...YOU KNOW I...I AIN'T NEVER STUCK MY NOSE IN YOUR BUSINESS BEFORE, MR. RATH, BUT, WELL...
I'M JUST GETTIN' A LOTTA *HEAT* ON THIS HERE CASE, YOU UNDERSTAND?
YOU'RE RIGHT. YOU AIN'T NEVER STUCK YOUR NOSE IN MY BUSINESS. AIN'T NEVER STUCK IT IN MUCH A' *NOTHIN'*, NEAR AS I CAN TELL. 'CEPT MAYBE A WHOLE MESS A' COBBLER.
MAYBE IF YOU'D JUST GO AND DO *YOUR JOB* EVERY ONCE IN A DAMN WHILE, SHERIFF...
I WOULDN'T HAVE TO DO *MINE* SO GODDAMN MUCH.
YOU'RE... YOU'RE *BLEEDIN'*, MR. RATH.
YEAH, HOW 'BOUT THAT? MUST BE GOIN' 'ROUND.

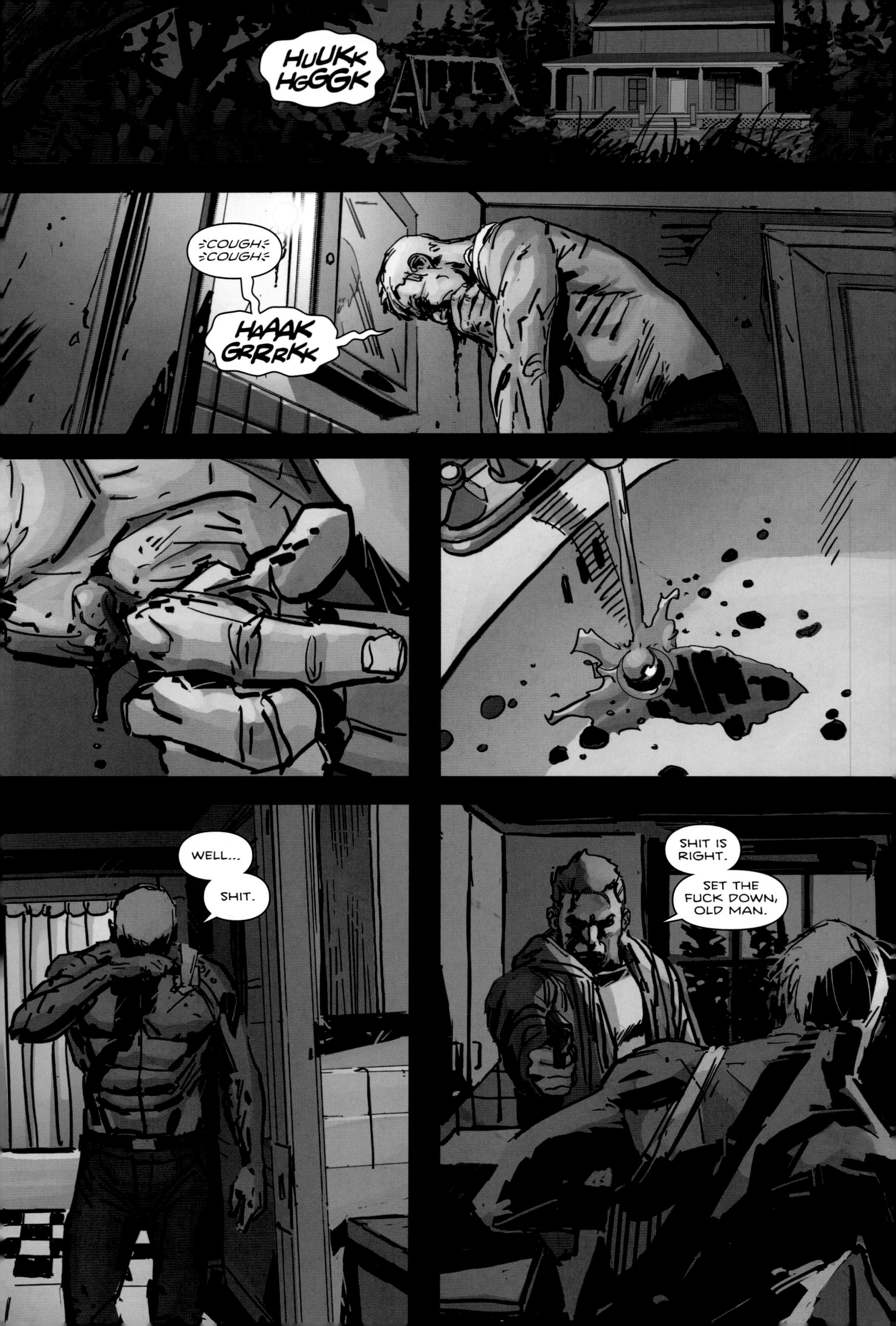
HUUKK HGGGK
COUGH COUGH
HAAAK GRRRKK
WELL...
SHIT.
SHIT IS RIGHT.
SET THE FUCK DOWN, OLD MAN.

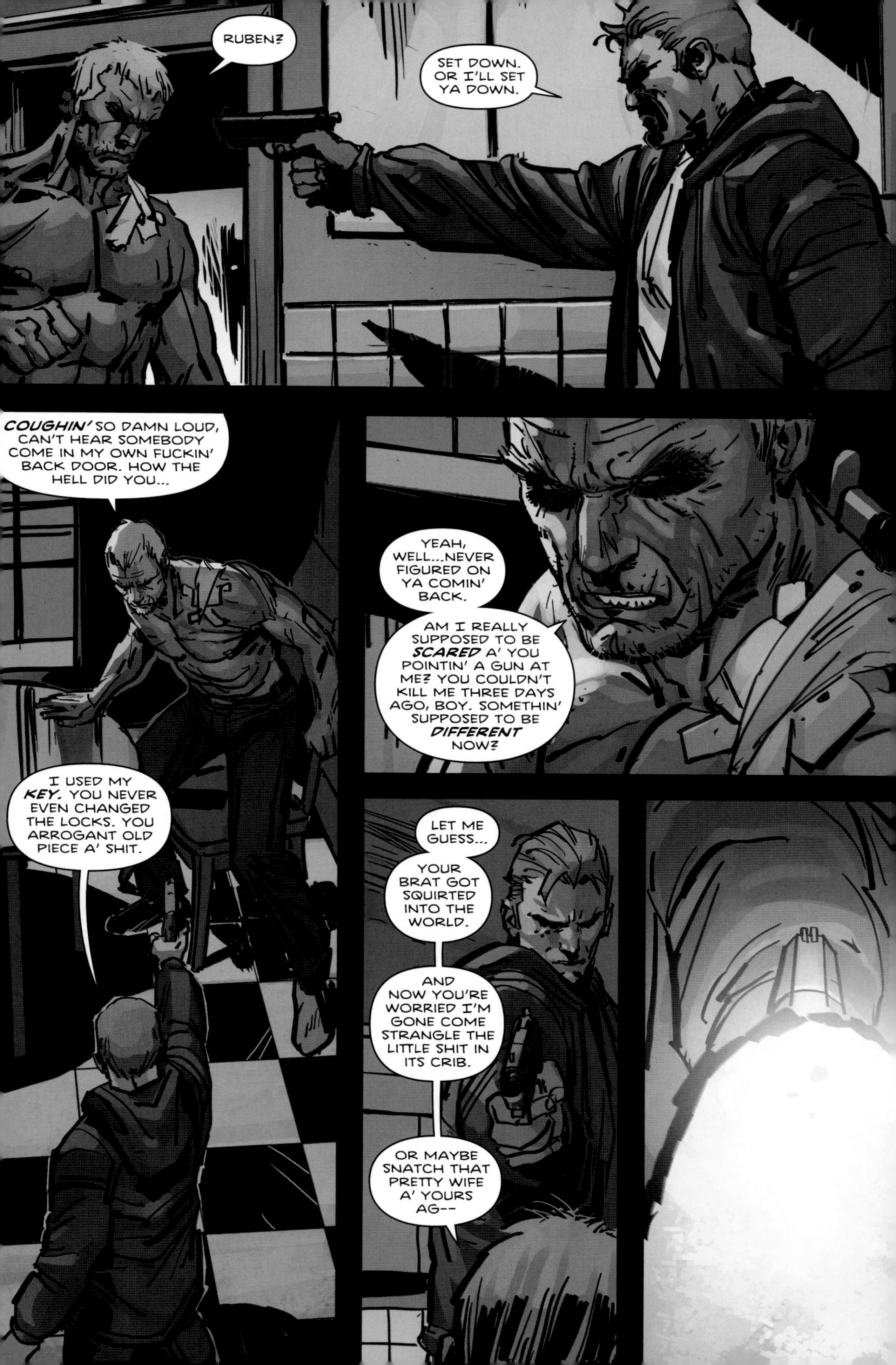
RUBEN?
SET DOWN. OR I'LL SET YA DOWN.
COUGHIN' SO DAMN LOUD, CAN'T HEAR SOMEBODY COME IN MY OWN FUCKIN' BACK DOOR. HOW THE HELL DID YOU...
I USED MY KEY. YOU NEVER EVEN CHANGED THE LOCKS. YOU ARROGANT OLD PIECE A' SHIT.
YEAH, WELL...NEVER FIGURED ON YA COMIN' BACK.
AM I REALLY SUPPOSED TO BE SCARED A' YOU POINTIN' A GUN AT ME? YOU COULDN'T KILL ME THREE DAYS AGO, BOY. SOMETHIN' SUPPOSED TO BE DIFFERENT NOW?
LET ME GUESS...
YOUR BRAT GOT SQUIRTED INTO THE WORLD.
AND NOW YOU'RE WORRIED I'M GONE COME STRANGLE THE LITTLE SHIT IN ITS CRIB.
OR MAYBE SNATCH THAT PRETTY WIFE A' YOURS AG--

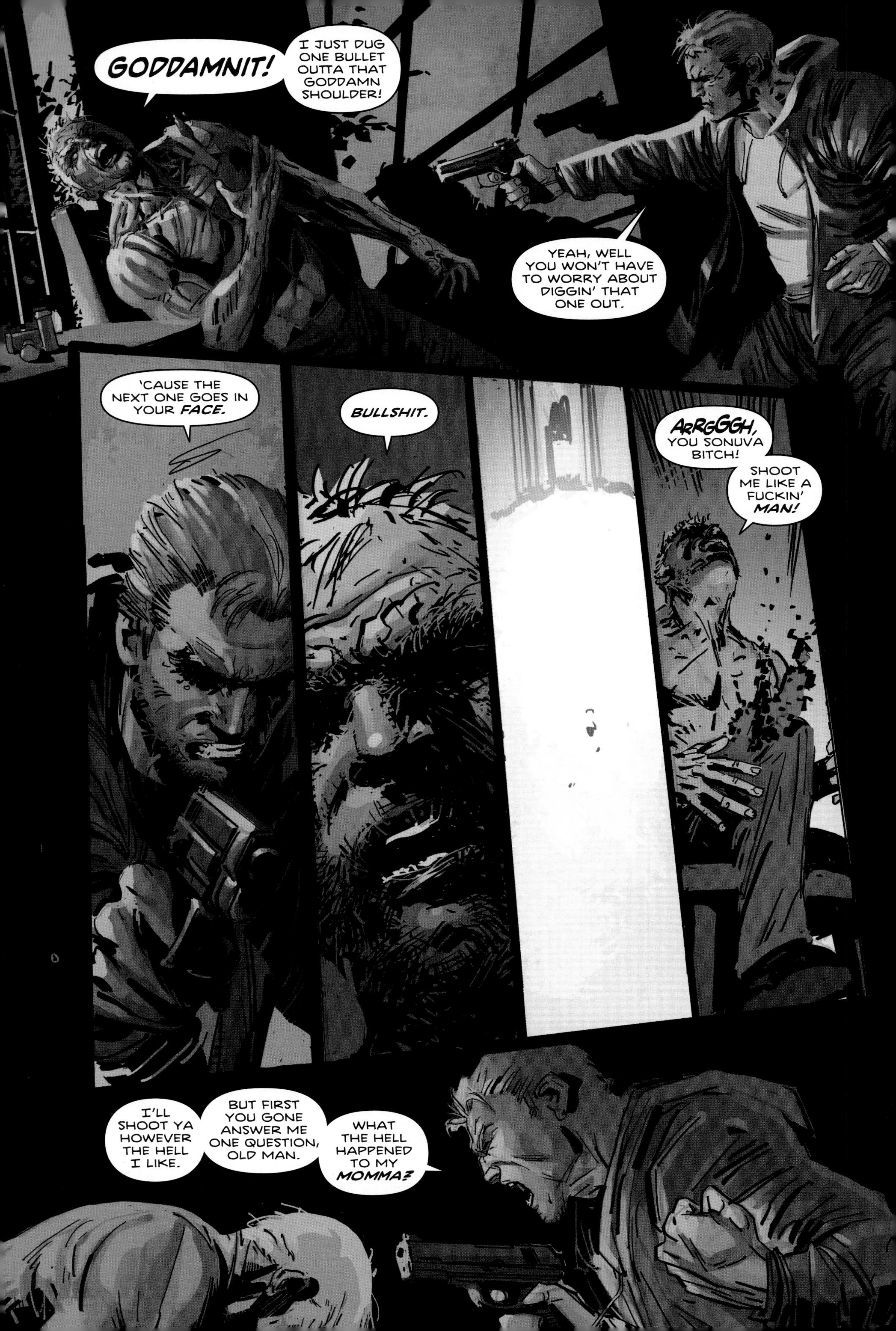
GODDAMNIT!
I JUST DUG ONE BULLET OUTTA THAT GODDAMN SHOULDER!
YEAH, WELL YOU WON'T HAVE TO WORRY ABOUT DIGGIN' THAT ONE OUT.
'CAUSE THE NEXT ONE GOES IN YOUR FACE.
BULLSHIT.
ARRGGGH, YOU SONUVA BITCH!
SHOOT ME LIKE A FUCKIN' MAN!
I'LL SHOOT YA HOWEVER THE HELL I LIKE.
BUT FIRST YOU GONE ANSWER ME ONE QUESTION, OLD MAN.
WHAT THE HELL HAPPENED TO MY MOMMA?

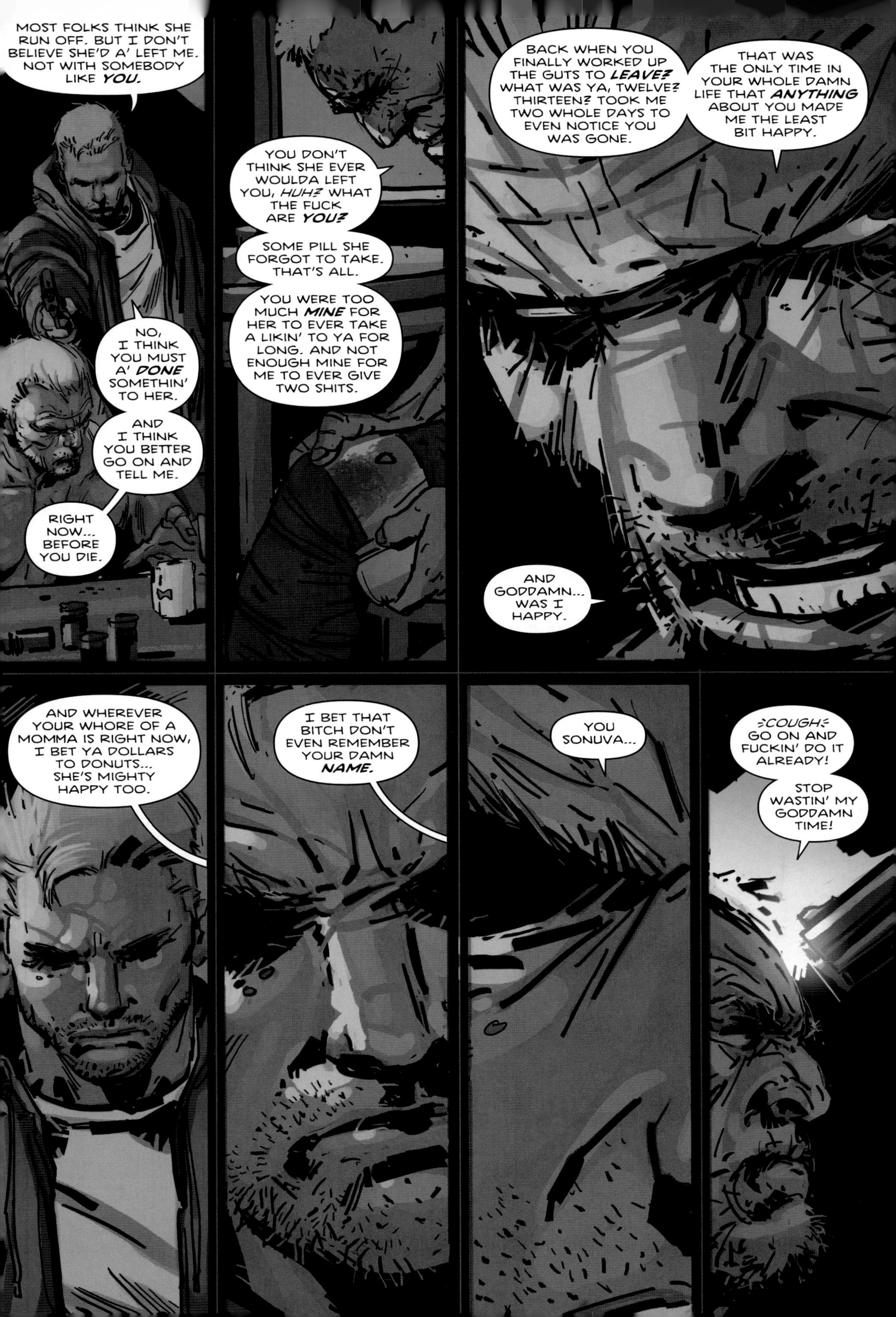
MOST FOLKS THINK SHE RUN OFF. BUT I DON'T BELIEVE SHE'D A' LEFT ME. NOT WITH SOMEBODY LIKE YOU.
NO, I THINK YOU MUST A' DONE SOMETHIN' TO HER.
AND I THINK YOU BETTER GO ON AND TELL ME.
RIGHT NOW... BEFORE YOU DIE.
YOU DON'T THINK SHE EVER WOULDA LEFT YOU, HUH? WHAT THE FUCK ARE YOU?
SOME PILL SHE FORGOT TO TAKE. THAT'S ALL.
YOU WERE TOO MUCH MINE FOR HER TO EVER TAKE A LIKIN' TO YA FOR LONG. AND NOT ENOUGH MINE FOR ME TO EVER GIVE TWO SHITS.
BACK WHEN YOU FINALLY WORKED UP THE GUTS TO LEAVE? WHAT WAS YA, TWELVE? THIRTEEN? TOOK ME TWO WHOLE DAYS TO EVEN NOTICE YOU WAS GONE.
THAT WAS THE ONLY TIME IN YOUR WHOLE DAMN LIFE THAT ANYTHING ABOUT YOU MADE ME THE LEAST BIT HAPPY.
AND GODDAMN... WAS I HAPPY.
AND WHEREVER YOUR WHORE OF A MOMMA IS RIGHT NOW, I BET YA DOLLARS TO DONUTS... SHE'S MIGHTY HAPPY TOO.
I BET THAT BITCH DON'T EVEN REMEMBER YOUR DAMN NAME.
YOU SONUVA...
COUGH GO ON AND FUCKIN' DO IT ALREADY!
STOP WASTIN' MY GODDAMN TIME!

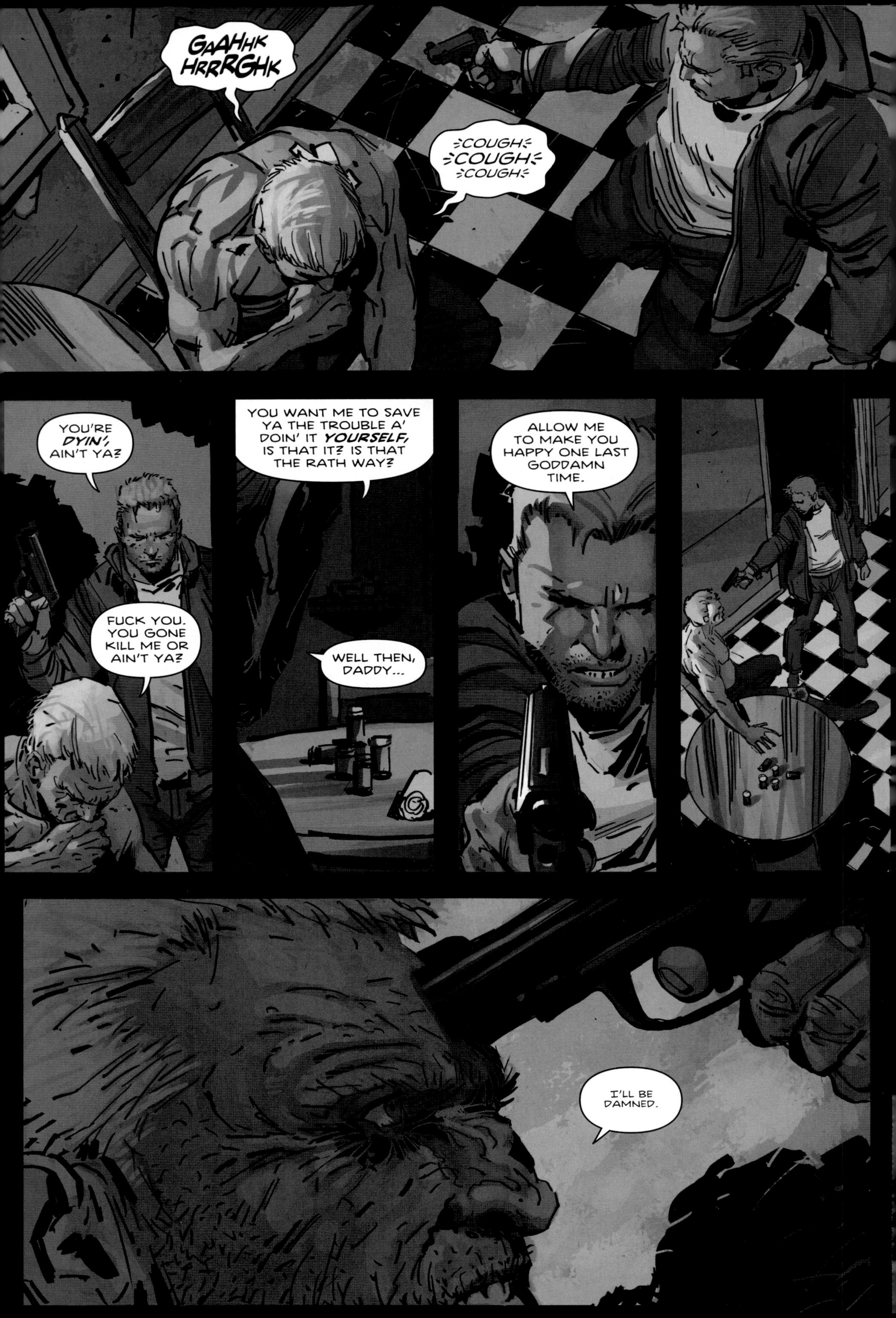
GAAHHK HRRRGHK
COUGH COUGH COUGH
YOU'RE DYIN', AIN'T YA?
FUCK YOU. YOU GONE KILL ME OR AIN'T YA?
YOU WANT ME TO SAVE YA THE TROUBLE A' DOIN' IT YOURSELF, IS THAT IT? IS THAT THE RATH WAY?
WELL THEN, DADDY...
ALLOW ME TO MAKE YOU HAPPY ONE LAST GODDAMN TIME.
I'LL BE DAMNED.

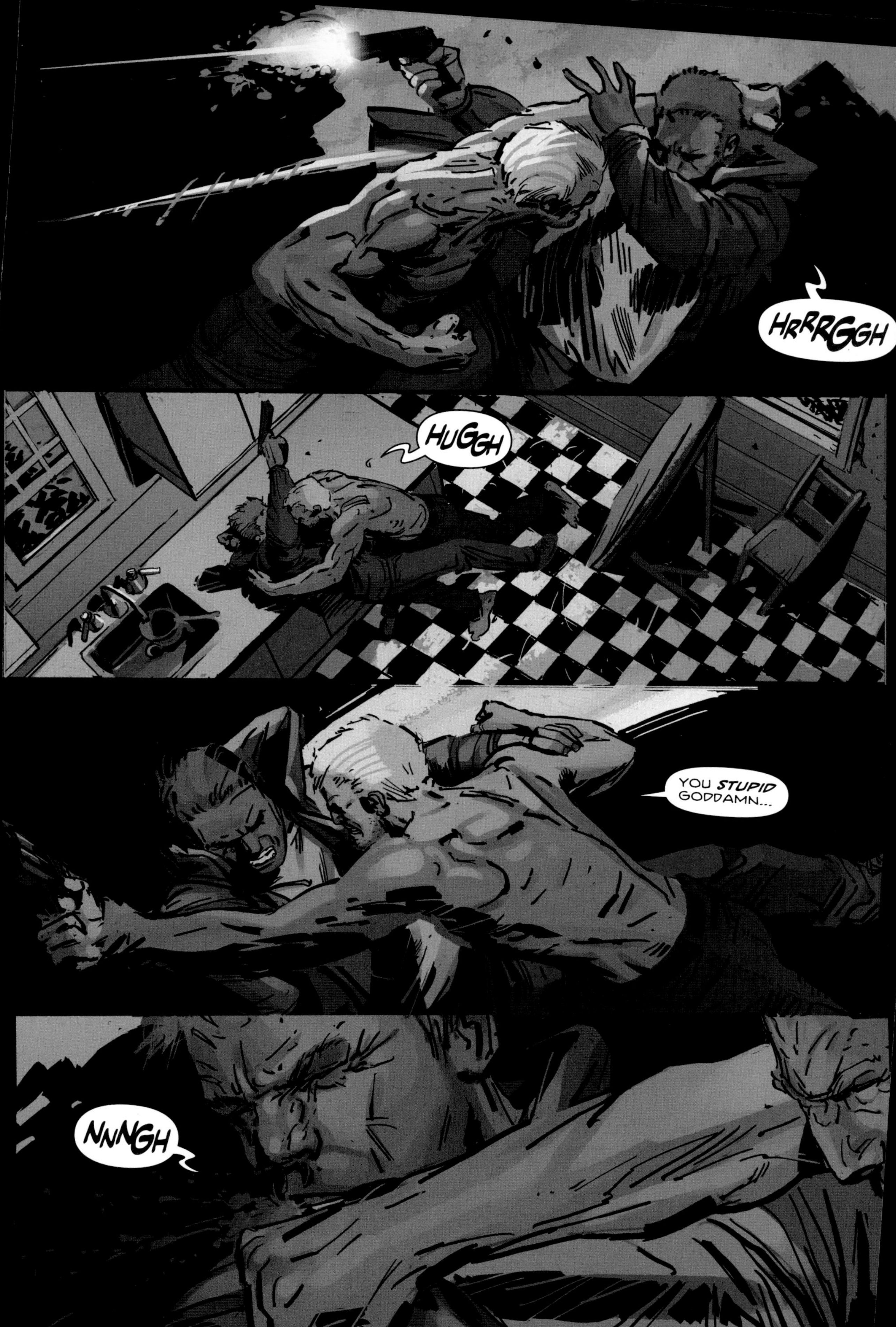
HRRRGGH
HUGGH
YOU STUPID GODDAMN...
NNNGH

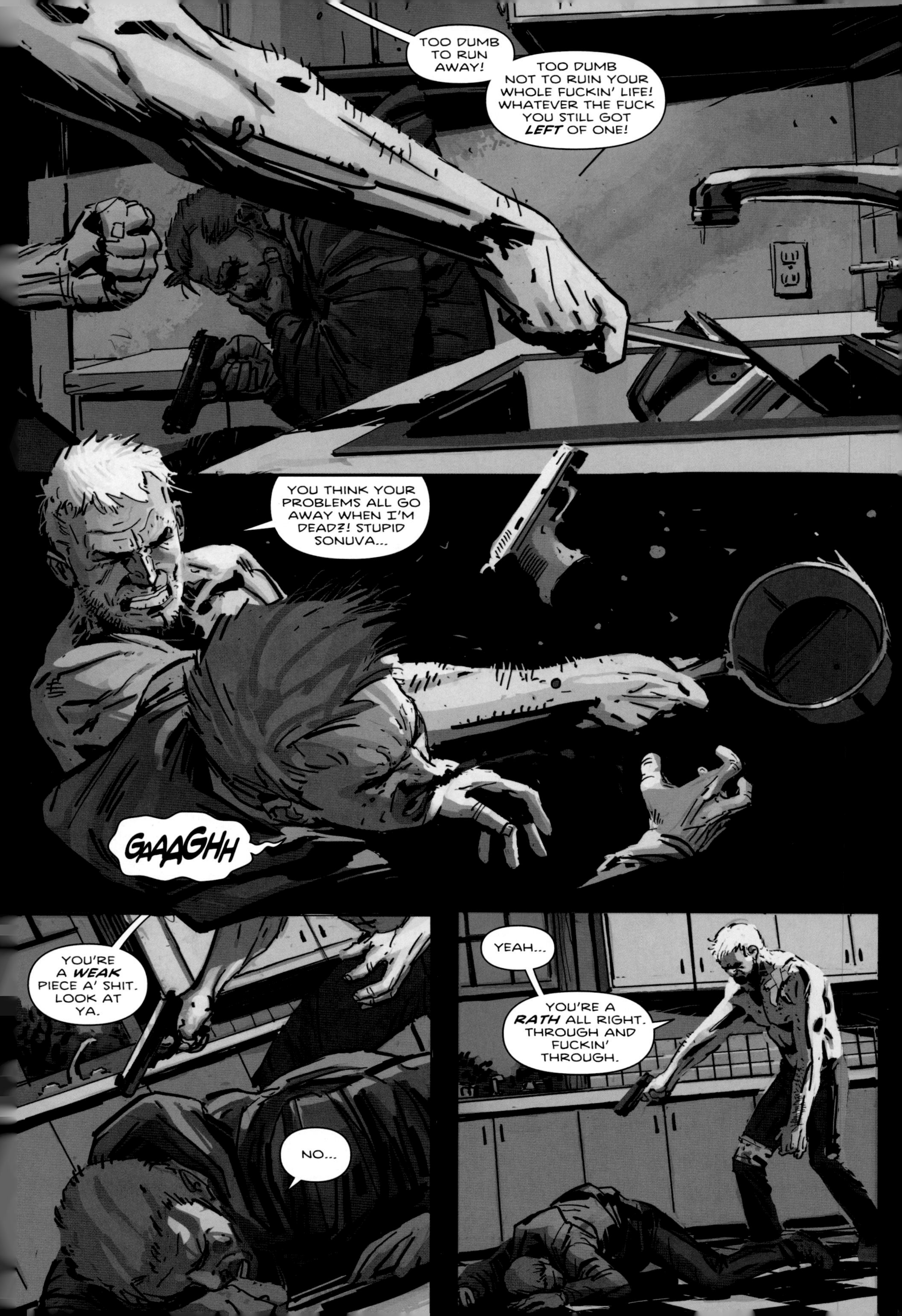
TOO DUMB TO RUN AWAY!
TOO DUMB NOT TO RUIN YOUR WHOLE FUCKIN' LIFE! WHATEVER THE FUCK YOU STILL GOT *LEFT* OF ONE!
YOU THINK YOUR PROBLEMS ALL GO AWAY WHEN I'M DEAD?! STUPID SONUVA...
GAAAGHH
YOU'RE A *WEAK* PIECE A' SHIT. LOOK AT YA.
NO...
YEAH...
YOU'RE A *RATH* ALL RIGHT. THROUGH AND FUCKIN' THROUGH.

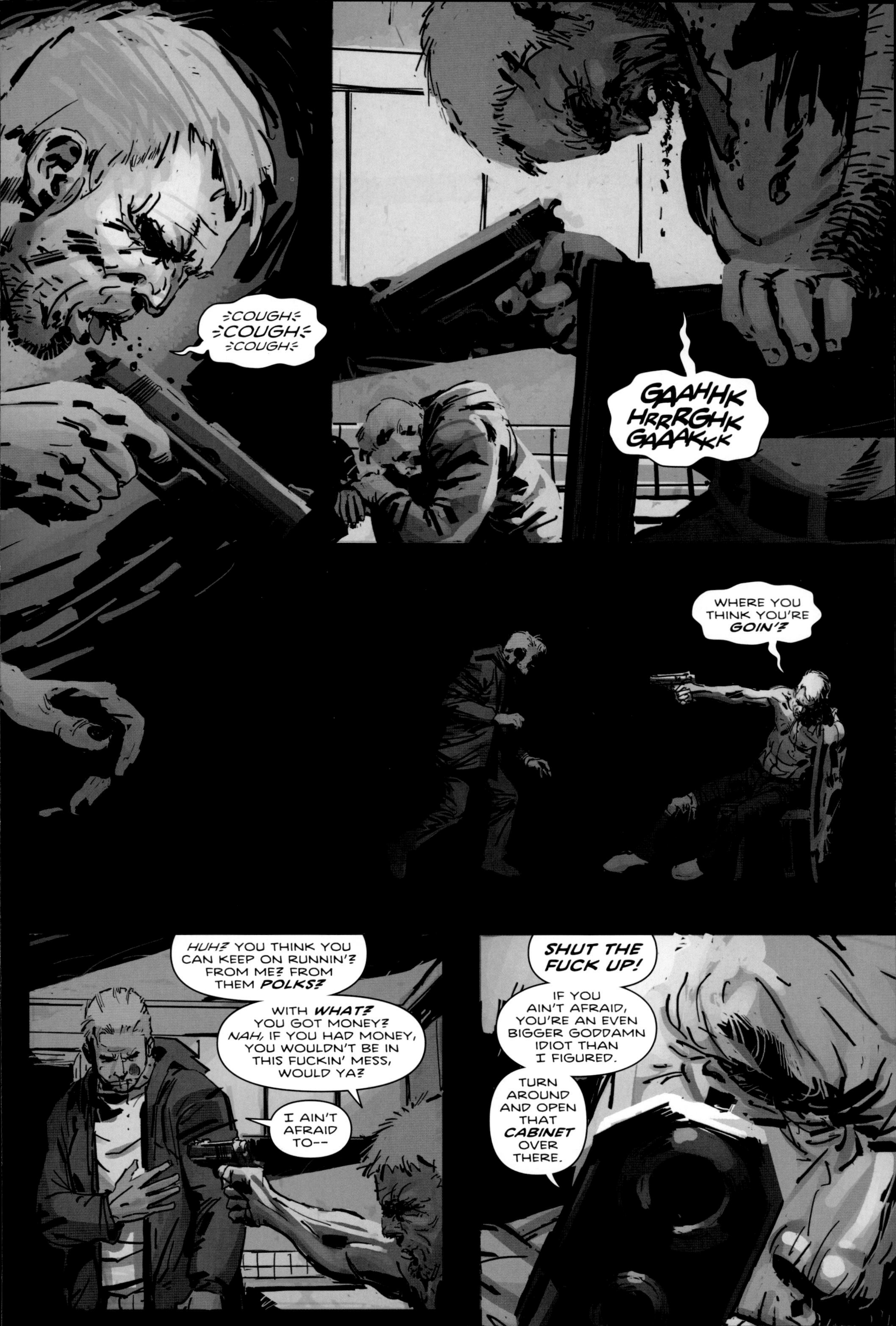

COUGH COUGH COUGH
GAAHHK HRRRGHK GAAAKKK
WHERE YOU THINK YOU'RE *GOIN'?*
*HUH?* YOU THINK YOU CAN KEEP ON RUNNIN'? FROM ME? FROM THEM *POLKS?*
WITH *WHAT?* YOU GOT MONEY? *NAH,* IF YOU HAD MONEY, YOU WOULDN'T BE IN THIS FUCKIN' MESS, WOULD YA?
I AIN'T AFRAID TO--
*SHUT THE FUCK UP!*
IF YOU AIN'T AFRAID, YOU'RE AN EVEN BIGGER GODDAMN IDIOT THAN I FIGURED.
TURN AROUND AND OPEN THAT *CABINET* OVER THERE.

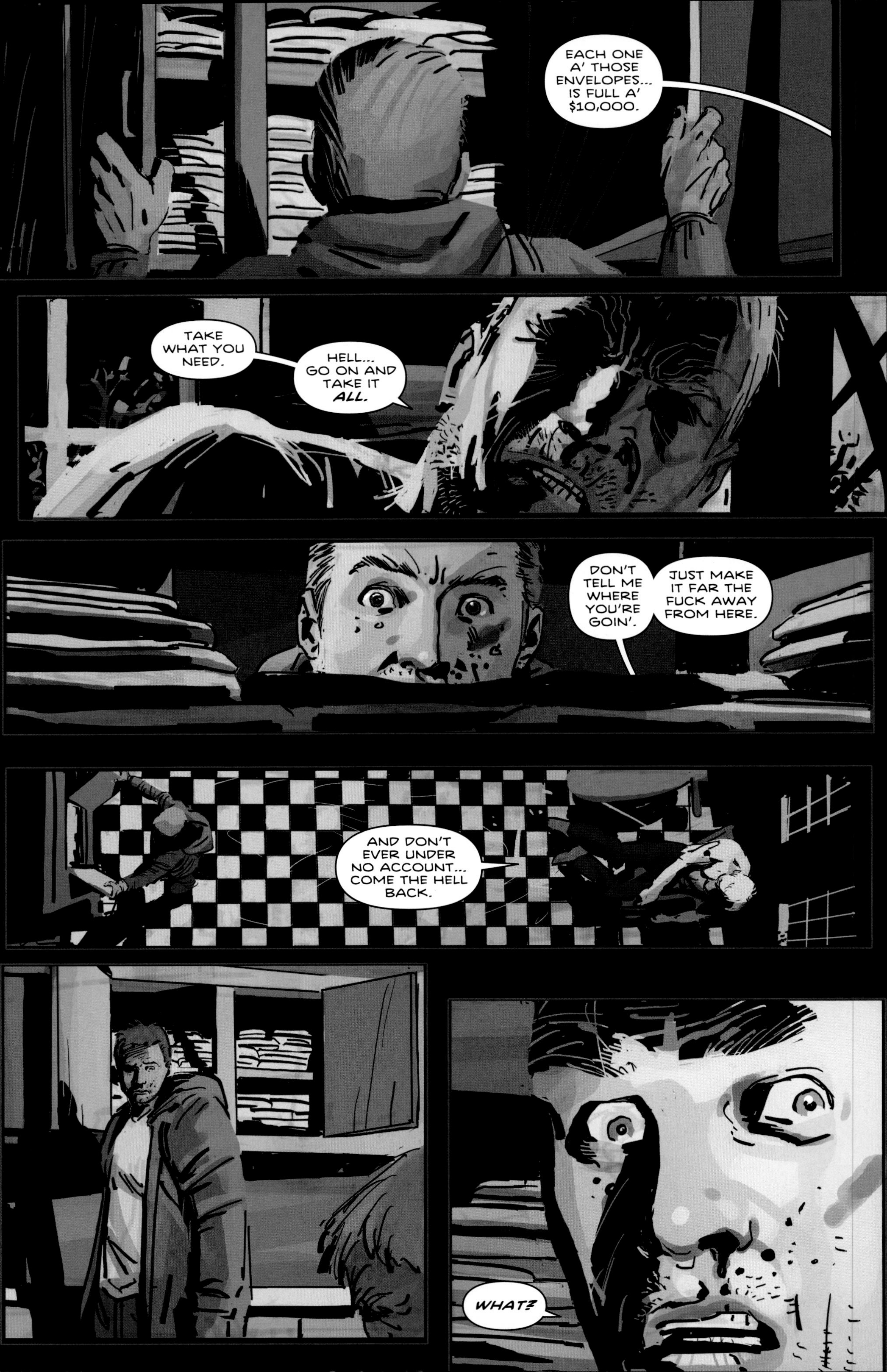
EACH ONE A' THOSE ENVELOPES... IS FULL A' $10,000.
TAKE WHAT YOU NEED.
HELL... GO ON AND TAKE IT *ALL.*
DON'T TELL ME WHERE YOU'RE GOIN'.
JUST MAKE IT FAR THE FUCK AWAY FROM HERE.
AND DON'T EVER UNDER NO ACCOUNT... COME THE HELL BACK.
*WHAT?*

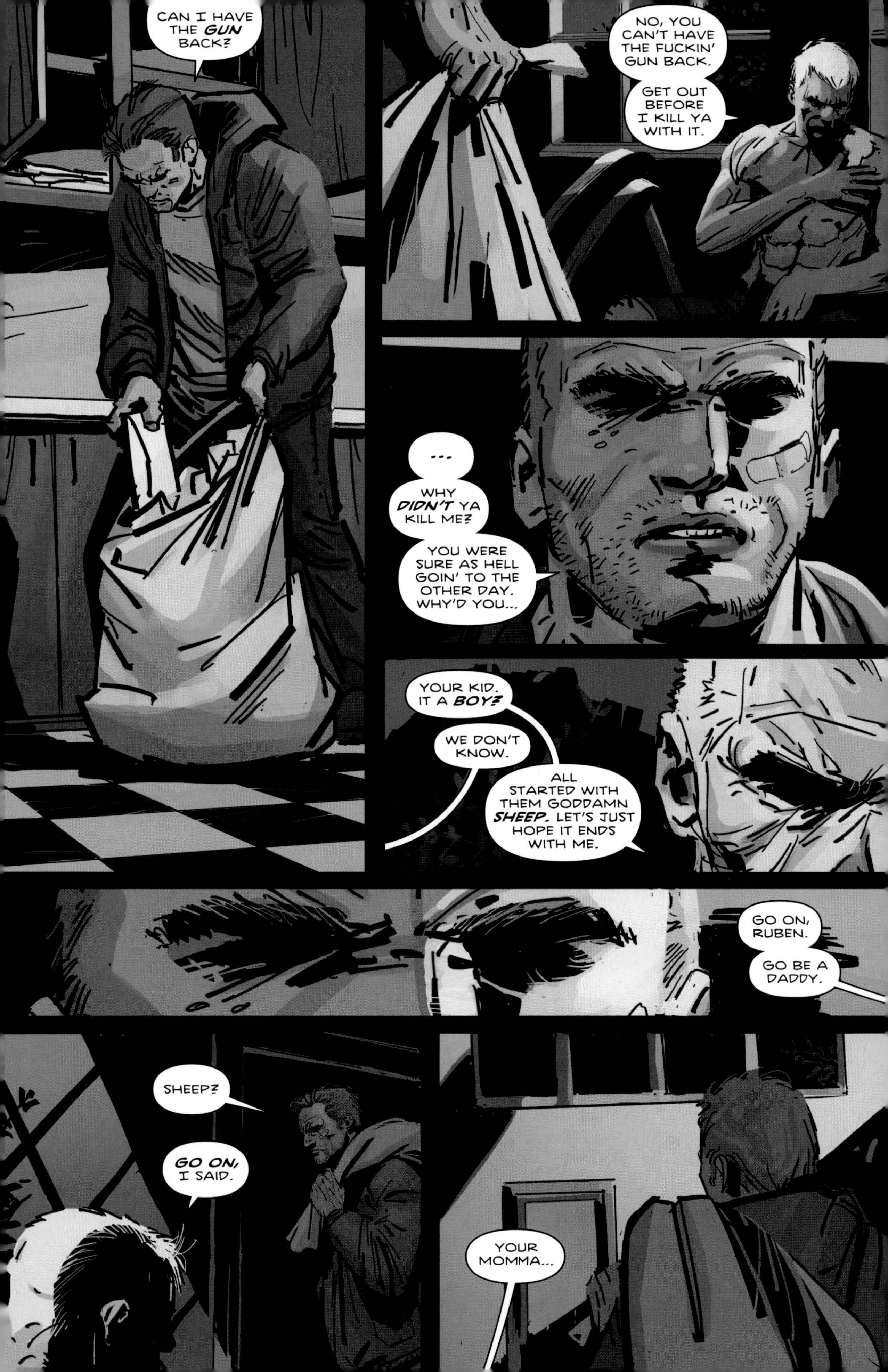
CAN I HAVE THE GUN BACK?
NO, YOU CAN'T HAVE THE FUCKIN' GUN BACK.
GET OUT BEFORE I KILL YA WITH IT.
...
WHY DIDN'T YA KILL ME?
YOU WERE SURE AS HELL GOIN' TO THE OTHER DAY. WHY'D YOU...
YOUR KID. IT A BOY?
WE DON'T KNOW.
ALL STARTED WITH THEM GODDAMN SHEEP. LET'S JUST HOPE IT ENDS WITH ME.
GO ON, RUBEN.
GO BE A DADDY.
SHEEP?
GO ON, I SAID.
YOUR MOMMA...

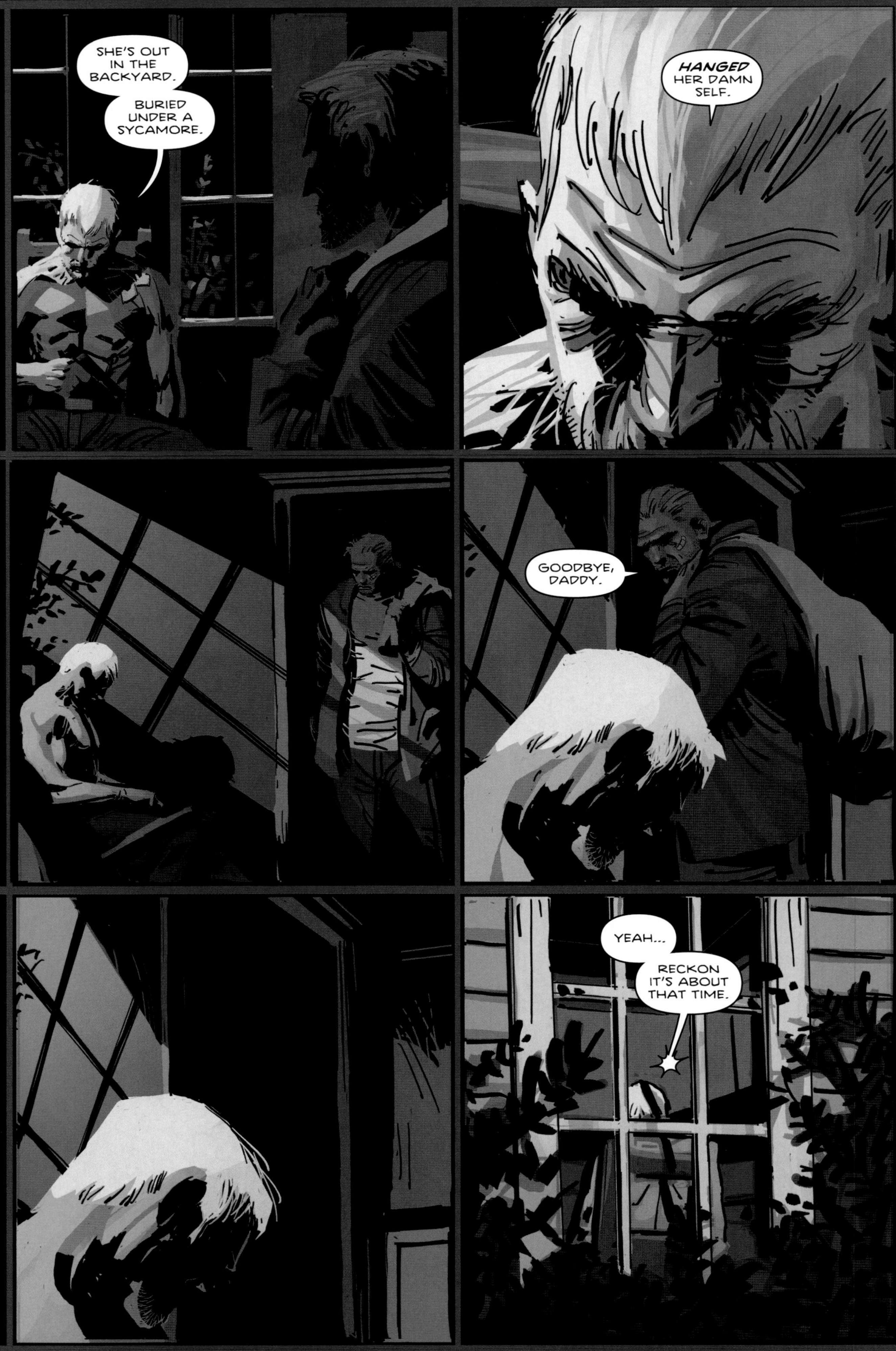
SHE'S OUT IN THE BACKYARD.
BURIED UNDER A SYCAMORE.
HANGED HER DAMN SELF.
GOODBYE, DADDY.
YEAH...
RECKON IT'S ABOUT THAT TIME.

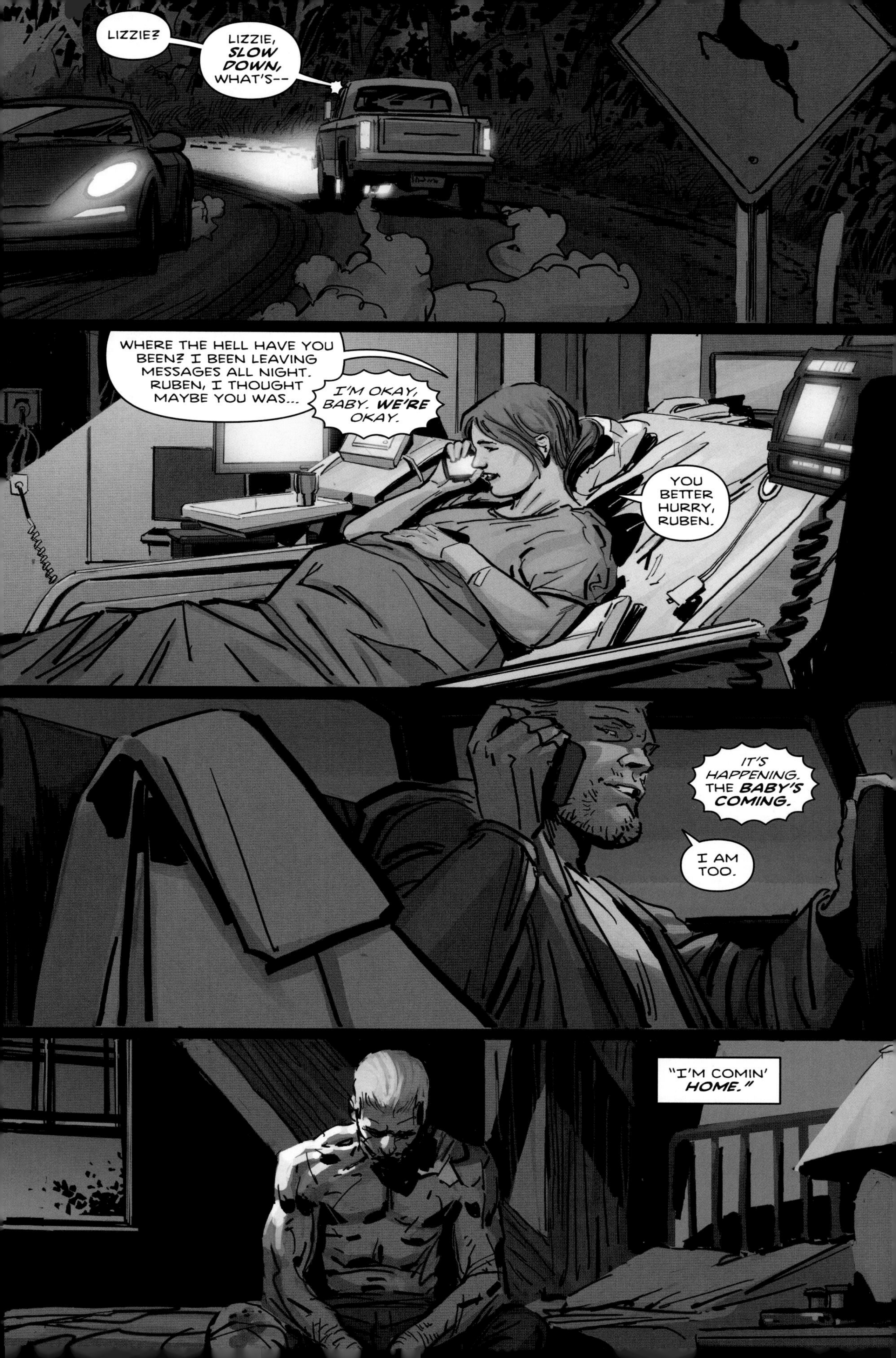
LIZZIE?
LIZZIE, SLOW DOWN, WHAT'S--
WHERE THE HELL HAVE YOU BEEN? I BEEN LEAVING MESSAGES ALL NIGHT. RUBEN, I THOUGHT MAYBE YOU WAS...
I'M OKAY, BABY. WE'RE OKAY.
YOU BETTER HURRY, RUBEN.
IT'S HAPPENING. THE BABY'S COMING.
I AM TOO.
"I'M COMIN' HOME."

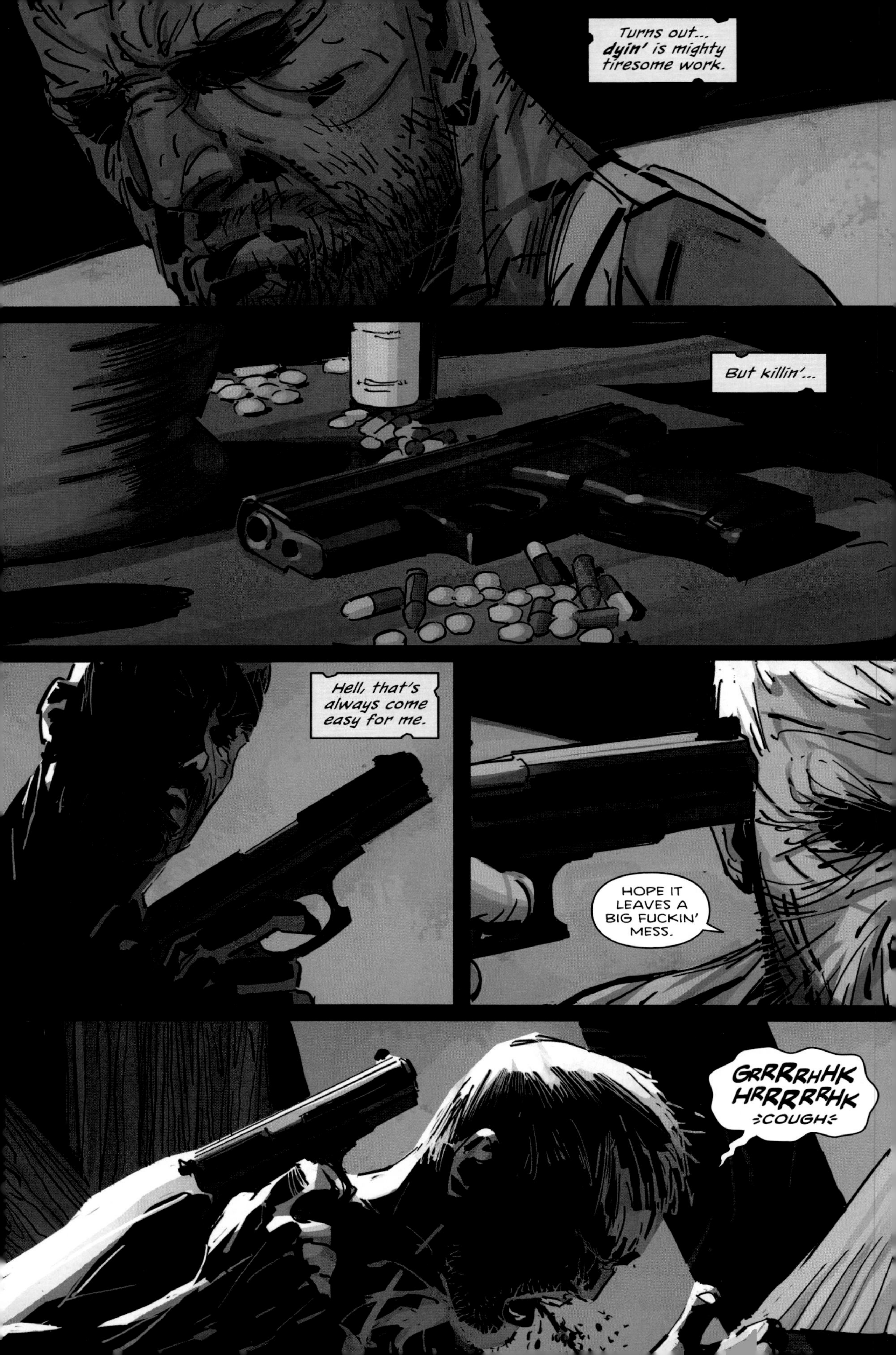
Turns out... dyin' is mighty tiresome work.
But killin'...
Hell, that's always come easy for me.
HOPE IT LEAVES A BIG FUCKIN' MESS.
GRRRRHHK HRRRRRHK
COUGH

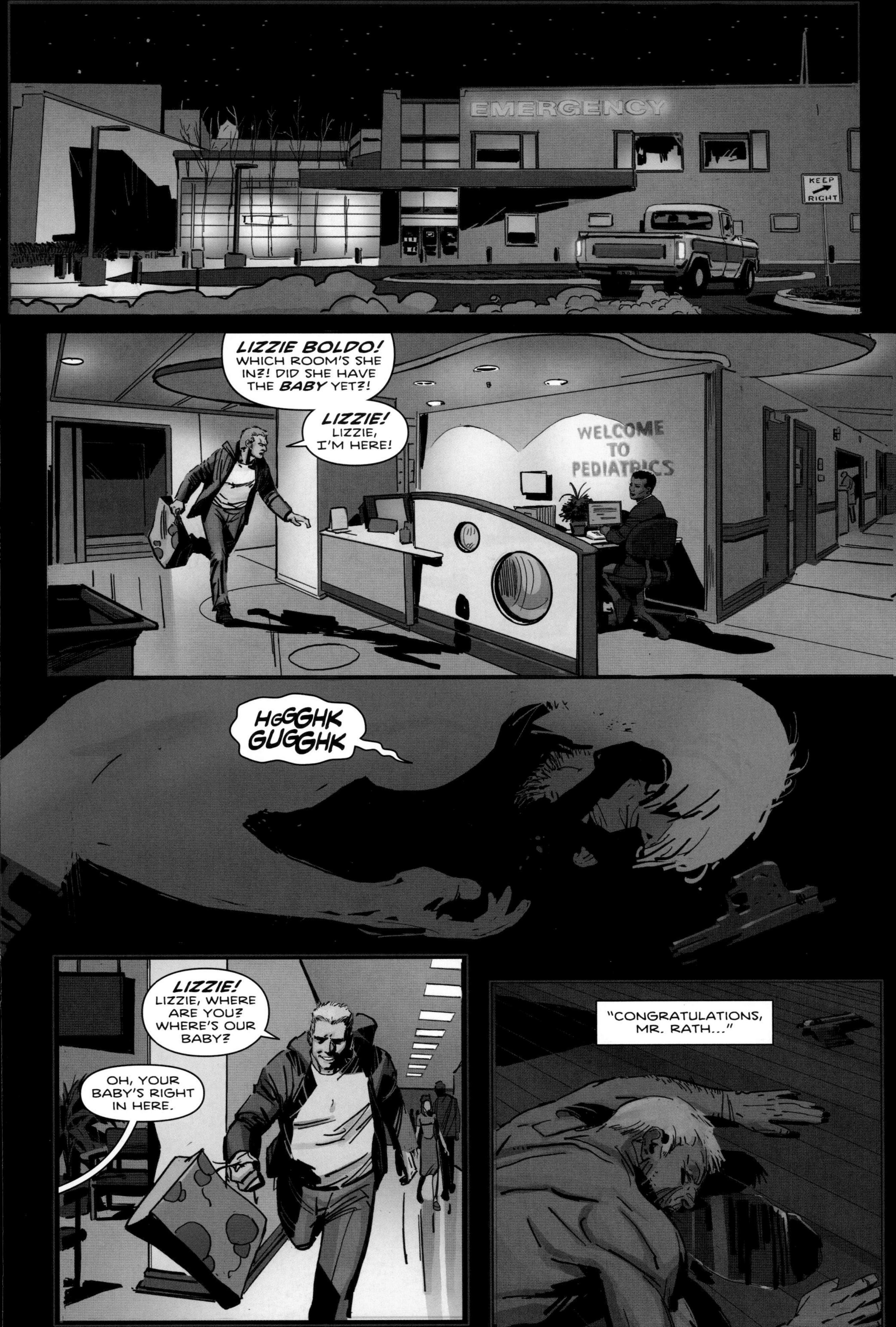
EMERGENCY
KEEP RIGHT
**LIZZIE BOLDO!** WHICH ROOM'S SHE IN?! DID SHE HAVE THE **BABY** YET?!
**LIZZIE!** LIZZIE, I'M HERE!
WELCOME TO PEDIATRICS
HGGGHK GUGGHK
**LIZZIE!** LIZZIE, WHERE ARE YOU? WHERE'S OUR BABY?
OH, YOUR BABY'S RIGHT IN HERE.
"CONGRATULATIONS, MR. RATH..."

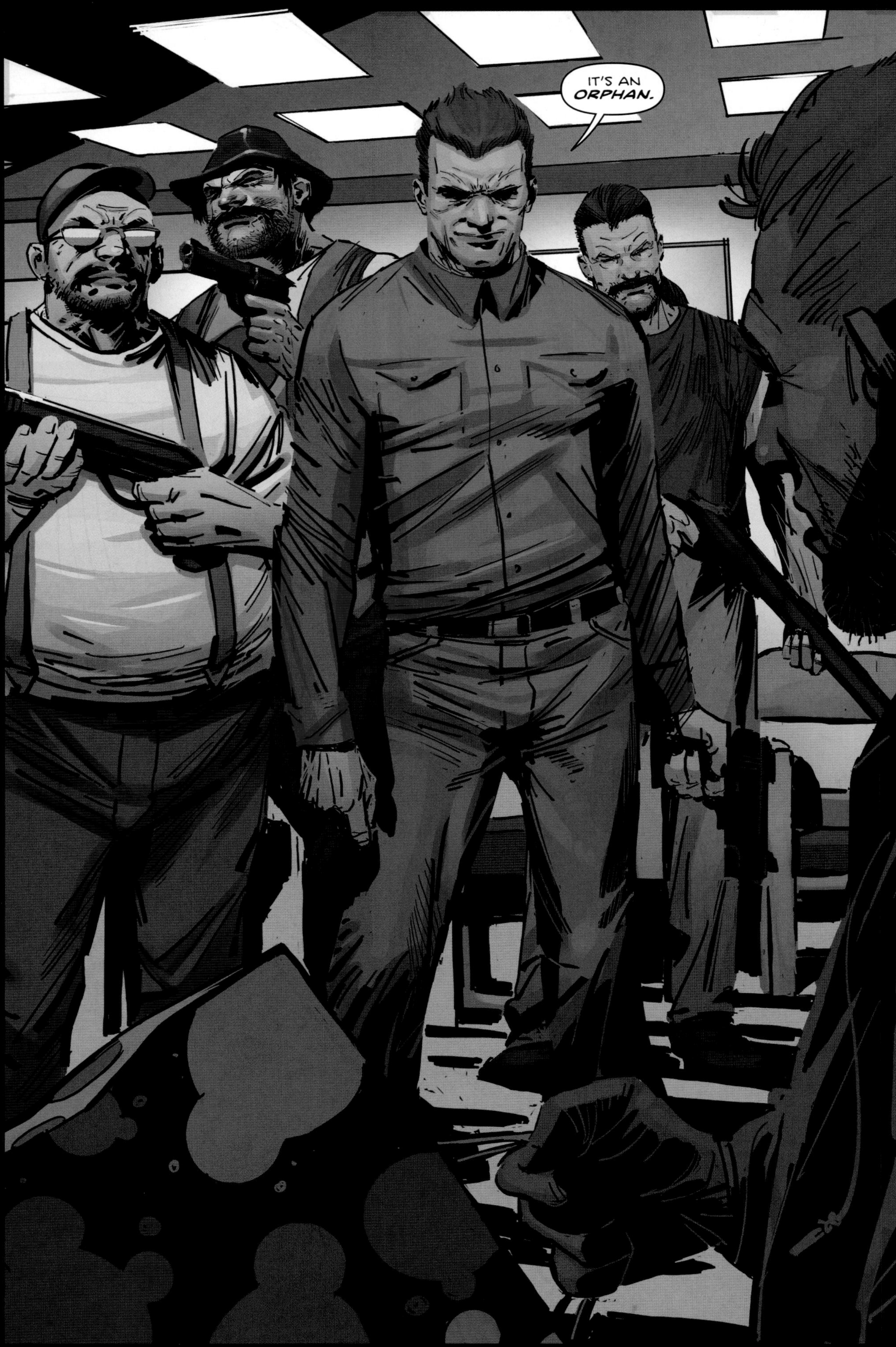
IT'S AN ORPHAN.

# CHAPTER FIVE

## WRATH'S END

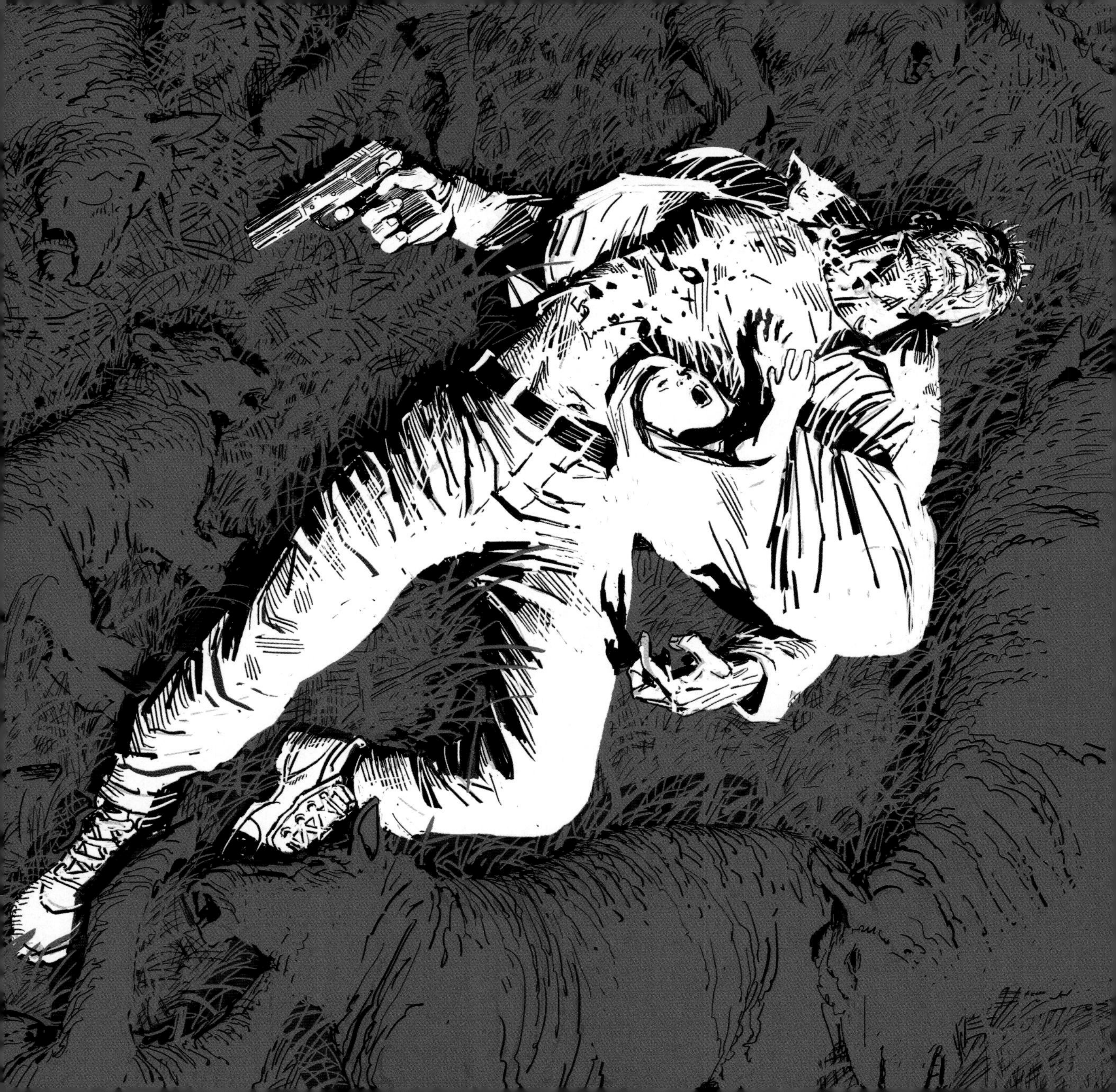

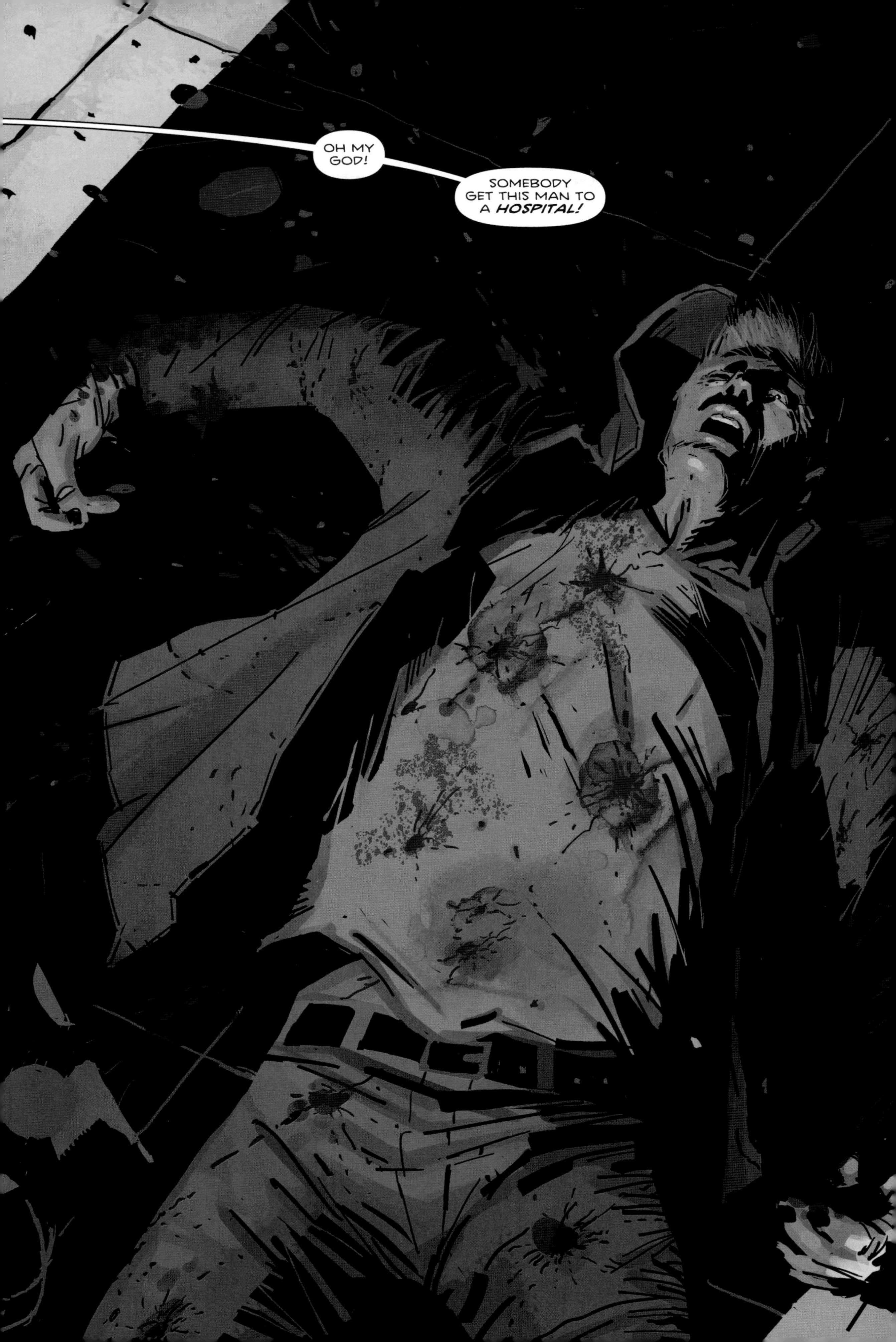
OH MY GOD!
SOMEBODY GET THIS MAN TO A HOSPITAL!

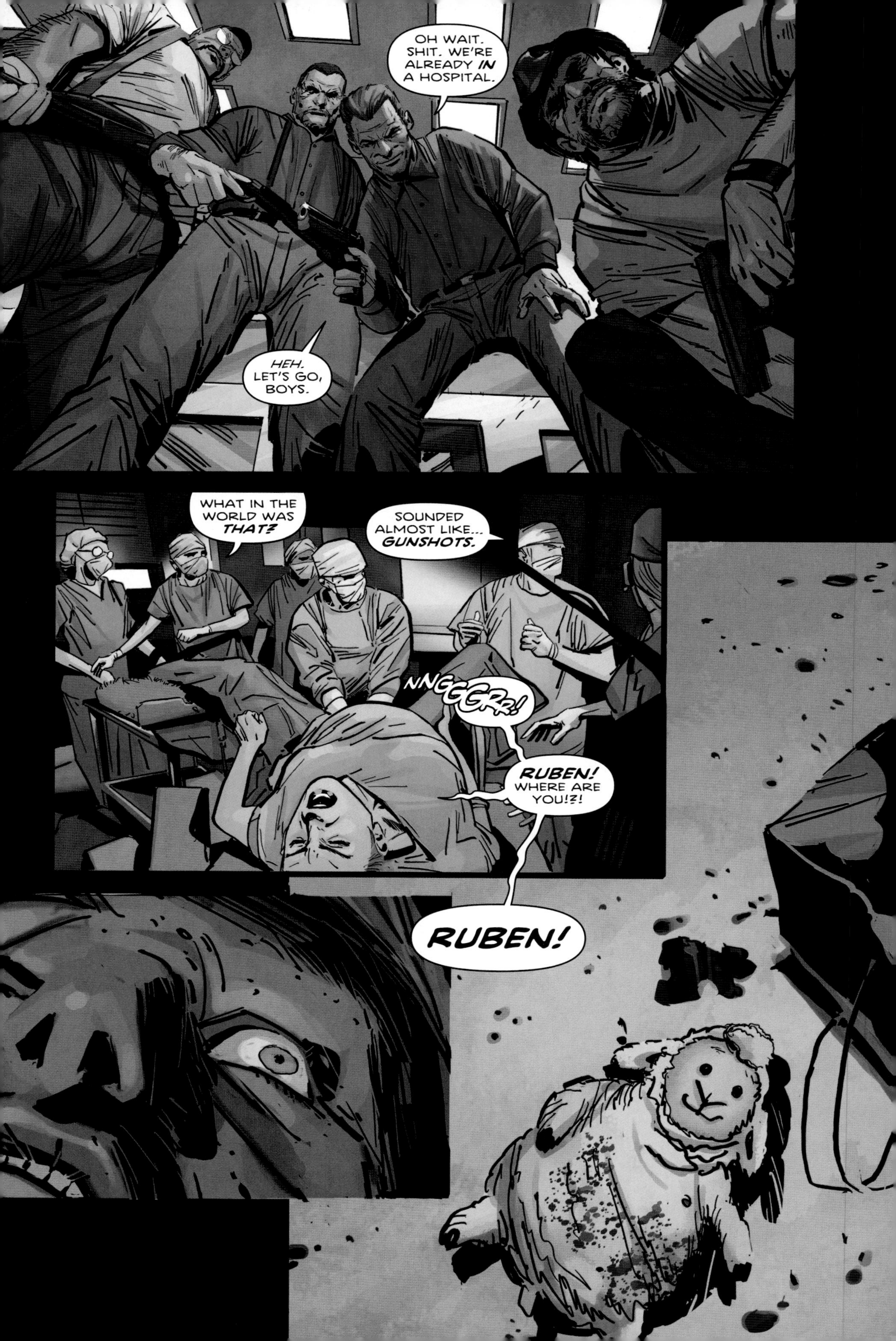
OH WAIT. SHIT. WE'RE ALREADY IN A HOSPITAL.
HEH. LET'S GO, BOYS.
WHAT IN THE WORLD WAS THAT?
SOUNDED ALMOST LIKE... GUNSHOTS.
NNGGGRR!
RUBEN! WHERE ARE YOU!?!
RUBEN!

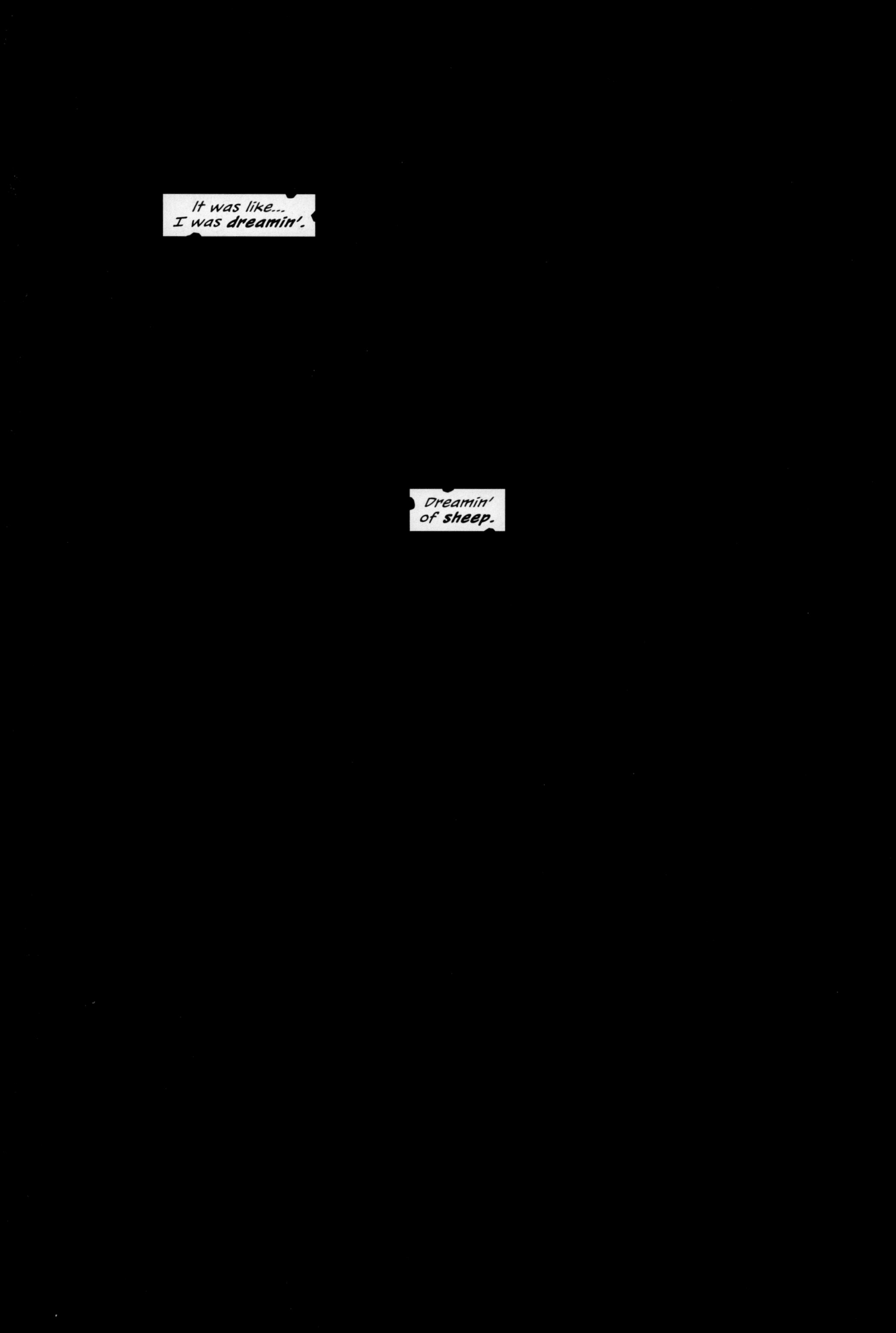
It was like... I was *dreamin'*.
Dreamin' of *sheep*.

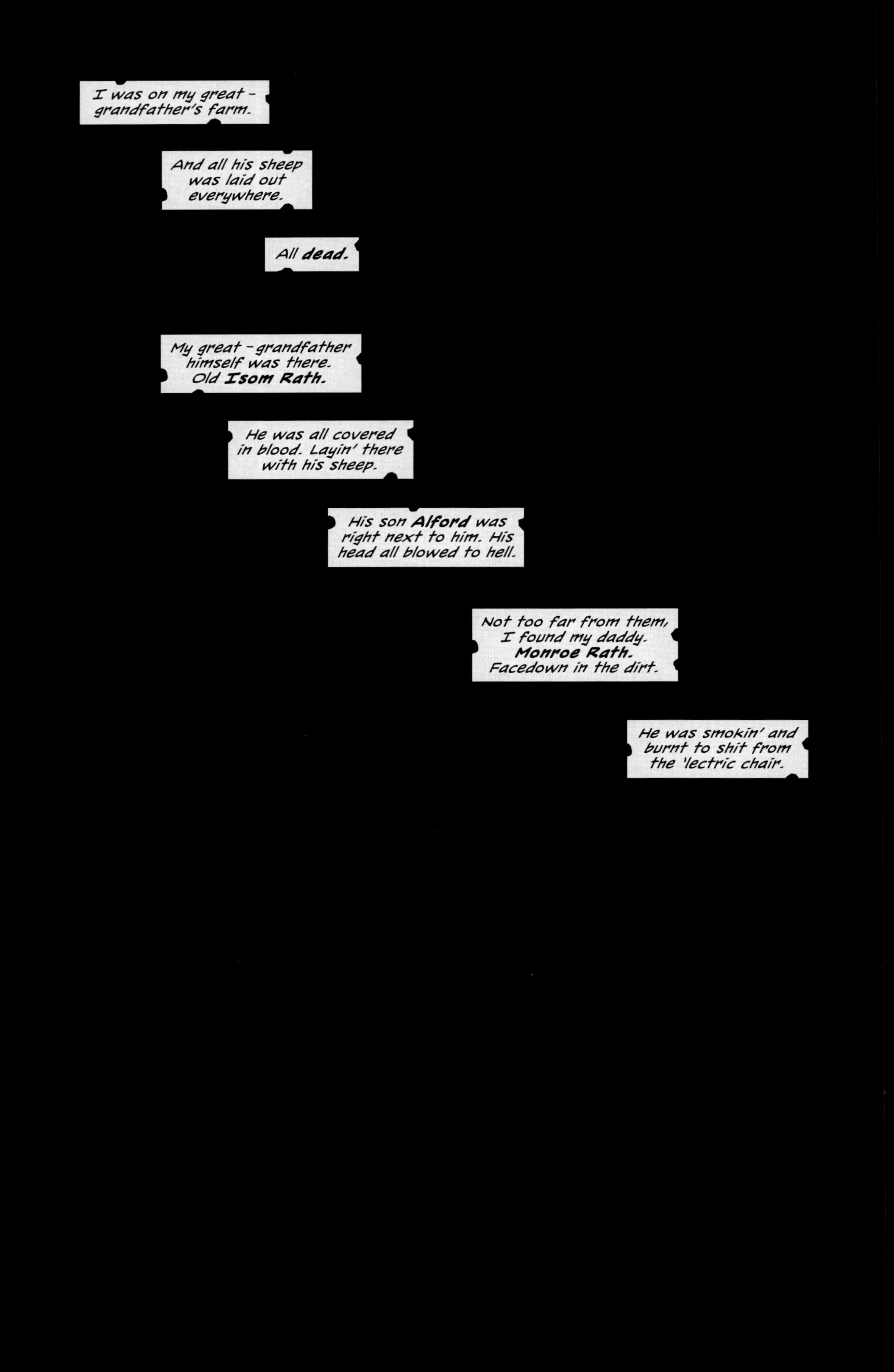
I was on my great-grandfather's farm.
And all his sheep was laid out everywhere.
All dead.
My great-grandfather himself was there. Old Isom Rath.
He was all covered in blood. Layin' there with his sheep.
His son Alford was right next to him. His head all blowed to hell.
Not too far from them, I found my daddy. Monroe Rath. Facedown in the dirt.
He was smokin' and burnt to shit from the 'lectric chair.

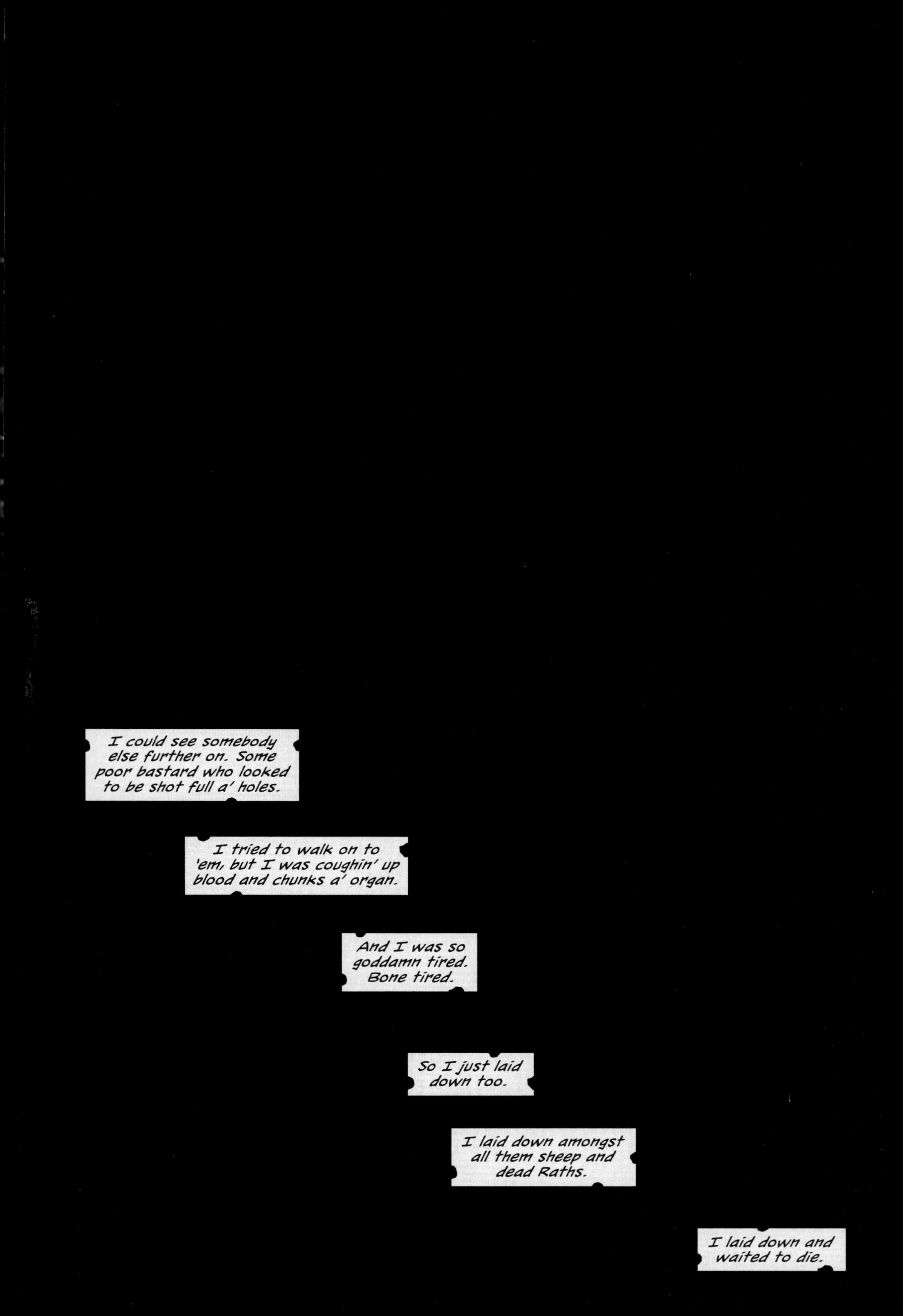
I could see somebody else further on. Some poor bastard who looked to be shot full a' holes.
I tried to walk on to 'em, but I was coughin' up blood and chunks a' organ.
And I was so goddamn tired. Bone tired.
So I just laid down too.
I laid down amongst all them sheep and dead Raths.
I laid down and waited to die.

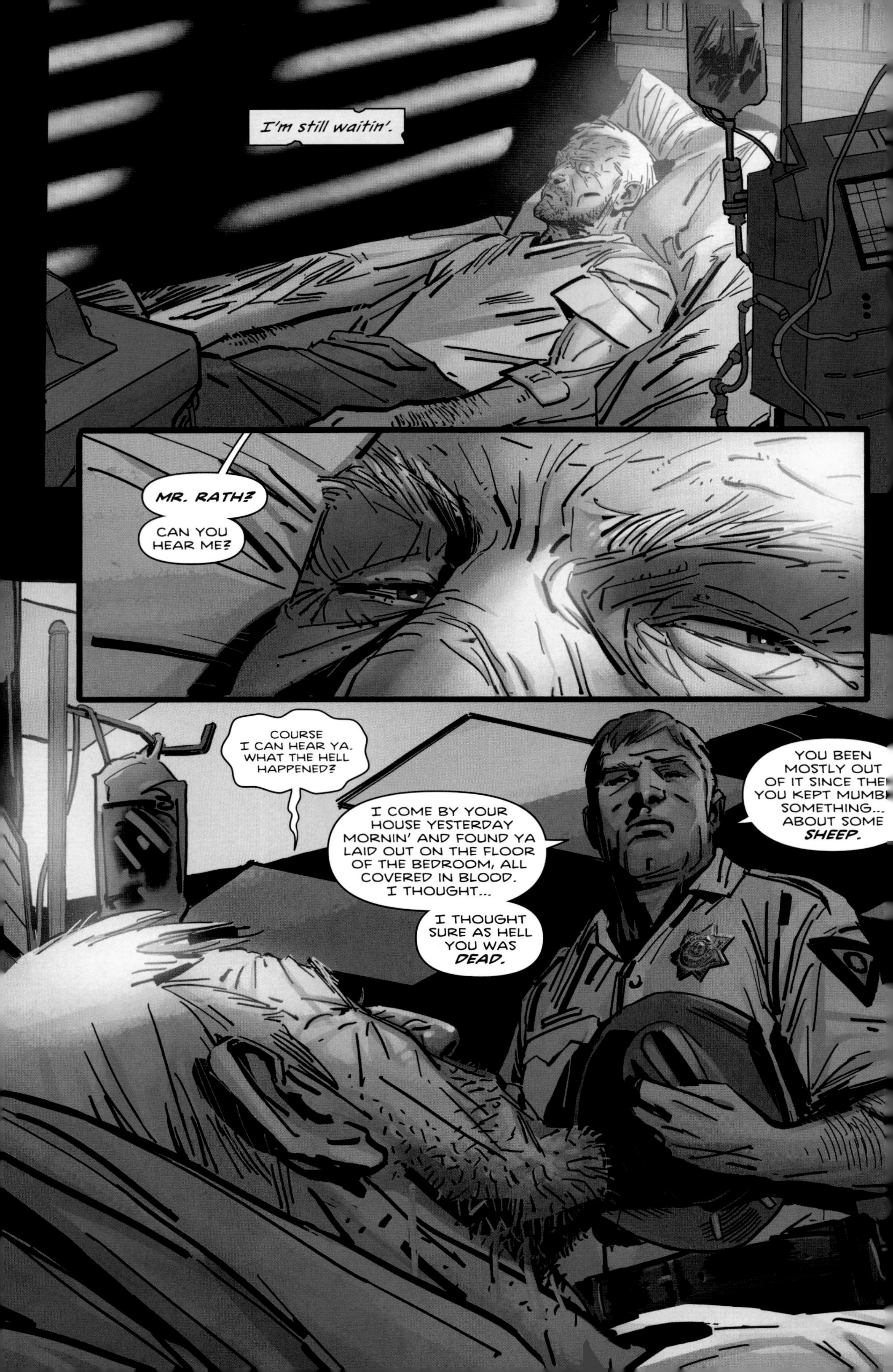
I'm still waitin'.
MR. RATH?
CAN YOU HEAR ME?
COURSE I CAN HEAR YA. WHAT THE HELL HAPPENED?
I COME BY YOUR HOUSE YESTERDAY MORNIN' AND FOUND YA LAID OUT ON THE FLOOR OF THE BEDROOM, ALL COVERED IN BLOOD. I THOUGHT...
I THOUGHT SURE AS HELL YOU WAS DEAD.
YOU BEEN MOSTLY OUT OF IT SINCE THE YOU KEPT MUMB SOMETHING... ABOUT SOME SHEEP.

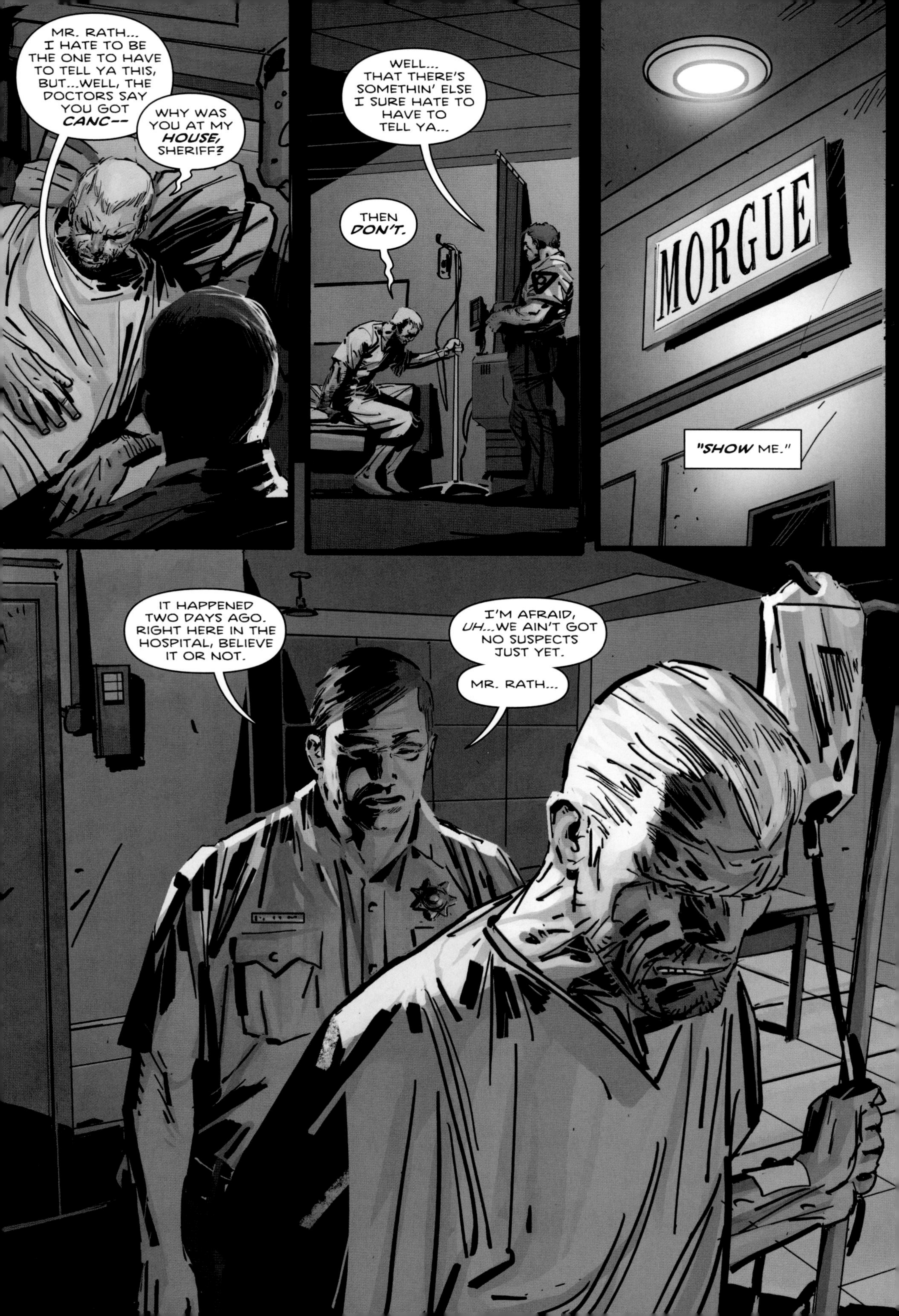
MR. RATH... I HATE TO BE THE ONE TO HAVE TO TELL YA THIS, BUT...WELL, THE DOCTORS SAY YOU GOT CANC--
WHY WAS YOU AT MY HOUSE, SHERIFF?
WELL... THAT THERE'S SOMETHIN' ELSE I SURE HATE TO HAVE TO TELL YA...
THEN DON'T.
MORGUE
"SHOW ME."
IT HAPPENED TWO DAYS AGO. RIGHT HERE IN THE HOSPITAL, BELIEVE IT OR NOT.
I'M AFRAID, UH...WE AIN'T GOT NO SUSPECTS JUST YET.
MR. RATH...

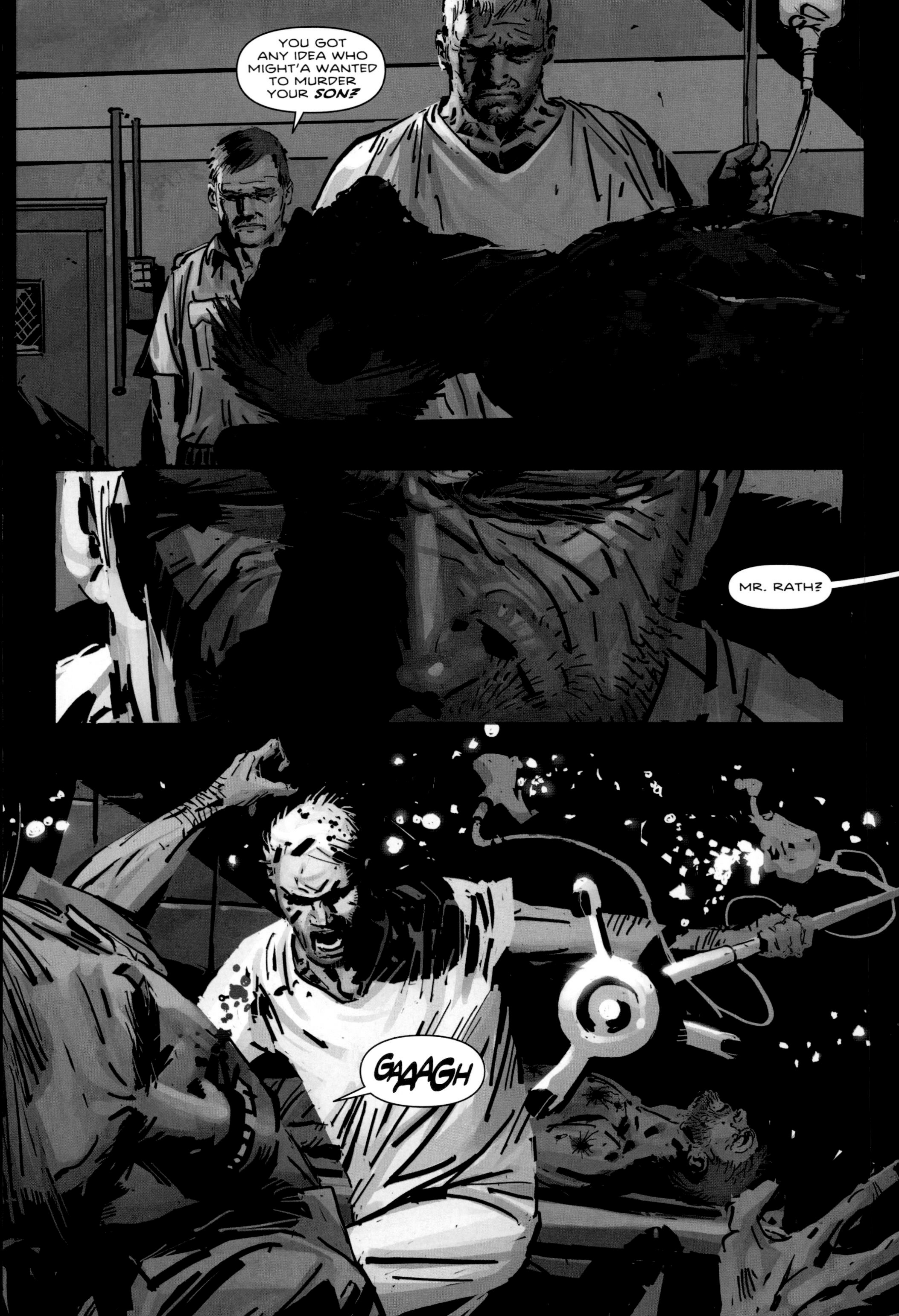
YOU GOT ANY IDEA WHO MIGHT'A WANTED TO MURDER YOUR SON?
MR. RATH?
GAAAGH

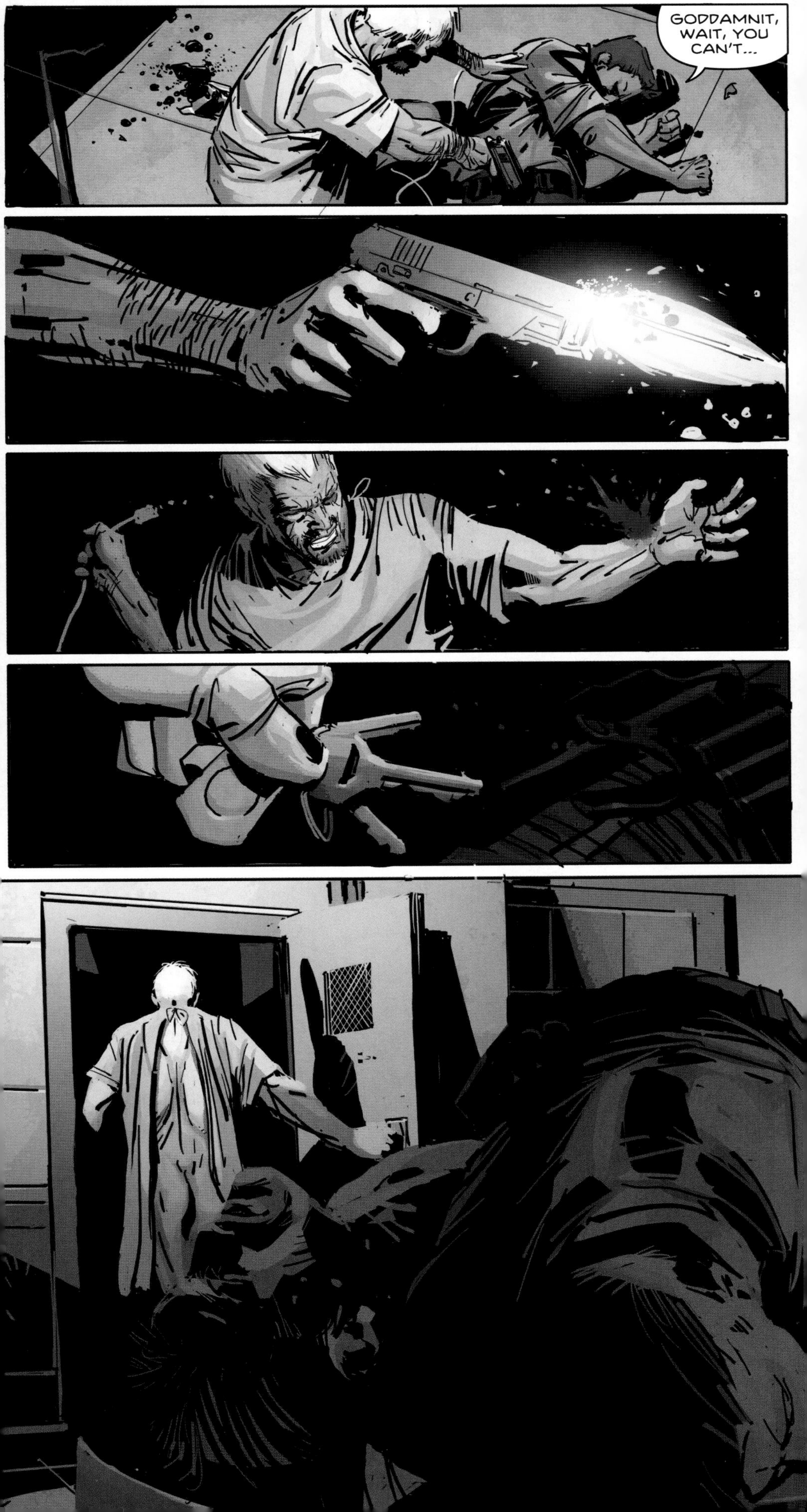
GODDAMNIT, WAIT, YOU CAN'T...

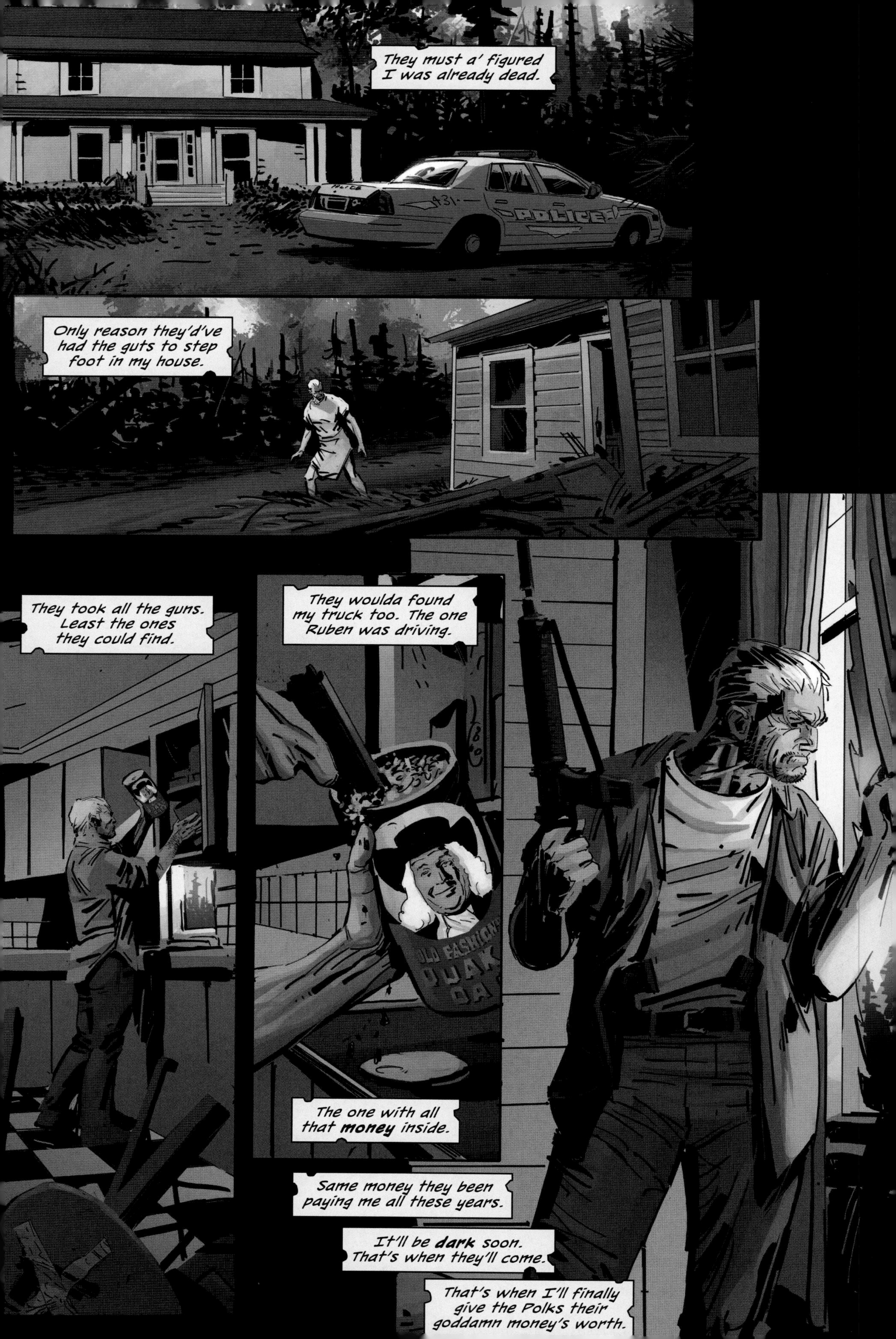
They must a' figured I was already dead.
Only reason they'd've had the guts to step foot in my house.
They took all the guns. Least the ones they could find.
They woulda found my truck too. The one Ruben was driving.
The one with all that **money** inside.
Same money they been paying me all these years.
It'll be **dark** soon. That's when they'll come.
That's when I'll finally give the Polks their goddamn money's worth.

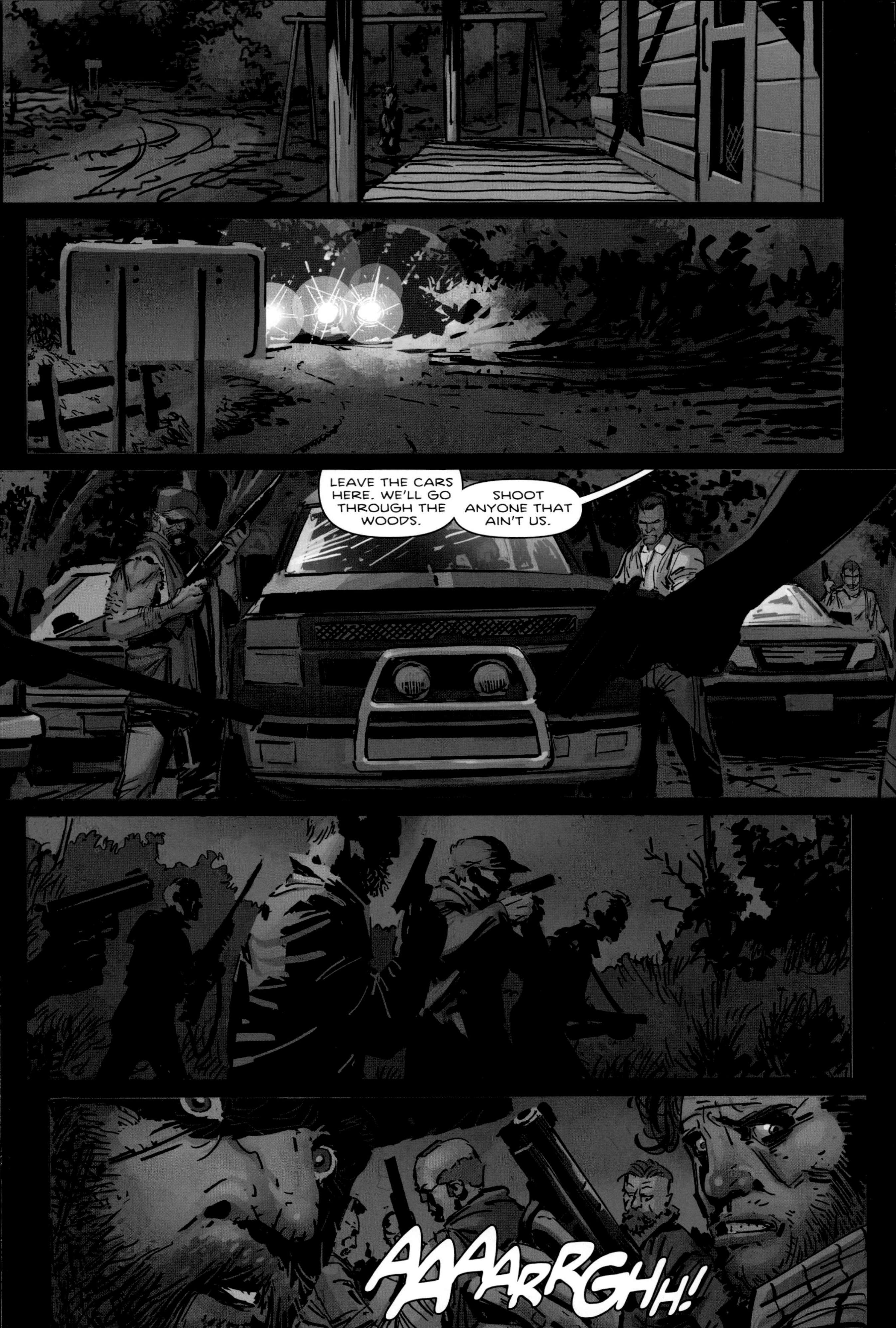
LEAVE THE CARS HERE. WE'LL GO THROUGH THE WOODS.
SHOOT ANYONE THAT AIN'T US.
AAAARRGHH!

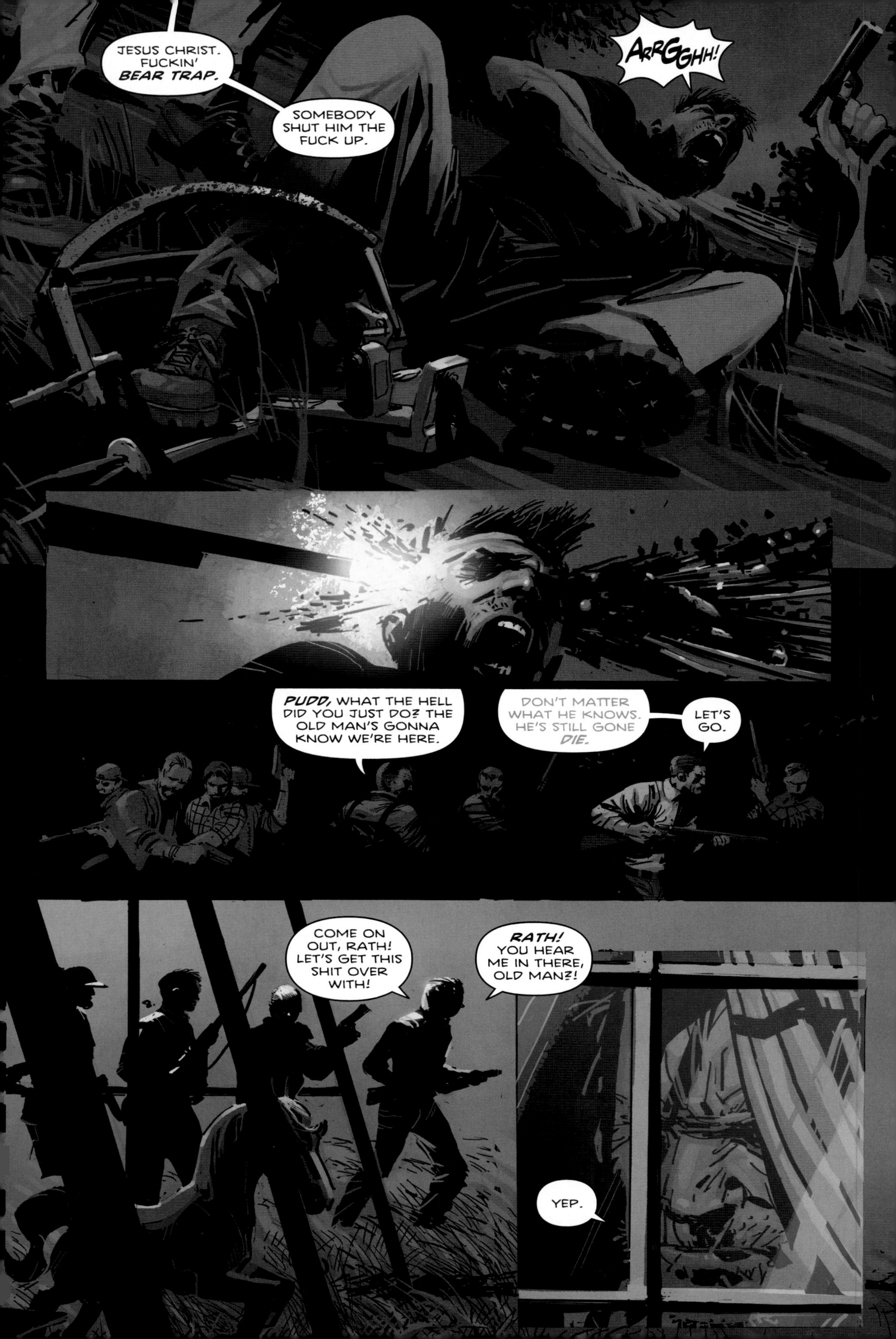
JESUS CHRIST. FUCKIN' BEAR TRAP.
SOMEBODY SHUT HIM THE FUCK UP.
ARRGGHH!
PUDD, WHAT THE HELL DID YOU JUST DO? THE OLD MAN'S GONNA KNOW WE'RE HERE.
DON'T MATTER WHAT HE KNOWS. HE'S STILL GONE DIE.
LET'S GO.
COME ON OUT, RATH! LET'S GET THIS SHIT OVER WITH!
RATH! YOU HEAR ME IN THERE, OLD MAN?!
YEP.

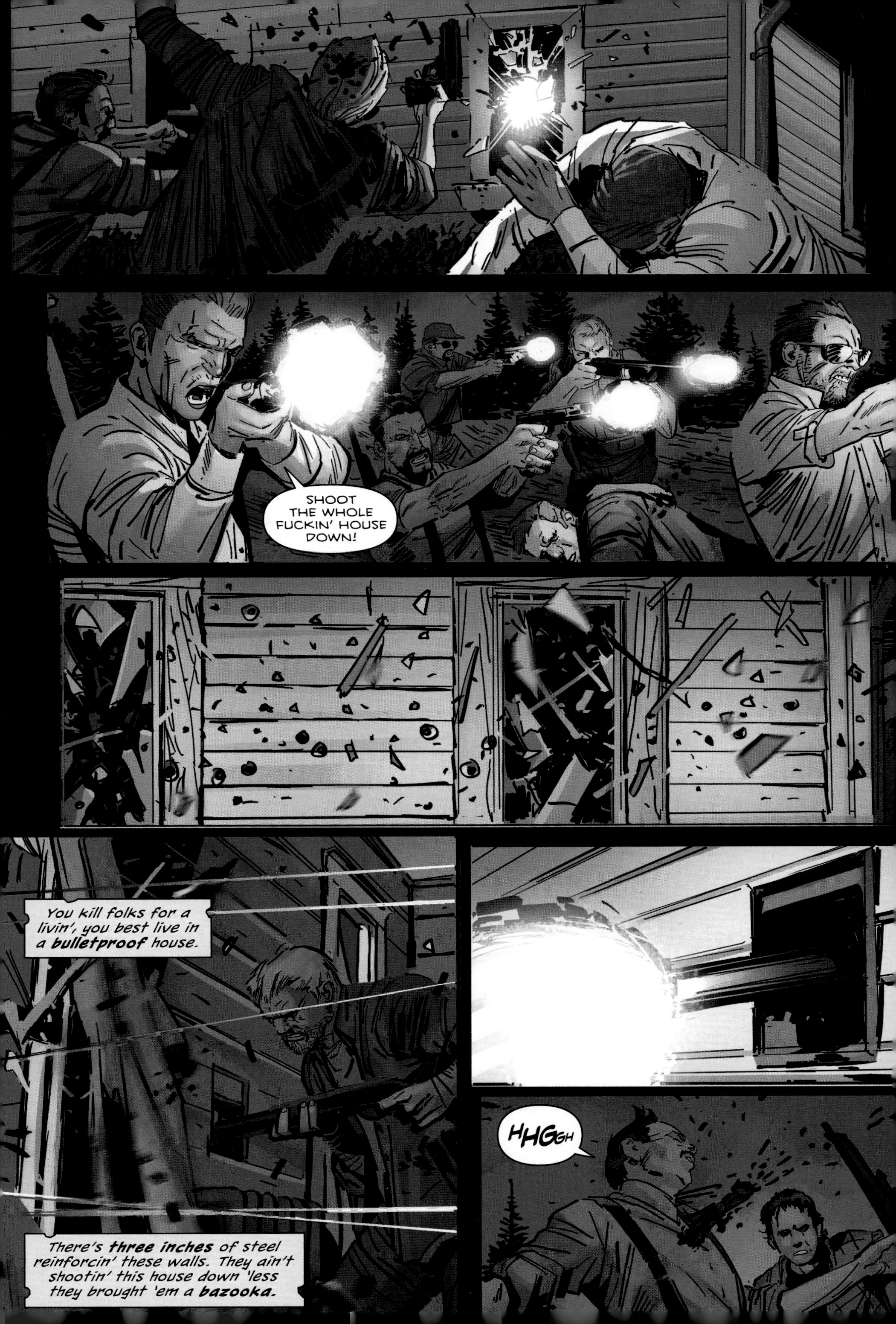
SHOOT THE WHOLE FUCKIN' HOUSE DOWN!
You kill folks for a livin', you best live in a **bulletproof** house.
There's **three inches** of steel reinforcin' these walls. They ain't shootin' this house down 'less they brought 'em a **bazooka.**
HHGGH

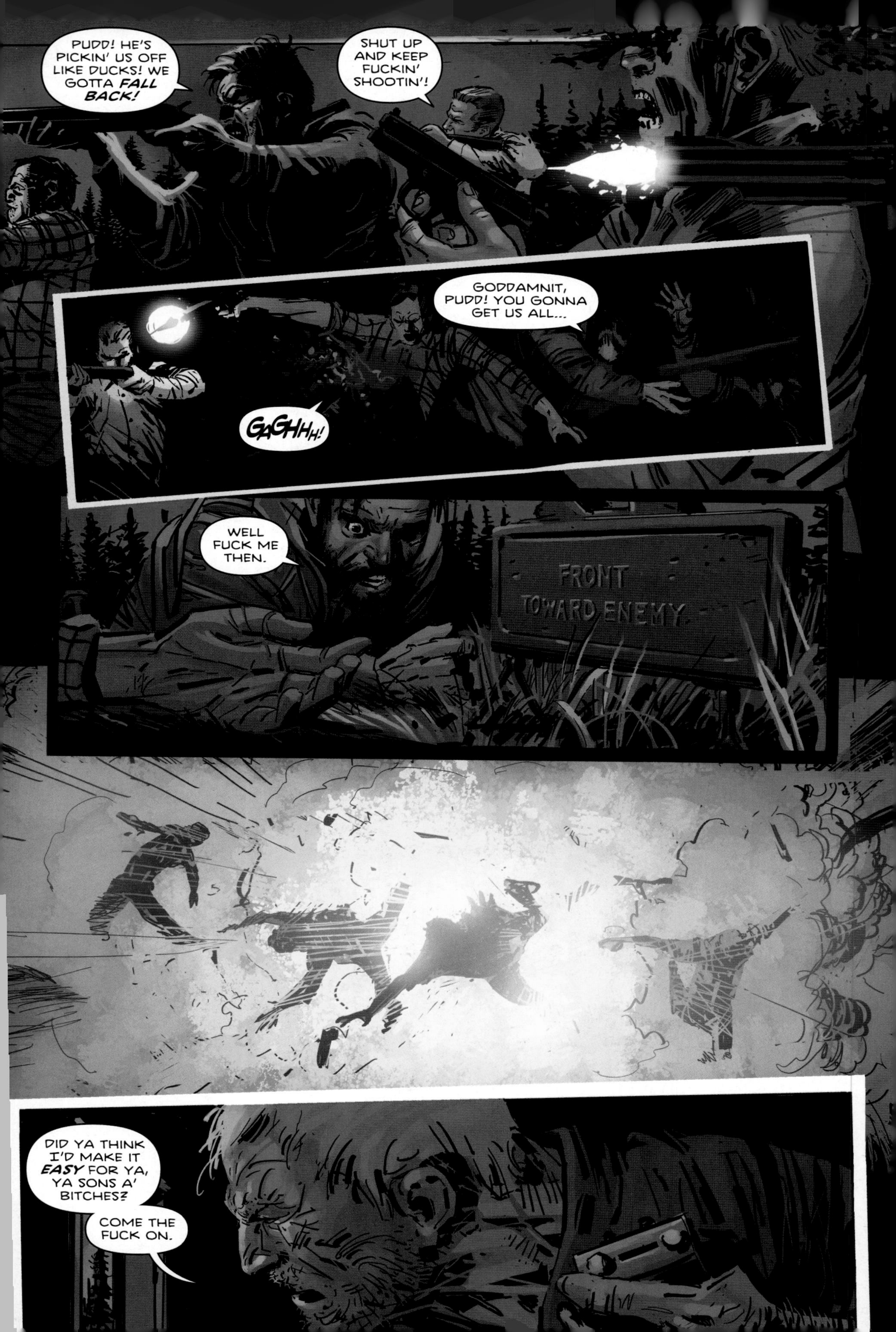
PUDD! HE'S PICKIN' US OFF LIKE DUCKS! WE GOTTA **FALL BACK!**
SHUT UP AND KEEP FUCKIN' SHOOTIN'!
GODDAMNIT, PUDD! YOU GONNA GET US ALL...
GAGHHH!
WELL FUCK ME THEN.
FRONT TOWARD ENEMY.
DID YA THINK I'D MAKE IT **EASY** FOR YA, YA SONS A' BITCHES?
COME THE FUCK ON.

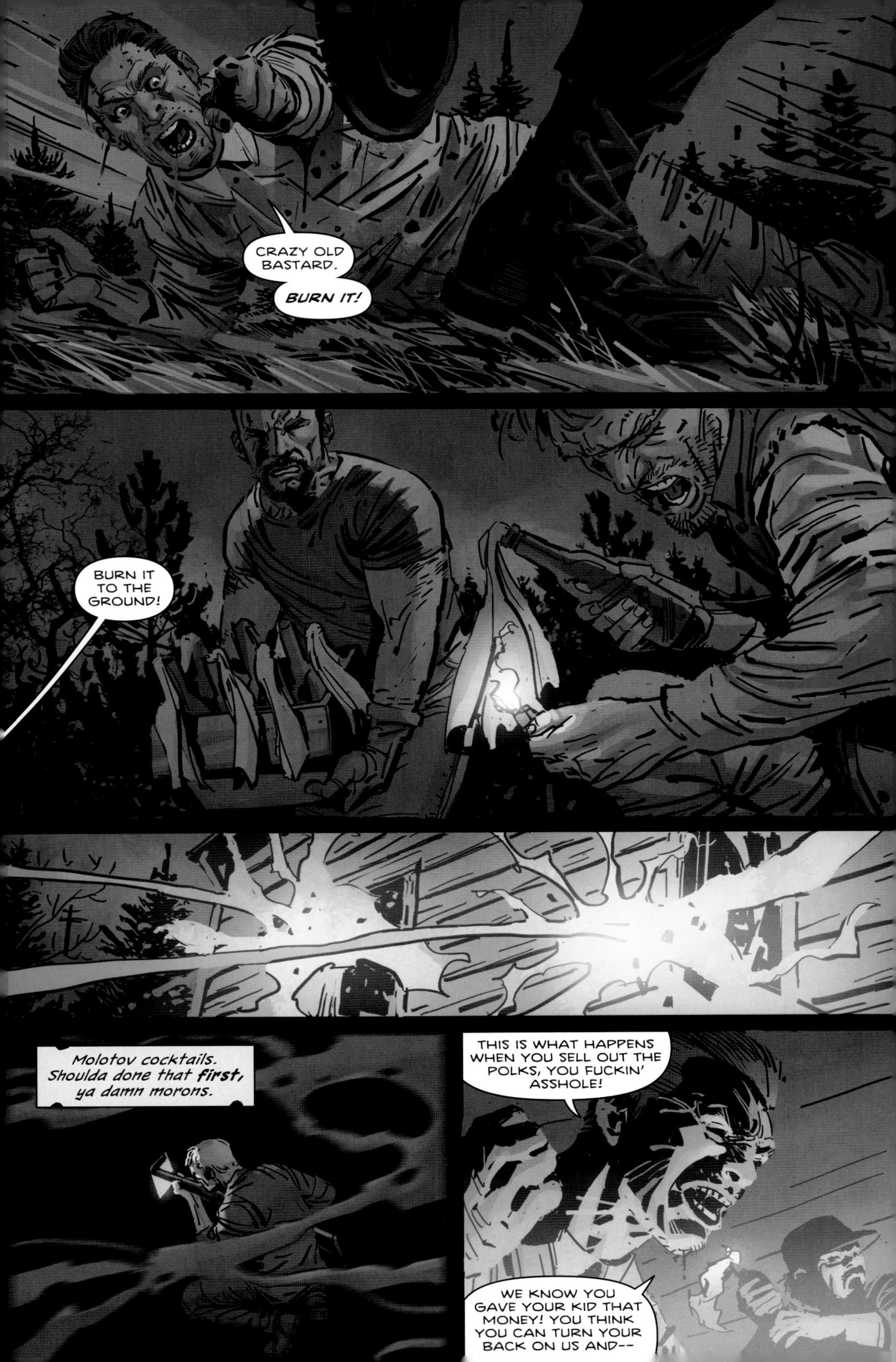
CRAZY OLD BASTARD.
*BURN IT!*
BURN IT TO THE GROUND!
Molotov cocktails. Shoulda done that **first**, ya damn morons.
THIS IS WHAT HAPPENS WHEN YOU SELL OUT THE POLKS, YOU FUCKIN' ASSHOLE!
WE KNOW YOU GAVE YOUR KID THAT MONEY! YOU THINK YOU CAN TURN YOUR BACK ON US AND--

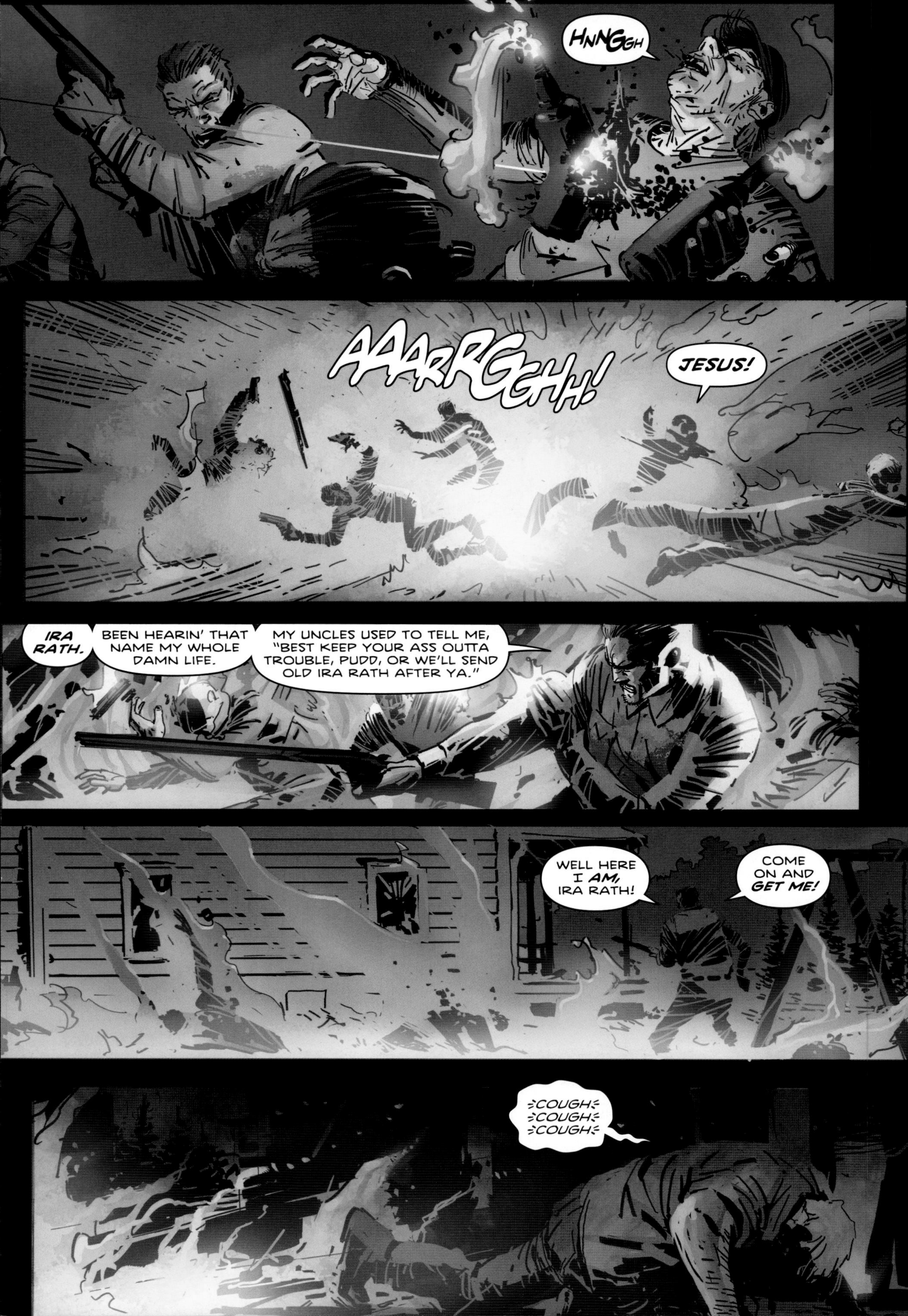
HNNGGH
AAARRGGHH!
JESUS!
IRA RATH.
BEEN HEARIN' THAT NAME MY WHOLE DAMN LIFE.
MY UNCLES USED TO TELL ME, "BEST KEEP YOUR ASS OUTTA TROUBLE, PUDD, OR WE'LL SEND OLD IRA RATH AFTER YA."
WELL HERE I AM, IRA RATH!
COME ON AND GET ME!
COUGH COUGH COUGH

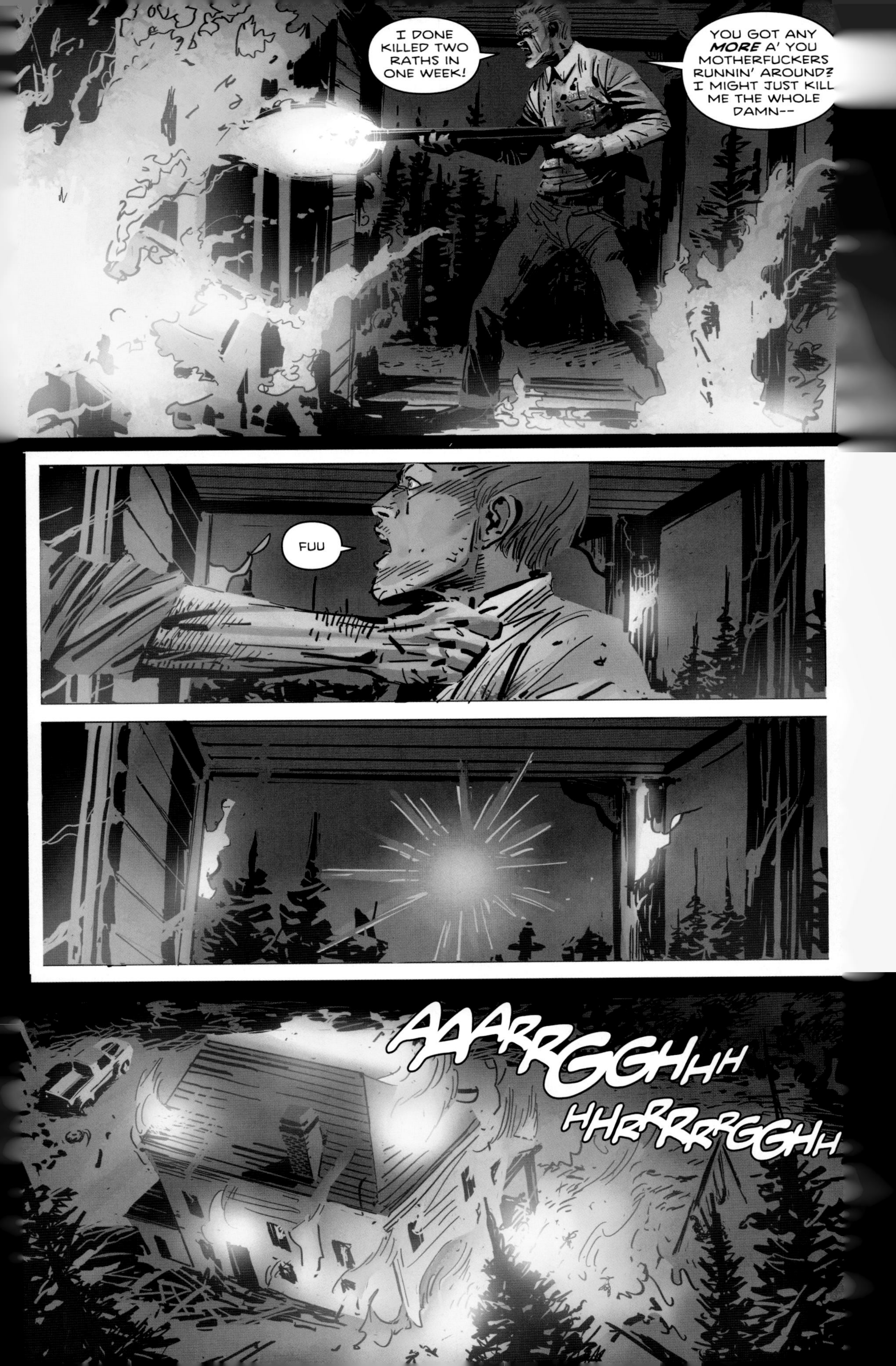
I DONE KILLED TWO RATHS IN ONE WEEK!
YOU GOT ANY MORE A' YOU MOTHERFUCKERS RUNNIN' AROUND? I MIGHT JUST KILL ME THE WHOLE DAMN--
FUU
AAARRGGHHH
HHRRRRRGGHH

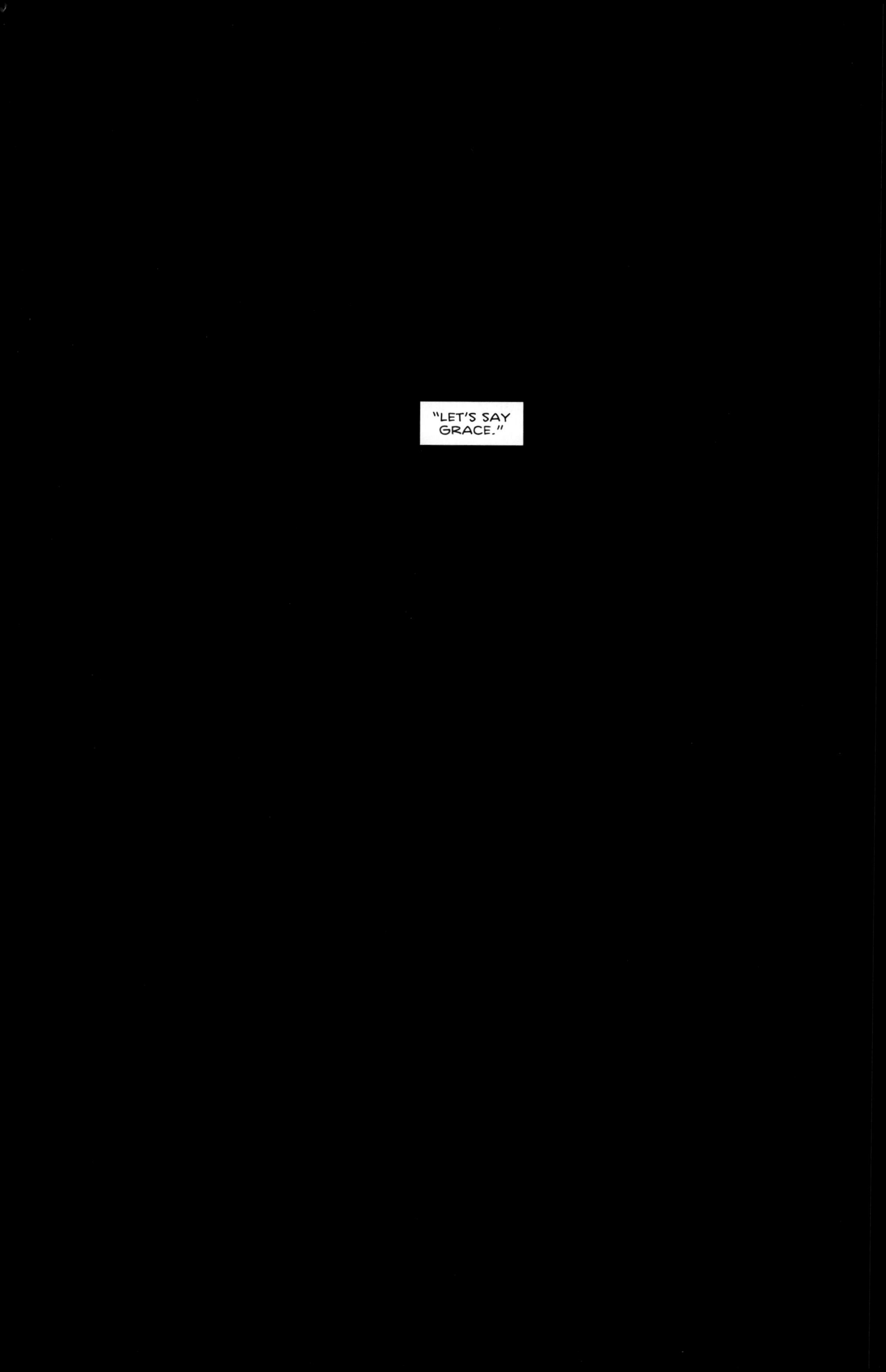
"LET'S SAY GRACE."

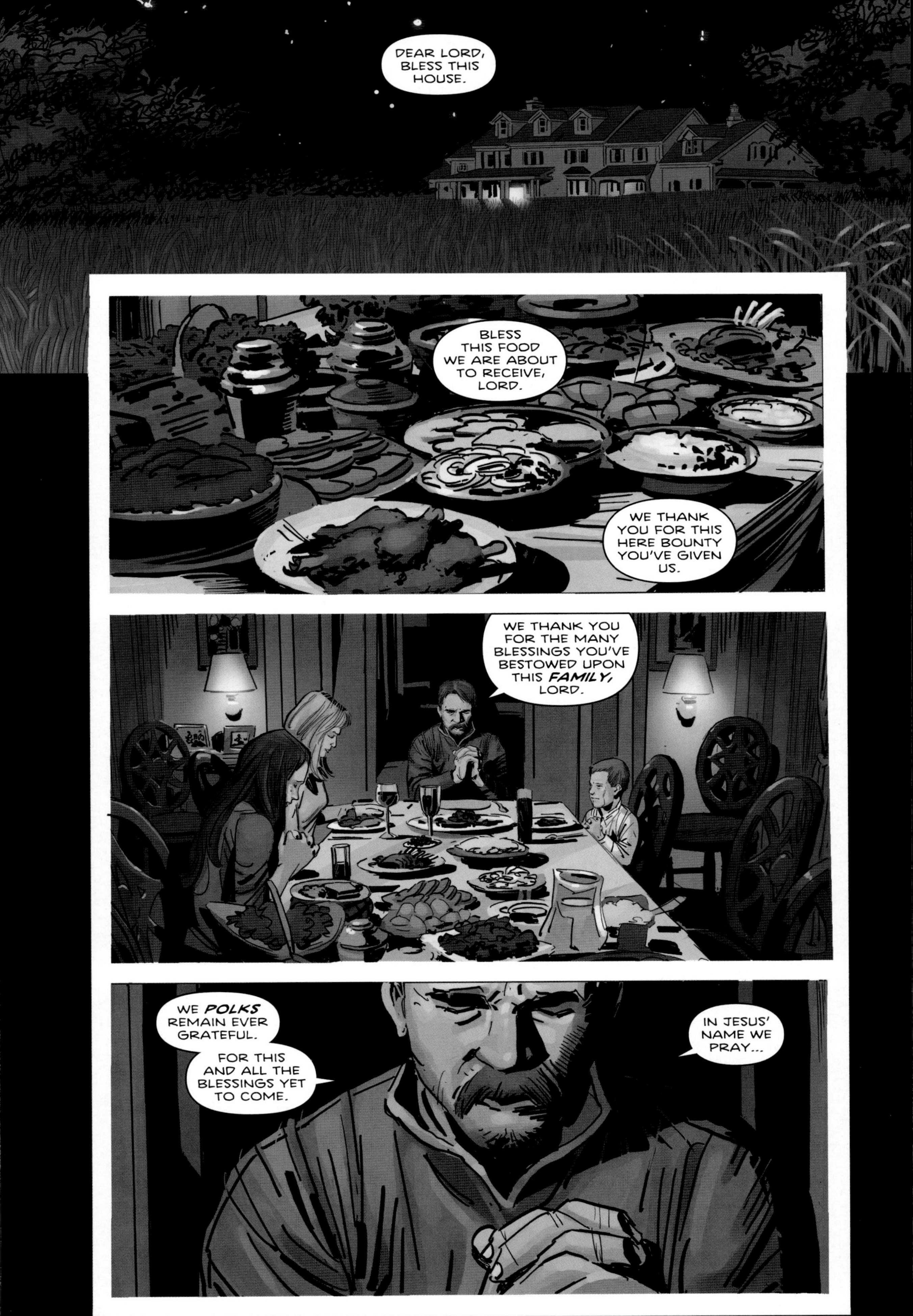
DEAR LORD, BLESS THIS HOUSE.
BLESS THIS FOOD WE ARE ABOUT TO RECEIVE, LORD.
WE THANK YOU FOR THIS HERE BOUNTY YOU'VE GIVEN US.
WE THANK YOU FOR THE MANY BLESSINGS YOU'VE BESTOWED UPON THIS *FAMILY,* LORD.
WE *POLKS* REMAIN EVER GRATEFUL.
FOR THIS AND ALL THE BLESSINGS YET TO COME.
IN JESUS' NAME WE PRAY...

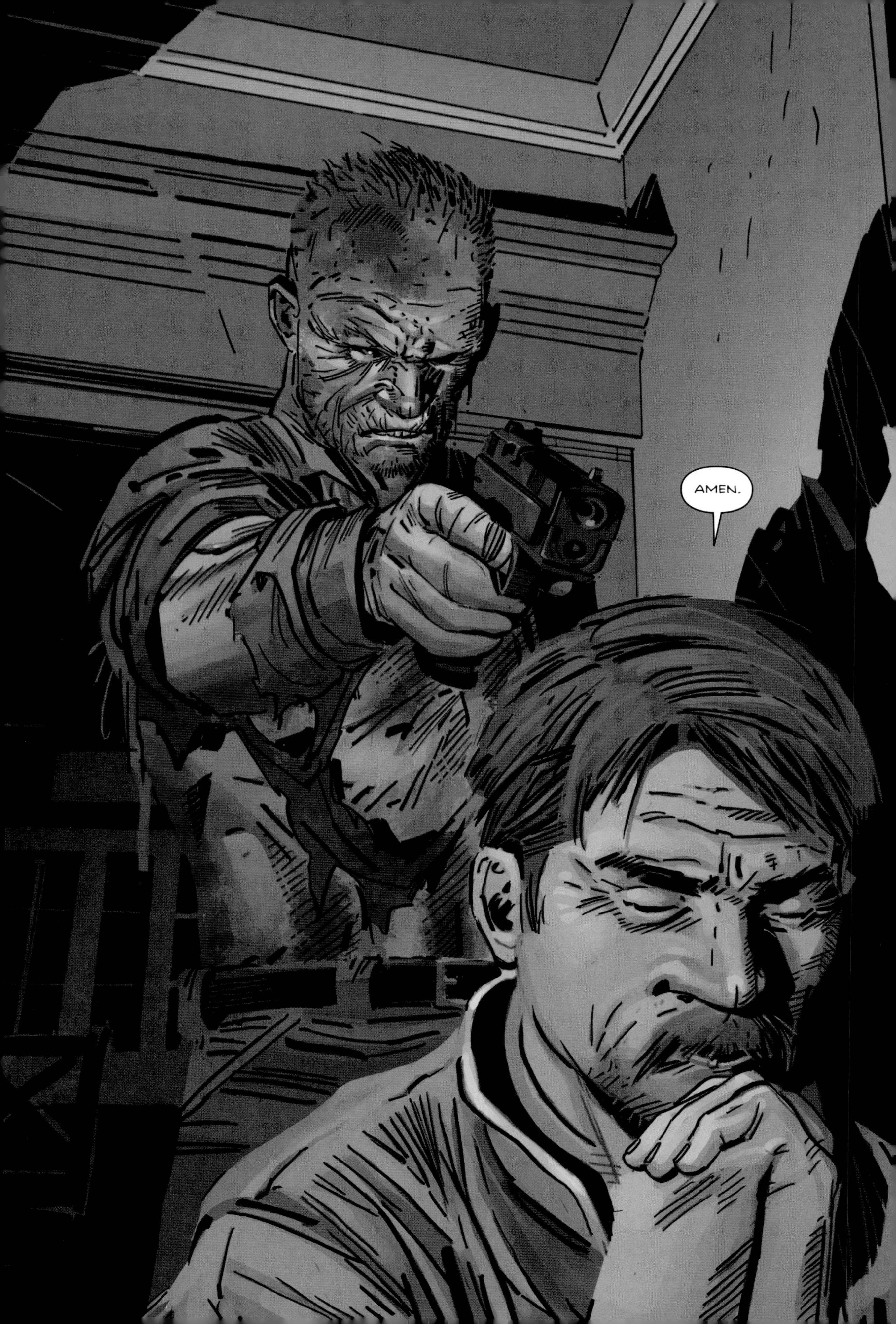
AMEN.

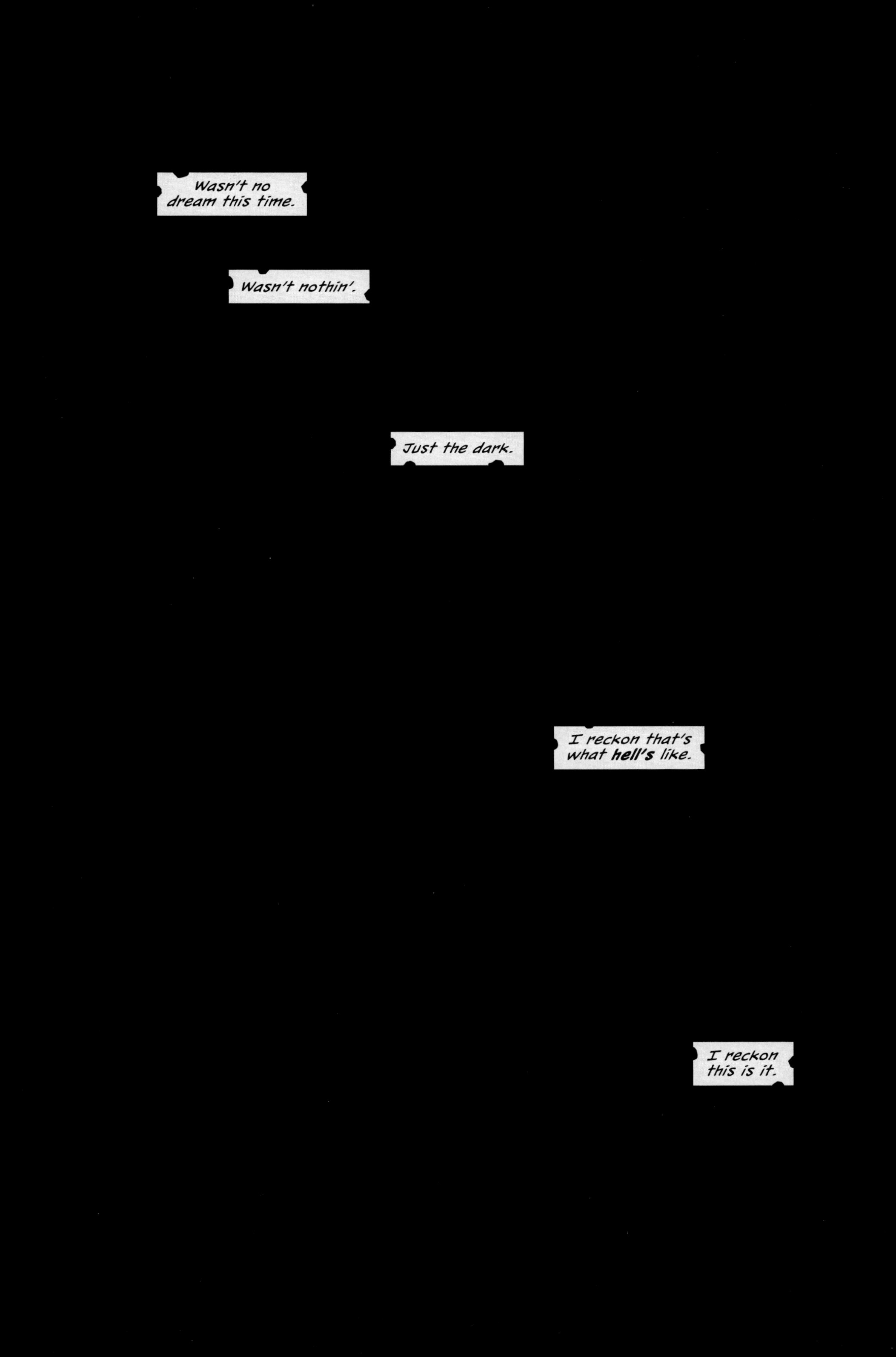
Wasn't no dream this time.
Wasn't nothin'.
Just the dark.
I reckon that's what **hell's** like.
I reckon this is it.

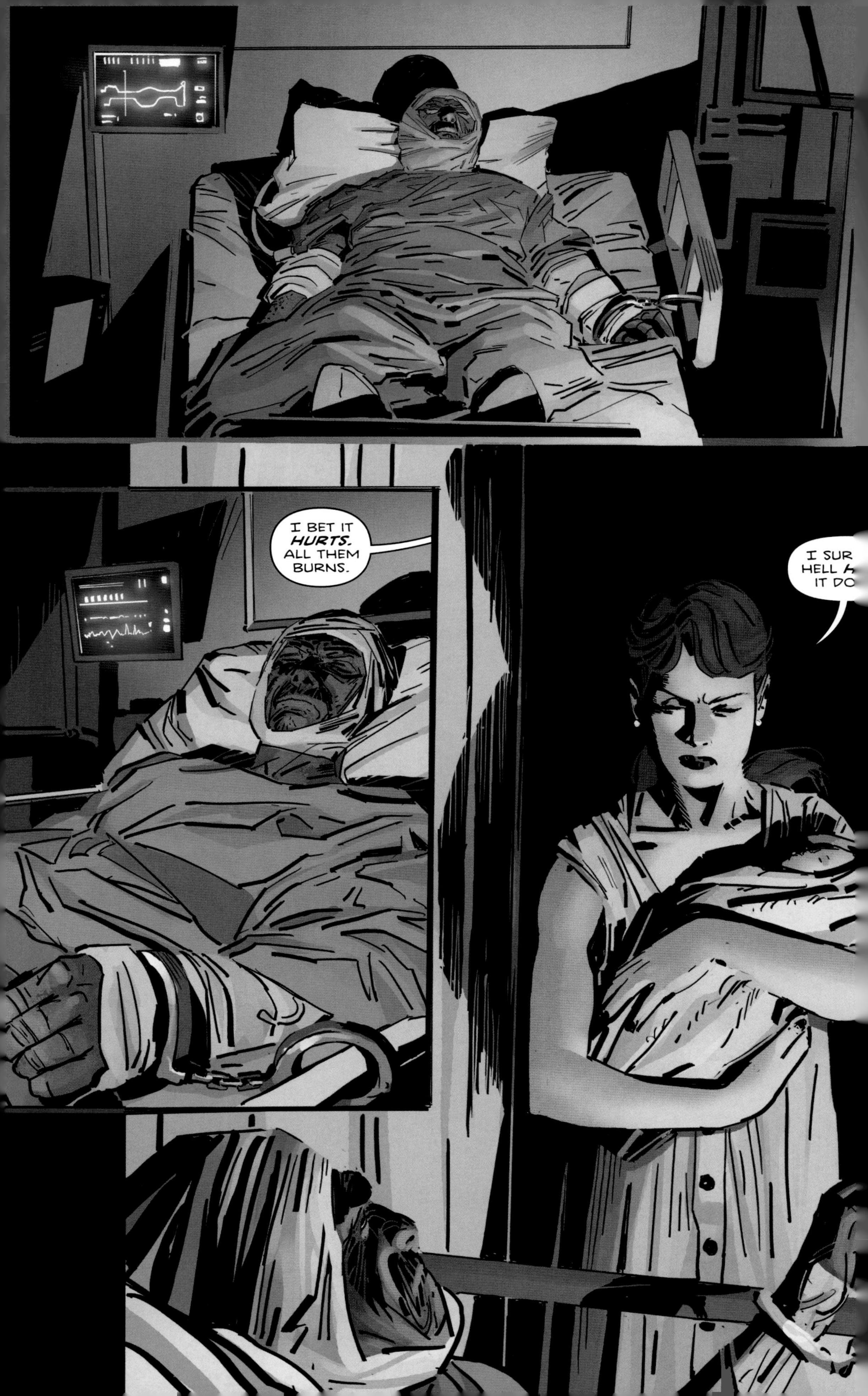
I BET IT *HURTS.* ALL THEM BURNS.

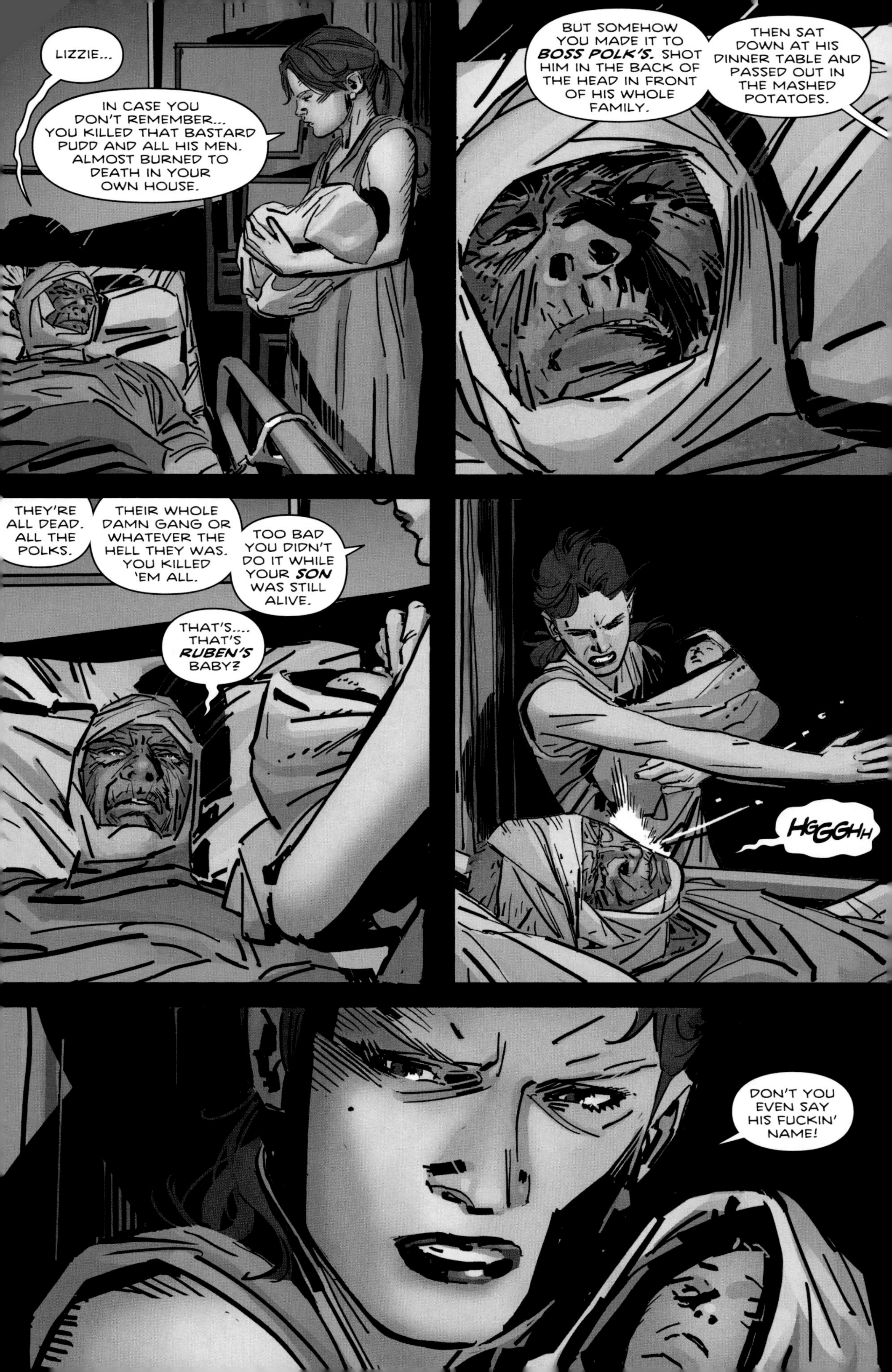
LIZZIE...
IN CASE YOU DON'T REMEMBER... YOU KILLED THAT BASTARD PUDD AND ALL HIS MEN. ALMOST BURNED TO DEATH IN YOUR OWN HOUSE.
BUT SOMEHOW YOU MADE IT TO BOSS POLK'S. SHOT HIM IN THE BACK OF THE HEAD IN FRONT OF HIS WHOLE FAMILY.
THEN SAT DOWN AT HIS DINNER TABLE AND PASSED OUT IN THE MASHED POTATOES.
THEY'RE ALL DEAD. ALL THE POLKS.
THEIR WHOLE DAMN GANG OR WHATEVER THE HELL THEY WAS. YOU KILLED 'EM ALL.
TOO BAD YOU DIDN'T DO IT WHILE YOUR SON WAS STILL ALIVE.
THAT'S.... THAT'S RUBEN'S BABY?
HGGGHH
DON'T YOU EVEN SAY HIS FUCKIN' NAME!

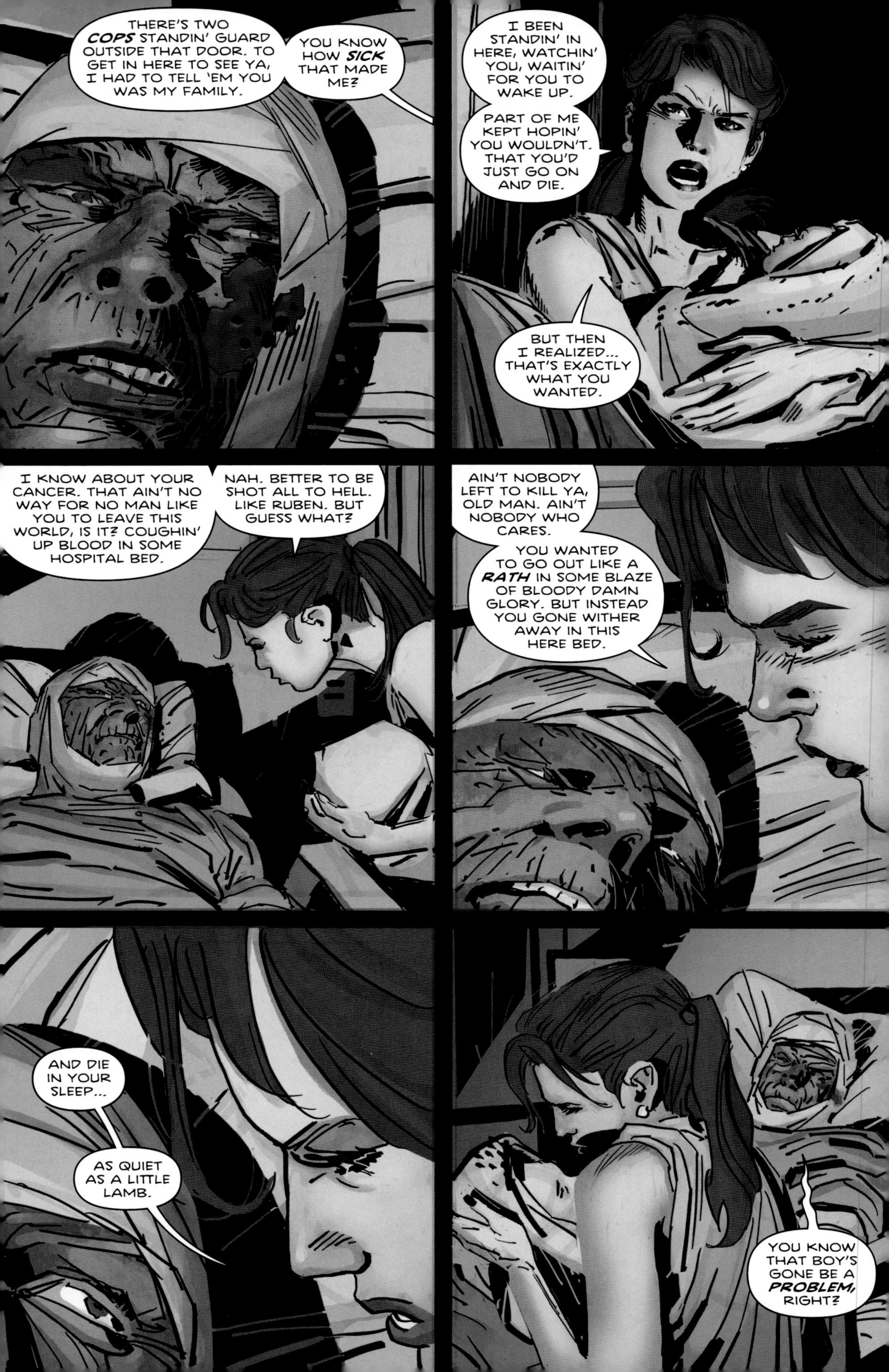
THERE'S TWO COPS STANDIN' GUARD OUTSIDE THAT DOOR. TO GET IN HERE TO SEE YA, I HAD TO TELL 'EM YOU WAS MY FAMILY.
YOU KNOW HOW SICK THAT MADE ME?
I BEEN STANDIN' IN HERE, WATCHIN' YOU, WAITIN' FOR YOU TO WAKE UP.
PART OF ME KEPT HOPIN' YOU WOULDN'T. THAT YOU'D JUST GO ON AND DIE.
BUT THEN I REALIZED... THAT'S EXACTLY WHAT YOU WANTED.
I KNOW ABOUT YOUR CANCER. THAT AIN'T NO WAY FOR NO MAN LIKE YOU TO LEAVE THIS WORLD, IS IT? COUGHIN' UP BLOOD IN SOME HOSPITAL BED.
NAH. BETTER TO BE SHOT ALL TO HELL. LIKE RUBEN. BUT GUESS WHAT?
AIN'T NOBODY LEFT TO KILL YA, OLD MAN. AIN'T NOBODY WHO CARES.
YOU WANTED TO GO OUT LIKE A RATH IN SOME BLAZE OF BLOODY DAMN GLORY. BUT INSTEAD YOU GONE WITHER AWAY IN THIS HERE BED.
AND DIE IN YOUR SLEEP...
AS QUIET AS A LITTLE LAMB.
YOU KNOW THAT BOY'S GONE BE A PROBLEM, RIGHT?

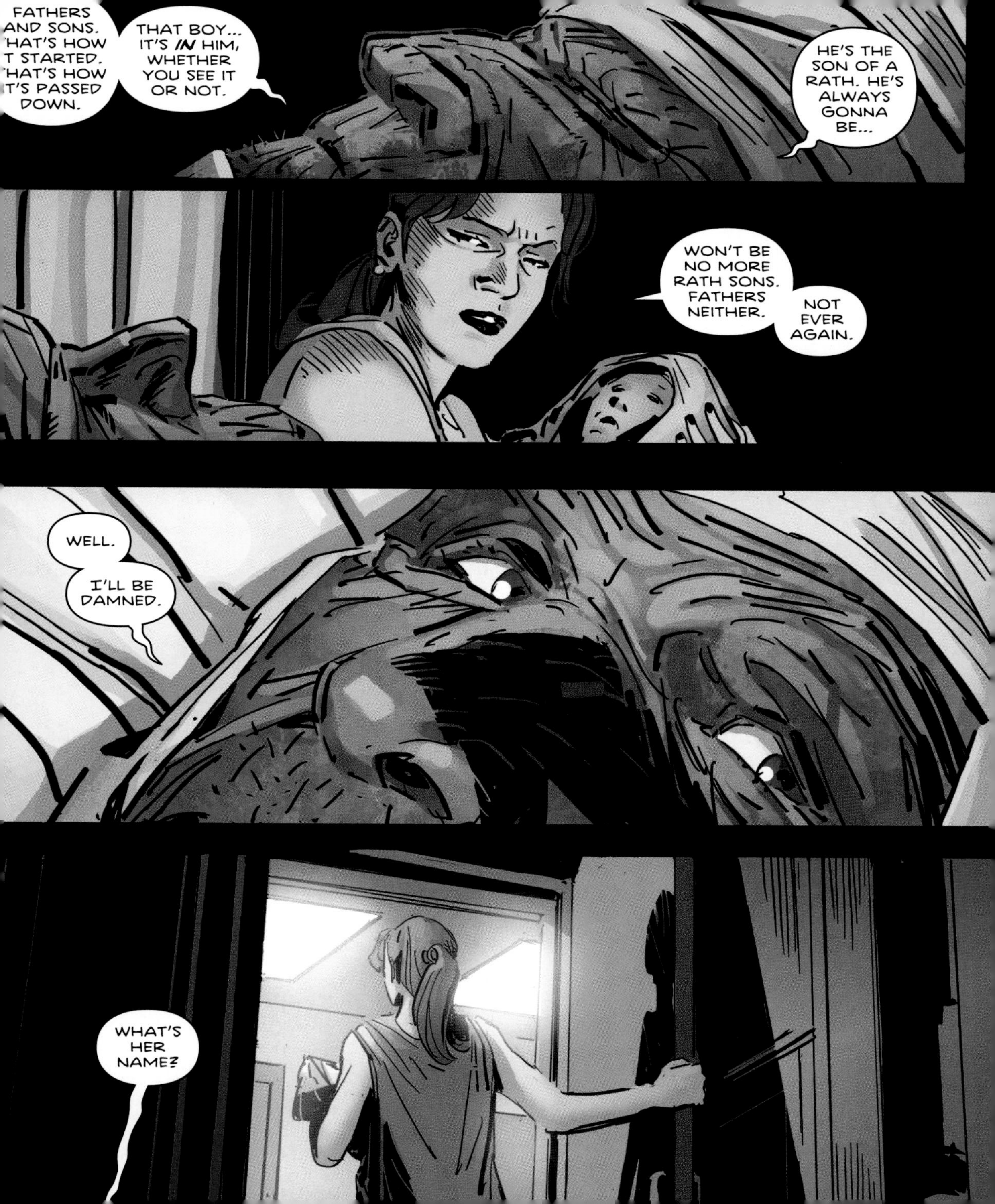
FATHERS AND SONS. THAT'S HOW IT STARTED. THAT'S HOW IT'S PASSED DOWN.
THAT BOY... IT'S *IN* HIM, WHETHER YOU SEE IT OR NOT.
HE'S THE SON OF A RATH. HE'S ALWAYS GONNA BE...
WON'T BE NO MORE RATH SONS. FATHERS NEITHER.
NOT EVER AGAIN.
WELL.
I'LL BE DAMNED.
WHAT'S HER NAME?

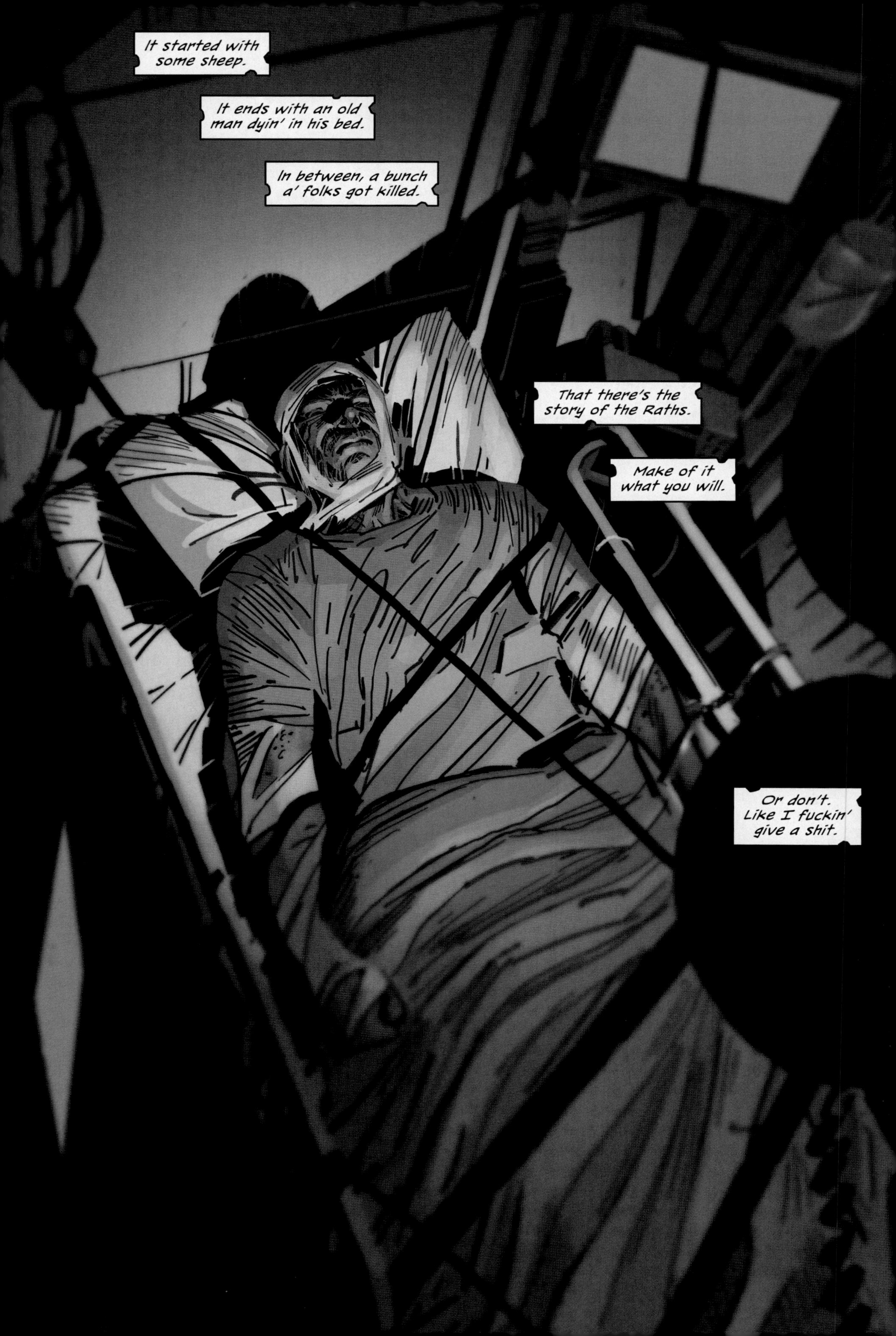
It started with some sheep.
It ends with an old man dyin' in his bed.
In between, a bunch a' folks got killed.
That there's the story of the Raths.
Make of it what you will.
Or don't. Like I fuckin' give a shit.

"MY JESUS YOUR GRACIOUS LOVE AND MERCY
TONIGHT I'M SORRY COULD NOT FILL
MY HEART LIKE ONE GOOD RIFLE
AND THE NAME OF WHO I OUGHTA KILL."

--BRUCE SPRINGSTEEN, "THE NEW TIMER"

# VARIANT COVER GALLERY

## STEVE DILLON

## RM GUERA

## TONY HARRIS

## DAVID LAPHAM
### WITH LEE LOUGHRIDGE

## ALEX ROSS

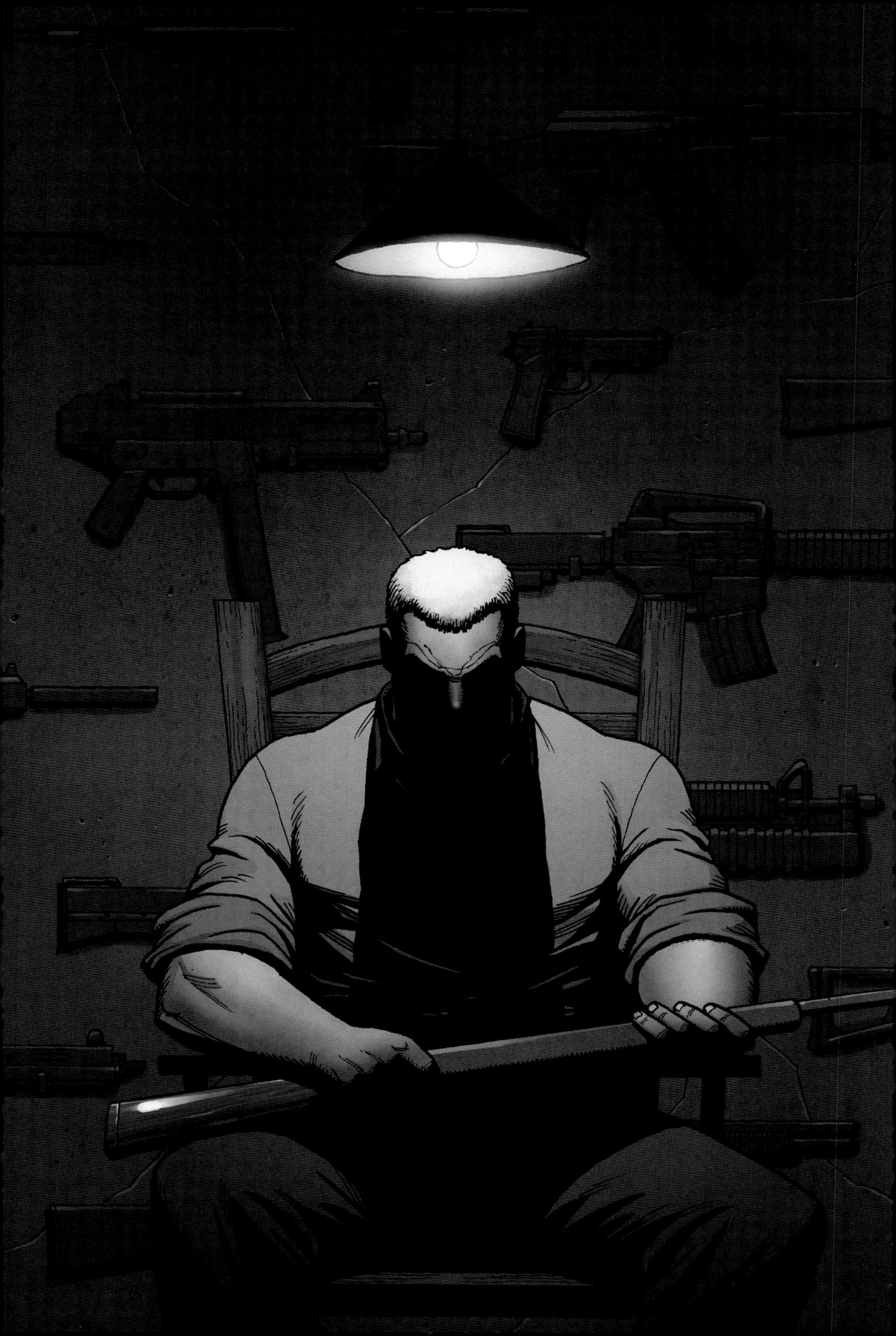

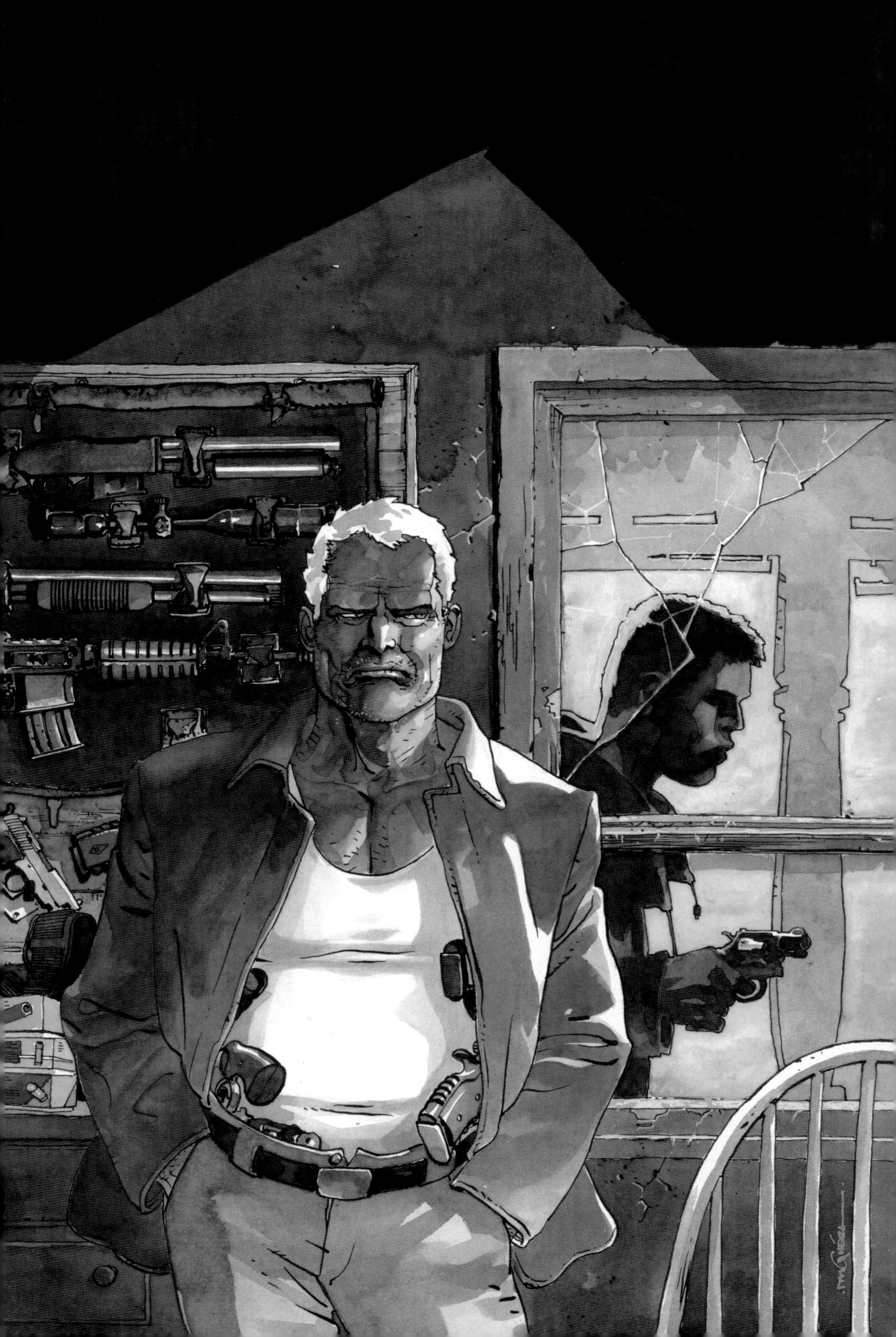

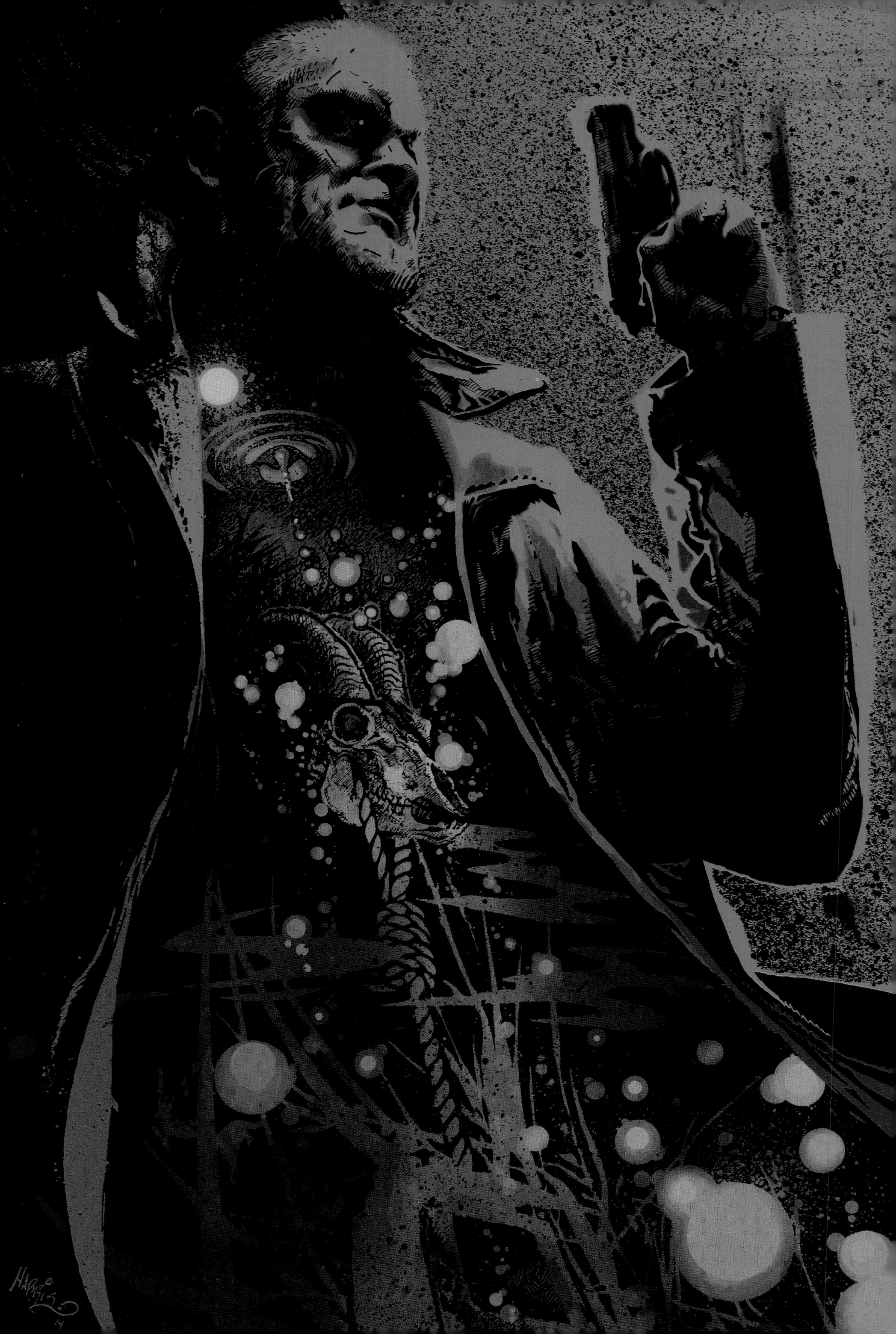
HARRIS
'14

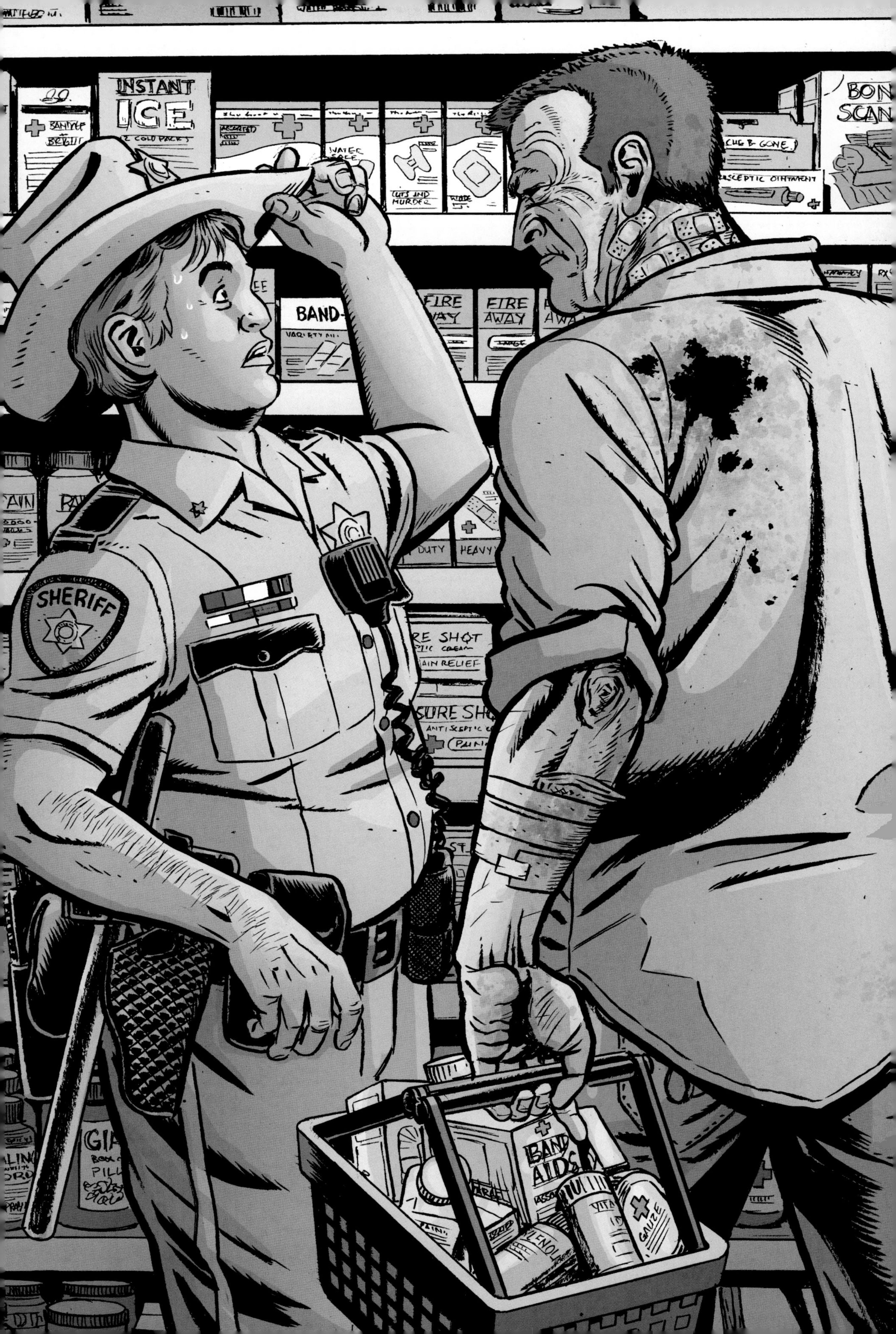
INSTANT ICE
CUTS AND MURDER
BAND-
FIRE AWAY
FIRE AWAY
SHERIFF
SURE SHOT
PAIN RELIEF
SURE SHO
BAND AIDS
GAUZE
BON SCAN
SCEPTIC OINTMENT
DUTY
HEAVY

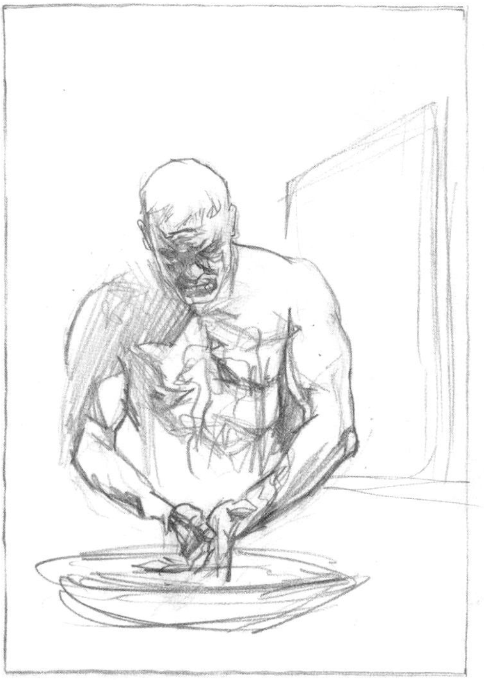

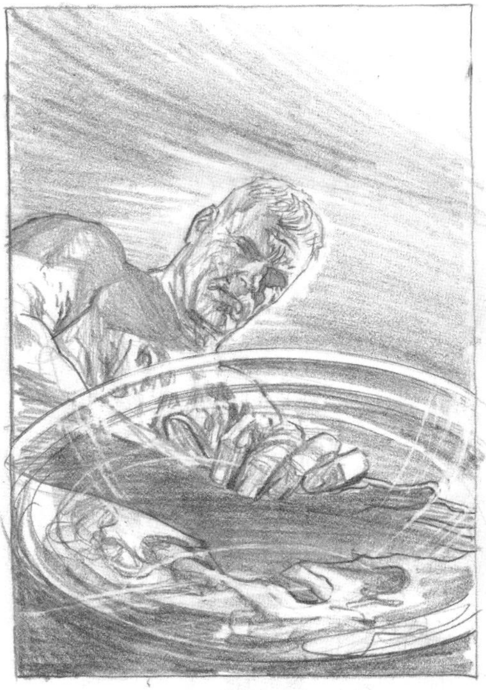

MEN OF WRATH

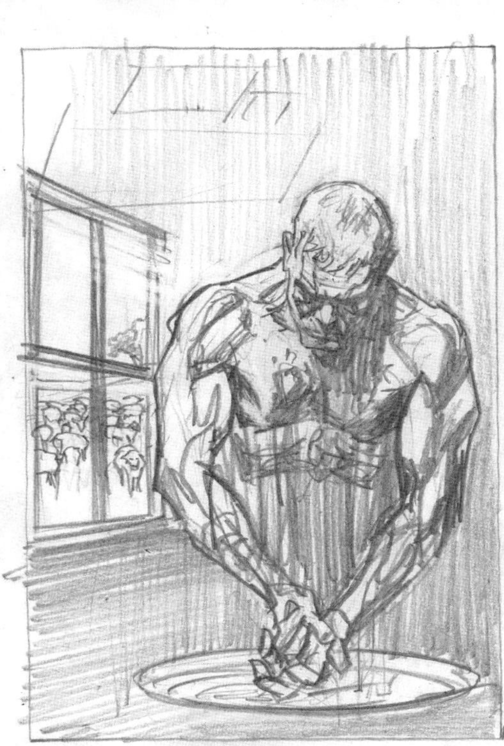

A

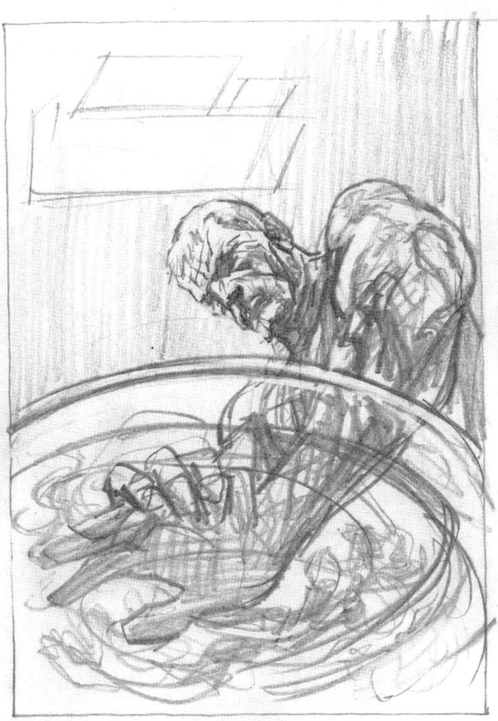

B

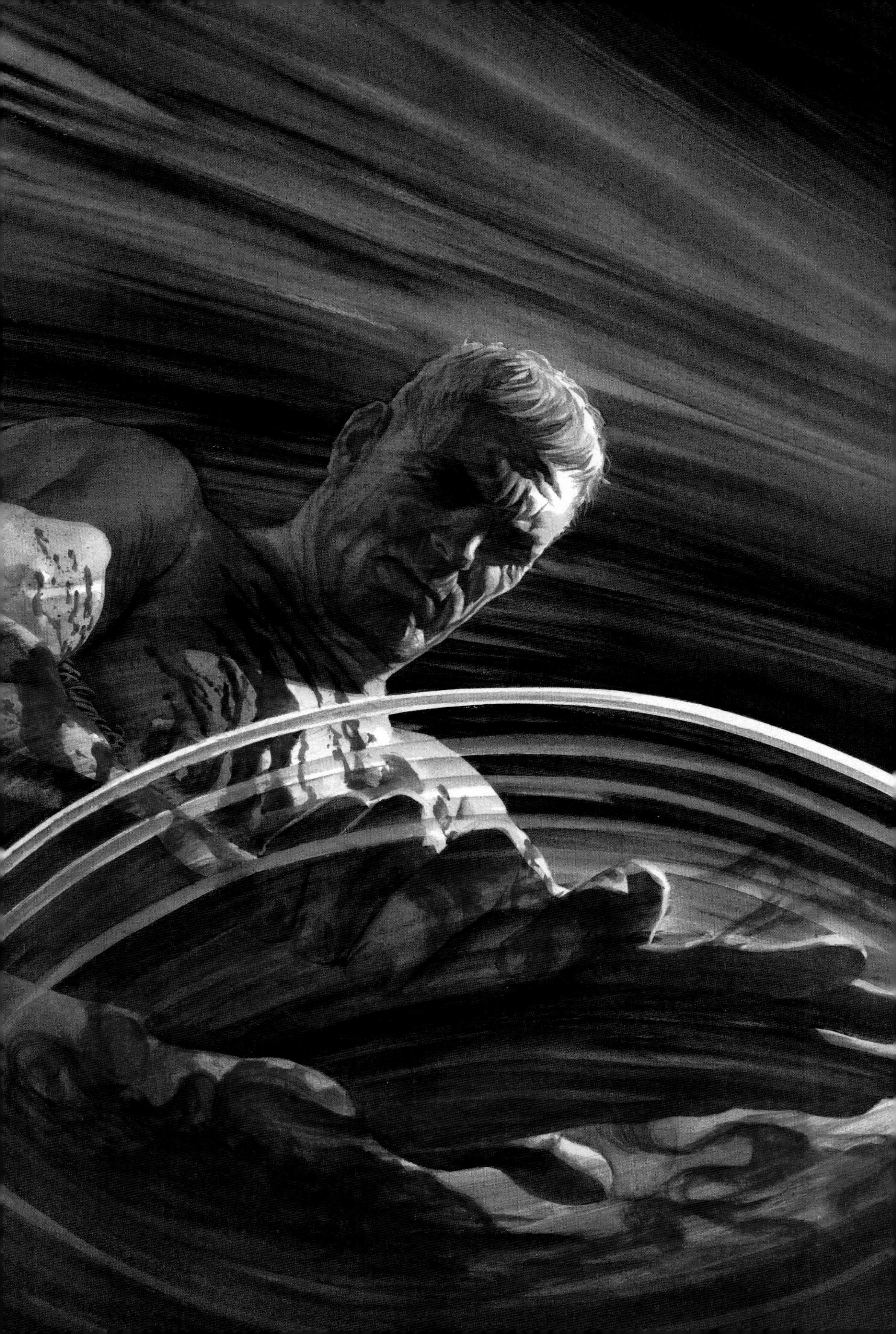

# SKETCH GALLERY

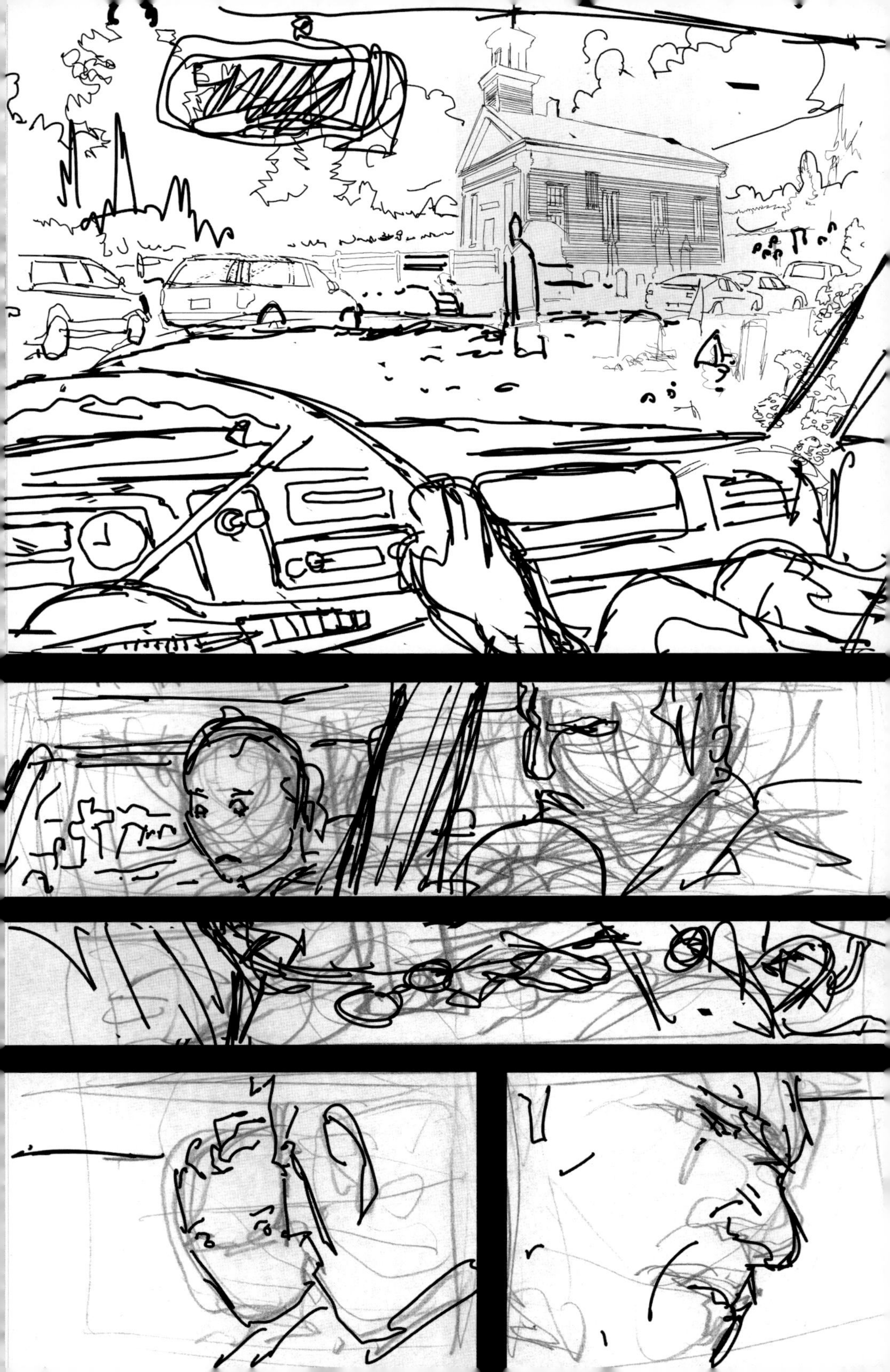

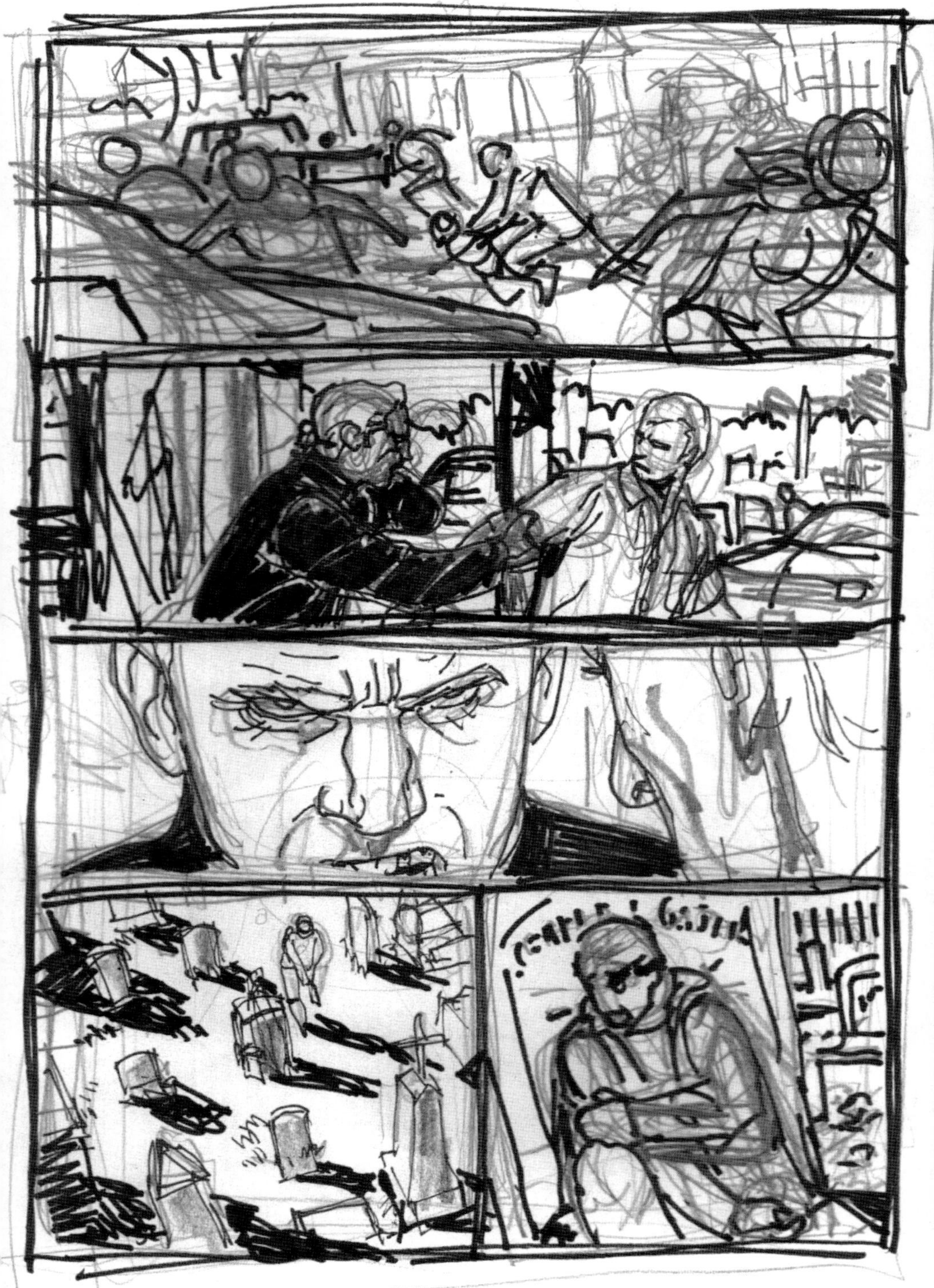

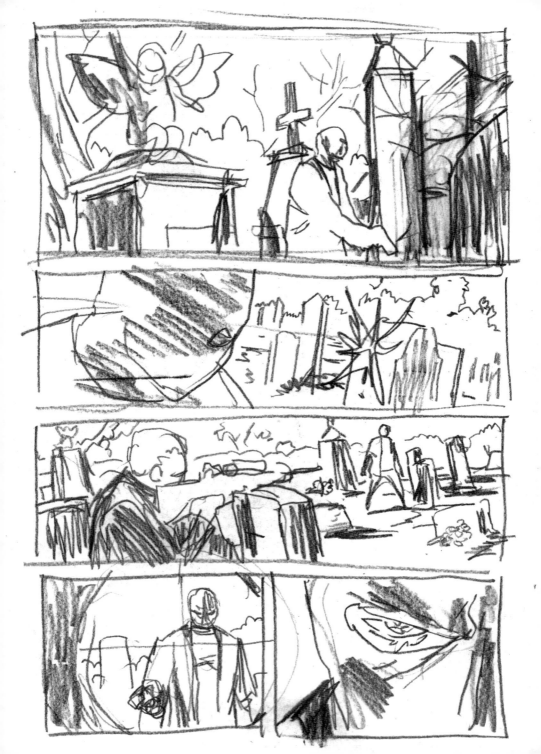

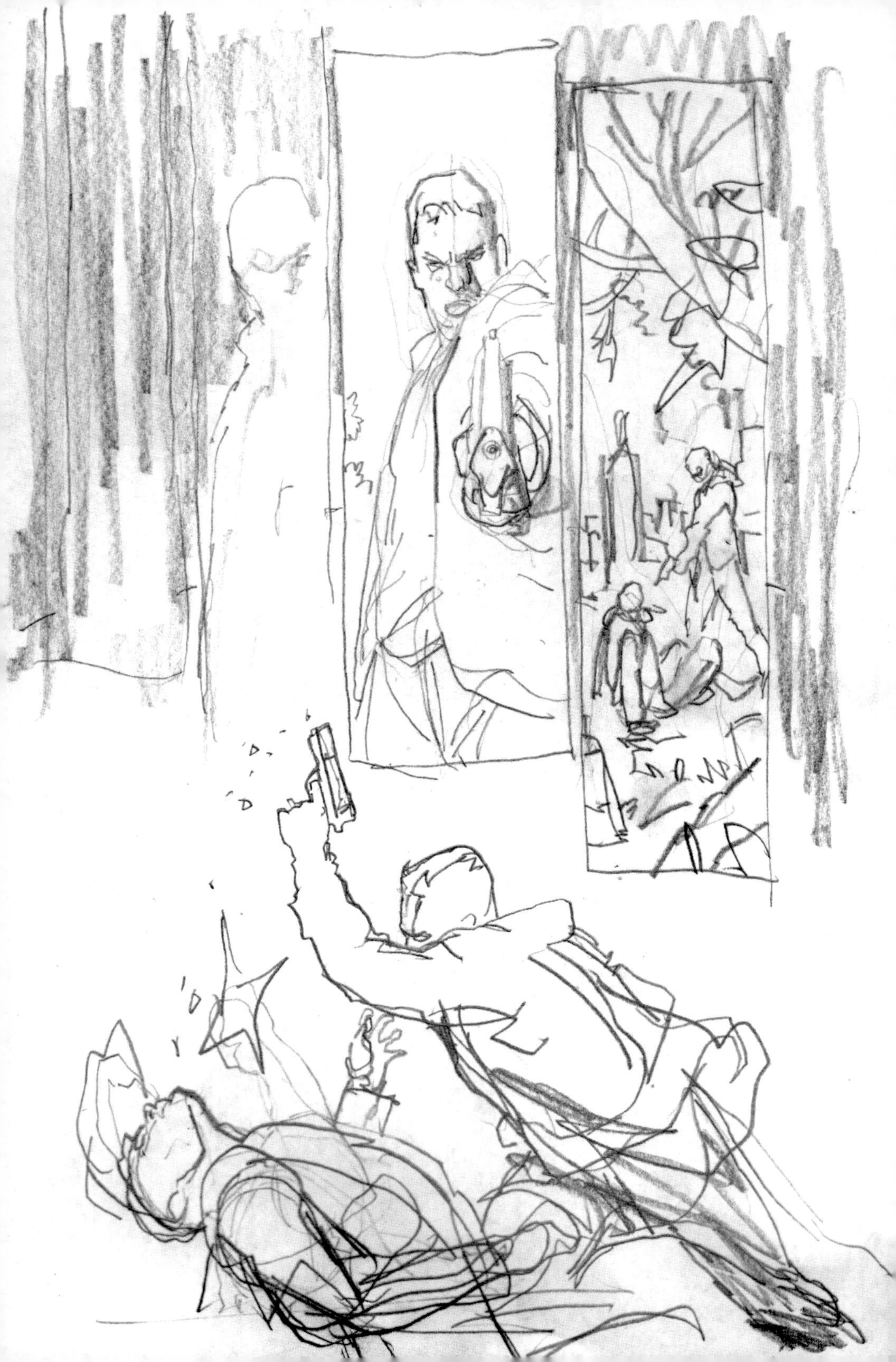

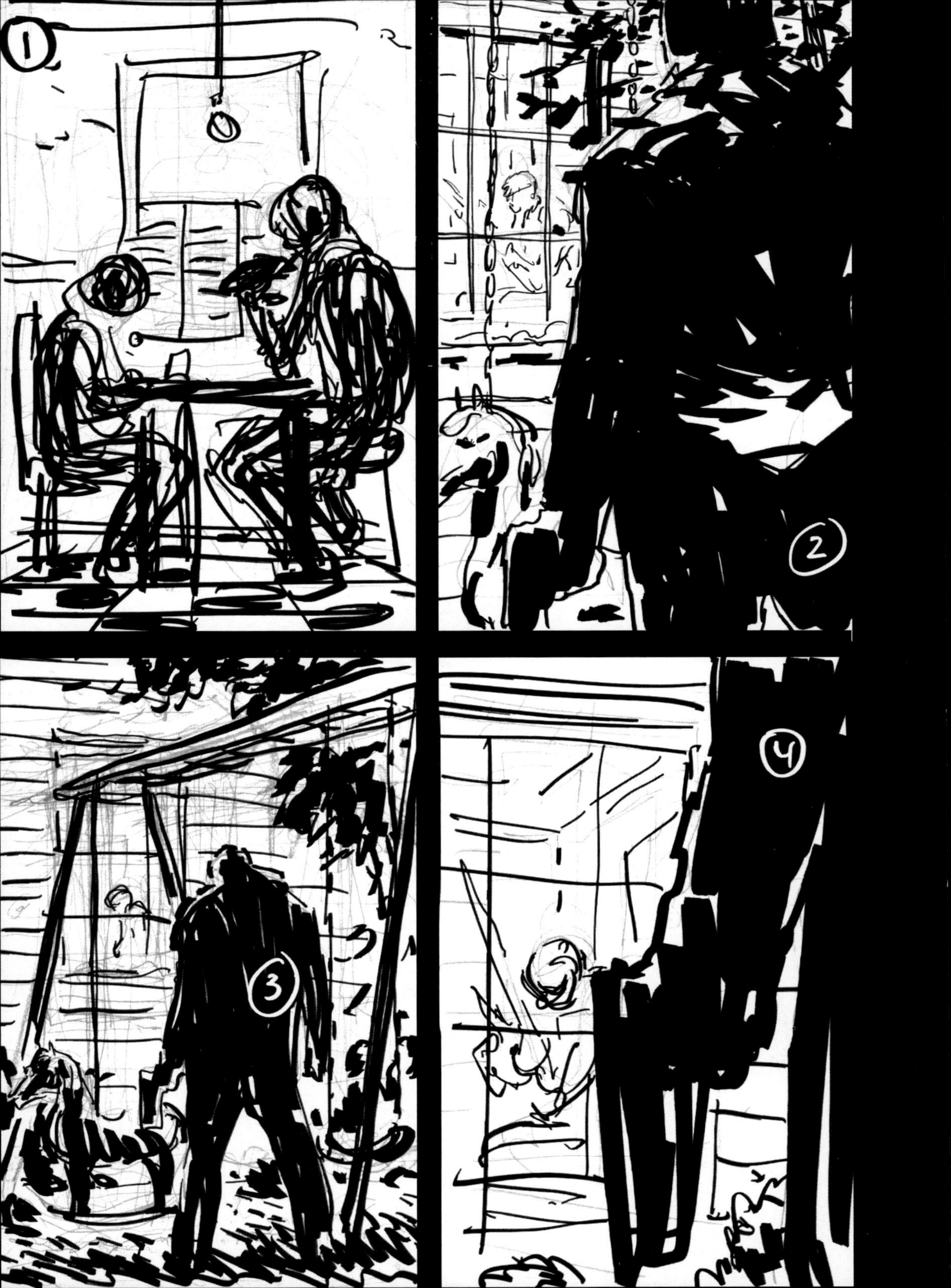

1
2
3
4

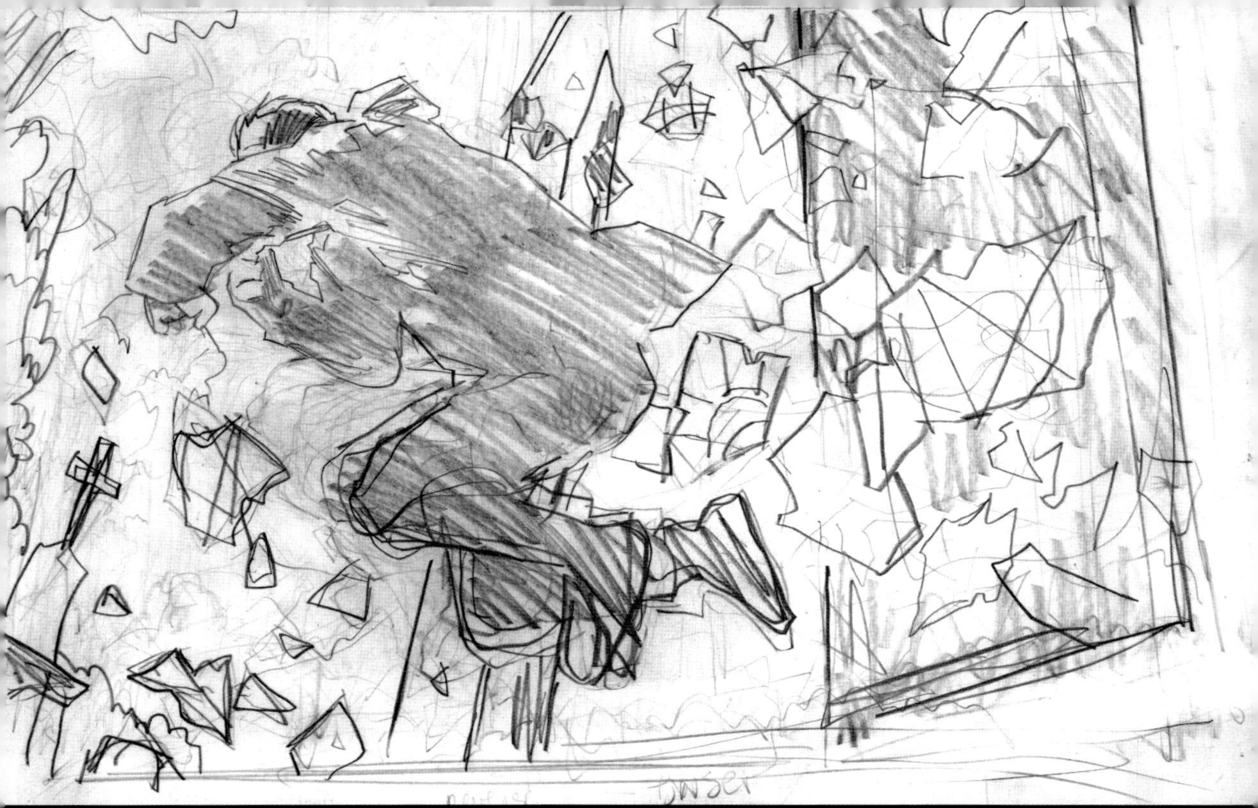

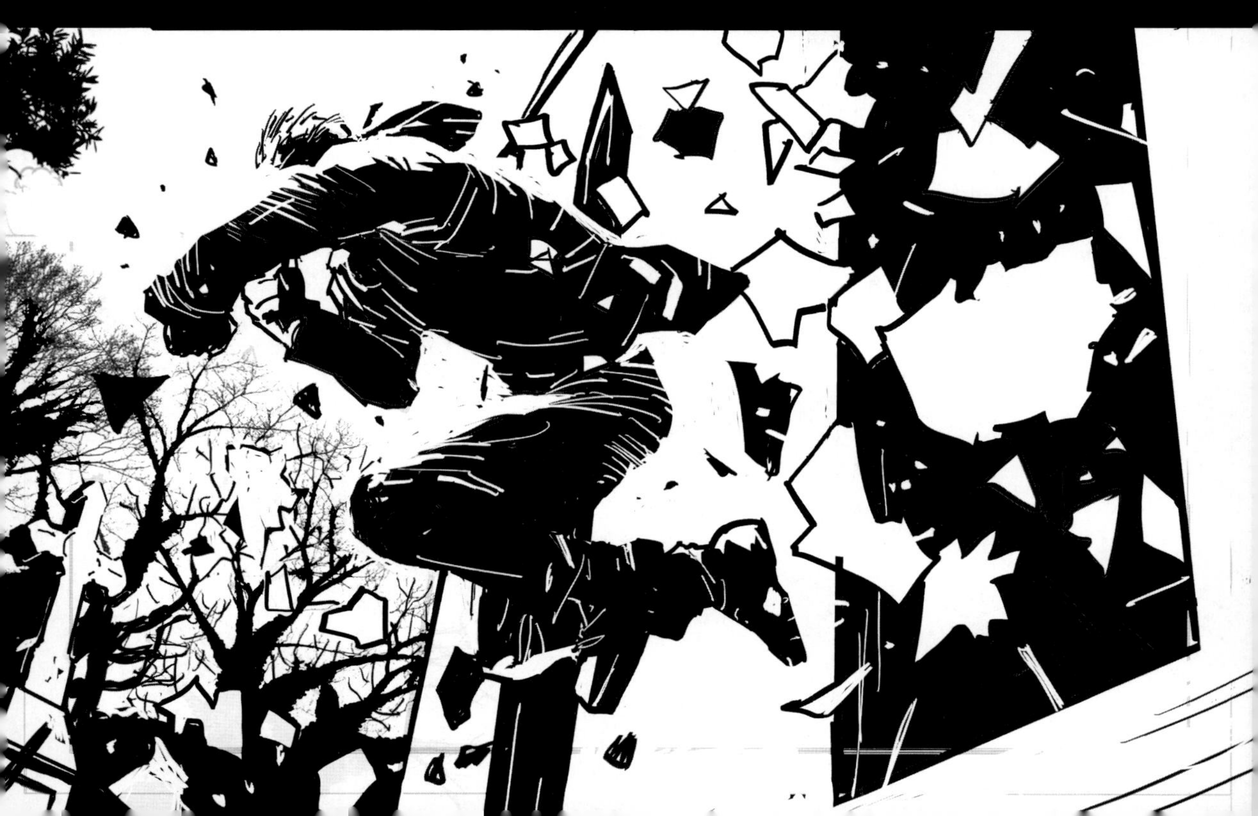

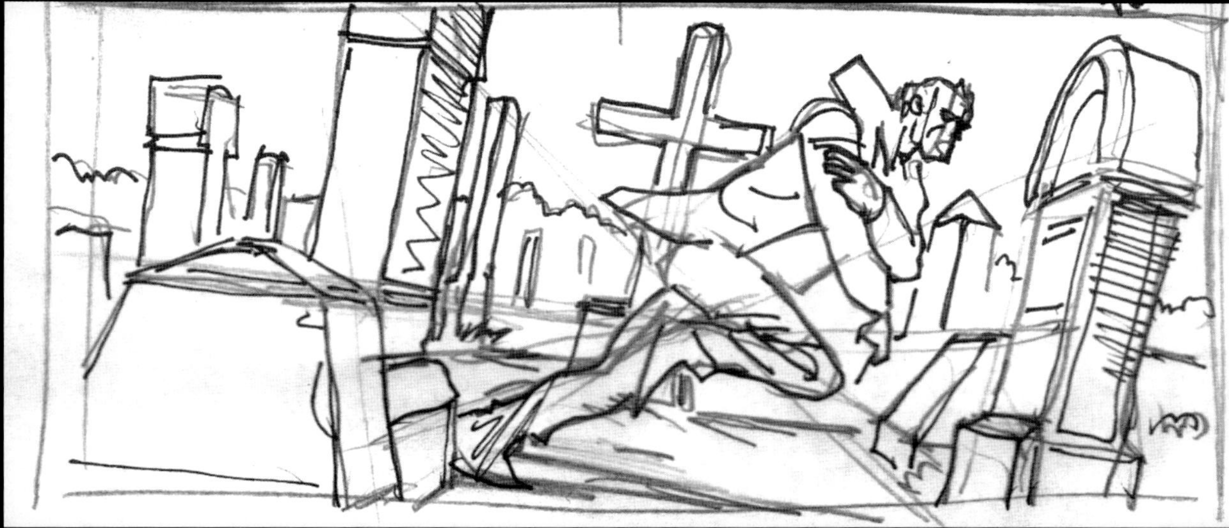

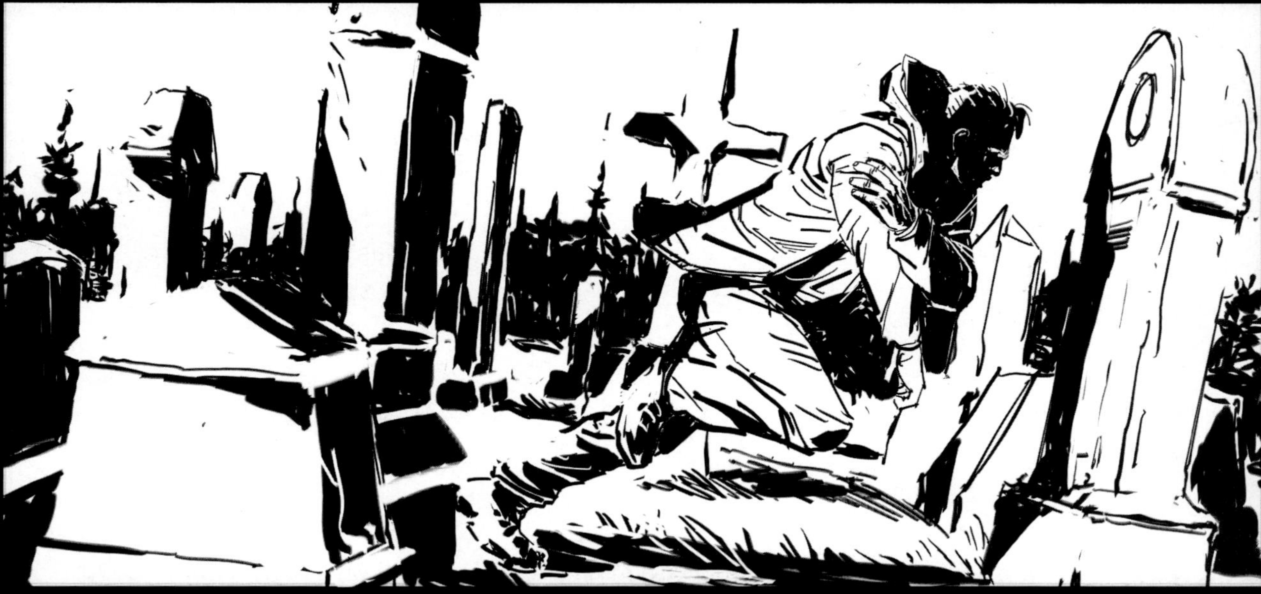

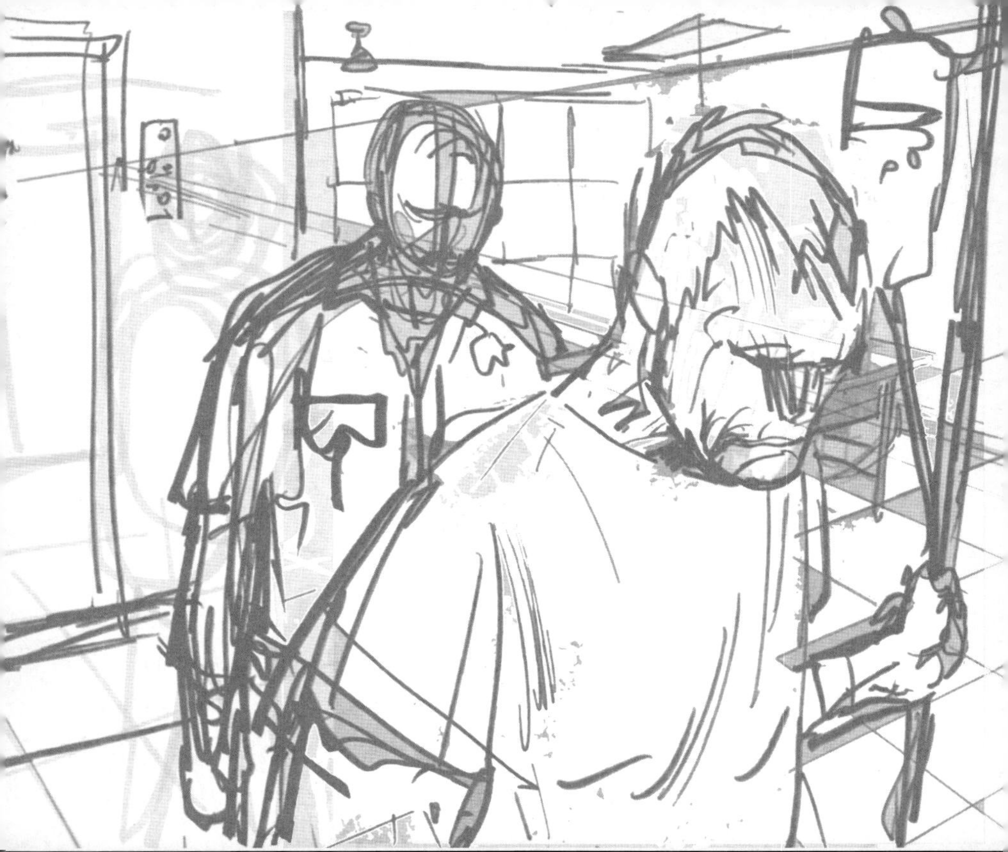

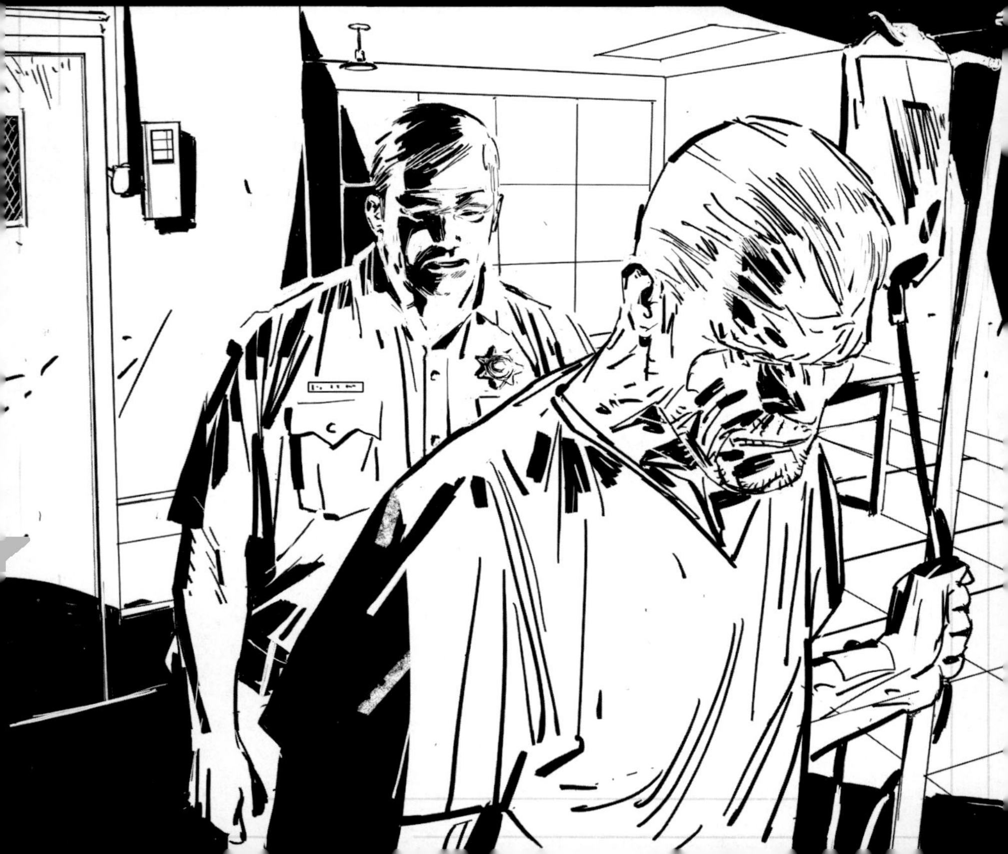